S0-BAU-462

Dear Reader,

This month, Harlequin Regency Romance will double your reading pleasure with two full-length stories by Brenda Hiatt and Paula Marshall. *Azalea* and *The Cyprian's Sister* are guaranteed to hold you spellbound until the very last page.

In October, we will be bringing you another very special book. *Untamed Heart,* by Georgina Devon, is a big book in every sense of the word. Look for it in your favourite bookstore!

Happy reading from Harlequin Regency Romance.

The Editor

REGENCY DIAMONDS

BRENDA HIATT
PAULA MARSHALL

Harlequin Books

TORONTO • NEW YORK • LONDON
AMSTERDAM • PARIS • SYDNEY • HAMBURG
STOCKHOLM • ATHENS • TOKYO • MILAN
MADRID • WARSAW • BUDAPEST • AUCKLAND

REGENCY DIAMONDS

Copyright © 1994 by Harlequin Enterprises B.V.

ISBN 0-373-31214-8

The publisher acknowledges the copyright holders of the individual works as follows:

AZALEA
Copyright © 1994 by Brenda H. Barber

THE CYPRIAN'S SISTER
Copyright © 1993 by Paula Marshall

Printed in U.S.A.

CONTENTS

ABOUT THE AUTHOR

The town of Williamsburg is especially dear to
Brenda Hiatt, since she attended the College of
William and Mary. So what could be more natural
than to write a Regency novel about a young
American girl from Williamsburg who takes
London by storm?

Brenda now lives in Texas with her husband and
two daughters.

Books by Brenda Hiatt

HARLEQUIN REGENCY ROMANCE

HARLEQUIN SUPERROMANCE

AZALEA
Brenda Hiatt

For my family.
Thank you for all
your patience.

PROLOGUE

March 1809

ANOTHER WAVE SWEPT across the pitching deck of the *Artemis,* almost wrenching Christian loose from the rail he grasped with one hand. Instead of alarm, he felt only exhilaration. For so long he had dreamed of this, his first sea voyage! The reality was even more exciting than he had imagined. Shaking the salt spray from his hair, he laughed into the screaming gale.

When his father had invited him to sail along on a business trip to America, Christian had jumped at the chance, the still-novel pleasures of London paling against the visions of adventure conjured up. What were gaming hells and cockfights, even the lights of the *demi-monde,* compared to this battle with the elements, the raw fury of wind and ocean? He had never felt more alive in all his eighteen years.

"It's gettin' mighty rough, lad. Best you go below with the other passengers." Captain Taylor, a stringy, dark-haired man with a clean-shaven, leathery face, clapped a gnarled hand on his shoulder. "I've told you what a storm at sea can do—haven't you seen enough?"

Christian breathed deeply of the fierce, fresh wind. "No, not really. I've never actually seen one before, you know. Are we in some danger then?"

The captain shrugged. "Any storm can spell trouble this far out...and I'd as lief not lose a paying guest overboard. Why, I remember a time... But there's his lordship, your father, come for you. We can talk later. I've work to do."

Captain Taylor turned to bellow orders at his crew, leaving Christian to grin after him. The captain's frequent tales of life at sea had been the best part of this voyage—up until now, anyway. Another splash of icy sea water caught Christian full in the face, making him gasp and sputter. Wiping the salt from his eyes, he saw his father beckoning him from the hatchway. With a last, reluctant look at the raging sea, he left the rail, stumbling slightly as the deck pitched beneath him.

"Here you are, son! Let's get below, where we'll be out of the crew's way." Lord Glaedon spoke heartily, but Christian couldn't mistake the concern in his eyes. "This looks like a bad blow."

His father had spent a great deal of time at sea in his youth, Christian knew, which meant his caution, based as it was on experience, could not be ignored. Still, the young man couldn't suppress a cocky grin as he stepped forward.

"Sailing is every bit the adventure you promised, Father," he said exultantly. "I hate to miss any of it. If you don't mind, I'd like to stay on deck for just a bit longer. Captain Taylor doesn't seem unduly worried—"

At that moment a falling spar, torn loose from the mast above, struck him a glancing blow on the shoulder, knocking him heavily to the deck.

For a few seconds he was dazed, not certain what had happened. Blinking as his vision cleared, he saw his father leaning over him, white-faced.

"My God, Chris, that was a close one!" He had never seen his father so shaken. "Can you stand?"

Christian nodded vigorously, though for the moment speech was beyond him. Scrambling to his feet, he followed the earl down the ladder that led to their cabin, his enthusiasm about the storm temporarily dampened.

The next morning dawned fair; a fresh breeze filled the sails while the sun sparkled on the deceptively innocent ocean. Christian, looking out from the same rail where he'd stood the evening before, marvelled at the change. It would seem that the sea was as fickle as he'd always heard.

Perhaps with the return of fine weather, Captain Taylor would have more time to answer his myriad questions about the New World they approached. Not for the first time, he thought about what it would be like to carve out a life for himself in that untamed wilderness—a far different life than that awaiting a second son back in England.

"Well, my boy, we'll be in sight of land in just over a week," said his father, coming up to stand beside him at the rail. "I suppose it's high time I told you the real reason I asked you to accompany me to America."

CHAPTER ONE

April 1809

"AZALEA! Are you out here?" The housekeeper's voice floated across the paddock to the stables, where a small, trousered figure was currying a dainty, silver-grey mare with long, brisk strokes.

"In here, Swannee!" the girl answered without pausing in her work. "What is it?"

"Your grandfather wants you up to the house right away. Visitors, I believe. And just look at you!" Mrs. Swann exclaimed in dismay. Azalea emerged from the stall, grinning impishly as she ran quick fingers through her tousled red curls. Enormous, grey-green eyes of startling beauty sparkled up at the distracted housekeeper, who at this moment was more inclined to notice the smear of stable dirt across the girl's left cheek than the flawlessness of the complexion it disguised.

Mrs. Swann sighed gustily and opened her mouth in preparation for a well-rehearsed homily on her young mistress's shortcomings, but Azalea forestalled her with an affectionate hug.

"Don't fuss, Swannee! Ten to one it's just Jonathan, and he won't mind seeing me in breeches. At any rate, I can go in by the pantry door and reach my bedroom without being seen."

Mrs. Swann, plump fists on plumper hips, shook her greying blond head in resignation and gazed fondly at the glowing, untidy girl before her. For the past eight years she had been the nearest thing to a mother Azalea had known, and in truth, she couldn't have loved her more had the girl been her own daughter.

Of course, who would not love such a beautiful child, with her bright, flame-coloured curls, thick-lashed liquid eyes and sweet, winning ways? But there was also a certain wildness about her that Mrs. Swann had done her best to control over the years—a task as futile as trying to control the fresh east wind that blew in from the coast.

"All right, miss," she conceded gruffly, "but do hurry. And I don't believe it is Master Jonathan coming to call. Your grandfather has ordered supper set back an hour and an extra chicken killed. He wouldn't likely do that for one of your young friends."

"Oh, how interesting—I shall hurry!"

Azalea raced across the field at a pace that caused the long-suffering Mrs. Swann to emit another sigh and hope the girl's grandfather was well away from the back windows. At this distance, Azalea looked more like a stable-lad than a young lady of Quality.

A scant fifteen minutes later, a hastily scrubbed and gowned Azalea clattered down to the library, where her grandfather customarily received callers. She was surprised to find the old gentleman quietly reading alone.

"Oh, have they gone already?" She stopped just inside the door, disappointed. "I did hurry, Grandfather, truly I did! Swannee said our guests would be staying for supper. Were they ladies or gentlemen? Are they staying here in Williamsburg? Or was it someone I already know? Was it Jonathan, after all? Why—"

"My dear, my dear, always leaping to conclusions," Reverend Simpson said, breaking in mildly. "Taking your questions in order, they have not yet arrived, but are due within the hour. They will be staying for supper, which has been set back to eight o'clock. They are gentlemen, two in number, and are staying at Wetherburn's Tavern until rooms can be prepared for them here. You have never met them, but have often heard me refer to the elder of the two, my old friend Howard Morely, Earl of Glaedon. The other gentleman is his second son, Christian, whom I have yet to meet. Obviously not Jonathan. Did I miss anything?" The old gentleman's austere, scholarly demeanour was softened by the twinkle in his bright blue eyes.

"You know you didn't." She smiled fondly at her grandfather. "But I still want to know all about them. Why have we had no word that they were coming? How long do they stay?" Azalea fairly danced with impatience. She could not recollect when they had last had overnight visitors. And Lord Glaedon! The hero of so many of Grandfather's tales about his time in India, the one with whom he had shared such splendid adventures...!

"Very well, my dear, stop twitching," the reverend said, relenting. "Due to a quirk of the mails, Howard's letter informing me of the date of his proposed visit arrived on the same ship that carried Christian and himself hither. They arrived in America only yesterday, and will probably stay with us but a few days, as Howard has pressing business in Richmond. However—" he interrupted himself with a brief fit of coughing "—I hope they will return for a longer visit when their affairs have been concluded."

This answer seemed clear enough, but there was something evasive in the old gentleman's manner that convinced Azalea there was more to the matter. "And?" she prompted. "What aren't you telling me, Grandfather?"

"Precocious child! Can you read my mind now?"

"If I could, I wouldn't need to ask. But I can tell when you've decided something doesn't concern me, or that I'm too young to hear all of the interesting details." Azalea almost pouted before hastily remembering that she was now too old for such behaviour.

Reverend Simpson sighed. "No, Azalea, young you may be, but this matter very definitely concerns you. Still, I would prefer to speak with Howard in person before acquainting you fully with the 'interesting details,' as you term them. I do promise to tell you all I can once I am completely in possession of the facts. Will that content you for now?"

Azalea smiled reluctantly. "I suppose it must."

"Good. Now perhaps you'd like to complete your toilette before supper—and I suggest you use a mirror this time. You missed a spot or two." He winked knowingly over his spectacles. Azalea grimaced, but hurried back upstairs to wash more thoroughly and put her hair in better order. She wanted to look her best for these distinguished visitors from England.

THE WARM SPRING AFTERNOON was beginning to cool when Azalea returned to the library. She stopped short on the threshold, startled to find their visitors already present. Her soft surprised, "Oh!" caused all three gentlemen to turn.

"Ah, my dear, here you are," exclaimed her grandfather, coming forward. "Let me present Lord Glaedon and his son, the Honourable Christian Morely. Gentlemen, my granddaughter, Miss Azalea Clayton."

She dropped a curtsy and lowered her gaze in confusion. "I—I beg pardon for not greeting you upon your arrival! I was in the garden and thought surely I would hear the approach of your carriage—"

"No need for apologies, child," the elder of the two visitors said, interrupting her warmly. "We have scarce been here ten minutes, and you could hardly have been expected to hear our carriage, as we rode instead. And let me say that I am delighted to make your acquaintance at last, though I feel I know you well from your grandfather's letters. You are even prettier than he described you."

Azalea looked up quickly at the unlikely words to find kindly grey eyes regarding her. Timidly, she returned the earl's smile.

Lord Glaedon was a hearty man in his late fifties, with very little grey in his thick black hair. He looked, Azalea thought, as an earl ought to: confident rather than arrogant, and dressed with a simple elegance that rendered him by far the most fashionable gentleman she'd ever seen. He was also the tallest man she could remember meeting. That is, unless she counted Judd Bellby, a local farmer's son who was certainly no gentleman.

"Thank you, my lord," answered Azalea, a heartbeat before she could be accused of staring. "Grandfather has told me much about you, also, and about the adventures you shared in India. Such wonderful stories!"

"And stories they no doubt were, for the most part," Lord Glaedon replied somewhat gruffly, glancing at the reverend. "Gregory ever had a tendency to exaggerate. Christian, my lad," he called, turning toward the other occupant of the room, "come forward and make Miss Clayton's acquaintance."

The younger gentleman turned away from the window, where he had apparently been admiring the spectacular sunset. He advanced two or three steps towards Azalea.

Looking up—far up—as he approached, Azalea realized that Christian was at least as tall as his father, and far more handsome. In fact, to her inexperienced eyes, he was the most perfect man she'd ever seen, with thick wavy hair, so dark it was almost black, and penetrating blue-grey eyes.

Exciting eyes, Azalea thought irrelevantly, the colour of thunderclouds just before a storm. At first glance, at least, the Honourable Christian Morely seemed the answer to a young girl's every romantic dream.

Blinking at the direction of her thoughts, Azalea had to suppress an urge to laugh at herself. *Romantic dreams, indeed!* Between studying, riding, gardening and other pursuits, she'd never wasted time on such fantasies. In fact, she had always scorned the other girls' sighs over a handsome new student or a visiting merchant's son. But of course, none of those young men had ever compared to Christian Morely.

"So this is little Miss Azalea! Not quite the child I was led to believe." His smile was condescending, Azalea thought, which immediately banished romance and put irritation in its place.

"I was thirteen in November, my lord, so I am scarcely a child," she retorted, standing up a little taller. She was suddenly glad she had given up her braids two months ago.

"Isn't that what I just said? And I understand that you have had a hand in the managing of this ... estate for the past year, as well."

Azalea regarded the young man suspiciously. Was he teasing her? Her grandfather's house and lands, while respectable, could hardly be called an estate. However, she could detect no trace of malice in Christian's amused expression and decided that he might merely be ignorant of the extent of an American plantation.

"That is true, sir," she finally conceded. "Mrs. Swann is gradually entrusting me with the duties that belonged to my grandmother many years ago. Part of my education, Grandfather tells me." She smiled a bit wryly.

"But not your favourite part, I take it?" He smiled back, a friendly smile that allayed her suspicions and put her at ease.

"Well, it's certainly more amusing than Latin, but I find I have less and less time to spend with the horses and plants...." Azalea broke off in some confusion, not certain whether she should have revealed these pastimes, which Swannee had informed her repeatedly were less than ladylike. She glanced in her grandfather's direction, but he was deep in conversation with the earl and appeared not to have heard.

"You like horses, then?" Christian prompted when she paused. He didn't look the least disapproving.

"Oh, yes! Above all things! Do you?" Azalea replied, caution vanishing as the conversation turned towards her favourite topic. "You'll have to meet Lindy, my mare," she continued when he nodded. "She's the most beautiful thing imaginable! Perfect lines, and the smoothest trot in Virginia. Do we have time to go down to the stables before supper, Grandfather?'' she asked eagerly, turning back to the older gentlemen.

"Certainly, my dear. You youngsters run along,'' Reverend Simpson replied with barely a glance in her direction. Azalea thought he looked grave. He obviously wanted to continue his discussion with Lord Glaedon. "Go for a ride if you wish. Supper will not be for an hour or more.''

"We'll return in time,'' Azalea promised, then turned back to Christian with sudden diffidence. "That is, if you wish to come, sir.'' He didn't seem at all like a "youngster'' to her!

"I'm quite counting on it,'' he responded with another warm smile. "And please, no more 'sirs'—it makes me feel positively ancient. Call me Chris.''

Azalea agreed delightedly. "You brought a horse from the inn, you said? I can have Lindy saddled in a flash. I'll show you a bit of Williamsburg before supper.''

Christian was finding young Miss Clayton unexpectedly likeable. He was not certain just what he had anticipated, but it was not this fresh, piquant womanchild.

When his father had first acquainted him with his plans, Christian had been dumbstruck and then affronted. The more the earl told him of the girl's circumstances, however, the more curious he had become. Now, very much to his surprise, he found himself actually giving his father's outrageous suggestion serious consideration.

"Grandfather keeps some prime bloods, as well as a couple of carriage horses,'' Azalea told him eagerly as her mare was saddled. "Lindy, of course, is my favourite, but I will be interested to know what you think of some of the others.''

Her enthusiasm made Christian smile, for horses were a passion of his, as well. It was...interesting to discover that they had that much in common, at least. ''I can scarcely wait. Perhaps tomorrow I might have opportunity to try the paces of one of them. I'm certain they will cast in the shade this nag I hired from the inn.''

A short time later, Chris accompanied Azalea down Queen Street toward the main thoroughfare of the town. He whistled tunefully as they went, to her secret delight. Whistling was something Swannee had often scolded her for doing. Still, even with his example before her she didn't quite dare to join in.

As it was late in the day, Duke of Gloucester Street was nearly deserted. ''I fear Williamsburg is not the hub of activity it was before the war,'' she told him apologetically as they turned their horses onto the wider road. ''Then, it was the capital of Virginia, and quite an important political centre for the whole country.''

Chris nodded. ''I read a bit of American history before leaving England. You seem quite thoroughly schooled in it, though.''

Azalea could feel herself blushing. ''Well, yes. I used to badger Grandfather to let me attend classes at the college.'' She pointed down the street the other way, to where a fine building, designed on noble lines by Sir Christopher Wren, was still visible in the failing light. ''Of course that was impossible, but he did arrange for a tutor. Dr. Jonas is so enraptured by Williamsburg's history, much of which, of course, he has lived through, that I couldn't help but get caught up in it.''

"Your grandfather teaches there as well, doesn't he?"

"Yes, as mathematician and grammarian. Do you know, he actually met Patrick Henry? That was the great orator who spoke out against the Stamp Act in that very building." She pointed to the capitol building. Now, however, that once-imposing structure stood empty, and signs of neglect were beginning to be visible. The focus of Williamsburg was now at the western end of Duke of Gloucester Street, where the College of William and Mary stood.

"We British were most unreasonable, were we not?"

The mildness of Chris's tone reminded Azalea abruptly that he and his countrymen doubtless viewed the outcome of the war rather differently than the Americans did. Casting about for another topic, she felt some relief when she noticed a sandy-haired youth approaching them on foot.

"Jonathan!" Azalea called, waving to the boy.

He quickened his pace. "Hullo, 'Zalea! You're out late. Who's your friend?"

She couldn't quite keep a trace of smugness from her tone as she answered. "This is Mr. Morely. He and his father, the Earl of Glaedon..." she paused to more fully enjoy Jonathan's expression of awe "...are visiting with us for a few days. Chris, this is my best friend, Jonathan Plummer."

To his credit, Jonathan recovered quickly. "Pleased to make your acquaintance, sir," he said with a shy grin. "Does this mean our picnic is off, 'Zalea?"

"Goodness, I'd forgotten! Yes, I suppose so, Jonathan. We can do it next week just as well." She blushed again, hoping Jonathan would not mention in front of Christian that their picnic was to take place in the branches of a tree. But he merely nodded, saluted Christian and sauntered on his way.

As he retreated, Azalea couldn't help comparing her old comrade to the gentleman at her side. Jonathan's father was a wealthy planter and had been a baronet before coming to America some twenty years ago. And his mother had been daughter to an English viscount, which, she had previously thought, made Jonathan nearly nobility.

Azalea had to laugh at such a notion now. Why, next to Chris, he was a simple country boy! She did not pause to consider that Jonathan's age, a mere year greater than her own, did him no good in the comparison. "I'll show you the magazine and guardhouse," she said to Chris, turning her mare. "Then I suppose we should return for supper."

AZALEA WAS IN HIGH spirits at breakfast the next morning. Christian and his father were due to return before dinnertime with their trunks. Rooms had been readied for them, and she and Chris were planning another, longer ride that afternoon.

She already regarded Chris as a friend. The fact that he seemed not to think of her as a mere child was a definite point in his favour. Of course, there was only a five-year difference in their ages, where Papa had been nine years older than Mama....

Abruptly, Azalea shook her head, causing the reverend to glance up from his morning papers. What on earth was she thinking of? Determinedly, she gave her attention to the ham and eggs before her.

A few minutes later, her grandfather put his papers aside. "When you've finished, my dear, could you give me a moment of your time in the library? I'll wait for you there."

"Of course, Grandfather. I'll only be a moment."

She was not especially curious. The reverend often requested her help in cataloguing or in reading the fine print that strained his eyes. He might even have a game of chess in mind, and Azalea had to admit she could use the practice. Quickly, she finished the last of her biscuit and milk and followed the old gentleman into the library.

"Yes, Grandfather? What is it you wish me to do?"

She breezed in, fresh as the bright spring morning in a pale green gown, her coppery curls bouncing at her shoulders. Reverend Simpson regarded her almost wistfully for a moment, then coughed and became very businesslike.

"I'd like you to take a seat and listen carefully to what I am about to tell you, with a minimum of questions, at least until I have finished."

Her curiosity now thoroughly aroused, Azalea sat in the chair he indicated and looked at him expectantly.

"After supper last night," he began, "I had a very long talk with Howard. As you know, my health is not what it once was. This infernal cough becomes worse by the month, and the doctor says that my heart is weak as well. No, no, my dear, I do not say this to alarm you," he said quickly when Azalea gasped with dismay, "but merely to help explain what I am about to suggest.

"Howard also acquainted me with some particulars regarding your English inheritance, which he looked into at my request. The means by which your uncle, Lord Kayce, gained possession of the properties is suspect, to say the least. So far, he seems unaware of your existence, but we cannot assume that he will remain so forever. Therefore, Howard and I both agree that you need stronger protection than I can provide you, especially given my present state of health. The most reasonable solution involves a marriage—"

"Marriage? Me? But I'm only thirteen! How—"

Her grandfather stopped the flow of questions with an upraised hand. "Azalea, please hear me out," he said in a firmer tone than usual.

Squelching her curiosity, she nodded meekly and he continued.

"Shortly after your birth, Howard and I discussed—not very seriously at the time, I must admit—the possibility of your eventual marriage to one of his sons. He has now made you an offer of marriage on behalf of his second son, Christian."

Azalea opened her mouth, but the reverend forestalled her with a glance.

"This would be an excellent match for both of you in worldly terms, of course," he went on, "but more importantly, it would give Howard legal authority to set about protecting your birthright. In addition, your marriage would afford you another kind of protection against your uncle, who may be less than pleased when he learns about you—which he will do, once Howard puts his plans into motion. Add to that the fact that Howard is my oldest and dearest friend—"

"You have betrothed me without my consent?" Azalea broke in indignantly, no longer able to contain herself. "Am I to be shipped across the ocean just like that? Grandfather, how could you?" She couldn't decide whether to scream or cry.

"You have been reading novels again and neglecting your studies, I perceive," the reverend said drily.

"Nothing so melodramatic as that, I assure you. One reason I waited until this morning to broach the subject was to give you an opportunity to meet Christian and form an opinion of him before being ... prejudiced ... by the reason for his visit. It *seems* that you like him quite well. In any event, no irrevocable steps have been taken, nor will they be, without your consent."

Reverend Simpson paused for a moment and made a great business of polishing his spectacles before continuing.

"Considering your youth, the marriage would be, ah, in name only for several years. It is my hope that you would remain here for at least a portion of that time, after which you would join Christian in England. You may now ask questions," he concluded, looking up at her with a resigned expression.

With that encouragement, Azalea found herself, for the first time since she had learned to talk, devoid of questions. Her mind was a whirl. With the fear of immediate removal from the only life she had ever known allayed, she began to view the prospect of marriage as exciting, rather than frightening.

And to Chris! Surely, even if she waited years and years, and had her pick of all the men in the world, she'd never find anyone so perfect, so handsome, so... interesting! Already teetering on the edge of her first romantic infatuation, Azalea tumbled headlong at the thought.

But what had Grandfather said? That the earl had made the offer "on Christian's behalf," whatever that meant.

"Does Christian know about this, Grandfather?" she asked, suddenly fearful of the answer.

"Why, of course. He was with us in the library after supper, if you recall. He offered no objections, if that is what worries you."

No objections. But also no assurances that she was the girl he would have chosen for a bride.

But she was being silly now. Of course Christian could not love her after only a few hours in her company. But once she was his wife, she thought, blithely, she could surely win his heart. And as for herself, if she was not a little in love with him already, she knew that she soon would be.

"All right, Grandfather. I will marry him."

"WELL, SON, HAVE YOU decided then?" Lord Glaedon enquired as the last of their luggage was loaded onto the hired carriage. "Don't feel that you have to take this step for my sake, or even the girl's, although I admit that is more of a consideration, in my opinion."

"Yes, Father," Christian replied, "I intend to go through with it—partly for your sake, partly for hers and even partly for my own. She's a taking little thing and shows promise of growing into quite a beauty. And I'm quite certain she won't bore me!" He grinned, recalling how her outspoken enthusiasm had led her into more than one social blunder at supper last night.

"In any event, I won't precisely be giving up my freedom for four or five years yet," he continued. "And if any of the young Marriage-Mart misses become too warm, I can always frighten them off with sentimental stories of my little American wife. An enviable position all round, I think."

His father glanced at him sharply, pausing in the act of climbing into the carriage. "I hope you intend to be discreet when we return to England, Christian. I'll withdraw the proposal at once if your recklessness is likely to cause Azalea pain. Gregory is my closest friend, and I feel rather a strong responsibility for his granddaughter, under the circumstances."

"As well you might, since you dreamed up this situation," retorted Christian, his smile fading. "But your worries are groundless, Father. I would never intentionally hurt a young innocent like Azalea. Indeed, I have hopes that in a few years we may deal quite famously together. She appears to be unusually intelligent and we share several interests already."

"Both horse mad, you mean," said Lord Glaedon with a chuckle, apparently reassured. "I suppose couples have entered into the married state with less in common, and still made a pretty good go of it. Do you plan to make her an offer in form?"

Christian swung up into the coach beside his father. "Why not? I know she's very young, but she'll no doubt enjoy it. And besides, every girl should have the right to at least one proposal of marriage in her life, shouldn't she?"

Christian smiled to himself, imagining Azalea's reaction when he proposed. Really, she was a most engaging child.

"I hadn't considered it quite in that light," said the earl, "but you are probably right."

DINNER WAS A RATHER uncomfortable meal for all concerned, as no opportunity had yet occurred for the reverend and the earl to compare notes on their private discussions with their respective charges.

Azalea kept stealing surreptitious glances at her soon-to-be betrothed, and Christian did likewise, attempting to discover from her manner whether her grandfather had mentioned anything to her.

This was going to be deuced awkward if he hadn't, Christian realized belatedly. Imagine proposing to a thirteen-year-old girl out of the blue—she would either swoon or think he had run mad. He was determined to get some indication of whether the ground had been prepared before proceeding, and began directing questioning looks, accompanied by much throat clearing, at Reverend Simpson.

Upon receiving a knowing wink and a slight nod in return, Christian was able to relax and enjoy the remainder of the meal. He realized, on reflection, that Azalea's very silence should have told him what he wished to know.

Shortly after dinner, the horses were saddled and brought round to the front of the house for the ride the young couple had agreed upon the previous evening. Azalea had changed into a charming grey riding habit that perfectly matched her silvery mare, Lindy. Chris was attired in a deeper shade of grey, his gleaming black boots mirroring the spirited stallion he was to ride.

"You so admired Spartan last night that I thought you might like to try his paces. He's the best mount in Grandfather's stables—excepting Lindy, here, of course." Azalea seemed to be recovering some of her usual animation with the arrival of the horses.

"You were very perceptive," replied Chris. "I was nearly drooling over this fellow yesterday, but didn't dare suggest you mount me on such an obviously valuable animal."

"Yes, I suppose he would bring a small fortune if he were sold, but of course we have no intention of parting with him. He was bred here, as was his dam. I daresay Grandfather's cattle would compare favourably with any stable in Virginia—and perhaps even in England!''

Chris could only agree. Chatting comfortably once again, the pair mounted and started down the broad gravelled drive at a brisk trot.

Azalea led Chris along one of her favourite routes, pointing out the particular beauties of the landscape. The apple and dogwood trees were in full bloom, transforming the countryside into a fairyland of white and palest pink.

Presently, they turned off into a narrow lane with a daisy-strewn field on one side and a large apple orchard on the other. The subject of horses and horsemanship had been temporarily exhausted, mainly because Azalea's thoughts were too busy for her to be her usual talkative self.

''Do you mind if I ask a rather personal question?'' Christian asked after a brief pause. Azalea's heart beat faster and she shook her head, hoping that the blush she could feel rising to her cheeks wasn't noticeable. Her reins slipped slightly in her suddenly damp hands.

''Well,'' he continued, ''it's your name. I've never heard it before and I wondered what it meant. Is it a family name or something?''

This was so completely opposite to what Azalea had expected to hear that she almost choked on a laugh.

''A family... No, not exactly. You see, my mother was very fond of the flora of the New World and experimented extensively with some of the wild species. Her favourite was the azalea, a flowering shrub. Surely you've noticed the large bushes round the house?''

"Yes, now that you mention it. The ones with the pink and purple flowers along the front, you mean?"

"Yes, those are the biggest ones. My mother planted those when she was only a year or two older than I am now. She also had some white ones brought down from the mountains by a friend of my grandfather's. I'll show them to you when we return." Next to horses, Azalea loved to discuss botany and gardening, which, perhaps in memory of her mother, she had studied in depth.

Christian nodded, but did not pursue the topic. They trotted along for several minutes, Azalea in silence and Chris whistling a stirring march. Azalea almost wished that her grandfather had never mentioned that marriage business. Then she'd be enjoying this ride as she had yesterday's, delighting in her new friend instead of worrying over how she ought to behave when—or if— he broached the subject.

"You are a very good whistler," she ventured after a moment.

Chris broke off with a laugh. "Funny you should say that. I consider it an almost guilty pleasure, since Father discourages it and Herschel, my older brother, positively loathes it, mainly because he's never learned himself. But here, why do we not take a rest for a moment?" He gestured toward a broad, mossy rock.

They both dismounted to rest on the cool surface in the shade of an unusually large and gnarled apple tree. Azalea spread her skirts about her, resisting the impulse to draw her knees up to her chin as she usually did.

Desperately, she tried to think of something else to say. The silence progressed from companionable to uncomfortable. Inspiration had yet to strike when

Christian turned to her and said, "I assume, Azalea, that your grandfather has spoken to you about the possible . . . alliance . . . between our families?"

He was watching her a bit anxiously, and that unaccountably put her more at ease. Realizing that Chris was nervous, too, made him less an object of awe. Her heart warmed towards him with an affection that was more sincere than the infatuation she had already admitted to herself.

She nodded silently, unable to meet his eyes. Had he changed his mind? She waited for him to continue.

"Now that we are alone, I'd . . . like to take this opportunity to ask you to marry me. Will you, Azalea?" he went on in a rush.

Startled, she turned her eyes to him, unable to believe that she had understood him correctly. "You . . . you're actually proposing to me?" she asked incredulously, unable to hide her sudden joy. This was much more romantic than the dry agreement she had expected. Perhaps he really did care for her a little.

Christian tried not to flinch at the expression in her eyes. How could he ever live up to such expectation, such adoration? He vowed silently to do his utmost to spare her disillusionment in the years ahead.

"It's appropriate that we settle this matter between ourselves, don't you think?" he asked in as casual a voice as he could manage. "After all, we are the ones who will be sharing forty or fifty years together, not the estimable gentlemen who concocted this rather unconventional arrangement."

Taking a deep breath, he continued. "I'm by no means perfect—" he frowned, for it seemed somehow imperative that she understand this "—and cannot promise to become so, but I would never knowingly cause you pain. Consider, also, that by marrying me at so young an age you will be cheating yourself of the chance to be courted by other, quite possibly more worthy, gentlemen later on."

Why should such an idea suddenly bother him?

"I want you to fully realize what you would be agreeing to," he concluded. To his surprise, he found himself holding his breath as he waited for her reply, watching her face closely to gauge her feelings.

"I realize," she said solemnly.

Christian let out his breath.

"I realized before I gave Grandfather my consent this morning, for he also wanted me to be very sure. I am. Yes, Chris, I will marry you, if you really don't mind being tied to a thirteen-year-old wife. I promise to grow up as quickly as I can!"

"Don't grow up too quickly, Azalea," said Christian quickly, surprising himself by his seriousness. "I may deprive you of other suitors, but I refuse to deprive you of your childhood. Enjoy it while you can. Promise me?"

"All—all right, I promise," Azalea answered, plainly startled by his earnestness.

"Thank you." The innocence in her wide green eyes moved him in a way he found hard to understand. "In return, I promise to make you as happy as I possibly can." He spoke it as a vow.

THE WEDDING TOOK PLACE three days later at Bruton Parish Church. Due to Azalea's youth, only the rector and his wife were present in addition to the four people principally concerned.

The usual announcement had not been placed in the local newspaper. Reverend Simpson had thought it best that Azalea's marriage not be publicized in Williamsburg. It might make her social life uncomfortable, he said, to be perceived as being "different" from her peers.

The rector's wife began to play the organ, signalling the start of the ceremony, and Azalea entered the sanctuary dressed, not in a real bridal gown, but in her best white poplin.

Glancing around nervously, she took in every detail of the familiar church, which she had attended weekly all her life. Everything now seemed new and different. For one thing, the rector was not perched in his customary place in the carved wooden pulpit, where he could look down on the congregation in their private pews. Instead, he stood at the front altar, as he normally did only for communion.

As the church was nearly empty, the usual rustlings and whisperings of the assembled congregation were strangely absent. The aisle appeared abnormally long as she slowly walked between the high wooden walls of the vacant pews. She hadn't thought she would be nervous, but now...

Christian watched her progress from his position next to the altar and couldn't help thinking how young and defenceless Azalea looked. An unexpected surge of protectiveness welled up in him. He suddenly regretted that he would have to leave her here, in the wilds of this new, untamed country. Of course, she would have her grandfather to watch over her, but still...

When Azalea finally reached the altar, the participants took their places and the rector began his homily. Neither bride nor groom heard much of his explanation of the purpose and responsibilities of marriage. It hardly seemed to apply in their case.

Abruptly, they were repeating the vows, and Azalea heard herself saying, " . . . until death us do part."

The very permanency of the oath made her tremble. How well did she know Chris, really? Glancing up, she met his eyes and he winked reassuringly. She sighed. Everything would be all right.

At the conclusion of the ceremony Christian hesitated, then kissed his new bride on the forehead. Azalea was slightly disappointed, but chided herself for the feeling. She knew it had been agreed that this would not be a true marriage for some years. Suddenly recalling what Clara Banks had told her about her sister's wedding night, she knew she should be relieved.

Then her new father-in-law was hugging her, the rector's wife offering congratulations and there was no more time for relief or regret. She was Mrs. Christian Morely.

WALKING HOME from Jonathan's farewell party, Azalea noticed the unmistakeable signs of autumn in the rosy blush of the dogwood leaves and the prominence of their berries. A few chrysanthemums bloomed in the tangle of weeds by the walls of the old magazine.

She did not pause long to admire such botanical delights this afternoon, for there was already a noticeable nip in the air, and dusk would be coming early. Azalea was going to miss Jonathan. True, they had not been as close this past year, but that was no doubt due mainly to the fact that they had less free time to spend together.

In the six months since her marriage, Azalea felt that she had hardly kept her promise to Christian not to grow up too fast. Everyone was pushing her to learn so many things. She had little time now for horses and gardens—or for romping with Jonathan.

And now her friend was leaving for England, to attend Oxford at his maternal grandfather, Lord Holte's, insistence. Perhaps she'd see him when she went to London in another few years. Wouldn't he be surprised!

For Azalea had reluctantly agreed to keep her marriage secret. Not even Swannee had been told. Although she knew that her friends would treat her differently if they knew, she would dearly have loved to tweak Missy Farmer's so superior nose with the news.

But the worst thing was not being able to confide in Jonathan. She knew he would never have been able to keep such a plum to himself, no matter how many promises she extracted from him. Perhaps it was just as well she had seen so little of him since the wedding.

She had managed to convince herself that having such a delicious secret more than made up for missing the satisfaction of seeing everybody's reaction to her news. It had helped to keep life interesting in the absence of the rather unconventional pastimes she had previously enjoyed. To think it had been three months, at least, since she had so much as climbed a tree!

Azalea sighed to herself as she pushed open the self-closing gate, weighted by an old cannon-ball on a chain, to enter the back gardens. If only the time would pass more quickly. The years stretching ahead of her before she could join Chris in England seemed like an eternity.

He and Lord Glaedon had returned after their trip to Richmond, but had been able to stay for a mere three days before meeting their ship. Wistfully, Azalea wished again that she and Chris could have had more time together.

Perhaps Grandfather could be persuaded that sixteen would be old enough for her to join her husband, she thought, returning to her favourite subject. After all, only two months ago Gwenny Pugh, the postmistress's youngest daughter, had married at sixteen.

With this argument in mind, Azalea skipped up the front porch steps and entered the house. She let the door slam behind her, and at once Millie, the young serving maid who doubled as Cook's assistant, scurried from the parlour, where she had apparently been waiting for her young mistress.

"Oh, miss, thank the good Lord you've come home at last!" she exclaimed in obvious agitation. "The reverend, he's been asking after you this past hour and more. Fair upset he seems to be! You'd best go to him at once."

"Upset? Do you mean he is angry with me?" Azalea asked in some confusion, unable to think of any scrapes she might have gotten into recently.

"Oh, no, miss!" replied Millie. "I only meant that he seems disturbed. He got some letter or message or some such, and he's been—"

Without waiting to hear the end of the girl's sentence, Azalea turned and ran to the library, a deep foreboding clutching at her heart.

Opening the door a crack, she cautiously peered inside to see her grandfather sitting before the dying fire, a crumpled paper in his lap. He seemed not to have heard her, but continued to stare unseeing into the flames. Azalea's apprehension increased.

"Grandfather?" she whispered.

The old man slowly turned towards her, and she was shocked at the change in his face. It was as though he had aged ten years in a few hours.

"What is it? What's wrong?" She could feel the blood draining from her face.

"You had better sit down, my dear. I'm afraid I have some very bad news," he said heavily.

He waited while Azalea shakily seated herself across from him.

"I don't know how to prepare you for this, child," he began in a voice devoid of expression. "I have received a letter from Herschel Morely, Howard's eldest son."

She closed her eyes, willing the words to stop, but her grandfather continued inexorably.

"The *Fortitude*, which was carrying his father and brother home to England, never reached port. It was lost in a storm at sea, along with its passengers and crew. No trace has been found of the ship, nor of any survivors. I'm sorry, Azalea."

CHAPTER TWO

September 1815

AZALEA CLOSED and fastened the valise containing the few clothes and essential toiletries she would need during her voyage. Everything else had already been packed in trunks and sent ahead. The sun was just rising, but in an hour's time a coach would arrive to carry her the forty miles to Hampton, where she would stay the night. The following day, she would board a ship for England.

She sighed as she contemplated the tedious journey before her. The months after her grandfather's death had been spent preparing for the voyage, down to the smallest detail, yet she felt far from prepared mentally. Mechanically, she walked to the window and gazed out over the lawns.

The past six years were almost a blur in her memory. Only a few events stood out clearly in her mind. One, of course, was the day she'd learned of Christian's death at sea. Her grandfather had suffered a seizure two days after receipt of that sad news, brought on, no doubt, by the stress of coping with both his own grief and Azalea's. He never fully recovered his faculties and for his final two years had been entirely bedridden.

Azalea had taken over all of his care completely, though her grandfather repeatedly expressed concern that such determined devotion, while touching, was an unhealthy escape from reality.

"The world goes on, my dear, and so must your life," he had said. "You cannot hide here with me forever. There is money to spare with which to hire a nurse for my care. An hour or two of your time in the evenings, playing chess or reading, would content me. I would not have you waste your youth at my bedside and then remember me with bitterness because of it when I am gone."

"You know how much you mean to me, Grandfather," she had replied. "It is my own choice to be here. The boys have all gone away to school or are tied up in their farming, and I never did have much in common with other girls and their silly, gossiping ways. I am much happier here with you, believe me."

Eventually, she allowed the persistent Mrs. Swann to share a bit in his nursing, but she used the time only to tend her neglected gardens and horses. Azalea had spoken truthfully when she'd said she had little desire for the society of others.

This was still true. Well-meaning neighbours came and went, their sympathy a cloak for curiosity. Especially unwelcome was the frequently asked question, "What will you do now?"

For Azalea's future seemed more of a blur than the past, even though her path had been carefully laid for her. Despite his infirmity, Reverend Simpson had prepared quite thoroughly for his granddaughter's future, she found. When it became clear that he could not linger much longer, he had summoned his lawyer, dictated letters and made certain changes to his will.

The reading of that will was another event that stood out clearly in her mind. Reverend Simpson had left all of his land and possessions to Azalea, which in itself had not surprised her. But the conditions of her inheritance did—that she sell the house and land and, with the proceeds, remove herself to England. There she was to establish herself in London and regain her inheritance, currently held by her uncle, Lord Kayce.

She had assumed her grandfather's primary motive in stipulating such a course was to prevent her from retreating further from society, but then she read the letters that accompanied the will.

The first must have been written early in his illness, as it was in her grandfather's hand. It detailed his suspicions of Lord Kayce, citing as evidence various things Azalea's own father had told him years ago. If these suspicions were to be believed, Lord Kayce had forced his elder brother to flee England in order to secure for himself the vast Kayce lands and wealth. Included in the letter was a stern warning to Azalea not to trust her uncle.

The second letter was from a Lady Beauforth, first cousin to Azalea's mother and niece to her grandfather. It was dated quite recently, and obviously in response to a query the reverend had sent some months earlier.

My dear Uncle Gregory:
I was delighted to hear from you after so many years. I remember you with affection from my childhood, and Mother always spoke lovingly of you. Of course, I would be delighted to offer my young cousin Azalea entrée to London Society. She will be wonderful company for my own

daughter, Marilyn, whom your Azalea cannot fail
to love as dearly as I do. And how exciting to have
a young American in our midst! Such a pity that
your health will prevent you from accompanying
her, but the whirl of London is always more enjoyable to the young, in any event.

I will endeavour to introduce Azalea about
without mentioning her American origin, unless
her accent should give her away—to avoid any
unpleasantness about the recent war, you understand. Of course, I have never much regarded
politics, nor have most of my friends, so do not
worry on that score. Please assure her that she will
be delighted with Town life. We shall await Azalea's arrival impatiently.

Your devoted niece, etc.
Alice Beauforth

A postscript to this letter, dictated by her grandfather, informed Azalea that for all of her apparent
flightiness, Lady Beauforth was very highly placed in
Society and would afford Azalea ample protection
while she regained her own fortune—protection he
could no longer give her.

Also enclosed with the letters were the proofs of
Azalea's marriage to Christian, with instructions to
use them, if necessary, to enlist the aid of Herschel
Morely, the new Lord Glaedon, in her mission.

Azalea had reluctantly answered Lady Beauforth's
somewhat disjointed missive, informing her cousin of
Reverend Simpson's death and of her own expected
arrival date in England. She had no intention of concealing her nationality, of course, but refrained from
mentioning this in her letter.

She also omitted any mention of Lord Kayce, her early marriage and her plans to gain her inheritance. If her uncle really were dangerous, no good could come of giving him advance warning of her arrival or her existence. And, after reading her rambling letter, she did not trust Lady Beauforth to remain silent on any point.

Thus it was a very brief, almost terse, note that Lady Beauforth received. No doubt that lady would attribute it to her young cousin's grief, or the influence of having been brought up in the wilds. Azalea could not bring herself to care overmuch which.

Absently, she fingered the large packet containing a copy of the will, the letters and the marriage lines. On impulse, she opened it again, to glance through the contents. There was the marriage certificate, with signatures of the rector, Dr. Wills, as having performed the ceremony and of Mrs. Wills as witness, as well as a document of consent signed by her grandfather.

Her throat tightened when she saw Christian's signature above her own childish one. Even after so many years, that loss still hurt.

She returned the certificate to the packet and tucked it into a compartment of her valise. Fastening it, she took a final glance around to assure herself that nothing had been forgotten and then turned and closed the door on the echoing chamber that had been her bedroom for most of her nineteen years.

The sound brought Millie, the mulatto servant, out of her own room at the end of the upstairs hallway. "Why, miss! I didn't know you was awake! I never heard a sound in your room all morning. You should have at least called me to help you dress—I could use the practice. Miz Swann says young ladies don't never

dress theirselves in Londonengland.'' Millie's hands
fluttered about her as she spoke.

"Yes, Millie, I'll have to get used to that myself, I
suppose. But for this morning, I was certain you would
have enough to do without helping me to dress. Besides, this gown fastens down the front, so it was no
trouble at all for me to do myself."

Azalea was clad in half mourning, her simple dress
of deep plum ornamented only by black lace at throat
and wrists. Her hair reached nearly to her waist, its
colour having deepened over the past few years to a
rich auburn. Her hermitlike existence had caused her
youthful tan to fade and her complexion was now of a
paleness to rival that of any London lady addicted to
creams and sunshades.

Her eyes, however, had not changed at all; they remained the deep grey-green of the Atlantic. The fairy-
like figure the young girl of thirteen had possessed had
ripened until, at nineteen, Azalea was endowed by nature with the full bust and tiny waist that so many
women of her time used padding and corsets to
achieve.

"Breakfast is ready, girls!" called Mrs. Swann from
the foot of the stairs.

Azalea thought the housekeeper looked younger,
somehow. Perhaps it was the excitement of setting out
on a journey that had put the sparkle in her eye; that,
or the knowledge that she was going back to her
homeland and a reunion with her two sisters.

Looking at Mrs. Swann, Azalea felt a small stirring
of anticipation in her own breast. Maybe she *had* been
cloistered away in this house for too long. Feeling suddenly more optimistic, she went down to breakfast.

The hired coach drew up to the front of the house just as the travellers finished breakfast. In a final flurry, cloaks, hats and gloves were found, and Mrs. Swann ushered the two girls out the door and down to the waiting coach.

Azalea was American to the core. Never having made much distinction of rank, she felt more as if she were travelling with an older and younger sister than with two servants. This was fortunate, as it made her departure from all she had ever known much less frightening.

With only a brief stop for refreshment at midday, they made good time over the surprisingly well-maintained roads, one of the few benefits of the recent war. They arrived at Hampton just after four o'clock.

Azalea was struck immediately by the unusual appearance of the town, which brought home to her the suffering caused by that second conflict with England, during which Hampton had been burned to the ground. In the intervening year much reconstruction had taken place, but stark, blackened ruins still dominated the scene.

Passing a large cathedral, she saw that some of the original structure remained, its red brick bell tower discolored by smoke, while two wooden wings were obviously newly built. The same combination of charred stone and recent woodwork, still under construction, could be seen throughout the busy town.

She realized how very fortunate they had been in Williamsburg to have escaped the worst ravages of this "Second War of Independence." Even there, though, where no English troops had come, the people had not gone unscathed. Several sons of local farmers and

merchants, and even two students she had known, had
departed to join the defending army and never returned.

A sudden surge of resentment against the British
startled her with its violence. How dared they! Her resolve to openly acknowledge herself an American became stronger, regardless of Cousin Alice or any other
squeamish family members.

The coach finally stopped in front of The Republic
Inn, a large, partially rebuilt house within sight of the
docks. The glass windows and fresh paint proclaimed
it a prosperous establishment and a well-maintained
one.

Alighting from the coach before the coachman could
climb down to assist her, Azalea turned to help Millie
and Mrs. Swann descend.

"Let's get inside for a hot meal and a good night's
sleep on dry land," Mrs. Swann recommended cheerfully. "We've got quite a day ahead of us tomorrow."

GAZING AROUND the drawing-room of the Beauforth
Town house on Curzon Street, Azalea was overcome by
depression. She did not doubt that this was one of the
finer houses in London, as Sir Matthew Beauforth had
possessed a fortune of no little consequence. But the
cold formality of the chamber, with its gilt chairs and
white upholstery, did nothing to lift her spirits, now
weighed down by apprehension, loneliness and fa-
tigue.

Immediately upon her arrival nearly an hour ago,
Mrs. Swann and Millie had been ushered off to the
servants' quarters by a housekeeper so stiff and fastid-
iously dressed that Azalea had at first mistaken her for
Lady Beauforth.

The butler, Smythe—if possible even more coldly formal than Mrs. Straite (whose name Azalea found peculiarly appropriate)—had shown her into this room with the intimation that Lady Beauforth would see her shortly.

Azalea's stomach growled. She was just wondering whether "shortly" meant something different in England than it had at home when a short, fat, gaudily gowned lady swept into the drawing-room, her bejeweled hands outstretched. An overpowering cloud of violet fragrance enveloped Azalea as the woman advanced.

"You must be little Azalea Clayton! Have you been *very* bored, my dear? I only just finished dressing after my afternoon nap."

Azalea was torn between an urge to laugh at the lady's appearance and a reluctance to breathe in her sickly sweet perfume. Collecting herself, she rose and extended her own hand.

"Lady Beauforth?" she asked uncertainly. After her experience with the housekeeper, she was afraid to jump to conclusions.

"Cousin Alice, my dear, please! Let us not stand on ceremony—we are kin, after all. Was your journey *dreadful?* You'll want to go straight to your room and sleep for *days,* I am certain. I was so sorry to hear about poor Uncle Gregory! You must feel the loss just *dreadfully,* my dear."

Azalea nodded noncommittally, wondering if this could possibly be her cousin's real speaking voice. Surely no one could feign that high-pitched tone indefinitely.

"Lady—Cousin Alice," Azalea said when it appeared that her hostess had temporarily run out of words, "I want to thank you so much for your willingness to take me in and sponsor me. I hope I won't be obliged to impose upon your kindness for too long."

"Tut, tut, my dear! What is family for? Besides, there is very little generosity in this case, as Uncle Gregory insisted on paying all of your expenses himself."

Azalea winced at this reminder of the terms of her grandfather's will, which she had not been certain Lady Beauforth understood. She was relieved to find that apparently she did, and that there was no chance of her being mistaken for a charity case.

Meanwhile Lady Beauforth, who was not quite so shatter-brained as she appeared, was making some calculations of her own regarding Azalea. With her air of maturity and grace, her unusual colouring and striking beauty, the girl was bound to cause a stir in the fashionable world of the ton. At first glance, she might not take—that gown was positively dowdy—but in a new wardrobe, with her hair stylishly cut...

"Now, my dear, I absolutely *insist* that you rest until tea," she said firmly. "If you're asleep, we shan't wake you till dinner, or even breakfast, if you prefer." Lady Beauforth needed some time to reorganize her thinking before her darling Marilyn made Azalea's acquaintance. This was not the rough savage they had both expected.

"Thank you, Cousin Alice, I am a bit fatigued. But please do not let me sleep through dinner, or I might well starve before breakfast." Azalea rose with a smile and followed a hovering maidservant out of the room.

As she climbed the curving oak staircase, she was struck again by the elegance of the furnishings she could see from this vantage point. Obviously someone other than Lady Beauforth had been in charge of decorating the house, unless her cousin's eccentricities were limited to matters of dress and speech, which Azalea somehow doubted. Most likely the bulk of it had been done by generations past, or perhaps by hired professionals.

"This here's your room, miss," the young maid said, interrupting Azalea's musings. "Her ladyship let Miss Marilyn choose the room, and she must have thought you'd be most comfortable here." She opened the door to the chamber and stepped aside. "My name's Junie, if you should be needing anything."

Azalea smiled warmly at the girl. "Thank you, Junie. I'm afraid I'm not very good company right now. I'm very tired. We'll have time for a good talk later, I'm sure."

"Of—of course, miss," the girl said, plainly disconcerted. "Will you be needing anything now? Her ladyship said as how I should unpack for you and act as your abigail, if you approve, of course." She smiled tentatively.

"That's very sweet, Junie, but I've already promised Millie, who travelled all the way from America with me, that she should have that post. I hope that won't cause a problem?"

"Oh, no, miss, I don't see how it would," Junie replied, though she looked a bit disappointed. "I'll just tell Mrs. Straite you've brought your own abigail. I'll continue on as upstairs maid. I was promoted just last month," she added proudly, with another shy smile.

Azalea realized that becoming her personal abigail would have represented an even greater promotion and thought she understood the girl's disappointment.

"How wonderful for you," she said warmly. "But I've just had an idea. Millie is an American, like myself, and has no real experience as a fashionable lady's maid. Do you suppose Mrs. Straite would consent to your training her? Both she and I would be very grateful, I assure you."

Junie's face broke into a delighted smile. "I'll ask her right away, miss! And thank you, miss!" she exclaimed, fairly skipping from the room.

Alone, Azalea finally had an opportunity to look about her room. Even at first glance it was apparent that the furnishings were not quite up to the standard of the rest of the house, though they were still far finer than any she had been used to. Azalea guessed that furniture a little too worn for the finer guest rooms had been put here, but she didn't mind a bit. The room was done in faded shades of green and gold, which she found soothing, and the bed and chairs looked more comfortable than newer ones might be.

Crossing to the window, Azalea caught her first glimpse of the gardens and gasped with delight. What a botanical wonderland! Even in late November, a few chrysanthemums were in bloom, and she could identify several species of ornamental shrubs.

She would explore the gardens as soon as she went back down—well, after some tea, anyway. She was famished—and tired. Removing her shoes, Azalea stretched out on the gold counterpane of the bed and closed her eyes. Just a few minutes rest . . .

Hunger awakened her several hours later. The sun had set, and Azalea found herself in almost total darkness. For a few moments she imagined she was still in the ship's cabin, but was recalled to her surround-

ings by the distant sound of hooves and carriage wheels
from the street.

Rising, she hurried to the window in an effort to de-
termine the hour. The last faint rays of the recently departed sun informed her that there should still be ample
time to dress before dinner. How late would that be,
here? Swannee had told her that Town meals were later
than those in the country, but she hadn't been specific. Perhaps each household kept its own hours.

Fumbling along the top of the dressing-table, Azalea
found a branch of candles and lit them from the em-
bers of what that afternoon had been a cheerful fire.
Opening the clothes-press in the corner of the chamber, she was pleased to find that the efficient Junie had
unpacked and hung her gowns, and had apparently
even shaken out the worst of the travel creases.

Selecting her best gown, a deep rust-coloured velvet, she donned it with full knowledge that it would
hardly stand comparison with the fashionable crea-
tions she had seen in a ladies' periodical on the drawing-room table earlier. Shopping for new clothes would
have to be high on her list of things to do.

Her hair was neat, but hardly attractive, drawn severely back from her face and twisted into a knot at the
base of her neck. However, this was the only style,
other than letting it hang loose, that she was capable of
on her own, and she knew that Millie could scarcely
have done better. Hairdressing was not one of the girl's
strong points.

Feeling very much the dowdy country cousin, Azalea
descended the stairs and paused at the bottom, listening for voices that might give her a clue as to where the
family was assembled at this hour. A murmur behind

the doors of the drawing-room encouraged her to approach.

Entering, she beheld her cousin, still attired in her brilliant rose, yellow and amethyst silks, speaking with a dazzling young lady dressed with impeccable and obviously expensive taste. At Azalea's entrance, the young lady turned wide, blandly interested eyes in her direction.

"Awake already, my dear?" Lady Beauforth asked solicitously. "I was going to have Junie check on you in half an hour, when I retired to my room to dress for dinner."

Azalea's imagination faltered at what her ladyship's idea of evening attire might be.

"Did you rest at all?"

"Oh, yes, Cousin Alice, I feel very refreshed. Truth to tell, it was hunger that awakened me, and not knowing the dinner hour here, I thought it best to dress and come down directly."

"How thoughtless of me! Of course, you would not be familiar with our customs yet. Dinner won't be for another hour and more—Marilyn and I were going upstairs to dress in a few more minutes."

Thus recalling Marilyn's presence, Lady Beauforth turned to introduce Azalea to her daughter, whose smile had become rather fixed.

"Marilyn, this is your cousin, Azalea Clayton, of course. Azalea, let me present my daughter, Miss Marilyn Beauforth." This last was said with a flourish, and her ladyship stepped back as if presenting a rare artwork to view.

Azalea was suitably impressed. She could scarcely conceive of a more perfect picture of fashion than the beautiful creature now facing her. Honey-coloured hair was piled artistically atop her graceful head in a style that caused Azalea an unfamiliar twinge of envy. The beautiful creature seemed a shade less than charmed, however.

"Pleased to make your acquaintance, I'm certain, Miss Clayton," Marilyn said with a slight nod. The formality of her words clashed oddly with her voice— a high, childish lisp that was still a good octave lower than her mother's.

"The honour is mine, Miss Beauforth," replied Azalea, following her cousin's lead. As Marilyn seemed disinclined to pursue the conversation further, Azalea turned back to Lady Beauforth.

"Ma'am, I could not help admiring your gardens from my window earlier. As I am down so early, would it be permissible for me to take a stroll through them before dinner?"

Though expressing surprise that Azalea should wish to walk out in the chill air after dark, Lady Beauforth saw no reason to disallow it, providing she was accompanied by Junie and wore a cloak.

Thanking her cousin with a warmth that drew surprised looks from both ladies, Azalea excused herself.

"Well!" Marilyn exclaimed pettishly as soon as the door had closed behind Azalea. "'Cousin Alice,' is it? And am I to be 'Cousin Marilyn'?" She shuddered delicately. "And her accent! Why, simply to be seen with her—was she really dressed for dinner, do you think?—may well lower me in Society."

Her mama tut-tutted and reassured her, but Marilyn seemed unwilling to clasp her new-found cousin to her bosom as Lady Beauforth had hoped she might.

Meanwhile, oblivious of the conversation within doors, Azalea was enjoying her tour of the gardens immensely. Led by her nose, she had discovered two late-blooming roses of a variety she had never encountered in Virginia.

Azalea appealed to Junie for information about this rare strain. Junie was forced to plead ignorance but, not wanting to disappoint her new idol, volunteered to introduce Azalea to the gardener on the morrow.

"He knows every flower and bush in the place, miss, and would dearly love to talk to someone what knows so much as yourself, I know."

"That would be lovely. Thank you, Junie," said Azalea. "But now, I suppose I had best hurry inside to comb my hair before dinner."

"Might I dress it for you, miss? I've been taught how, and even did Miss Marilyn's once, when her abigail was sick," Junie offered eagerly.

"Could you? That's one thing I'm certain Millie cannot do yet. Perhaps you can be my personal hairdresser, as well as Millie's tutor."

When Azalea descended to the dining-room half an hour later, her confidence was bolstered by the knowledge that her hairstyle, at least, rivaled that of her cousin Marilyn. True to her word, Junie knew her business and had arranged Azalea's hair beautifully, with curling tendrils escaping from a high crown to frame her face.

Junie had assured her that with a little more time and a little less hair she could have done even better. After seeing Junie's ability, Azalea had promised to have her hair cut in the morning, even before visiting a dressmaker. She realized that she would need her cousins' advice on these matters, and determined to bring up the subject at dinner.

Proceeding to the place at table indicated by Smythe, Azalea was gratified by the slight widening of Miss Beauforth's eyes, taking it as a compliment to Junie's skill. Lady Beauforth was more outspoken, cheerfully greeting Azalea from her place at the head of the table.

"Why, what a difference that hairstyle makes, my dear! I declare, you look like a new person. Don't you agree, darling?" she asked hopefully, turning toward her daughter.

Marilyn responded with an insincere smile. "Indeed, it makes you look almost English. A definite improvement."

Azalea had to bite her tongue to suppress the angry retort that rose to her lips. If it were not so absurd, she might almost think Marilyn was jealous of her. However, it would not do to antagonize her relatives on her first evening in their home.

"Thank you," she forced herself to say. "I thought perhaps tomorrow I might have it cut as well. Junie tells me it is far too long and thick to be fashionable."

"Junie?" Marilyn looked blank.

"The upstairs maid. It was she who styled my hair."

Marilyn's glance slid negligently away to focus on her mother, who had already launched into a stream of advice to Azalea concerning the only hairdressers and modistes worth visiting.

"I vow, you'll be quite a credit to us when you are properly attired," she declared. "We'll have you betrothed by the end of the Season, I doubt not. It is most fortunate that you have come to us now, when we shall have all winter to bring you smack up to the nines."

"Mama, I was just thinking about *my* wedding clothes," Marilyn interrupted with a sidelong glance at

Azalea. "I saw a new watered silk yesterday that would do admirably for my travelling dress."

"Are you to be wed soon, Cousin?" asked Azalea politely, to cover her dismay at Lady Beauforth's words. It had not occurred to her that she might be expected to marry. She didn't want another husband, at least not now. Not after Chris.... She hurriedly thrust the memory aside.

"Oh, yes, Marilyn has made *such* a conquest!" gushed Lady Beauforth before her daughter could answer. "And Lord Glaedon, old friend and neighbour that he is, has been *quite* flatteringly insistent on an early wedding date. It will scarce give us time to ready a suitable trousseau."

"No, Glaedon would not be put off till June, but must needs marry me in February," Marilyn tittered. "I must say he has been most attentive of late, as well." Demurely casting her eyes down, Marilyn glanced sideways through her lashes at her cousin, as though to ascertain if she was paying proper attention.

Azalea scarcely noticed. "Lord Glaedon, did you say, ma'am?" she asked in a tight, strained voice. Suddenly, it seemed difficult to breathe. "I—I did not know that you were acquainted with him."

She hardly knew what she was saying, the shock of hearing the name was so great. Of course, she had known that if she stayed permanently in England, she would likely encounter Christian's older brother eventually, but she had pushed that thought far to the back of her mind. The news that he was apparently a frequent visitor to this very house had taken her completely off guard.

Struggling to regain her composure, she noticed that her cousins were regarding her rather strangely. "What did you say, ma'am?'' Belatedly, she realized that Lady Beauforth had asked her a question.

"I asked how you come to know of Lord Glaedon, my dear. Are you all right? Your colour is quite gone. You are not about to swoon, are you?''

"Oh, no ma'am, I—I'm fine,'' Azalea answered in a tolerably steady voice. "I was merely startled.''

She took a few deep breaths to calm herself before explaining. "The previous earl, Lord Glaedon's father, was a close friend of my grandfather's, you see. He spoke of Lord Glaedon frequently, and was devastated by the news of his death. It—it is my belief that the shock played a large part in the illness to which he eventually succumbed.''

"Oh! Oh, I see,'' said her ladyship with a nod, her curiosity apparently satisfied. "No wonder mention of the name distressed you. But I do hope you won't mind meeting the present Earl of Glaedon. As he is Marilyn's fiancé, we encounter him frequently in Society, as well as here at home.''

Lady Beauforth's tone, while concerned, did not indicate any suspicion that Azalea had told considerably less than the truth. For that, Azalea could only be relieved. She had no intention of acquainting her cousins with the details of her early life. Of course, she had no reason to believe that Lord Glaedon would be so reticent once he knew who she was. It was even possible he might hold her partially responsible for the deaths of his father and younger brother.

She stifled a sigh. That was one problem she refused to worry about before it materialized.

"No, I'm certain I will be able to encounter his lordship with composure, Cousin Alice,'' Azalea assured her, hoping she spoke the truth. "It was merely the unexpectedness of hearing his name that overset me for a moment.''

Reassured on that point, Lady Beauforth resumed her instructions to the girls on where they were to shop on the morrow, since she would be unable to accompany them.

''I find my uncertain state of health makes it difficult for me to get about. I quite rejoice at the idea of your being able to accompany Marilyn to the shops and functions when I am unable to, Azalea—though of course we are delighted to have you here for your own sake, as well.''

This last statement was added almost as an afterthought, and gave Azalea some insight into her cousin's real motive for offering her a home. It also helped to explain the contradictory nature of the letter sent to her grandfather. The thought bothered Azalea very little. She liked to know where she stood with people, and acting as Marilyn's companion made staying here smack even less of accepting charity.

BACK IN HER ROOM, Azalea dismissed Junie for the night, after repeating Lady Beauforth's compliments on her hairstyle. Feeling no inclination to sleep, due, no doubt, to her nap earlier, Azalea reviewed her first day in London. In all, she found more to be pleased with than she had expected.

She had doubts whether she would ever become close to her cousins, but they had treated her cordially enough and she saw no cause for complaint. By the end of the week, she would begin her campaign to regain her inheritance.

Since leaving America, she had thought of little else, regarding that as her grandfather's dying wish. If nothing more, dwelling on it served to distract her from her grief over her grandfather, and yes, over Christian as well. That loss still had the power to cause her pain, even after all this time.

On the passage from America, she had found the very sea a constant reminder of him. She had tried to spend as little time as possible on deck, devoting her days instead to needlework and to Millie, who had been seasick for most of the passage. Occasionally, however, she had been irresistibly drawn to the railings of the foredeck, where she would gaze out across that beautiful, treacherous expanse, keeping her mind carefully blank.

The only time she allowed herself to think of Christian was in her prayers, when, against all reason, she would unfailingly ask for a miracle to bring him back. She had done so every night since learning of his death six years ago.

Staring sightlessly down at the gardens, where wisps of fog trailed across the paths, Azalea deliberately lowered her rigid shield and allowed herself the luxury of remembering.

Immediately, Christian arose vividly in her mind, just as he had appeared the first evening they had met—handsome, carefree and self-assured. The few conversations they had shared replayed themselves word for word, until Azalea glanced over her shoulder, so strongly did she feel his presence.

She stopped her reverie abruptly on arriving at that fatal day that had destroyed her happy dreams and shook her head fiercely, surprised to find her cheeks wet with tears. For she was not really sad.

Instead, she felt oddly cleansed by the memories she had suppressed for so long. It was as if a tight knot within her had become untied, releasing her and allowing a freedom she had forgotten existed.

After six long years, Azalea was finally able to let Christian go, into the past where he now belonged. Suddenly tired, she turned back to the bed and slipped beneath the quilts. With a little sigh, she drifted off to sleep, dreaming of the future, rather than the past.

CHAPTER THREE

AZALEA DESCENDED at eight o'clock the next morning in search of breakfast, only to be informed by a startled maidservant that the ladies were still abed. In fact, the girl stammered, they did not customarily appear before ten o'clock—and then, only after an early evening.

The bright morning sunshine helped to relieve the sombreness of the dining-room, with its dark panelled wainscotting and beige-and-brown-figured wallpaper, making it bearable if not cheerful. Still, it was hardly in keeping with her high spirits. Azalea hoped that the sunshine was a good omen for her first full day in London.

"Could I perhaps have some breakfast in the garden?" she asked the little maid. "I'm very hungry." She smiled hopefully at the nervous girl, whose mouth twitched timidly in return.

"Certainly, miss! I'll fetch it at once."

"Or perhaps you could have Millie, the girl I brought with me, bring it out?" suggested Azalea. "And I'd very much like to speak with Mrs. Swann, as well, if that can be arranged." She broadened her smile to disguise her discomfort at dispensing orders. She wondered if she'd ever get used to it.

When Millie and Mrs. Swann joined her in the gardens, they compared notes as Azalea ate. Mrs. Swann professed herself content, relating that Mrs. Straite had agreed to keep her on as under-housekeeper and still-room maid until she could find a housekeeping position elsewhere. She pursed her mouth as she spoke of the housekeeper.

"Not to worry, miss," she said with a sniff. "I'll stay here as long as you have any need of me."

Azalea knew that it must be galling to her to be relegated to such a position, but was too grateful for her support to say so.

"Have you located your sisters, Swannee?" she asked her old friend with a smile. "Are they still living in London?"

"Drusilla is, I think, for I had a letter from her after I wrote that we might be coming. Margaret moved to Yorkshire some years back, though, so I don't expect I'll be seeing her any time soon."

Azalea nodded and turned to Millie.

The younger girl seemed quite uncomfortable with her prospective position as Azalea's abigail. "Folks do seem to stare at me a bit, Miss Azalea. I never thought much about my looks back home, but here... Couldn't I find some sort of work to do in the kitchens? I've already made friends with the scullery maid and one or two others there."

Her mixed ancestry had caused little comment in Virginia, where free Negroes and mulattos were not uncommon. But for the first time, Azalea realized how noticeable Millie must be in London. She agreed to this arrangement, recognizing that the shy girl might be happier occupying a less-conspicuous position than that of abigail.

With this matter settled to the satisfaction of all concerned, Azalea returned to the house to discover that Lady Beauforth was awake, but had sent word that she would remain in her room until nuncheon.

Marilyn descended half an hour later and asked if Azalea were ready to commence their shopping expedition.

"More than ready," Azalea replied. She had grown a bit bored with no one to talk to and no duties to perform. "I am eager to make myself presentable for London Society. I will appreciate any advice you can spare me, Cousin Marilyn, for I can see that your taste is flawless." She was determined to do what she could to overcome the young lady's animosity, whatever its cause.

Seemingly gratified by the compliment, Marilyn bestowed a brief, dazzling smile on her cousin and agreed to guide her selections if necessary.

The girls' first stop was at the establishment of Madame Jeannine, the hairdresser Lady Beauforth had proclaimed to be superior to all others. That lady exclaimed over the thickness and rich auburn colour of Azalea's hair as she deftly cut and styled it with rapidly moving scissors and comb.

"A delight to work with, *mademoiselle*," she said more than once as she worked.

In a surprisingly short time, she handed Azalea a mirror and invited her to view the result. Azalea gasped with pleasure as she did so. Relieved of excess weight, her natural curls had reasserted themselves and framed her face charmingly. The back remained long, though not so heavy, and was piled loosely but artfully on top of her head.

She looked questioningly at Marilyn, who reluctantly admitted that it looked very well. Azalea thanked Madame Jeannine as they took their leave of her with a profuseness that Marilyn appeared to consider slightly ill-bred.

En route to their next destination, the shop of a very fashionable modiste on Bond Street, Azalea couldn't help noticing the unusual level of noise in the streets. She commented on it to her companion.

"What do you mean? I perceive nothing out of the ordinary," said Marilyn in some surprise.

"Why all the shouting, singing and street shows. See those *jongleurs* over there? I thought some type of fair or festival might be in Town."

"No, my dear, it is merely London." Marilyn's breathy voice held amused condescension. "Do you mean to say there are no hawkers or entertainers on the streets in America?" she asked, betraying more interest than she had yet shown in a conversation with her cousin.

"Why, no. At least, not in Williamsburg. The merchants confine their selling to their shops, for the most part, and the public entertainment is to be found in the theatres, or in the town square during summer lay-by festivals. But I find all of this most interesting and exciting," she added quickly, not wishing Marilyn to think her critical of London.

Her cousin merely looked thoughtful, however.

Azalea was entranced by the dazzling array of silks, satins, velvets, muslins and laces paraded before her at Madame Clarisse's exclusive shop. Still, she was not so dazzled that she neglected to enquire about prices before ordering anything to be made up for her. She was secretly shocked by the replies, delivered in an accent that belied *Madame*'s fashionably French name.

It took little of her mathematical training to tell her that her small competence could quickly be consumed by far less than Lady Beauforth's idea of an adequate wardrobe. Nevertheless, she ordered three morning dresses and an evening gown, slightly less elaborate than what the modiste recommended. She also purchased a pair of stockings, some drawing-room slippers and a parasol.

"I believe that will be all for today, thank you. Shall we return home for nuncheon, Cousin?" she enquired brightly, turning to Marilyn.

"All?" repeated Marilyn in obvious disbelief.

Before she could continue, Azalea spoke again. She was not about to mention her lack of funds in front of the sharp-eared modiste, who had shared enough gossip during the past hour to demonstrate how carefully she listened to her customers' chance comments.

"For the present. I find myself quite fatigued, as well as hungry." Luckily Marilyn was not aware of the hearty breakfast she had enjoyed three hours earlier.

"Very well. I must not forget you are new to Town and unaccustomed to the exertions of shopping," said Marilyn pityingly.

Nor do I sleep until ten o'clock, thought Azalea, though she only nodded in reply.

During the carriage ride back to Curzon Street, Marilyn kindly offered to bring her cousin up to date on the current gossip. While she chattered on, Azalea was busy planning an early, discreet visit to the solicitor her grandfather had mentioned. It was obvious her present funds would scarcely last the Season if she were to enter Society as planned.

Why had no one told her London was so expensive? She determined to have a private conference with Lady Beauforth at the earliest opportunity. She thought it might be unwise to mention her problem to Marilyn, who seemed as prone to carrying tales as the modiste had been.

Upon their return, the ladies were informed by Smythe that Lord Glaedon had called in their absence and would look to see them in the Park that afternoon. Azalea was glad they had missed him. She needed a chance to compose herself first, and to decide what sort of enquiries about his family would be appropriate.

She wondered whether Marilyn or her mother had told him of their American cousin's visit. It seemed likely, given the degree of intimacy Marilyn had claimed last night. If so, it seemed odd that he had mentioned no connection between the two families. She finally decided that her best course would be to take her cue from him, and to neither volunteer nor request any information unless he seemed disposed to be friendly.

After the meal, Azalea rang for Junie and asked if it would be possible to speak with Lady Beauforth, as she had not appeared at table. Junie seemed doubtful, but went to enquire. She returned after a moment to say that her ladyship was resting, and then asked how the morning's shopping had gone.

"I can see you took my advice about your hair, miss. It looks lovely!" she declared.

"Thank you, Junie. Perhaps you can advise me again," said Azalea tentatively. It had occurred to her that Lady Beauforth might not entirely welcome the news of her guest's lack of funds.

"Of course, Miss Azalea," said Junie importantly. Plainly, she was enjoying her new role as abigail/adviser to the American girl.

"Well, I seem to have a problem. I hadn't realized London would be so...well, expensive. Can you tell me if there is any way to make over my wardrobe without squandering all I have in the world? I'm afraid Lady Beauforth might not understand. After all, she recommended the modiste I visited today, so she must not consider her prices outrageous. But I don't see how I can possibly purchase one fourth of what my cousin seems to think necessary for the coming Season on what my grandfather left me."

Junie fairly swelled with pride at this evidence of Azalea's reliance on both her judgement and her discretion. "Well, miss, I know there are stalls down in Soho where there are bargains to be had, but it would never do for you to be seen there. I could go for you, with your permission. We're much the same size, and I'm handy enough with a needle to make what changes might be necessary."

"Oh, Junie, would you? That would be famous! But...do you think Lady Beauforth would be angry if she found out?" Azalea suddenly sobered. "I won't allow you to run that risk on my account."

Junie smiled with genuine affection for this unique young lady who actually put concern for an abigail above her own wants. "I'll just be certain she don't find out, that's all," she replied confidently. "You be thinking of a way to account for the new clothes you'll be having shortly, and I'll leave this very moment!"

Impulsively, Azalea hugged the girl, assuring her that she could come up with a plausible story.

When Junie returned, less than an hour before Azalea and Marilyn were to leave for the Park, she brought with her four dresses that rivalled those ordered that morning at Madame Clarisse's.

"There were lots to choose from, miss, but I thought you might need me to help you dress. I can go back tomorrow, if you like." Junie was nearly breathless, making Azalea wonder if she had run part of the way home in order to be back in time to help her new mistress.

Azalea was astonished and delighted when the abigail revealed what the gowns had cost—a mere fraction of the modiste's prices. Junie explained that most of the gowns at the Soho markets had been worn only once or twice, since it was considered bad ton to be seen twice in the same dress, particularly a ball gown.

"Then won't the ladies who originally had these made up recognize them if I wear them in public?" asked Azalea uneasily. That would be a snag in their ingenious plan.

"Not if I make a few little changes—add a ruffle here, remove some artificial flowers there. So many dresses are nearly alike anyway, no one will notice," Junie reassured her. "Now, what will you wear for your drive in the Park?"

Half an hour later, Azalea descended wearing one of the new gowns, hastily basted in at the waist. She felt positively elegant. True, there was a small stain near the hem at the back, which there had not been time to remove, but if she remained seated in the carriage, no one should notice it.

Marilyn joined her a few moments later, resplendent in jonquil silk. "We must hurry," she said as they proceeded to the waiting barouche. "Lord Glaedon dislikes to keep his horse standing in the Park."

Azalea wondered why Lord Glaedon had not come to fetch them, but refrained from voicing her thoughts. The drive to Hyde Park was short and in the opposite direction from Bond Street, affording her a look at more of Mayfair's imposing homes. The atmosphere here was far quieter than it had been in the shopping district, she noticed.

When they turned into the Park, Azalea had to stifle a gasp. So this was where everyone was! Lady Beauforth had complained last night that London was thin of company, but it seemed to Azalea that a veritable horde of fashionable people were here to take advantage of the fine weather, walking, riding and driving. How on earth did Marilyn intend to find her betrothed in this throng?

As if in answer, the girl at her side waved as a tall man in a dark blue riding coat trotted up on an enormous black gelding. "Lord Glaedon! I trust we have not kept you waiting long?"

"Not at all, my dear," he said smoothly, as he bent over her extended hand. Marilyn simpered prettily for a moment before belatedly recalling her manners.

"This is my cousin, Miss Clayton," she said, and Lord Glaedon turned his attention to Azalea.

As he bowed in acknowledgement, his eyes fastened on her face with an expression of mingled curiosity and bemusement.

Azalea felt similarly bemused, and only just remembered to nod in return. She had expected some slight resemblance to Christian but now that Lord Glaedon faced her, the likeness was so striking it left her momentarily speechless. Herschel had the same dark hair and stormy blue-grey eyes as his younger brother. Even his voice was amazingly similar. He could have been Christian himself, risen from the dead.

Suddenly aware that they had been staring at one another, she made a determined effort to pull herself together.

"I'm pleased to make your acquaintance, my lord," she said rather lamely.

As she spoke, his gaze seemed to harden slightly and he hastily withdrew his hand before it could touch hers. He flicked a glance at Marilyn.

"Perhaps I should have warned you that my cousin is newly come from—from America to live with us," she stammered. "Nothing was really settled until she arrived yesterday, so I did not mention it before."

Her cousin seemed almost to be apologizing, Azalea thought indignantly.

"Yes. Quite," was all he said in reply. "Shall we commence our tour of the Park?"

Marilyn assented eagerly and the coachman urged the horses on. Lord Glaedon rode comfortably alongside, listening to his fiancée's chatter, and carefully avoided any glance in Azalea's direction. This afforded her an excellent opportunity to examine him at leisure, though she was careful not to stare, as Marilyn might misinterpret her reasons.

Yes, she had been right. The earl's resemblance to his younger brother was indeed striking.

There were subtle differences, however, which became apparent as she watched him. For one thing, he looked—and acted—far older than Chris would have been if he had lived, though Herschel was only a year or two older than Christian, if her memory served her.

His manners were certainly inferior to his brother's. Even his smile had a decidedly cynical twist, exaggerated by a faint scar that traced a line from his left ear to the corner of his mouth. It gave him a mysterious, almost sinister expression.... Perhaps the resemblance was not so strong after all, she decided.

He obviously had not recognized the name Clayton, but then the marriage had been no certain thing when Chris and his father had set out from England. Perhaps it was not so remarkable that Herschel had not been informed of it. His hostility had seemed directed not so much at her as at Americans in general. A holdover from the recent war, perhaps?

Watching him surreptitiously, she also decided that his attitude towards Marilyn was not what it should be. There was no real warmth in his manner, for all her cousin's earlier boasting about his impatient ardour. Of course, her own presence might be inhibiting him somewhat, Azalea supposed, but really, he looked almost bored.

Their circuit of the Park was finished long before Marilyn exhausted her store of gossip.

"May I call on you tomorrow?" Lord Glaedon asked, almost perfunctorily.

"You know you may, my lord," replied Marilyn, dimpling at him. "We shall look forward to your visit."

He touched his hat to both of them and turned his horse. As he rode away, he began to whistle a lilting Irish tune. Frozen in sudden shock, Azalea was left staring open-mouthed at his retreating back.

CHAPTER FOUR

AZALEA TOOK IN NONE of the scenery during the drive back to Beauforth House. Fortunately, Marilyn's aimless chatter did not require anything in the way of a thoughtful response. At any rate, her cousin seemed to detect nothing wrong in her manner.

Still trembling from the discovery she had made, Azalea stared ahead blindly, trying desperately to force her mind to function. She felt as if her whole world had just been turned upside down without warning. Blinking rapidly against the darkness that seemed to be advancing on the edges of her sight, she nodded vaguely to something her cousin had said.

Think! Think!

Christian had distinctly told her, once upon a time, that Herschel not only detested whistling, but that he had never learned to do it. And that tune—it had been the same one she had heard Christian whistle in Williamsburg. Azalea herself had been struck by Lord Glaedon's uncanny resemblance to the Chris she remembered. Could he possibly be her husband? How? *How?*

Clasping her hands tightly together in her lap, Azalea strove to organize her whirling thoughts. That he had not recognized her, was patently obvious.

Or... was he merely pretending not to?

She didn't think so. Surely he would have betrayed himself somehow, if only with a flash of awareness at his first sight of her.

And what of Herschel? If Christian was now the Earl of Glaedon, then Herschel must also be dead. She and her grandfather had heard no word of that tragedy, though she doubted anyone would have informed them. But how could Christian possibly have been alive all these years without her knowledge? And could he have changed so much?

The Christian she remembered had been a carefree, easygoing young man, with engaging manners, nothing at all like the curt, cynical fellow she had met an hour ago. And he could never have aged that much in only six years. She supposed he could have received that scar in the shipwreck, but how could his whole personality have changed so completely?

What was far more likely was that Herschel had taken up whistling late in life, perhaps even in tribute to the younger brother he had lost. But somehow she didn't think so. That sense of familiarity had nagged at her from the first moment she had seen Lord Glaedon. And when she'd heard him whistling, she had known beyond any doubt, for one crystal-clear moment, that he was indeed her Chris.

But without any facts, she realized, her guess was only wild conjecture. She must have the facts.

Would they be common knowledge? If so, Lady Beauforth could undoubtedly tell her what she so urgently needed to know—she had heard enough at dinner last night to realize that very little of what went on in the fashionable world escaped her ladyship's notice.

The moment she had put off her cloak, Azalea went in search of her hostess.

Glancing up and down the empty upstairs hallway, she decided that the corner room at the far end was most likely Lady Beauforth's, as it was undoubtedly the largest. Before she could reconsider, she walked quickly to the door and knocked, more loudly than she had intended. Her cousin's startled "Yes?" told her that she had guessed correctly.

"It is I, Cousin Alice. Azalea. May I speak to you for a moment?"

"Of course, dear, come in."

Azalea opened the door and found herself in a chamber that bore no resemblance to the tasteful décor of the rest of the house. Cousin Alice's boudoir was a hodgepodge of antique and modern tables, chairs, étagères, pillows and ottomans. Incredibly, there was even a stuffed elephant's foot in one corner, with a bright pink cloth on top.

Every colour of the rainbow was present, though red and purple predominated, and every available surface, including the elephant's foot, was crowded with ornaments of incredible variety. Valuable works of art competed for space with obvious trumpery pieces.

After a moment, Azalea succeeded in locating her cousin among the startling assortment. Dressed in a magenta wrapper, Lady Beauforth reclined on a chaise longue in the centre of the room.

"Yes, dear child, what is it?" she asked, completely at home in her astonishing surroundings. "Is something troubling you?"

With a start, Azalea recalled her purpose. "Not troubling me precisely, Cousin Alice," she began with studied casualness, "but I am curious about something and was hoping that you could enlighten me."

Ever eager to be a source of information, Lady Beauforth beamed at her young relative. "Of *course*, dear! I'll be delighted to be of assistance."

"Miss Beauforth and I just encountered Lord Glaedon in the Park. As I, ah, mentioned last night, my grandfather was well acquainted with his father, the fourth earl. He spoke of the family to me on more than one occasion, and it was my understanding that it was Herschel who was next in the succession?" Azalea could not quite bring herself to say Christian's name. She paused, hoping that Lady Beauforth would take it from there. She was not disappointed.

"Oh, my *dear*, I assumed you knew! It's best you did, I suppose, all things considered. After all, if there were any unpleasantness in that quarter, it's only fair you should know why, don't you think?"

Azalea nodded vaguely, having absolutely no idea what her cousin was talking about.

Lady Beauforth continued. "What I mean to say is that Herschel was killed two years ago in the war—the American war, you understand, not the French. Marilyn was *quite* devastated, I assure you. You may not have known it, but it was planned almost from her infancy that she would marry poor Herschel. Our lands run with theirs, you see.

"At any rate, Christian seems to have taken all Americans in dislike because of his brother's death. Quite understandable, I suppose. Not that it is *your* fault, of course, or anyone else's who wasn't actually in the fighting.... But I'm sure you understand."

Azalea was beginning to, though the suddenness of having her suspicion confirmed almost took away her capacity for thought. "But, my lady—" A light tap on the door interrupted her, and Marilyn's abigail entered with a note for Lady Beauforth.

As her cousin read the message, Azalea had time to consider what she had just learned and to be glad of the interruption. She had been on the point of asking how Christian had escaped the shipwreck, a question that would have demanded more explanations than she was ready to give at the moment. There was another matter she could bring up, however.

"Tell my daughter that we'll discuss this at dinner. Perhaps we can contrive to make an appearance at both," said Lady Beauforth to the maid, dismissing her.

She turned her attention back to Azalea. "Now, my dear, where were we? Oh, yes, dear Christian. I pray you'll not take offence at his manner if he should, ah, treat you less than charmingly, now that you know the cause. And I suppose it would be quite proper if you were to make some show of sympathy over poor Herschel, seeing how you know the family, so to speak. But let me tell you the most interesting on dit— Oh, was there any other advice you needed?" Lady Beauforth interrupted herself, apparently remembering her current role as social advisor.

"As a matter of fact, Cousin Alice, there is," said Azalea reluctantly. She thought she might have liked to hear that particular on dit. "I find myself in need of visiting my grandfather's London solicitor, a Mr. John Timmons, and have no idea how to go about doing so."

"Oh, surely there will be no need to actually visit the man," said Lady Beauforth, clearly disappointed by the mundane request. "Indeed, most solicitors very much dislike women in their offices, I understand. I know dear Sir Matthew's lawyers always called on me here at the house after he went to his reward. Your best course would be to send a message round, asking him to visit you.''

Azalea doubted this very much. After all, she was hardly of her cousin's social standing, which would likely make this Mr. Timmons reluctant to take so much time out of his busy schedule to cater to her whims. In addition, if she were to decide to ask his advice about her six-year-old marriage, she had no desire to be overheard by any member of her cousin's household. She decided to confide in Lady Beauforth about the lesser of her problems.

''The truth is, Cousin Alice, I need to speak to him about a rather delicate matter. I find that what my grandfather left me, which seemed so ample in America, will hardly support a London Season and certainly would leave me nothing to live on once it is over. I wish to enquire into the particulars of my paternal grandfather's will, to see if I have any money coming to me from the Kayce estates.''

''Oh, my dear, I had no idea! How very dreadful for you, to be sure!'' exclaimed Lady Beauforth, struggling up into a sitting position. ''I naturally assumed that you were sufficiently well set up... but enough of that. Of course, under such circumstances it would be best for you to visit him. He would likely refuse to come to you, anyway, if he knew the truth. But in the meantime, what shall we do for you?'' She appeared to be genuinely concerned, perhaps partially out of a fear that she might be expected to finance Azalea's Season herself.

"I shall be fine, Cousin, really," said Azalea quickly, banishing such an uncharitable thought. "Junie has been telling me about some places in Soho—"

"That's *it!*" Lady Beauforth's brow cleared as if by magic. "The very thing, if we are discreet. You wouldn't *believe* how many ladies of the ton shop there—by proxy, of course—because of the nip-farthing allowances their husbands give them. I daresay one or two of Marilyn's old gowns might be altered to fit you as well, as you are neither as plump nor as tall as she."

Azalea was relieved at her cousin's enthusiastic reception of the idea and it emboldened her to continue. "To tell the truth, Cousin Alice, Junie already made a brief trip to Soho for me early this afternoon. The dress I am wearing now came from one of the markets, though we only had time enough to take it in at the waist. She assures me that she can refurbish it to make it even more modish."

Lady Beauforth waved this idea aside and assured her that her own dressmaker could make any necessary alterations, as her taste was exquisite. Relieved of the possibility of having to fund Azalea's comeout herself, she seemed disposed to be generous.

"Now run along, my dear, and I'll have Marilyn's abigail look over her gowns from last Season. We are fortunate that the styles have not changed very much. I'm certain Mrs. Osgood can bring them bang up to the nines for you." She dismissed Azalea with the most unaffected smile she had yet bestowed on her.

THE NEXT MORNING Junie appeared with a breakfast tray almost the instant Azalea awoke. An envelope rested on the tray next to the cup of chocolate and Azalea picked it up. "What is this?"

"I couldn't say, miss. It was given to me last night by Cartwright, her ladyship's dresser, to bring to you first thing. I set it on your tray so I wouldn't forget."

Azalea opened the envelope to find that it contained the direction of Mr. John J. Timmons, Esq., and the information that Lady Beauforth's carriage would convey her there in the course of the morning, if she so wished.

"Why, how kind," Azalea exclaimed. "I'll go directly after breakfast. Junie, do you suppose you could order her ladyship's carriage to be ready in three-quarters of an hour?"

"It's early yet, miss, but I'll try," answered the abigail doubtfully.

"Don't put the coachman to any trouble. I'll wait until he's had a chance to eat something. There is no real hurry, I suppose." But Azalea's heightened complexion told the observant Junie that she was anxious to carry out whatever business she intended.

"It will be ready inside an hour, miss, for certain," she promised, and left the room with a militant gleam in her eye.

Junie returned in a few minutes to inform her mistress that the carriage could indeed be ready by nine o'clock, or even sooner if she wished.

"Thank you, Junie. You take very good care of me," said Azalea warmly, making the abigail flush with pleasure.

"No more than you deserve, miss," she said brusquely. "Now, which dress will you wear? I got that stain out of the white one, and hemmed up the blue."

At precisely nine o'clock Azalea descended the front steps to the waiting carriage, wearing a charming morning dress of sky blue. She was accompanied by a smart-looking Junie, who had bought herself a dress at the market yesterday as well, in keeping with her new post as a fashionable lady's maid. She had informed Azalea that young ladies of Quality simply did not go about in public alone, and stubbornly insisted upon coming with her.

Azalea thought it absurd for Junie to waste a whole morning trailing after her as if she were a child, but finally agreed to abide by the social customs of the London ton. And since she was somewhat nervous about the coming interview, she was glad to have Junie's company today.

Leaning back against the velvet squabs in the elegant carriage, Azalea tried to organize her thoughts for the ordeal ahead. She had brought along every bit of legal documentation she possessed and hoped it would be enough to satisfy Mr. Timmons of the validity of her claims, at least regarding the Kayce estate.

The marriage papers resided in her reticule, separate from the rest. Two days ago she had regarded them as mere sentimental keepsakes, but she now realized that they might well be vitally important, in a legal sense, at least.

The mansions of the elite and fashionable West End had been left behind and they were now travelling through a less attractive part of London. Peering out of the carriage window, Azalea was shocked at the squalor that existed less than ten minutes from the elegant Mayfair neighbourhood where her cousins lived. Nowhere in America had she seen such filth and human degradation.

Slovenly and obviously inebriated women lounged in gloomy doorways, many nursing infants. Azalea saw one woman offer her baby something out of a bottle and she turned to Junie in dismay.

"Look at that woman! Surely she is not giving that poor baby liquor to drink?"

"Like as not, miss," replied the abigail after a brief glance. "In these parts, gin is the lifeblood of the poor folks. No doubt the child would get nearly as drunk on its mother's milk."

"But that's terrible! Why doesn't someone do something?"

Junie looked at her in amazement. "It's her babe, to raise or kill as she sees fit."

Azalea lapsed into silence, feeling immeasurably depressed by the scene of degrading poverty she had just witnessed. In America, at least in the part of it she had known, the poor worked where they could and kept their dignity. If jobs were not to be had, they moved west, where there was farmland for the taking.

A few minutes later her spirits revived somewhat as the scene changed again to what was obviously a business district. Well-dressed merchants and gentlemen moved purposefully along the streets. No women were in evidence. The carriage came to a stop in front of an imposing redbrick edifice identified by a brass plate simply as the Law Offices.

Stepping out of the carriage, Azalea told her maid firmly to remain where she was. Though Junie looked as though she would have liked to argue, she obeyed.

Following the directions she had been given, Azalea proceeded to a suite on the second floor of the Law Offices with a door plate reading John J. Timmons, Esq., Barr. Opening the door, she found herself in a plush but rather musty chamber facing an owlish man of indeterminate age seated at an enormous wooden desk.

He looked up from his sheaf of papers with a frown that gave way to blank astonishment as he beheld a lady in these sacred male precincts.

As the man appeared totally bereft of speech, Azalea opened the conversation herself, speaking quickly before she could lose her courage.

"Mr. Timmons? I am Azalea Clayton. I was referred to you by my grandfather, the Reverend Gregory Simpson. I believe you handled his business when he was young, as well as that of his father, Sir Philip Simpson."

She was running out of opening remarks when he finally recovered himself enough to speak.

"Oh, uh . . . no, ma'am. I mean, I'm not Mr. Timmons at all. I am Peter Greene, his clerk. I—I'll tell him you're here. Miss Clayton, was it?"

Mr. Greene disappeared through a heavy door at the rear of the room, obviously more intimidated by her presence than by the task of informing his employer of it, however unwelcome such information might be.

Looking absently around at the innumerable leather-bound volumes lining the walls and stacked on the floor, Azalea mentally prepared her arguments against the possibility of Mr. Timmons refusing to see her. She had worked herself into a state of imaginary indignation when Mr. Greene reappeared and indicated, mainly by gesture, that she could proceed into the inner sanctum.

The second office was immaculate in comparison to the dusty disorder of the first. An elderly and rather

stout gentleman rose to greet her, bowing with old-
fashioned courtesy.

"Miss Clayton? I am honoured to make your acquaintance. Pray sit down. In what way may I be of
service to you?" His tone was formally polite, but
Azalea thought the man looked puzzled, and wondered what garbled account of her connections Mr.
Greene had given him.

"Mr. Timmons," she began tentatively, perching on
the edge of the overstuffed leather chair opposite the
desk, "I believe you knew my grandfather slightly and
conducted business for his father, Sir Philip Simpson,
before his death."

"Of course, of course," replied the lawyer, now
more at ease. "I remember young Gregory well, though
I suppose I shouldn't say young exactly, as we are almost of an age. Is he still in Virginia? How is he?"

"He died eight months ago, which is why I am here."

"I am sorry," said Mr. Timmons sincerely. "I remember him as an unusually intelligent man. He went
to America to teach at one of the universities, I recollect."

Azalea lost some of her diffidence. "Yes, at the
College of William and Mary, in Williamsburg. He
became one of their most respected faculty members," she added with unconscious pride.

"And in what circumstances are you left? He was
your guardian?" She nodded. "What became of your
parents?"

"Both died when I was very young. My mother was
his only daughter. My father was Walter Clayton, fifth
Baron Kayce. On his death, my grandfather left me
everything he had, on the condition that I sell the

property and come to England. I am presently staying with my cousin, Lady Beauforth, in Curzon Street.''

"I know of Lady Beauforth," said Mr. Timmons mildly when she paused. "An estimable woman, I believe.''

Azalea took a deep breath before continuing. "Grandfather wished me to take steps to reclaim my inheritance. Indeed, I have found that I must do so, as a Season with Lady Beauforth will cost a great deal more than I can presently afford. On my grandfather's recommendation, I would like to engage you as my man of business here in London, if that would be acceptable to you?''

"Why, of course, my child. I thought that was settled already." Mr. Timmons's eyes twinkled with a trace of humour. "It appears you have a measure of your grandfather's independence, and likely his intelligence as well. Otherwise, you wouldn't have come to me.''

Gratefully, Azalea pushed the packet of papers across the desk to him. "Here is a summary of the fourth Lord Kayce's will, which was sent to my father on his death. The estate itself, as I understand it, was entailed, but there was a substantial sum that was brought into the family by marriage and that should have come to me at my father's death.''

Mr. Timmons opened the packet and began sorting through the papers it contained. "I shall need to look over the original will, of course. It should be filed at Somerset House. I assume your father left none?''

Azalea shook her head.

"Not unusual in so young a man. We shall also need indisputable proof of your own identity—ah, here we are. Yes, these will be more than sufficient.''

He met her eyes solemnly. "I shall not attempt to deceive you, Miss Clayton. Lord Kayce, your uncle, is a very powerful man. He may very well attempt to counter your claims. After all, he could stand to lose a good deal of money as a result. Have you communicated with him at all?"

"No, I haven't. From certain things my grandfather told me, I thought that might be...unwise. In fact, I'm not even sure he's aware of my existence." Mr. Timmons raised his brows at this and she hurried on. "In any event, I arrived in London only the day before yesterday, and thought it would be prudent to consult with an expert in legal matters before deciding upon any course of action."

"A wise precaution," the lawyer replied noncommittally. "However, as you are under age, Miss Clayton, you will need a guardian—and the most natural person for that role would be your uncle."

Azalea stared at the lawyer in dismay. "But I am perfectly happy with Lady Beauforth, and it was my grandfather's express wish that she act as my guardian. And...suppose Lord Kayce wishes me ill?"

Mr. Timmons blinked.

"Well," she continued more cautiously, "Grandfather once hinted at something like that, though he was sick at the time and I suppose I might have misunderstood him." All of a sudden, her grandfather's accusations seemed rather unlikely.

"As to that, I cannot say." Mr. Timmons had retreated into cool professionalism now. "Though I would imagine that any danger from your uncle would be financial rather than physical. But the fact remains that in the normal course of things, Lord Kayce would legally be named your guardian, until you come of age or, of course, marry.''

At this last word, her head came up. She believed that Mr. Timmons was a man she could trust, and that he had a certain interest in her welfare, if only because of his memories of her grandfather. Decisively, she pulled the remaining papers from her reticule and handed them to the lawyer.

''Perhaps this will make a difference.''

Frowning puzzlement gave way to incredulous amazement as the lawyer unfolded and perused the documents. ''These appear to be genuine. Why did you say nothing of this before?''

Azalea thought she detected a hint of suspicion behind the kindly brown eyes. She knew instinctively that her only course must be one of total honesty if she were not to lose Mr. Timmons as an ally.

Adhering strictly to the facts, she explained the circumstances of her marriage and subsequent supposed widowhood. She then confided her belief that grief at Howard Morely's death had precipitated her grandfather's decline and eventual demise. Throughout the recital, she kept her voice carefully level, drawing on the control she had cultivated over the past six years.

''It was only yesterday that I discovered that Christian Morely, now Earl of Glaedon, is still alive,'' she concluded. ''I still do not understand how that can be, but I met him myself in Hyde Park.''

''I do seem to remember some furor over the earl, or perhaps it was his brother, a year or two ago,'' said Mr. Timmons thoughtfully. ''I cannot seem to recall the details, but something was in the papers, I believe. However, this would seem to be the answer to both of your problems. Glaedon is not so wealthy as your uncle, but he is quite well situated, I believe."

He turned his keen gaze back to Azalea. "What is it, my dear? Is he unwilling to acknowledge you?" When she did not answer, his brows drew together. "I assure you he can be legally forced to do so. These documents constitute sufficient proof—"

"Not precisely that, Mr. Timmons," Azalea broke in. "At least, I'm not certain that is the case. When I met him yesterday, he seemed not to recognize me, even when we were introduced. As a matter of fact, he was almost rude to me."

Mr. Timmons opened his mouth, but Azalea hurried on. "So, if you don't mind, I'd rather not make these documents public just yet. I want to discover what is going on first. Perhaps it will transpire that I don't care to acknowledge *him!*" she concluded with a defiant lift of her chin.

A half smile played about the old solicitor's mouth, but he seemed compelled to try again. "Understand, my dear lady... or Miss Clayton, if you will, that the resources you would have at your disposal as Countess of Glaedon could make all the difference in the world to your legal battle with Lord Kayce. It is unlikely—"

"Please, Mr. Timmons, can you not understand?" she interrupted urgently. "Lord Glaedon already dislikes Americans. If I were to declare myself his wife now, not only might he not believe me, but it could serve to confirm his negative opinion. I also think it would not be very conducive to my future happiness in marriage. Promise me you will say nothing of this to anyone, at least for the present."

Mr. Timmons could not hold out against the plea in Azalea's voice and finally nodded slowly. "Very well, my dear. For the present, though it goes against my better judgement. I shall see what I can manage with the other documents you have given me. And I must recommend that you entrust the marriage papers to me as well, for safe keeping."

"Of course." She leaned forward. "And you won't inform my uncle about my presence in London just yet either, will you?"

He shook his head. "No, though he must be told eventually, of course. I am sure he will be very surprised. But you have given me enough to work on for the present, I believe, without complicating matters further. I shall send word when I have made some progress. My first step will be to obtain your grandfather's will."

Azalea thanked the older man warmly and rose. Nothing of substance had been accomplished yet, but her spirits were higher than they had been half an hour earlier. Merely sharing her dilemma with the capable solicitor was a vast relief, and it was with a renewed lightness in her step that she left Mr. Timmons's offices.

Smiling brilliantly at Mr. Greene simply for the pleasure of watching him stammer in confusion, she tripped out the door and down the stairs to the waiting carriage.

CHAPTER FIVE

AZALEA'S RELIEF WAS short-lived, however, for Marilyn's greeting upon her return to Beauforth House served to remind her of the difficulties she had yet to overcome.

"Cousin, I thought you would never return! Have you forgotten that my dear Glaedon is to call on us this morning?" she exclaimed as Azalea took off her cloak. "He would find it most odd, even rude, if you were out when he arrived. You would not wish to give him yet a lower opinion of Americans, I am sure."

"Oh, heavens no," replied Azalea, but her sarcasm was lost on her cousin.

"I thought not," Marilyn said with a satisfied nod. "And pray try as much as possible to refrain from speaking while he is here," she added. "I saw yesterday how little he liked hearing your accent. Oh! One of my curls is come undone!"

Marilyn hurried upstairs to find her maid before Azalea could respond to her outrageous suggestion. It was probably just as well, she realized belatedly. The retort she'd almost made would not have contributed to cousinly feeling at all. But neither that nor any other consideration would persuade her to apologize for her nationality!

She was still seething when Lord Glaedon was announced a moment later.

"Good day, Miss...Clayton, is it not?" he said as he entered the parlour behind the butler.

"Yes, that's right. Good day, my lord. And how are you this fine morning?" Marilyn's recent caution prompted her to intensify her accent. She was rewarded by a slight tightening around Lord Glaedon's mouth.

"Very well, I thank you," he replied tersely. "Is Lady Beauforth not in?"

"Oh, yes. She and Miss Beauforth should be down at any moment, I should think. They have been kindness itself to me since my arrival from America," Azalea said deliberately. His presence was unsettling, especially now that she knew who he was. But that did not stop her from baiting him. She had to know just how deep his animosity went. And surely, if she mentioned America he must realize who she was and recall the claim she had upon him!

"You arrived only a few days ago, I believe?" was all he said, however.

"The day before yesterday. And already I am finding that England is vastly different from America."

"I would imagine so," he said before she could elaborate. "We have had the benefit of several more centuries in which to become civilized. But then, our civilization is one thing you colonists fought so hard to free yourselves from, is it not?"

Azalea blinked at this sudden attack. "Indeed—" she began indignantly, but broke off at the sound of Cousin Alice's voice.

"Good afternoon, my lord. I hope you haven't been waiting long," Lady Beauforth called out. She was dressed today in varying shades of bright pink silk. "Ah, but I see Miss Clayton has been here to keep you company. You two met in the Park yesterday, I believe?''

Marilyn came in on her mother's heels with a brilliant smile for Lord Glaedon and a breathless reply to the offhand compliment he made her. Both ladies had eyes only for their gentleman caller, allowing Azalea a chance to compose herself and subdue her sudden anger.

Ringing for tea, Lady Beauforth waved Lord Glaedon into the most ornate, and least comfortable, chair in the room. Marilyn lost no time in seating herself by his right hand, while her mother, chattering gaily, moved to his left. Azalea was left to shift for herself.

"Do you still leave for your estates tomorrow, my lord?" asked Marilyn as soon as her mother paused in her recital of the past week's scandals. "I do hope you will return to Town in time for our theatre engagement the week after next."

Her fluttering lashes and shy smiles amused Azalea, for they had plainly been cultivated for his lordship's benefit—or perhaps for the benefit of gentlemen in general. The effect was undeniably attractive, and for a moment Azalea toyed with the idea of learning to emulate this behaviour, before regretfully deciding that it simply wasn't her style.

Watching Lord Glaedon as he responded to Marilyn's flirtatious sallies, Azalea found it hard to believe that this was the same man she had befriended, married and, yes, even loved, six years ago. This Christian was solemn and almost dour, not laughing and carefree, as she remembered him. Could the deaths of his father and brother have wrought such a change in him?

Realizing that she was staring, Azalea pulled her attention back to the conversation, hoping to gain some useful insight into the intricacies of London Society.

"...and Lady Gascombe cut her *dead,* can you imagine," Lady Beauforth was saying, "because her sister had become engaged to a merchant! But then, everyone knows what a high stickler Harriet Gascombe is—not that that's a bad thing in itself, of course. But poor Miss Fenworth is lost now, I fear. No one will receive her after that, I daresay."

Despite her intention to listen quietly, Azalea burst in on the conversation. "I cannot believe anyone of sense would hold a young lady responsible for her sister's actions! Surely others have survived worse family connections than a merchant."

Everyone round the tea table started as though one of the chairs had spoken. After a slight, uncomfortable pause, Marilyn tittered and Lady Beauforth answered, "Not after being cut at a public theatre by someone of Lady Gascombe's standing, I assure you, my dear. Though it is possible that her ladyship had another motive for her actions, I admit. It is rumoured that her own daughter and Miss Fenworth are rivals for at least one titled gentleman."

"But how infamous!" exclaimed Azalea, forgetting that her purpose was to learn London customs rather than condemn them. "Surely anyone who knew that would see Lady Gascombe's actions for what they were?"

"Now, now, my dear," Lady Beauforth said soothingly. "Remember, you are new to London and our ways. Marilyn, you must be sure to acquaint Azalea with some of the more notable names before we spring her on Society. We don't want her to offend." Lady

Beauforth looked rather alarmed at the mere possibility of such a *faux pas*.

But Lord Glaedon was looking at Azalea rather strangely. "Azalea?" he repeated when Lady Beauforth fell momentarily silent. "What an unusual name. I believe I once knew someone with that name—as a child, perhaps." He was frowning slightly in concentration.

"My mother named me so, after a flowering shrub native to Virginia," she offered, hoping to jog his memory. Marilyn, however, glared at her.

"Azalea, dear, would you be so kind as to pour out for us?" asked Lady Beauforth hastily, intercepting the glare.

"Yes, they still teach that skill in the colonies, do they not?" said Marilyn with a honeyed smile.

So much for avoiding all mention of my origins, thought Azalea cynically, though her smile of acquiescence matched her cousin's for sweetness.

As she poured, Azalea realized that her own personality was as far removed from what it had been six years ago as Christian's appeared to be. Glancing involuntarily at him at the thought, she found him regarding her intently, his black brows drawn down in a frown.

"Oh! I do beg your pardon, Cousin Alice," Azalea exclaimed as she sloshed a little tea into Lady Beauforth's lap. "The—the pot was hotter than I expected." She cursed her inattention, especially when she saw Marilyn's smirk.

"Mama, your faith appears to have been misplaced," Miss Beauforth commented liltingly. "I suppose I'd best do the honours myself. You'd not wish to risk hot tea on your own person, would you, my lord?"

she cooed, fluttering her lashes at the earl as she
wrested the pot from Azalea's hands.

For an instant, Azalea considered deliberately spilling the remainder of the tea over Miss Beauforth. As
it was, she resisted just long enough so that when she
released it, Marilyn narrowly escaped spilling it herself. Quickly, Azalea turned to Lady Beauforth.

"I'm truly sorry, ma'am. Do allow me to blot that
from your gown before it sets." Her irritation towards
Marilyn was swallowed by dismay at the sight of the
brown rivulets on Cousin Alice's fuschia day dress.
Ineffectually, she dabbed at the stains with her nap-
kin.

"Pray do not regard it, my dear." Lady Beauforth
pushed her hands away gently. "Cartwright will have
it good as new by morning."

Azalea resumed her seat, trying vainly to control the
colour she could feel rising in her face. Perhaps she
hadn't grown up so much after all! Another quick
glance at the earl showed that he was studying her
again, but now his look was thoughtful rather than
forbidding.

She immediately returned her gaze to her lap, but
that brief glimpse had done nothing to calm her rapid
pulse. Those blue-grey eyes, which had affected her so
deeply when she was a girl, had a far stronger and more
profound impact on her as a woman.

"Well, this has been delightful," said the earl, before she could think of anything else that might remind him of his time in Virginia, "but I really must be
going. I have several matters to attend to before leaving London. I shouldn't have spared even this much
time, but I did promise to call."

A polite smile at Marilyn accompanied this statement, and she simpered back at him.

"Very well, if you must," said Lady Beauforth with a slight pout, "but we shall hope to see you at Lady Burnham's card party, if not before. Oh, and Christian, give my regards to your grandmother. It has been an age since we've seen her in Town."

"Of course, my lady. Miss Beauforth, Miss Clayton." Bowing to all of them collectively, he departed.

"WELCOME HOME, my boy!" The Dowager Countess of Glaedon greeted Christian at the door of Glaedon Oaks the next day, unwilling as usual to await him in the parlour. "I have missed you. Do you stay through the Christmas season?"

"I fear not, though I shall return for it," Christian replied. "I have another week's worth of business awaiting me in Town before then."

"To do with your recent betrothal, no doubt." The dowager, undisputed matriarch of the family, put her head on one side as she gazed lovingly up at her grandson. "What is this I hear about a February wedding? Dare I hope that means you are truly smitten with the girl?"

"Come, Grandmother, let us go in by the fire. I am chilled from my long ride."

Though she docilely allowed herself to be led back into the parlour, the dowager did not relinquish her topic so easily. After ringing for a bowl of hot punch, she returned to the attack. "Well? And how goes your courtship of Miss Beauforth?"

Christian blinked. "Courtship? It is done, I imagine, as we are betrothed. Now I have merely to do the pretty by her until the wedding."

His grandmother's face fell noticeably. "So that is the reason for the early date? I had so hoped—"

"Don't be absurd," he said, more sharply than he had intended. "I have known Marilyn Beauforth most of my life, and she is still the vain, silly thing she ever was. I only offered for her because it seemed the honourable thing to do, now that Herschel is gone."

"Goodness, Christian, you were in no way bound by that old promise your father made to Sir Matthew Beauforth! Herschel planned to offer for the girl because he wanted to, I assure you. If you do not care for her there is no need for you to wed her. The family honour will not suffer in the least—or would not have, had you not offered."

Christian shrugged, though in truth his grandmother had hit on the heart of the matter. He had done enough to blacken the family honour already without disregarding old promises. "'Tis as good a way to ensure the succession as any," he said negligently, "especially as it will unite our two estates."

The dowager frowned. "Christian, I do not like to hear you speak so. I shall be the first to admit that in many, if not most, marriages, love follows later rather than coming before. But I cannot think it proper to enter the married state without *some* degree of affection for one's future spouse."

"I apologize, Grandmother. Miss Beauforth has grown into a diamond of the first water, and I would be blind not to appreciate that fact. Perhaps my admiration of her person will later develop into something stronger, as you suggest. It is not as though I harbour a *tendre* for another."

He paused, suddenly recalling another young lady he had met lately.

From the moment he had first laid eyes on Miss
Clayton, something about her had profoundly disturbed him. She was lovely, certainly, even more striking than Miss Beauforth with her unusual colouring,
but that was not it—or at least he didn't think so. He'd
never been particularly swayed by mere beauty before.

At any rate, Miss Clayton's beauty could hardly
make up for her origins. Doubtless it was her accent
combined with that beauty that had so unsettled him.
Christian was not accustomed to feeling unsettled.
That must be why he had allowed himself to be goaded
into open criticism of her homeland on the second occasion they'd met.

It hadn't been like him at all, for he had always
prided himself on his coolness in uncomfortable situ-
ations. His grandmother, not to mention his few
friends, would have been amazed had they witnessed
his rudeness to Miss Clayton.

Azalea. That's what Lady Beauforth had called her.
Again that vague disquiet crept over him, though his
lips curved in a smile of their own volition. Such a
pretty name. So unusual. He was certain he'd heard it
before....

"What? What is it, Christian?" His grandmother's
voice recalled him to the present.

Christian shook his head. "Nothing, Grandmother."

There was no point dwelling on it now. Most likely,
Lady Beauforth had mentioned the girl's name when
she'd told him her cousin would be coming to live with
her. He didn't recall her doing so, but it seemed a reasonable explanation. If he *had* known someone of that
name before, it would come to him in time.

He swallowed his punch and stood to ring the bell. "I may as well ride over the grounds with the steward before changing out of my travelling clothes," he said. "There is no point wasting what little daylight remains."

Lady Glaedon watched him go, shaking her head with a mixture of sadness and fondness. She had noticed the preoccupation in her grandson's manner, obvious to one who had raised him as her own from the time his mother had died, shortly after his eighth birthday. She hoped that all would work out well for him. The last few years had not been easy for Christian.

They had not been easy for the dowager, either. She had lost her son and, she had then believed, her favourite grandson to a shipwreck. Then, only four years later, her other grandson, the new earl, had been killed in the war in America, which Herschel had insisted on participating in despite his family responsibilities.

Herschel's death had been the final straw. Lady Glaedon had become a virtual recluse, refusing to see anyone but family. Then Christian's miraculous return had restored hope and meaning to her life.

The two of them had always been close, probably closer than would have been possible were she truly his mother. After Christian's arrival back in England, she had reentered Society to some small extent, more for his sake than for her own.

She had been saddened by the singular change in Christian, once so fun loving and easygoing. His experiences, which he refused to discuss with her, had somehow turned him into a taciturn, cynical man. She had become determined to do everything in her power to ensure his happiness, and thereby her own.

To that end, she had tried her hand at some subtle matchmaking. There were certainly plenty of young ladies to choose from in London. Lord Glaedon's romantic good looks, combined with the air of mystery surrounding his sudden reappearance on the scene, caused feminine hearts to flutter wherever he went.

He had never shown the slightest interest in any of them, however. And then, without warning, he had offered for Miss Beauforth. Lady Glaedon had hoped that he had fallen in love at long last, but plainly that was not the case.

Sighing, she picked up her embroidery. If anyone deserved happiness, Christian did. But she feared he was far from finding it.

THE NEXT TWO WEEKS were relatively happy ones for Azalea. Since Lord Glaedon had gone from London, she'd been able to push her problems to the back of her mind for the present.

She had the pleasure of seeing Millie comfortably accepted by the staff at Curzon Street as an under kitchen maid. Mrs. Swann, meanwhile, had received a letter from her sister in Yorkshire, inviting her for an extended visit. Azalea convinced her to accept. It had become obvious that Mrs. Swann was unhappy under the supercilious eye of Mrs. Straite and that it was only a matter of time before a confrontation occurred between the two women.

In addition, Azalea feared that Swannee might complicate the situation with Lord Glaedon. Though the housekeeper had never been told of the marriage, Azalea had often suspected that her old friend knew the truth. There was no knowing what she might do or say if she learned that Lord Glaedon was still alive. It

would be best if Mrs. Swann were out of London until
Azalea had a chance to settle the matter for herself.

Though it was long past the autumn Little Season,
Azalea made a few fashionable acquaintances among
the callers at Lady Beauforth's home. Her wardrobe
had grown to an adequate size for a winter in London,
although she realized much more would be needed for
the spring Season. A dozen bargain gowns had been
purchased for refurbishing, and two new outfits were
being made up: a riding habit of rich green-and-gold
velvet and a ball gown in a pale green satin that Azalea
had found irresistible.

Her relationship with her cousins was improving as
well. Lady Beauforth had warmed towards her until
she no longer felt herself a charity case in the household. Marilyn still persisted in holding her at a distance, but she, too, showed some signs of thawing.

The two young ladies were in each other's company
most mornings. While shopping, receiving and returning calls, Azalea had ample opportunity to observe
Miss Beauforth's character. She came to the conclusion that while Marilyn was spoiled, certainly, and had
done little to improve her mind, she was not actually
malicious or stupid. In time Azalea hoped that they
might truly become friends.

One blustery afternoon in early December, she sat in
the library, writing a letter to a young lady in Williamsburg who had extracted a promise from her to
correspond upon her arrival in England. A two-month
separation, combined with the stiff formality of the
English ladies she had met, caused Azalea to remember Miss Severson with more fondness than she'd ever
felt towards her in Virginia. As she was closing her

surprisingly affectionate missive, Lady Beauforth bustled into the room, in obvious high spirits.

"Ah, *there* you are, my dear! I have the most *splendid* news! I have just received an invitation to a Christmas ball at Lady Queesley's on Thursday. She is leaving for the country and wishes to give a farewell entertainment. No doubt she feels the need to fortify herself for the dull weeks ahead. I must say I find London, even thin of company, far preferable to rusticating over the holidays. But that is neither here nor there. I vow, I had *quite* given up being able to present you to Society before spring, but this will be a *marvellous* opportunity! This will be your debut, in a manner of speaking, so we must choose your outfit with care."

This speech left Azalea nearly as breathless as it did Lady Beauforth, but she recovered quickly. She was pleased at the news, partly because of the qualms she had felt over the expensive ball gown she had purchased with the Season still some months away. And, of course, what female could suppress a flutter of pleasure at the prospect of her first ball?

She turned to Lady Beauforth with a smile, her letter forgotten. "Oh, Cousin Alice, how delightful! Are you certain I am invited? I do not recollect ever having met Lady Queesley."

"Yes, she enclosed cards for each of us. Indeed, it would be strange if you were *not* invited, as it is generally known that you are staying with us. And Lady Queesley never does anything shabbily, I assure you," said Lady Beauforth in a tone that quite settled the matter.

"In that case, dear cousin, I can look forward to the ball with all my heart," said Azalea cheerfully. "Will my new green satin be appropriate, do you think?"

"The very thing, my dear! We'll have to see about finding you some matching flowers for your hair. But I must get back upstairs to Marilyn—I promised her I would only be a moment. Oh, I *do* hope dear Glaedon returns in time for this ball...." So saying, Lady Beauforth departed as quickly as she had come, her words trailing behind her.

Azalea's pleasure dimmed abruptly at this reminder of the very real problems she still faced. If Lord Glaedon *were* at the ball, she would have to make some attempt to solve them, though as yet she hadn't a clue how she was to do so. Frowning, she turned back to her letter.

As SHE DRESSED for the ball a few nights later, Azalea's thoughts kept straying to Lord Glaedon and the dilemma he represented. He was back in Town, she knew, for Lady Beauforth had announced that tidbit at nuncheon. How her cousin could have discovered the fact so quickly Azalea did not know. Lady Beauforth apparently had her sources.

Still, she refused to let that problem, or the one concerning Lord Kayce, whom she had all but forgotten, completely destroy her enjoyment of the evening ahead. This was to be her first ball, after all. Surely everything would work itself out in time.

Junie put the finishing touches to her hair and invited Azalea to view the result in the long glass on the wardrobe door. "You'll be the belle of the ball, Miss Azalea, that's certain," she announced proudly.

Looking into the mirror, Azalea could almost agree with her. Surely, the exquisitely gowned and coiffed young lady gazing back at her bore no resemblance to the rough provincial she had been two weeks earlier.

Pale green satin gleamed richly through the overskirt of matching net. The waist was high, just under her full breasts, with a low neckline—so low, in fact, that she had protested to Madame Clarisse, the modiste, only to be assured that she would see many more-revealing gowns, and that this one was in the best possible taste for a young girl making her comeout.

Her white throat was adorned by a single strand of small but perfectly matched pearls that had been her mother's, and white flowers wreathed her hair. The colour of the gown intensified the green of her eyes, the deep red of her hair, just as its lines emphasized the best points of her figure. She felt that the overall effect was pleasing and that her appearance, at least, would hardly cause her cousins embarrassment.

She was able to judge their reactions a few moments later when she nervously descended the long staircase. Lady Beauforth's face lit up immediately upon perceiving Azalea above. Her pleased smile quickly allayed any doubts about her approval.

Marilyn's feelings were more difficult to fathom, but Azalea thought she could construe her slight frown and the widening of her blue eyes as an oblique sort of compliment. Marilyn herself was a veritable vision of loveliness in ethereal white.

Azalea had to wonder again how her cousin could be jealous of her—and more importantly, how she could possibly win Lord Glaedon away from such a beauty. She suppressed a small sigh as they slipped into their wraps and out the door to the waiting carriage.

"What a pleasant evening," she remarked to her cousins, in an attempt to ignore the trembling in her midsection that seemed to increase as they neared Lady Queesley's mansion. "In Virginia, the December winds are quite bitter, compared to this."

"But I had understood the colonies—er, the United States—to be quite warm. I'm certain Mr. Symes, who was in Charleston several years ago, said that the summers there were unbearably hot, and plagued by insects," said Marilyn, sitting up a little straighter and looking directly at her cousin for the first time since leaving Curzon Street.

Azalea had once or twice before noticed her cousin's interest in her chance comments about America. "Yes, that's true as well," she agreed. "I haven't spent a summer here, of course, but I understand that your climate is not subject to the extremes we experience in the New World. Perhaps the surrounding ocean acts as a buffer to the elements here." She was about to expand on this theory, which Reverend Marston, one of her numerous tutors, had once put forth, but she sensed she was losing the attention of her audience.

"In any event," she went on, "in Virginia we have both extremes. Summer and winter both can be rather unpleasant at times, but spring and autumn are generally delightful, with colours as vivid as the temperatures are pleasant. And we only rarely see fog there."

She continued discussing Virginia's seasons, with more and more frequent questions from Marilyn and an occasional comment from Lady Beauforth. In this manner, the time passed pleasantly for Azalea as the coach inched forward in the long queue before Lady Queesley's doorstep. Finally, it was their turn to alight, and Azalea's anxiety returned suddenly and in full force.

As if reading her mind, Lady Beauforth gently patted her shoulder and said, "Chin up, my dear. One's first ball is exciting, but can be a bit terrifying also. Just pretend you've done it all before, and don't forget to breathe!"

Lady Queesley greeted Lady Beauforth warmly, exchanging the latest news of some mutual acquaintances, before turning to the two younger ladies.

"Why, Marilyn, I declare you become more beautiful by the day," the countess exclaimed, in a fair imitation of Lady Beauforth's style. Azalea had noticed that this affected, gushing manner was the rule rather the exception among the older ladies of the ton.

"Your mother must be very proud. It's no wonder you managed to snare the pick of the Season." This last was directed at Lady Beauforth with a knowing smile and the ghost of a wink. "But pray present me to your little American relative! Your niece, did you say?" Lady Queesley's overpowering smile was now turned on Azalea.

"My second cousin, actually, Lydia," returned Lady Beauforth, smiling every bit as broadly as her hostess. "This is Miss Azalea Clayton, lately from Williamsburg, Virginia. Azalea, Lady Queesley."

Azalea dropped a curtsy of the proper depth and murmured that she was honoured to meet her ladyship.

Plainly pleased by the girl's respectful manner, a contrast to Marilyn's bored observance of the proprieties, Lady Queesley offered her opinion that a delightful surprise was in store for the young men lucky enough to be present tonight. She concluded by promising to present her son, Lord Mallows, to the new-comer as soon as she could resign her post by the door.

As the trio progressed into the ballroom, Lady Beauforth whispered, "That is quite a triumph already, my dear! Everyone knows dear Lydia is absurdly protective of her son. She would hardly have made such a promise if she were not vastly taken with you."

Azalea could not help but be gratified by such a compliment, but before she could reply, her attention was claimed by the scene before her. The enormous ballroom glittered with gold and white in the light of what seemed to be thousands of candles in sconces and chandeliers.

As the Beauforth party was announced, a veritable sea of faces turned toward them, and Azalea was seized by an almost overwhelming desire to turn tail and flee. She mastered the impulse quickly, by necessity—her cousins were advancing into the crowd at a steady pace, and she had no wish to be left on her own among this throng of strangers.

"I thought you said everyone was away from London this close to Christmas!" she said to Lady Beauforth, raising her voice slightly to be heard over the collective, well-modulated tones of the guests.

"Oh, they are, my dear!" replied her cousin. "You will see the difference next spring, when the Season has begun. This is a fairly intimate and quite comfortable gathering. I assure you, at a successful ball at the height of the Season, one can scarcely breathe, much less move. Not nearly so pleasant as a small party like this one, in my opinion."

Azalea shook her head and looked around her in disbelief. A small party? She was certain she had never in her life seen so many people gathered under one roof.

Marilyn, meanwhile, had already located—or been located by—several admirers and was happily chatting and flirting with no less than four young men at once. As she made no move to introduce any of them to her cousin, Azalea turned away to observe another portion of the crowd.

The sea of faces was beginning to resolve into individuals and Azalea noticed a few people she had met on morning calls with her cousins. Seeing Lady Dinsmore, a young matron she had befriended, a short distance away, she turned to ask Lady Beauforth whether it would be acceptable to approach her alone. Before she had opened her mouth, however, she saw the unmistakable figure of Lord Glaedon coming towards them.

CHAPTER SIX

AZALEA WAS COMPLETELY unprepared for the riot of emotions that assaulted her at her first sight of Lord Glaedon after his absence. She felt now that she must have been blind at their first meeting not to have realized instantly that he was Chris, the Christian Morely she had been so infatuated with in her youth. His height, his colouring, his stance and especially his eyes shouted his identity at her, though he was not even looking her way. In fact, he was making a beeline towards Marilyn.

With a sinking sensation, she watched as he bent over her cousin's hand and neatly extricated her from the knot of admirers, to his apparent amusement and their equally obvious chagrin. He looked almost unbearably handsome to Azalea, his dark blue superfine coat matching his eyes, and the whiteness of his intricately tied cravat emphasizing the near blackness of his carefully disordered hair.

Though she could not hear what was being said, she assumed from Marilyn's flirtatious fan and fluttering lashes that it was complimentary. Azalea's excitement at her first ball suddenly fell rather flat.

Still, determined to enjoy herself as much as possible, she turned her back on Lord Glaedon and made her way over to Lady Dinsmore.

That lady seemed sincerely delighted to renew their brief acquaintance, and they chatted for some minutes about botany and gardening, a shared passion. They debated the likely source of the potted holly bushes that had been placed about the ballroom in the spirit of the season, presenting a considerable hazard to those who carelessly passed too close to them. This led to a comparison of English and American hollies by Azalea, followed by a discussion of other differences between the flora of the two countries.

"I hear that there are countless varieties of wild-flowers in America that we never see here. I would love some descriptions," Lady Dinsmore was saying, when a slight "ahem" at her elbow caused Azalea to start and look around.

Their hostess, Lady Queesley, stood there, accompanied by a fair, stout young man who had presumably been the one clearing his throat. Lady Dinsmore discreetly excused herself.

"Miss Clayton, I promised to introduce you to my son," the countess said with a smile. "Viscount Mallows." Lady Queesley gestured grandly toward her treasure. "George, do show Miss Clayton about and introduce her to some of the young people," she added in an audible undertone before fading into the crowd.

Lord Mallows seemed somewhat ill at ease and Azalea concluded that he was unused to being thrust forward by his mother. *Overprotective* was the word Cousin Alice had used, and Azalea suspected that it might be quite accurate. He seemed to be searching almost desperately for something to say, so she broke the awkward silence herself.

"This is a lovely room, my lord. We have nothing to compare with such elegance in Williamsburg, I assure you." There. She had given him an opening, and she hoped he would have the courage to pick it up.

"Will-Williamsburg?" he asked with a slight stammer. "That is in Virginia, is it not?"

"Yes, in the southern part of the state."

"I have a friend from that part of the world," Lord Mallows continued, obviously pleased to have something to say for himself. "I'll introduce you if I can find him. He—he's here somewhere." Whereupon he stood on tiptoe, being only an inch or two taller than Azalea herself, and scanned the room.

"How kind of you!" she exclaimed. "But you needn't search for him this instant, surely." She was rather hoping to have her first public dance with the viscount, since she was certain he wouldn't be too critical of any mistakes she might make. But it was too late. He was already gesturing, quite conspicuously, to someone across the room.

"He's on his way," Lord Mallows said smugly, turning back to Azalea with a smile. It was clear to her that he was extremely eager to escape her presence, but she could not take offence. She suspected that he behaved similarly with all ladies.

"You wanted me, George?" A tall, sandy-haired young man shouldered his way between two imposing dowagers who blocked his path, ignoring their outraged murmurs. "What was so important that you had to summon me from the side of one of the most fascinating... But who's this?"

His glance fell on Azalea and remained there. "If this is the reason for my summons, I forgive you, George. Might you introduce me to Miss..."

"Jonathan?" gasped Azalea incredulously.

The young man's mouth fell open. "Azalea?" he exclaimed, equally taken aback.

Thrown off his stride by their behaviour, the viscount tried to steer the conversation back into more conventional channels. "Miss Clayton, I—I'd like to present Mr. Jonathan P-Plummer," he said as quickly as his stammer would allow.

"It *is* you!" she cried. "I knew I could not be mistaken!"

After gazing at one another for a few seconds, both began talking excitedly, almost as if trying to cover the last six years in ten minutes.

"I vow I would never have known you...."

"Yes, when I left your father was well...."

"How are Missy and James and the others...?"

"...with my cousins, in Curzon Street..."

Finally, Lord Mallows's repeated attempts to take his leave brought them back to their surroundings.

"Yes, George, off to the cards with you. I am deeply in your debt," said Jonathan, smiling broadly. Then, turning back to Azalea as if still unable to believe that this exquisite creature was the friend he had romped with in childhood, he bowed and said with mock formality, "Miss Clayton, may I have this dance?"

Still dimpling with the pleasure of finding a friend from home among the cold London ton, Azalea dipped him a flawless half curtsy and replied in the same vein.

"But of course, Mr. Plummer." Then she marred the effect by whispering, "You must not mind if I forget a few of the steps—I have only just learned to dance, and have never done so in public before."

Jonathan chuckled as he led her onto the floor, where the first set was just forming. "I'm glad to see you haven't changed completely, 'Zalea," he said.

The dance began and Azalea had opportunity to discover that Jonathan, at least, knew all the steps. He was, in fact, a very accomplished dancer and neatly covered her few mistakes. She was relieved to find dancing less of a trial than she had expected, and as the set progressed, her steps became surer. Nor could she be especially conspicuous, she thought, with so many other couples whirling about the floor.

In this last thought, however, Azalea was not quite correct. The two young Americans made a striking couple and drew glances from several quarters, some admiring, some envious and some merely thoughtful. Among the latter was Lord Kayce, who had discovered her identity by chance, having overheard a conversation between two of the envious watchers, a pair of spinsters about to enter their fourth Season.

He had first learned of Azalea's existence less than a week ago, so he saw no immediate need to play the part of the devoted long-lost uncle. No, he was willing to await a more opportune moment for introductions. As he watched Azalea twirl past, her lovely face alight with laughter at some comment her partner had made, his pale brown eyes narrowed thoughtfully.

Lord Glaedon was another thoughtful observer, watching the pair speculatively and trying, still unsuccessfully, to remember who the girl reminded him of. She had continued to thrust her way into his thoughts frequently during the past two weeks, sometimes at the most inopportune of times. It was the primary reason he had neglected to call at Beauforth House upon his return to Town yesterday, in fact.

He could not deny that she was very beautiful, but he was certain now that that was not the reason behind her disturbing effect on him. It was almost as if she were trying to tell him something—not in words, but by her very presence. Shaking his head to clear it of such thoughts, he turned back to Marilyn, who had apparently not noticed his momentary defection and continued her avid recital of Miss Belgrave's most recent fall from grace.

Suddenly, her manner irritated him. It occurred to him that Miss Beauforth's conversation consisted almost entirely of gossip. Though he had been about to ask her for another dance, he now chose not to intervene when young Smallwood stepped up and requested the honour. Christian glanced around as the couples took their places and, seeing no sign of the disturbing American beauty, retired to the terrace to think.

Meanwhile, Azalea was having a better time than she would have thought possible a scant half-hour before. Jonathan had introduced her to his circle of friends, a lively group of young people, and several of the gentlemen were already vying for her attention.

Never having flirted before, Azalea was surprised to discover how easy and amusing it was, with no expectations raised on either side. She had essentially cut herself off from Society for the past six years, but now, surrounded by the light banter of her new acquaintances, she found herself opening up.

Returning breathless and smiling from the exertions of a country dance with Lord Soames, Azalea suddenly found herself face-to-face with Lord Glaedon. Still in high spirits, she mastered the sudden shyness that threatened and dropped a quick curtsy, saying brightly, "How nice to see you again, my lord. I trust you are enjoying the evening?" Marilyn was nowhere to be seen.

"Indeed, yes, Miss Clayton," replied the earl gravely. "I was hoping to persuade you to stand up with me for the next dance in order to increase that enjoyment."

He spoke so stiffly that Azalea was tempted to refuse, but realized that this might be a perfect opportunity to untangle some of the mystery surrounding him.

"Of course, my lord," she answered, after only the briefest pause.

Then, to her consternation, the orchestra proceeded to strike up a waltz. Chiding herself for her alarm, she told herself that this would make it that much easier to engage him in conversation.

Still, Azalea was glad that it was not her first waltz of the evening, otherwise nervousness would have been sure to make her stumble. At his first touch, a light, perfectly proper clasp on her waist and hand, she had to struggle to keep her features composed.

His palm seemed to burn against the small of her back, while his hand meshed with hers as no other gentleman's had. After the first shock, however, she floated almost effortlessly in his arms.

His nearness, his touch, made her throat dry and took away her capacity of thought, and it began to appear that they would pass the entire dance without a word. Determined that this not be the case, Azalea had just steeled herself to ask her partner if he had ever been to America, when he caught her off guard with a question of his own.

"Is it possible that we have met before, Miss Clayton? I felt when I first saw you that day in the Park that you reminded me of someone, and I have been unable to shake the impression." He spoke warily, as though expecting a rebuff.

"It is possible, of course, my lord," she answered, seizing the opening. "Have you ever been to Virginia?"

Lord Glaedon stiffened. "I fear not, Miss Clayton. I intended to visit it at one time, but the ship foundered in the crossing and my father, I regret to say, died at sea. I could never bring myself to repeat the trip."

His tone was cold and emotionless, but Azalea was moved regardless. She remembered how close he and his father had been and realized that this must be one more grudge Christian bore against Americans. For the moment, she ignored his baffling assertion that the shipwreck had taken place on the outward voyage.

"I am sorry, my lord. I, too, once lost a loved one at sea." How, she wondered, would he respond to that? But not even a flicker indicated that he was aware of her intent.

"The sea, at least, takes life without motive or malice," Lord Glaedon replied after a moment. "So much cannot be said of people who kill and degrade their fellow human beings. Tell me, Miss Clayton, as an American, what are your views on slavery? Do you consider it a 'sad necessity,' as I hear is the fashionable view among your countrymen?"

Although his sudden change of topic surprised her, Azalea answered without hesitation, for this was a subject near to her heart.

"Slavery is 'necessary' only to the rich, my lord, so that they can remain so. Money is a paltry excuse for turning humans into possessions, and I am confident that the majority of Americans—voting Americans—feel the same way, and that the days of that reprehensible institution are numbered." She spoke with conviction, but Lord Glaedon's expression was cynical.

"How touching, to be sure," he said. "But I'll wager you're not above eating the sugar or wearing the cotton that slave labourers have gathered. And how willing would you be, I wonder, to forgo any part of your personal comfort to change that institution? I have heard such high-sounding words from Americans before, but it would seem that words are all they are. Something must be fundamentally wrong with the citizens of a nation that would condone such inhumanity."

Azalea was struck momentarily speechless. She felt as strongly about the matter as he did and knew full well that many of her countrymen were hypocrites on the subject. But she was furious that he should so deliberately choose to doubt her sincerity.

The music had stopped, but he continued to look down at her, waiting sardonically for her answer.

"You asked for my opinion and I gave it, my lord," said Azalea with deceptive sweetness. "I see it was not the opinion you expected or wished to hear. Obviously, you would rather mock me than believe me sincere, since to do that would be to admit that all Americans are not the heartless villains you wish to think us. What of your countrymen who must serve in the Royal Navy against their will? I don't believe America has a monopoly on inhumanity. Or on hypocrisy and deceit!"

With that parting shot, Azalea turned and left him without a backward glance.

Luckily, the next dance was a cotillion and afforded little chance for conversation with her partner. As Azalea focused on the intricate steps of the dance, her temper cooled somewhat, though she still deeply resented Glaedon's assumption that she shared the mercenary motives of the worst of her countrymen.

Looking around at the outrageously expensive splendour of the ballroom, she suddenly felt a desire to laugh. Obviously wealth, and especially the ostentatious display of it, was as important to the English ton as to any American! By the end of the dance, she found she was looking forward to crossing swords with Lord Glaedon again.

CHRISTIAN WATCHED AZALEA as she flounced away, struck less by her words than by the sweet seductiveness of her hips as they moved beneath the green satin of her gown. He had intended to discover more about her during that dance, in an attempt to allay the disquiet he felt in her presence. Instead, he had again been drawn into an attack on her homeland.

As she danced the cotillion with another admirer, Christian was forced to admit that he was far more drawn than repelled by Miss Clayton. Not that it mattered, of course. He had already committed his future to Miss Beauforth and nothing could change that. After the mess he had already made of his life, he owed it to the family to marry her, a woman of fortune and impeccable breeding. The marriage would bring to fruition the honourable plans of his father and brother, now dead.

But for the first time since his betrothal, those ringing, lofty arguments sounded hollow. Whatever his feelings, however, he would stand by his given word. To do otherwise would be unworthy of the name he bore, a name he had damaged enough. Rapping out an

oath under his breath, he went in search of his fiancée
to secure her for the supper dance.

ON HER WAY IN TO SUPPER with Jonathan and a group
of his friends, Azalea came face-to-face with Lord
Glaedon once again. Marilyn clung to one of his arms
and Lady Beauforth rested a hand on the other.

After one brief glance at the earl, Azalea turned
quickly to her cousins. "Ma'am, may I present a very
old friend of mine from Williamsburg? Jonathan
Plummer, Lady Beauforth, Miss Beauforth... and
Lord Glaedon." She had not hesitated quite long
enough to be rude.

Glaedon's nod, however, was curt. "Servant,
Plummer. Miss Beauforth, my lady, I'll go ahead to
reserve a table."

Azalea nearly gaped at his retreating back, but before she could exclaim at his incivility, Lady Beauforth spoke.

"Mr. Plummer, how charming to meet you. You
knew our Azalea in America then?"

Marilyn had looked as though she were about to
follow Lord Glaedon's example, but at the sound of
Jonathan's voice, she hesitated.

"The pleasure is all mine, Lady Beauforth. Yes, I
lived in Williamsburg until my grandfather, Lord
Holte, insisted I attend Oxford. As he was footing the
bills, my father sent me off with his blessing. Since
finishing, I have found several reasons to prolong my
stay in England." This was said with a lingering look
at Marilyn, who fluttered her lashes in return.

"You must come to call on us in Curzon Street, Mr.
Plummer," insisted Lady Beauforth, all smiles.

Azalea's estimation of Jonathan's social standing rose precipitously at this unusual mark of distinction. She knew by now that her cousins were considered "high sticklers" and were very particular about who they deigned to name their friends.

She said as much to Jonathan as they proceeded to the supper table where a few of his friends were already assembled.

"Yes, I don't often invoke Grandfather's name like that, but I wanted to be sure of seeing you often. I thought it would be more convenient if I were allowed to run tame at Beauforth House. What can you tell me of your fair cousin?" He glanced over to where the young lady in question sat at a nearby table.

He appeared vaguely disappointed when she informed him that Marilyn was betrothed to Lord Glaedon. "Ah, well, I can but dream," he said philosophically.

Just in time, Azalea stopped herself from hinting that the marriage would not take place at all if she had any say in the matter. Even after several years' separation, she found it hard to be guarded with Jonathan. Instead, she followed his glance, to find Lord Glaedon's eyes on her, his expression unreadable.

Turning away hastily, she said, "Pray do not get your hopes up, Jonathan. Even were the match broken off, I can't think Miss Beauforth would care for life in the colonies."

This drew a general chuckle from Jonathan's set, and a lively discussion of the relative rigours of fashionable life in America and England ensued.

At the other table, Christian continued to regard Miss Clayton for a moment, admiring the way her green eyes flashed and sparkled as she laughed with her

young American friend. Turning back to Miss Beauforth, he was struck anew at the contrast between his
betrothed and her colonial cousin.

Though Azalea was the elder by a year, a fact which
Marilyn had brought to his attention three times now,
she gave an impression of youthful innocence that Miss
Beauforth singularly lacked. While Miss Clayton
seemed completely unaware of her physical charms, his
fiancée made full use of her own with a sophistication
that would have done credit to a woman twice her age.

"You must try the ham, my lord," cooed Marilyn at
that moment, leaning far forward to afford him a tantalizing glimpse of cleavage. "It is sliced so thin it nigh
melts in your mouth." She smiled seductively as she
licked the corners of her full lips.

With an effort, he smiled back. "I'm sure it is delicious."

She tittered and batted her eyes, and he realized that
she took his words as a veiled compliment, when in fact
they had been no more than inattention. Mentally, he
shrugged. What did it matter, as long as she was content?

Though he strove to attend to the conversation between Miss Beauforth and her mother, Christian was
keenly aware of the laughter from Miss Clayton's table. In spite of himself, he rather wished he were there
instead.

AZALEA REFLECTED ON the events of the evening with
a measure of satisfaction during the carriage ride back
to Curzon Street.

After supper, she had been engaged for every dance,
and not just with members of Jonathan's youthful set.

Several titled gentlemen, including Lord Chilton, a dandified marquess, had also vied for her attention.

She had not seen Lord Glaedon again after supper; from something Marilyn said to her mother, she gathered that he had taken his leave early, a circumstance that had disappointed both her cousins. For herself, she felt it was just as well, as she wanted to prepare a few unanswerable arguments before speaking to him again.

Her plan had not gone especially well, she had to admit. She had intended to fascinate Lord Glaedon, to get him talking about himself, to discover what lay behind his refusal to acknowledge her. Instead, she had fallen to arguing politics with the man.

Instead of charming him away from Marilyn, she had no doubt deepened his dislike of her. Nor was she any closer to solving the mystery of his escape from the shipwreck. Even more alarming, she found that she was more strongly attracted to him than ever!

But even had she found him repugnant, she could not allow him to go through with his intended marriage to Marilyn. Perhaps something *had* happened to make him forget their wedding. Something to do with the shipwreck, perhaps? If that were the case, she would be party to the crime of bigamy if she stood by silently.

She owed it to Lady Beauforth, not to mention Marilyn and Christian, to prevent such a thing. And somehow she would, even if it meant alienating Lord Glaedon forever by pressing her claim. But first she would try other, more subtle means.

No, she could not regret attending the ball. Everything had been new to her, and Jonathan and his friends had been more than pleasant. She had discovered that she could dance without embarrassing herself, and had made dozens of acquaintances. In fact, she had enjoyed every moment—even her argument with Lord Glaedon. Especially her argument with Lord Glaedon.

All in all, she thought, as the carriage rolled to a stop before the Beauforth Town house, it had been a satisfactory first ball. So why didn't she feel more satisfied?

CHAPTER SEVEN

WHEN SHE AWOKE the next morning from a deep, dreamless sleep, Azalea was amazed at the lateness of the hour. Why, it must be near eleven o'clock! She could not remember ever having slept so late in her life. Junie had apparently been at the keyhole, for she entered mere seconds after Azalea stirred.

"Well, miss, I trust you slept well after your grand night?" she asked with a smile, setting a tray of toast and chocolate on the bedside stand.

"Like a stone, Junie, thank you," Azalea answered. "I must have been more tired than I realized."

"'Twas the excitement, Miss Azalea, as much as the dancing, I'll warrant. A first ball will do that to a body, so I hear. Now, have a bite to eat, and I'll be back in a few minutes to help you dress. You're certain to have some morning callers within the half hour, or I miss my guess. Didn't I say you'd be a sure success?" she asked smugly as she left the room, leaving Azalea to marvel at the speed of the below-stairs gossip network.

Descending to the front parlour some twenty minutes later in a flattering new gown of fine peach wool, Azalea saw that Junie had been correct, as usual. Her hostesses were already entertaining no fewer than five callers, four of whom were among Azalea's admirers from the previous evening.

The fifth was a middle-aged gentleman unknown to her. Several bouquets of hothouse flowers reposed in vases about the room, she noted with pleasure. She could hardly wait to examine them, as she was certain at least one of the varieties represented was unfamiliar to her. Right now, though, she must greet the guests.

Every gentleman present rose at her entrance, and Lady Beauforth turned to beam at her. Marilyn, who had been enjoying the undivided attention of the visitors in her cousin's absence, offered a smile that was a tinge less welcoming.

Azalea nodded to each of the gentlemen in turn, with a light comment to each about last night's ball. Mr. Gresham, she noticed, seemed content to resume his flirtation with Marilyn after greeting her, but the others, including Lord Chilton, were flatteringly attentive, clustering about her as she took her seat. Before conversation could resume, however, Lady Beauforth drew her attention to the older gentleman at her side.

"My dear Azalea," she exclaimed, "let me present your uncle, Lord Kayce. I collect that you did not make his acquaintance last night, though he was in attendance, were you not, sir?"

"I was indeed, my lady," Lord Kayce returned in an affectedly nasal tone as he bowed in Azalea's direction. "There was such a flock about my young niece, however, that I forbore to intrude the presence of a stodgy old man like myself on her obvious enjoyment." A pleasant smile accompanied this remark, and Azalea felt her shock at his identity giving way to surprise at his manner.

Lord Kayce was thin, slightly over middle height, and possessed an expressive, if not a handsome, countenance. He was dressed in the absolute height of ele-

gance, with a froth of rich, cream-coloured lace at his
throat and wrists setting off the deep green of his embroidered waistcoat and matching jacket. His hair,
which he wore tied back with a green ribbon in an old-
fashioned style, had apparently been the same deep
auburn as his niece's in his youth, though now it was
heavily threaded with grey. Azalea couldn't help
thinking that this was what her father might have
looked like had he still been alive. The thought warred
with her misgivings.

"I wish you had approached me, my lord. Surely
you don't think me such a pleasure seeker that I would
regret time spent with my nearest kinsman!" she said,
the warmth in her tone not entirely feigned.

"You reassure me, my dear," he replied. "But
please, no more 'my lording.' As you remind me, we
are the only members left of the Clayton family, so it
must be Uncle Simon."

He was all affability, apparently eager to welcome
her both to England and into his life. He certainly did
not resemble the calculating, ruthless mercenary her
grandfather had led her to expect.

"Of course. And you must call me Azalea." She
wished she had the courage to ask him outright what he
meant to do about her share of her father's estate.
Could Grandfather have been mistaken about him?

As they chatted of America and of Azalea's impres-
sions of London for a few minutes, Azalea found herself unwillingly drawn to her new-found kinsman,
although his effeminate way of speaking and gesturing with his hands reminded her of Lord Chilton. Her
uncle was not a member of the dandy set, however—
one had only to look at his clothing, which was far
more subdued than Lord Chilton's, to ascertain that.

Though distracting, the affectedness of his manner along with his self-deprecating air only served to make him appear that much more harmless. The unworthy thought occurred to Azalea that this might be the reason for its cultivation.

"I really must be going, but I do trust we shall see each other often, my dear child," said Kayce, rising smoothly after a glance at his pocket watch. "Perhaps, once the Season is under way in the spring, we can collaborate on a comeout ball for our young relative," he suggested lightly to Lady Beauforth as he took his leave.

"Of course, if you would care to, my lord," she answered, simpering as fulsomely as Marilyn did with the younger gentlemen.

"We'll discuss it at some future date," he assured her. "Oh, and I pray you will allow me to send round a token of my affection, my dear," he said to Azalea. With another warm smile for his niece, he bowed smoothly and departed.

Before he was out of the room, Azalea's gallants returned to their various assaults on her heart, and she was soon laughing at their outrageous flattery. Her enjoyment of the moment was only marred by the absence of one particular gentleman, but she refused to dwell on it just then.

"*Well,* my dear, I would say that your social position is assured now that Lord Kayce has decided to recognize you," Lady Beauforth said as the last of their callers departed. "He is incredibly wealthy, as well as influential among the ton. With his patronage and, of course, my own, which is not inconsequential, I assure you, you are sure to take next Season. We'll have you married to a lord or I miss my guess!"

"But why should he not recognize me, Cousin Alice?" asked Azalea choosing to ignore Lady Beauforth's increasingly frequent references to finding her a husband. "The family connection cannot be doubted, so would he not look foolish to ignore it?"

"Foolish? Kayce?" Lady Beauforth was plainly shocked. "Nothing of the sort, my dear! It is scarcely possible for a man of his standing to look foolish, whatever the circumstances. Had he decided to ignore the connection, you would have stood in grave danger of being cut on the mere notion that he must have some reason for not acknowledging you. I am very happy for you that it will not come to that!"

"But why should he do such a thing?" Azalea persisted suspiciously. "He *seemed* a most pleasant man. I concluded from his manner that he became aware of my presence in London only last night, else he would have called sooner."

"Yes, he did say that, didn't he?" Lady Beauforth looked thoughtful. "Normally, absolutely *nothing* goes on in London of which Lord Kayce is unaware. I'd have expected him to know of your presence the day of your arrival, or the day after at the very latest. Perhaps he has merely been deciding what to do. Your success last night may have clinched the matter for him. If you are going to take, he will certainly want some of the credit, and would not wish to look foolish by ignoring his niece when she becomes a Toast next spring," she concluded, blithely unaware, as always, that she had contradicted herself.

Azalea was accustomed to Cousin Alice's confusing speeches and had learned by now not to take her every utterance at face value. It could not be denied, however, that Lady Beauforth was nearly as well-informed as she claimed Lord Kayce was, and Azalea could not lightly dismiss everything she had said. Especially given her grandfather's warnings. But could her uncle—or anyone—really be capable of such duplicity?

Perhaps so. She recalled a time when her cousins had encountered on the street two ladies they apparently despised, judging by previous conversations. To watch that meeting, one would have thought it a reunion of the dearest of friends.

The English, she reminded herself, were not nearly so open as Americans were, so it might be possible that her uncle would conceal any dislike of herself that he might feel. She decided to go slowly with him, and make more of an effort to discover his true feelings. After all, she could hardly judge his character accurately on the basis of a single fifteen-minute interview!

"SECURE THAT LINE!" bellowed the captain, his black hair dripping with sea water. "Furl the main topsail!"

"This looks like a bad blow." Christian's father sounded concerned.

Suddenly, flowers were everywhere. Apple blossoms. Daisies. A soft breeze was blowing. What was everyone worried about? he wondered.

"My God, Chris!" His father's face was white. The sky behind him had gone from blue to leaden, an odd, yellowish grey.

"Man overboard!" shouted the captain, red hair and beard now whipping in the gale. Chris turned to see a crate of chickens wash over the rail, then another. The brown-and-white birds squawked in terror, their feathers flying, then they were gone.

"That was a close one!" His father's voice again.

Christian awoke with a start, sweat beading his brow. The bed linens were damp around him.

"Damn," he muttered. It had been months since he'd last had that nightmare, and he had begun to hope he was finally free of it.

Still shaken, he rose to light the oil lamp on the desk, determined this time to write it down while it was fresh in his mind. Before he could dip his pen, however, it was gone—again. All that remained was a vague memory of wind and waves, and his father's voice. It always happened like this. Somehow, he was certain that if he could just remember it long enough to commit it to paper, the dreams would cease plaguing him. But he never could.

Fiercely, he scoured his memory, but all that came to him were more recent recollections. Port cities in the tropics, nights of celebration so decadent they made the amusements offered in London seem like nursery games by comparison. Quickly, he thrust the distasteful memories from his mind.

That was before, he told himself. When he hadn't known any better. He was not like that now, and would never be again. Now he was head of the Morely family, sixth Earl of Glaedon. No one must ever know how he'd stained the proud name he bore. He would forget it himself. He must.

Christian pulled out some papers he had brought with him from Glaedon Oaks and read through them until his eyes began to grow heavy. The day was well advanced when he finally awoke again.

Feeling remarkably refreshed, he rang for his valet. He had been remiss since his return to Town. It was time he paid a social call at Lady Beauforth's. He was, after all, betrothed to her daughter. It was not Marilyn's face, however, that arose before him as he tied his cravat. Humming cheerfully for a reason he refused to examine, he picked up his hat and gloves and strode purposefully into the chill December afternoon.

AZALEA AND HER COUSINS were just sitting down to tea when Smythe entered stiffly, announcing, "Mr. Plummer," in his formal, slightly bored tone. Jonathan strolled in nearly on his heels, encompassing the three ladies with his engaging smile and offering a vivid contrast to the starchy butler.

"So good to see you again, Lady Beauforth, Miss Beauforth, Azalea. I trust I'm not intruding? I had planned to come this morning, but I'm afraid I didn't feel quite the thing. Fully recovered now, though, I assure you." He sat next to Marilyn and helped himself to three buttered scones in proof of his words.

"Of course you're not intruding, dear boy," gushed Lady Beauforth as her daughter nodded in agreement. "We're delighted to see you again! As you are such an old friend of Azalea's you must regard us as family and drop in whenever the fancy strikes you."

Jonathan merely nodded, his mouth too full to allow any audible reply.

"How is Lord Holte?" Lady Beauforth continued, without regard to her guest's inability to answer. "I don't remember if you said whether you were staying with him in Town or have your own lodgings, as you young gentlemen so often do these days."

With the assistance of a judicious sip of tea, Jonathan managed to swallow. "Grandfather is still in Essex at present, so I am perforce in lodgings. I plan to join him at Bitters for Christmas and try to persuade him to accompany me back to Town in the spring, as this will be my last Season for some time to come."

"Do you go abroad, then, sir?" asked Marilyn. Azalea thought she detected a trace of disappointment in her cousin's voice.

"Not precisely, Miss Beauforth. I return to my home in Virginia this summer. Father is not as young as he once was, and he has been hinting in his letters that he could use my help, particularly at harvest time. Filial duty, or guilt, if you will, is finally getting the better of me."

"How very responsible of you!" exclaimed Marilyn warmly. "Dear Azalea has been telling me a bit about America, and I'm certain you must have even more exciting stories to tell of life there," she added, to Azalea's surprise. "What is it you will be helping your father to harvest?"

"Apples, mostly," replied Jonathan, then proceeded to describe his father's orchards and the surrounding countryside in some detail.

Azalea took little part in the discussion, content to watch with some amusement the conversation between her cousin and her erstwhile best friend. Marilyn leaned toward him, asking question after question, appearing genuinely fascinated by the topic. In fact, she was so absorbed in the conversation that she scarcely flirted at all.

Without her assumed airs, she appeared even more attractive than usual, Azalea thought. Her fine blue eyes sparkled, and as she leaned forward she displayed an eagerness that seemed genuine, not flirtatious.

Azalea did not mind Marilyn's monopolization of her old friend—on the contrary, she was delighted. For all of Jonathan's outrageous compliments the night before, Azalea knew he would never see her as more than a little sister grown up. And at least one of her problems would be closer to a solution if Marilyn were to form an attachment for Jonathan, in lieu of Lord Glaedon.

As if on cue, Smythe entered the parlour to announce his lordship. Marilyn looked up with a brilliant smile, her affections obviously not yet engaged to the point of whistling an earl and his fortune down the wind.

Azalea felt her heart beat faster as she stole a glimpse at him, looking unbelievably handsome in a rust-coloured coat and fawn buckskins, then quickly turned her attention back to her plate.

"My lord, how good of you to call," Lady Beauforth exclaimed delightedly. "Pray take a seat while I ring for a fresh pot of tea." After only the briefest hesitation, Lord Glaedon seated himself in the remaining empty chair, which happened to be next to Azalea.

"How do you do, my lord," she murmured, not quite meeting his eyes. She was remembering their rather heated "discussion" last night and was suddenly embarrassed. How forward he must think her! And then there was that hint she had thrown out about his deceitfulness, perhaps undeserved.

Or perhaps not. She stiffened her spine and raised her head to attend to the conversation.

Marilyn was enthusiastically recounting one of the anecdotes Jonathan had just shared, apparently forgetting for the moment the earl's dislike of America and its inhabitants. He did not seem especially put out, however, listening with polite interest as she concluded and Jonathan took up the story where she had left off.

Marilyn's unusual animation did not escape Christian's notice any more than it had escaped Azalea's, and he also was able to make a shrewd guess as to its cause. He was surprised to realize that the idea did not disturb him in the least. Instead, he was aware of a distinct sense of relief that it was Marilyn and not her cousin who drew Mr. Plummer here.

And surely he had not engaged Miss Beauforth's affections to the extent she had led him to believe. Of a certainty, he had never been able to evoke the animation of spirits she was evincing now at the rustic tales of this colonial.

To be fair, the fellow seemed likable enough, and did tell a good story. But who was he? Plummer? Christian couldn't remember ever having heard the name before last night. A friend of Miss Clayton's, Lady Beauforth had said.

He listened more closely to the conversation in hopes of discovering more about him—and, perhaps, about the intriguing, maddening Miss Clayton as well. Though she sat in silence beside him, he was profoundly aware of her nearness.

"So you see," Jonathan was saying, "my grandfather had to be obeyed, even if it meant travelling half-way around the world for my education when there was a perfectly adequate, probably superior, university within walking distance of my home."

"And what school might that be?" asked Christian, raising one brow sceptically. He seriously doubted that any "higher education" the colonies had to offer could compare to Cambridge or Oxford.

"Why, the College of William and Mary, of course!" answered Jonathan with some surprise. "Like Azalea, I am from Williamsburg," he said carefully. "We both grew up practically in the shadow of the college. It so dominated our lives that it is difficult to remember that there are those, especially here across the Atlantic, who may be unaware of its very existence." Jonathan regarded Lord Glaedon rather strangely.

"No, not quite that, I assure you. As a matter of fact, my father had a very close friend who, I believe, was a professor at that school."

Jonathan glanced at Azalea, but she seemed completely absorbed in examining the lace edging of her sleeve. "Who might that have been, my lord?" he asked after a moment. "I knew several of the faculty, and I believe Miss Clayton was well acquainted with nearly all of them through her grandfather, who also taught there."

Christian turned to the young woman at his side, but she still did not look up. Lady Beauforth began hastily to clear her throat, apparently preparatory to changing the subject, but Christian answered Jonathan's question without hesitation.

"A Reverend Gregory Simpson," he said. "He teaches, or taught, mathematics, I believe."

"Well, if it ain't a small world!" exclaimed Jonathan. He looked again at Azalea, who this time was moved to speak.

"He was my grandfather, my lord," she said quietly, meeting Christian's eyes for the first time since his arrival. "He died last spring, which is why I find myself in England. I—I knew of his friendship with the late earl, but there seemed no opportunity, or reason, to mention it before this." She looked as though she were about to say more, but then decided against it.

"I'm sorry, Miss Clayton," he said sincerely. "Believe me, I had no wish to distress you with painful recollections."

He continued to regard her intently for a moment and was startled to see her colour rise. His own body began to stir in response and his pulse quickened.

Christian had done his best to put Miss Clayton from his mind since last night's ball, and he'd thought he'd succeeded. But now, in her presence, he found himself as disturbed by her face and voice as he'd been before. It was almost as though a part of him, deeply buried, was linked to a similar part of her. It made no sense.

At this point, Lady Beauforth broke in with an observation on the decorations used at the Queesley's ball and Jonathan joined in determinedly, giving both Azalea and Christian a chance to reflect while appearing politely interested in the conversation.

Azalea had known it was inevitable that the bond between their two families would come out in conversation sooner or later. She had even hoped for an opportunity to bring it up so that she could watch Lord Glaedon's expression for evidence of deception.

His face had told her precisely nothing.

He seemed genuinely sorry for her loss, and had betrayed not the slightest consciousness at the disclosure. For a moment, there *had* been something else in his eyes, a warmth that went beyond sympathy, but then it was gone.

Now he merely looked thoughtful. Either Lord Glaedon was such an accomplished actor that he could give Edmund Keane a run for his money, or he honestly had no recollection of his weeks in Virginia.

Or I'm losing my mind, and the marriage never took place.

No! She had the papers to prove it.

Christian, meanwhile, was every bit as preoccupied as the girl sitting beside him.

Had his father mentioned Simpson's granddaughter? Was that why her name seemed familiar to him? It seemed the most probable explanation yet. He recalled that their disastrous trip to America was to have included a visit to Simpson's home, and she would likely have been mentioned in that context, though she could have been little more than a child at that time.

But what of that elusive familiarity? Was it possible that Reverend Simpson had sent a likeness of the girl to his father and that he himself had seen it years ago? He could not remember such a thing among the old earl's belongings. He resolved to go through them more carefully when he was next at Glaedon Oaks. He had to discover why she affected him so strongly.

When Lady Beauforth had exhausted the subject of last night's decorations and began criticizing the refreshments served, Lord Glaedon rose and rather absently took his leave.

Azalea was not sorry to see him go. She tried to enter more fully into the discussion so that her companions would not notice her distraction, but Jonathan seemed well aware of the constraint in his friend's manner. He shot several significant looks her way, particularly when Lady Beauforth mentioned Lord Kayce's visit, making Azalea wonder if he knew something about her uncle.

When Jonathan rose to leave, she quickly asked him to accompany her to the library to see a letter she had just received from a mutual friend in Williamsburg. He acceded willingly, and to her relief, neither of her cousins seemed inclined to join them.

His first words when they were alone, however, had nothing to do with Lord Kayce. "Say, 'Zalea, that fellow who just left, Lord Glaedon—isn't he the one who came to visit you in Williamsburg? I thought for certain it was when I first saw him, but then when he started talking, I wasn't so sure."

Azalea froze. She had totally forgotten that brief meeting with Jonathan all those years ago. Swiftly, she made a decision. "No, that was his brother, who died in the recent war. I'm told they looked very much alike."

To her relief, Jonathan appeared to accept her fabrication. She hated to lie, but she was completely unprepared to offer an explanation for Lord Glaedon's memory lapse, especially since she herself did not know what had caused it. Before he could ask any more questions, she changed the subject.

"Tell me, Jonathan, what do you know of my uncle, Lord Kayce? You looked startled, even displeased, when Lady Beauforth mentioned him." Azalea realized that a man was more likely to have accurate information than even the best-informed female, and Jonathan moved in circles that would allow him to hear more than Mr. Timmons might ever discover.

Jonathan looked uncomfortable. "I'll admit I have heard a few unpleasant things about him. Kayce has a reputation as a hard man, for all that soft front he puts on. I've even heard rumours he may actually be dishonest."

"Dishonest?" Azalea asked sharply. "Have you specifics?"

"Well, nothing's been proven," Jonathan replied. "But poor Jim Sykes challenged him to a duel last year over some business deal where he claimed Kayce cheated him, and was found dead—killed by footpads, it was said—before the meeting ever took place. My guess is Kayce didn't want to risk his precious person any more than his honour. Don't trust him, Azalea."

"Thank you, Jonathan, I won't. Don't bruit it about just yet that he is my uncle, please. And let me know if you hear anything that you think I should know."

She wished suddenly that she could ask him about Lord Glaedon, too. No doubt Jonathan could find out what sort of a reputation he had, and perhaps other things about him, as well. But she could not, not without giving explanations that she was not yet ready to give.

Preoccupied with such thoughts, she bade him farewell.

"Mr. Plummer seems a fine young man," declared Lady Beauforth when Jonathan had gone.

"Did you not say he was but a year older than yourself?" asked Marilyn. "He seems far older, somehow. Doubtless due to his life in the wilds of America." A smile played about her lips.

"And grandson to Lord Holte!" continued her mother. "Why did you never tell us before last night that you were acquainted with such an eligible gentleman, Azalea?"

"Eligible, ma'am?" asked Azalea, startled to hear Jonathan mentioned in those terms.

"Oh, quite!" Lady Beauforth assured her. "And he seems greatly taken with you, I notice. I doubt not with a little encouragement, he could be brought to make you an offer.''

Marilyn's delicate brows drew down in a quick frown, but Azalea almost choked on a laugh. "An offer? From Jonathan? I assure you, ma'am, that he regards me with nothing more than brotherly affection. Why, we practically grew up together!''

Immediately, Marilyn's expression cleared. "Yes, Mama, you speak foolishness, surely,'' she said with something suspiciously like relief.

Azalea did not hear Lady Beauforth's reply. She was struck by a sudden realization—that some gentleman might very well make her an offer if she continued to go on as she had last night, flirting and accepting dances as though she were in fact seeking a husband. It would not at all do to forget, amid the excitement of making new friends in London, that she was already a married woman.

She would be more careful from now on, she vowed, and not encourage any such expectations. On no account would she risk breaking some poor man's heart; she knew only too well how it felt.

CHAPTER EIGHT

"I'M SORRY, MY LORD. I have looked into every point of law that could be even remotely relevant to our case, but there is nothing we can do. The girl's claim cannot be doubted. Timmons, her man of business, has all the necessary proofs."

"Yes, yes, you told me that before. 'Tis why I called on her today." Lord Kayce eyed the fat solicitor with disfavour. "I pay you an exorbitant fee to protect my interests, Mr. Greely. Those interests are now threatened by a mere slip of a girl—a girl whose existence you somehow failed to apprise me of until last month. I must wonder whether you are worth your keep after all."

The lawyer mopped his brow with an already damp handkerchief. "My lord, her claim against the Kayce estates is insignificant in comparison to the total. Your interests—"

"That is not the point," snapped Kayce. "Why was I never informed that my fool of a brother had offspring? Is that not what I employ you for? I dislike surprises, Mr. Greely."

"It is usual that such heirs make application to the estate upon the decease of the holder, my lord. I have no idea why Miss Clayton or her representatives never wrote to us after your brother's death. Naturally, I assumed—"

"I do not pay you to assume. What we must do now is figure a way out of this predicament. While the money involved may represent but a fraction of my holdings, I would prefer not to lose that particular acreage. If you recall, I had made certain arrangements that might be an, ah, embarrassment if they came to light."

Mr. Greely paled visibly. "The right of way. I had forgotten, my lord. And if your niece contests the property, there will certainly be a full investigation." He appeared to think hard for a moment. "I cannot think she will care overmuch whether she receives the land itself, my lord. Perhaps she can be bought off. If you were to offer her a fair price for the acreage, she'd likely take it, particularly if she is as short of funds as you say."

Kayce nodded slowly. "Perhaps. She would not be sending her maid to buy gowns for her in Soho were she well-fixed."

Heartened, the lawyer went on eagerly. "She must surely be grateful for the way you have increased her inheritance over the years. It may even be possible to induce her to accept the original value rather than what it is worth now. That seems only fair. The extent of the Kayce holdings, to include her small piece of it, are solely to your credit. You had little enough to work with when your father died."

That much was true. Though he had successfully forced his elder brother, Walter, to leave England permanently after their father's death, Simon had still struggled to bring profit out of the estates. The fourth baron's gaming and spendthrift ways had all but depleted his resources. Simon had succeeded beyond anyone's expectations. He rather regretted that his father, who had always favoured Walter, could not have lived to see it.

Word of Walter's death had changed nothing for Simon, except that he could now claim the title he had already felt entitled to by his brother's long absence. The fact that he had contrived that absence himself was yet another matter he preferred not come to light. Not even Greely knew of it.

With the entire fortune indisputably his, Kayce had redoubled his efforts accordingly, with spectacular results. Until last week, it had never occurred to him that his unmourned brother might have left anything behind besides the estates and title.

Today Simon Clayton, sixth Baron Kayce, was one of the wealthiest men in England—and one of the most feared. His reputation for ruthlessness was well deserved; he let no consideration of compassion or common decency stand in the way of his advancement. He lived for money and the power that came with it—and now found himself in the position of losing a galling amount to this upstart niece, unless she could somehow be disposed of.

"It would be well if we could possess ourselves of those proofs you mentioned. Timmons, you said?"

Mr. Greely nodded. "At the Law Offices."

Kayce nodded absently, his agile mind toying with the options. "I had thought a discreet accident might be necessary—indeed, certain arrangements have already been made that may bear fruit. But now I am entertaining other ideas. My niece is actually quite a beauty, I have discovered. I almost hate to see such a commodity go to waste if I could possibly turn it to my advantage."

"Of course!" exclaimed Mr. Greely, struggling to sit up straighter in the overstuffed library chair. "Miss Clayton is but twenty years old!"

Kayce began to smile. "Precisely. Who more appropriate for the role of guardian than her closest living relative? And as her guardian, it would be up to me to say where she weds."

"If the girl is as attractive as you say, you might get two or three times the price of her inheritance in a marriage settlement," said the solicitor.

"That and more, I should say." Kayce lapsed into thought. "Yes, that will do nicely, I think. Greely, ring for my valet. I believe a few discreet enquiries are in order."

TWO AFTERNOONS LATER Azalea was still wrestling with her options, along with her latest attempt at embroidery. The Beauforth ladies were gossiping with Lady Mountheath and her acid-tongued daughters, who seemed to take an unholy glee in the shredding of reputations. Azalea had therefore retreated to needlework to avoid embarrassing her cousins with another outburst.

English ladies, she had found, seemed to consider needlework an absolutely necessary accomplishment for any woman with pretensions to quality, so Azalea had spent several fruitless hours since her arrival in London trying to master that feminine art. After much frustrating effort, she had finally reached a point where she could appear to be occupying herself with a canvas, so long as the observer did not examine her rather unusual designs too closely.

At length, Lady Mountheath took herself and her daughters off, just in time for Lady Beauforth and

Marilyn to go upstairs to change for dinner. Azalea was debating whether to follow them when Smythe announced a Mr. Greely, identifying him as Lord Kayce's man of business. Azalea put her embroidery aside most willingly to receive him.

Mr. Greely was only a slight improvement over embroidery, unfortunately; Azalea disliked him on sight, and his obsequious manner set her teeth on edge. He was dressed quietly and expensively, as one might expect of Lord Kayce's personal aide, but his hair and nails were considerably less than clean and he seemed unable to meet her direct gaze.

"My dear Miss Clayton," he said silkily, "it is such an honour to make your acquaintance. Lord Kayce's only living relative—you can have no idea how overjoyed he was to learn of your existence."

Was it her imagination or did she detect a note of irony in the man's voice? Entirely likely, given the circumstances, Azalea thought. And this man must know her uncle's mind as well as any person could.

"Thank you, Mr. Greely," was all she said, but her attention sharpened to catch any accidental information the solicitor might let drop by word or tone.

"Your uncle means to call on you again in the very near future, but in the meantime he has sent me to take care of some pressing legal matters and to advance you a few hundred pounds on your inheritance." Mr. Greely beamed, obviously expecting the girl to be overwhelmed by Lord Kayce's generosity.

While surprised and pleased that she was to receive such a sum so promptly, Azalea knew that it represented but a tiny fraction of what was rightfully hers. Still, it implied that Lord Kayce did not intend to dispute her claims after all.

"Has Mr. Timmons spoken with my uncle then?" she asked.

Mr. Greely blinked, but answered quickly. "I have seen Mr. Timmons myself, actually. He and your uncle agree that it will be best for all concerned if Lord Kayce is named your guardian without delay. That way your uncle will be in a position to smooth your entry into London Society." He smiled his oily smile again.

Azalea suspected that Mr. Greely, and most likely her uncle as well, thought her an empty-headed miss who would believe whatever they chose to tell her. She saw no reason at present to disabuse them of that notion. In fact, she thought she might manage to use it to her advantage.

"Must I go to live with my uncle then?" she asked with wide-eyed innocence.

"Oh, I doubt it, Miss Clayton. Your uncle said nothing of your removal to his house." Mr. Greely looked almost alarmed at the suggestion.

After a few more pleasantries, Mr. Greely produced several documents requiring her signature, which Azalea glanced over with assumed ignorance.

Lord Kayce had apparently arranged for her to receive a generous allowance, she saw, for which she could only be grateful. The document making him her guardian, however, was cleverly worded to sound as though she were merely allowing her uncle to oversee her affairs, while in reality she would be giving him complete authority over her person and property. This contract might possibly be binding even should Lord Kayce's guardianship cease—which she now began to hope it might do very soon.

To sign it was obviously out of the question, but she had no wish to arouse Mr. Greely's suspicions. She put on her sweetest smile.

"I'd love to oblige you, Mr. Greely, but I did promise my grandfather that I would let Mr. Timmons look over any papers before I signed them. As it was practically his dying wish, I would feel just terrible if I disregarded it. Surely you understand?" Azalea allowed a quaver to enter her voice as she spoke of her grandfather, then held her breath, afraid that she might have overplayed her role of sorrowing innocent.

She need not have feared. After a slight hesitation, Mr. Greely returned her smile indulgently. "Of course I understand, Miss Clayton. It sounds as though your grandfather was a wise and prudent man. I will just take these papers to Mr. Timmons myself in the morning. He can bring them here for you to sign once he has, er, approved them."

Azalea rather doubted that Mr. Timmons would see this precise document, as no lawyer worth the name would let his client sign it, but she merely smiled and thanked Mr. Greely for his understanding.

"Before I leave, Miss Clayton, I would like to present you with a gift from your uncle. It is his way of welcoming you to England and to the family. If you would accompany me outside?"

Azalea was wary after reading those documents, nor was Mr. Greely himself a man to inspire trust, but she could think of no gracious way to refuse. Once on the steps, however, her wariness evaporated.

Held by a groom just beyond the front railings was the daintiest, most beautiful bay mare she had ever seen.

"Is she for me?" Azalea gasped, turning to Mr. Greely with her face aglow.

That mercenary gentleman blinked, as though momentarily dazzled. "Indeed she is. A small token of your uncle's affection," he said with the closet thing to a genuine smile she had yet seen from him.

"Has she a name?" asked Azalea, her gaze quickly returning to the lovely animal.

"You may name her what you wish. Lord Kayce will be pleased that you approve of her," replied Mr. Greely blandly.

"Oh, yes! Yes, I do!" Azalea's eyes never left the mare. "Please convey to him my most heartfelt thanks!"

"I'll do that, Miss Clayton. Good day." Mr. Greely descended the steps to the waiting carriage, but Azalea barely noticed his departure. Slowly she approached the waiting mare, still unable to believe that this beautiful creature was really hers. Her uncle was obviously a skilled judge of horseflesh, whatever else he might be.

"I shall name you Virginia—Ginny for short," said Azalea softly, stroking the mare's black, velvety nose. Her problems were by no means solved, but she allowed them to slip from her mind for the moment. It appeared that there were to be some advantages to her connection with Lord Kayce after all.

From what Lady Beauforth had said after her uncle's call, Azalea suspected that this development would please her cousins. She determined to tell them over the meal.

"Gracious!" exclaimed Lady Beauforth, when Azalea had made her announcement. "I wonder... I mean, how wonderful for you, my dear! And you are certain he means for you to remain with us?"

"That is what Mr. Greely implied, though of course none of the details have been worked out as of yet. I think I would prefer to remain here—if you don't mind, that is, Cousin Alice," she concluded hastily. She realized that she would be more than a little sorry to leave this household, which was beginning to feel like home.

"Mind?" cried Lady Beauforth, plainly touched by the plea in Azalea's voice. "My dear, I would be most distressed to have it any other way. Already you are almost a second daughter to me, and I am certain Marilyn quite regards you as a sister."

Surprisingly, a tight smile and nod from Miss Beauforth acknowledged the sentiment. This response, slight as it was, encouraged Azalea.

"Thank you," she said warmly to her cousins. "Thank you both. As I barely know my uncle as yet, I would very much rather stay here in familiar surroundings with those I have grown to care for." She realized as she spoke that this was only a slight exaggeration, and was gratified by the glow her words produced on Lady Beauforth's countenance.

"I'll let you know instantly, of course, when I have more information," she continued, thrusting back a sudden pang of conscience at her concealment of one particular fact that would by comparison eclipse this latest news. "Perhaps when my uncle calls in a day or two he can give us the details of the arrangement."

To divert her thoughts, Azalea mentioned the generous allowance her uncle meant to give her, a topic of great interest to both of her cousins. That subject dominated their conversation for the remainder of the meal.

AZALEA WAS UP at first light the next morning, eager
to try the paces of her new mare. It would be her first
ride in London—and on her very own horse!

She dressed quickly in the new green-and-gold velvet riding habit she had purchased in case such an opportunity arose, and descended to the kitchen before
Junie had even begun her vigil at the keyhole. Cook
readily acceded to her request for a sweet roll for herself and some sugar for Ginny, and Azalea proceeded
to the stables with her mouth and pockets full.

She breathed deeply as she entered the stables, rev-
elling in the almost-forgotten scent. Why had she not
spent time here before this?

Tom, the head groom, noticed her at that moment
and hurried forward with a broad smile. "You'll be
wanting to see the new arrival, I don't doubt, Miss
Azalea."

"Indeed I will, Tom," she replied, returning his
smile. "And I'd like to take her out for a turn in the
Park before breakfast as well, if you would be so kind
as to have her saddled."

"I thought you might, miss. She'll be ready in a trice
and I'll accompany you myself."

Azalea started to protest that he need not go to that
trouble, but stopped when she saw the set of his jaw.
Junie was not the only one determined to see that she
stayed within the bounds of propriety, it seemed. She
could not be vexed, however, for she knew that they
were only trying to protect her from unpleasant gossip—and perhaps from physical harm.

While Tom cinched the beautiful sidesaddle that had
been delivered with the mare, Azalea introduced herself to Ginny and fed her the sugar she had brought.
Her soft voice and gentle, non-threatening movements

quickly overcame the little mare's initial shyness, and by the time Tom handed her into the saddle, they were becoming friends.

"A trifle skittish she is, miss, and a bit spirited for a lady's mount, I thought. You ride well, though, I take it?" asked Tom, observing her easy seat with appreciation.

"It has been a few months, and I'll no doubt be sore later, but I'll have no trouble handling her, Tom. Thank you for your concern." The groom mounted a roan gelding and they headed for the Park at a brisk trot.

As they entered the gates, Azalea looked around in delight. There had been a frost during the night, and the grass and trees were lightly glazed with white. The fairyland effect, temporary as it might be, almost made up for the lack of foliage and flowers.

Few people were about; a pair of grooms exercised their masters' horses and a few vendors were setting up their carts for the day's business. The cold air fairly sparkled in the sun, and Azalea could see her breath when she spoke to Tom. She trotted onto the bridle-path and urged her new mount to a canter more brisk than she would have dared had the Park been more crowded.

Rounding a turn past a clump of evergreens, Azalea saw a gentleman approaching on a large black stallion at a pace even quicker than her own. As he rapidly drew closer, she realized with a strange lurch of her heart that the rider was Lord Glaedon.

CHAPTER NINE

"MISS CLAYTON!" Lord Glaedon exclaimed, with every appearance of pleasure. "I did not know you were in the habit of riding before breakfast. Might I join you? It is rare to see a lady abroad so early." He pulled up when his horse drew even with hers.

"So I have discovered, my lord," Azalea replied, wondering if he could hear the hammering of her heart. "I have always been an early riser, and here I am frequently hard-pressed to find anything to do before the household is awake." She noticed that Tom had dropped back out of earshot, though he kept her well within view.

"You have taken to riding to relieve your boredom?" Lord Glaedon asked with a hint of his usual sardonic manner.

"As a matter of fact, this is my first ride since coming to London. I have only just acquired this mare and was anxious to try her paces."

"She's quite a little beauty," said Lord Glaedon appreciatively, casting a knowing eye over the horse. "Did you choose her yourself?"

"Actually, no," replied Azalea, reluctant to mention Lord Kayce. "But I doubt I could have done any better if I had." Reaching forward, she patted the mare on her beautifully arched neck. "She has the cleanest lines I've ever seen, and in Virginia I had the chance to see some absolutely prime animals, I can assure you."

Azalea glanced quickly at the earl, watching again for any flicker of recognition or anger at her mention of America. Again she detected nothing. His eyes were still on the mare.

"Yes, I had heard that there were some exceptional breeding farms in the New World," he said after a moment. "Perhaps someday I'll attempt the trip again."

A fleeting expression of pain crossed his handsome face, but Azalea thought that only natural considering his loss on the last crossing. She was almost—*almost*—convinced that he truly had no memory of his time in Virginia.

"That stallion is nothing to cough at, either," she said, in an attempt to change the subject. She had no wish to antagonize him—at least not right now.

"Yes, Sultan is my pride and joy. And I did choose him myself," said Lord Glaedon with the first twinkle she had seen in his eyes since she first met him again in London. She felt a flutter of response deep within her.

"I would never have suspected otherwise, with your knowledge of horses," she returned with a tentative smile.

She vividly remembered how enthusiastic he had been on the subject of horses six years ago. Perhaps if she could keep him on that topic, some spark of their old friendship, along with a glimmer of memory, might be rekindled.

"And how did you know of that, may I ask? Is it such common knowledge?" asked Lord Glaedon, with a surprised lift of his brows.

Azalea swallowed, but covered her momentary confusion quickly, replying lightly, "But of course, my lord. You must know that any gallant such as yourself is much discussed among the ladies."

"Perhaps," he said sceptically. "But I would not have thought my judgement of horseflesh one of the topics to interest them."

"Oh, anything to do with you is, I assure you. Shall we ride on?" she asked hurriedly, anxious for a chance to gather her scattered wits before she betrayed herself further.

"Certainly," responded the earl, obediently turning his horse.

As they cantered along the bridle-path, Azalea felt her confusion give way once again to the exultant pleasure of riding. She had missed it so! Though neither spoke for several minutes, their spirits seemed somehow in tune. Azalea found it unexpectedly pleasant to share this favourite pastime with another enthusiast, even under such awkward circumstances.

As they drew near to the Park gates once again, Azalea finally broke their companionable silence. "I don't suppose you would care to race, my lord?" she asked hopefully. For the moment, her intention of pricking his memory had been forgotten in the exhilaration of riding.

"I would dearly love to," he replied, "but it would certainly be frowned on if we were seen, and I have no desire to be barred from riding in Hyde Park. A pity."

He was smiling down at Azalea as he spoke, and she felt her heart beating faster than the exercise could account for.

"A pity indeed," she said wistfully, slanting a glance up at him. "I remember how I used to race across the fields back home with none to see or criticize. Here, I feel I am constantly being observed—and judged." She recalled with a rush of homesickness the lovely flowered fields and woodlands of Virginia and the solitary rides she used to enjoy there.

"Observed, perhaps," agreed Lord Glaedon with an appreciative glance at her face and figure. "But I cannot imagine anyone criticizing your riding. You are quite an accomplished horsewoman. In fact..." He glanced about them. "Is that groom of yours to be trusted?"

"What do you mean, my lord?" asked Azalea curiously.

"This area of the Park appears to be deserted, except for ourselves. Perhaps we might manage a very *brief* gallop, if you are game."

He sent her a mischievous look, reminding her forcefully of the Chris she had known in Williamsburg. Her heart seemed to stop for a moment.

She smiled back roguishly. "Of course I am game." With that, she flicked the reins and sent Ginny off at a thundering pace.

After a startled instant, Lord Glaedon followed, catching up fairly easily. "I did not mean this to be a race, you know," he called out.

But Azalea scarcely heard him. When her mare lurched into a gallop, she had felt something slightly amiss, and now the feeling intensified. Her saddle was slipping!

Alarmed, she pulled back on the reins, realizing only then that Ginny had managed to take the bit between her teeth. Ears back, the mare was fully into the spirit of the race, apparently unaware of her mistress's difficulty.

Locked into the sidesaddle as she was, Azalea realized that she could be badly hurt if the cinch gave way
completely. Transferring the reins to one hand, she
desperately tried to extricate her knee from around the
horn so that she could leap off if necessary. Before she
could manage it, however, the saddle made a sickening slip sideways.

"I've got you!" Lord Glaedon, leaning over as he
drove his own horse up against hers, grabbed her
around the waist.

Ginny responded by shying violently, then half rear-
ing. Lord Glaedon was on the ground by now, however, and pulled Azalea away from her.

"Th-thank you!" she stammered. "I have no idea
what got into her!"

The mare was becoming calmer now, though she still
skittered away from Sultan when he tossed his head in
her direction.

"You said you obtained her only yesterday," Lord
Glaedon reminded her. "I suspect she is not as thoroughly broken to riding as you were led to believe."

His arms remained around her as he spoke, giving
Azalea a warm sense of security that she ached to prolong. But already the groom was upon them, and at his
first words, Lord Glaedon released her.

"Good God, Miss! What happened? I told you that
mare was too spirited for a lady."

Azalea tried to subdue the trembling that started the
moment she was out of Lord Glaedon's grasp. "Nonsense, Tom," she said briskly, to hide the emotions as-
saulting her. "She merely needs a bit of work. I'd have
been fine had the saddle not slipped."

"Slipped? Why, I cinched it myself!" Effortlessly,
the groom captured the mare and examined the sad-

dle, which had slid around to her side. "Why, look here," he said after a moment. "This part ain't even leather. It's some sort of cloth, and it's stretched out. Pretty shoddy way to make a saddle, if you ask me."

Shaken though she was, Azalea felt a nasty suspicion leap into her mind. "The saddle came with the mare, did it not?" She still did not name her uncle. If Lord Kayce had an unsavoury reputation, as Jonathan had implied, she did not want Lord Glaedon to learn of the connection just yet.

Tom was nodding. "Aye. Looks fancy enough, too." He fingered the girth. "I think I can tighten this up enough to get you home, miss, but I'll replace the cinch before you ride out again."

"I should say the entire saddle should be disposed of," said Lord Glaedon firmly. "And I don't recommend you attempt another gallop on that mare for quite some time, Miss Clayton. You should probably hold her to a trot, until you know her temperament better."

Reluctantly, Azalea agreed. "It is just as well that our gallop was cut short, I suppose, as I will probably be sore enough tomorrow as it is," she added, with an attempt at lightness.

"My dear Miss Clayton! I had quite forgotten that this was your first ride in some time. I am doubly at fault for suggesting that damned gallop." Lord Glaedon's eyes were concerned again and Azalea felt warmth flow through her.

"Pray do not blame yourself, my lord. I was enjoying myself immensely and had no wish to stop."

"Still, if you wish to minimize your discomfort, I recommend you walk for a bit before returning home.

Trust me, I speak from experience," he concluded wryly.

She smiled. "Very well. It will take Tom a few minutes to see to that strap, anyway."

Christian felt a tremor go through him in response to that smile. Doubtless it was simply reaction to the excitement they had been through, he chided himself. Casting about for a safe topic, he recalled that his father had known Miss Clayton's grandfather.

"I was surprised to learn of the connection between our families," he began as they strolled down the path.

His companion coughed delicately. If he didn't know better, he might have thought she was disguising a chuckle. "My—my grandfather spoke of your father often. I believe they served together in India in their youth," she said.

"So you did not share my surprise. I rather received that impression at the time." Lovely, thick-fringed green eyes watched him expectantly, giving Christian the odd feeling that he was somehow disappointing her.

"You might have told me earlier, you know," he said, more severely than he had intended. What did she want from him?

At his words, she frowned, and he discovered that even her frown was charming.

"And how was I to know that you were ignorant of their friendship? For all I knew, you might have been perfectly aware of who I was but had decided not to recognize the connection."

Christian was taken aback. "What reason could I possibly have for snubbing the granddaughter of my father's closest friend?"

"That is best known to yourself, my lord," she returned primly.

"Come, Miss Clayton, let us cry friends. Now that you know it was mere ignorance on my part, surely you cannot hold my earlier behaviour against me." Suddenly, it seemed imperative that she forgive him.

Azalea looked thoughtful. "I think I can," she said after a moment. "You were rude to me on the mere grounds of my nationality, which is not something you could reasonably expect me to be responsible for, even if it were cause for shame. Which it is not!" She flashed a speaking glance up at him.

Increasingly bewitched by her, Christian fought valiantly against a smile. He nodded. "You are right, of course, and I humbly beg your pardon."

She regarded him steadily, and he felt his pulse accelerate. He would not look away, however, and after a brief silence she nodded in turn.

"Very well," she said. "If you will consent to learn a little about America before you condemn us out of hand, I think we could even become friends." Her look challenged him now.

"You drive a hard bargain, Miss Clayton, as I think you know," said Christian half-seriously. "Very well, I agree to learn more about America in general and Virginia in particular if you will be my tutor."

Azalea regarded him suspiciously. Was he flirting with her? She could not account for the sudden change in his attitude, unless it were merely the discovery that she was Gregory Simpson's granddaughter.

Such old obligations, she thought, must have more hold on Lord Glaedon than she would have imagined. It was probably all tied up with that unfathomable male code of honour.

But honour played very little part in Christian's present thoughts. He was finding Miss Clayton more delightful with every word that passed her lips, though her beauty was already alluring enough. She seemed both intelligent and naïve—a combination he found totally enchanting and quite irresistible.

"Well, Miss Clayton? Have we a bargain?" he prompted when she did not immediately speak.

"Certainly, my lord," she replied decisively. "How can I refuse, when it was I who demanded your further education? What would you like to know?"

"Everything, of course," he said laughingly. "But you can begin by telling me more about the excellent horseflesh you claim to have seen there."

This was a topic with which Azalea was completely at home. She proceeded to describe the breeding programs of some of the landowners of her acquaintance, as well as those of the more famous Virginia horse farms.

As she pursued the topic, she realized that she was repeating almost word for word much of what she had told this same man six years ago. Noticing his occasional slight frowns, she could not help but wonder whether he remembered at least parts of that prior conversation. Then another possibility occurred to her.

"I fear this has become quite a lecture, my lord. I do tend to run on when discussing a subject that interests me, and I have no wish to bore you."

"Bore me? With talk of horses? Impossible! If I seemed distracted, it was merely that I was considering ways of implementing these American innovations in my own stables. Pray continue," he said with every appearance of sincerity.

Azalea thought this explanation likely enough and resumed her "lecture."

In fact, Christian had been less than candid. He was certainly not bored; he suspected that Miss Clayton could discuss Greek history without losing his attention. But he was feeling the oddest sensation of having been here before—of having heard these same words spoken in that same voice.

Flashes of sunlit fields and apple blossoms arose in his mind, and suddenly he was reminded of his nightmares. He realized that Azalea had stopped speaking, and he looked at her questioningly.

"My lord, I must get back," she said with an apologetic smile. "I will likely be missed as it is. At any rate, you have heard most of what I can remember at the moment about Virginia's best-known stables."

"Very well, Miss Clayton," said Christian reluctantly. He found he was very much loath to let her go. "I shall look for you to continue my lessons very soon."

They returned to the horses, where Tom had finished his repairs, and Christian helped Azalea to remount. Retaining her hand for a moment, he brushed her gloved fingertips with his lips. Then, without a word, he swung up into his own saddle and rode off.

Azalea gazed after him until she suddenly remembered Tom's presence. Almost guiltily, she removed her hand from her cheek, where it had unaccountably strayed, and turned thoughtfully towards the gates.

On re-entering Beauforth House, Azalea was extremely relieved to encounter neither of her cousins. The details of her outing would be sure to cause some awkwardness.

If asked directly about her ride, she would mention the meeting with Lord Glaedon, of course. Otherwise, her cousins might very well discover it from Tom, or even the earl himself, and would think her reticence suspicious. Somehow, though, she rather doubted that Lord Glaedon would mention it.

Still, she was glad that her resolve to be truthful was not to be immediately put to the test. Reaching her bedchamber undetected, Azalea quietly opened the door, only to be confronted by a reproachful Junie.

"Thank heaven you're back, miss! It's 'most ten o'clock, and I was near frantic, not knowing where you'd gone off to! I didn't dare ask anyone, for you know how servants gossip," she said self-righteously, "but if her ladyship had asked for you there'd have been the devil to pay, and no mistake."

"Oh, nonsense, Junie." Azalea laughed to cover her alarm. "I only went riding in the Park to try out my new mare. Tom accompanied me, so everything was perfectly proper. Cook knew where I was also. If you had asked him, you could have spared yourself your mother-hen worrying."

She knew Junie genuinely cared about her, but it did get tiresome now and again to be treated as though she were an ignorant child.

"Well, that's all right then, miss," said Junie, only slightly mollified. "I don't suppose you've breakfasted yet?"

"No, not really. Could you bring me up a tray? I'd like to change before going back down."

By the time Junie returned, Azalea was clad in a fashionable powder blue cambric gown and had taken the pins from her hair in an attempt to rearrange it. She gratefully allowed Junie to take over that task, then proceeded to do full justice to the ample breakfast provided. By now it was nearly eleven o'clock, and she was scarcely surprised when she was summoned downstairs to greet a caller.

She entered the parlour to discover Lord Kayce engaged in desultory conversation with her cousins. The sight of her uncle immediately recalled to her mind her earlier suspicions about the saddle, but now, in retrospect, she decided they were rather absurd.

Upon seeing her, Lady Beauforth immediately made excuses to both Azalea and her uncle, saying that she and Marilyn were expected at Madame Clarisse's shop, where they were to meet Lady Silverton and her two daughters. Without giving her own daughter a chance to speak, she bustled her out the door, leaving Azalea alone with Lord Kayce.

"It is good to see you again, my lord," Azalea said cautiously.

"The pleasure is entirely mine, my dear, I assure you. And have you forgotten so soon that I am to be Uncle Simon?" He was dressed as elegantly as before, his exquisitely tailored maroon jacket opening over a matching waistcoat richly embroidered with silver. "Now that I am officially your guardian, I thought a personal visit in order."

"Is it completely settled then, Uncle Simon?" asked Azalea, surprised that she had not heard from Mr. Timmons.

"But for a few legal formalities." He airily waved those aside. "I came to assure you that I have all well in hand regarding your future."

"My—my future?" asked Azalea.

"Certainly. As my ward, your future is my concern, and I did not wish you to spend a moment worrying your pretty head over it."

Lord Kayce was smiling benignly, almost smugly, Azalea thought, and her uneasiness grew.

"I am to remain in this house for the present, am I not, Uncle?"

"Of course," he replied reassuringly, having apparently noticed her anxiety in spite of her effort to conceal it. Her uncle was far more astute than his man of business, Azalea realized.

"It would be inappropriate for you to reside with me, unless a suitable female companion could be found for you," he continued, "and, as Lady Beauforth is willing to house you and act as chaperon, the need does not arise. However, I would like to ask a favour of you while we are on that subject."

"Yes?" Her most immediate concern had been allayed, but she still did not wholly trust him. Was he going to ask her again to sign those documents? How could she refuse a second time?

"I shall be having a small dinner party Friday evening and I would be honoured if you would consent to act as hostess. I am anxious to show off my new-found niece to a few of my oldest friends. Will you be so kind as to do this for me?"

"Of course, Uncle Simon, I would be delighted to." Azalea was so relieved by this apparently innocent request after what she had feared that she missed the avaricious gleam in Kayce's eyes. "What time shall I be ready?"

"I'll send a carriage for you at seven-thirty," said Lord Kayce with barely concealed satisfaction. "Are you happy with the mount I purchased for you?" he asked, neatly changing the subject before she could question him further.

"Oh, she's marvellous," exclaimed Azalea. "Did not your Mr. Greely convey my thanks? I rode her this morning, and her paces are like silk, though her manners are just the slightest bit rough, I fear. We nearly had a mishap. But I have no doubt she will improve with training." She couldn't quite bring herself to mention the saddle, though she watched him closely as she spoke.

"Indeed! My apologies, in that case. I assure you she came highly recommended." Was it her imagination, or did she detect a certain wariness in his expression?

"No apology necessary, Uncle Simon, I assure you. She's a splendid animal, really."

He smiled thinly. "I am happy that she pleases you. And now, I really must be going. I'll see you a few days hence." Lord Kayce rose smoothly, executed a graceful half bow and departed.

Perhaps he really did mean well, she thought hopefully after he was gone. Still, she would call on Mr. Timmons in a few days if she had not heard from him, to see whether Mr. Greely had indeed brought him those documents.

A LITTLE OVER AN HOUR later Lady Beauforth and Marilyn returned, accompanied by Jonathan Plummer, who, Marilyn said, they had encountered upon leaving Madame Clarisse's shop. Naturally, they had invited him for nuncheon, knowing what a good friend of Azalea's he was.

Watching Marilyn's rapt expression when she looked at Jonathan, Azalea doubted whether this last consideration had actually carried much weight, but she was happy to see her old playmate in any event. She carefully observed both his behaviour and Marilyn's, and was able to conclude that her hopes in that direction were not completely unfounded. There was obviously a fair degree of attraction on both sides.

Nuncheon was a lively meal, with Jonathan and Lady Beauforth carrying the bulk of the conversation, though by no means excluding the others. As before, Azalea noticed that Marilyn's speech was far less affected when she spoke to Jonathan.

Between anecdotes, Azalea managed to relate Lord Kayce's invitation. Jonathan's look of concern reminded her of his earlier cautions, and after the meal she again contrived to have a brief moment alone with him.

"I fear you may have been quite right about my uncle," she told him without preamble as they lingered in the dining-room after her cousins had proceeded to the parlour. "He seems uncommonly anxious to be made my guardian, and now I have reason to suspect he may actually wish me ill." She related the story of that morning's mishap, omitting, however, any mention of Lord Glaedon.

Jonathan nodded grimly. "You never were anyone's fool, 'Zalea," he said. "You look so much like the other London belles now, I had dashed near forgotten how sharp you can be. Just as well you are, though, with the likes of Kayce to deal with."

"I'm beginning to realize that. I'll be careful, though, I promise you. Should I refuse his invitation to dinner, do you think?"

Jonathan thought for a moment. "No, it should be all right. He'll hardly try to harm you in front of a crowd, and it would be well known to your cousins that you were in his company. My advice is to play along— for now—but keep your eyes open."

"That's precisely what I had intended to do," she agreed.

Lady Beauforth called to them from the parlour then, querying about their tardiness.

"Don't forget, 'Zalea—if you need a friend, I'm always here," Jonathan whispered hastily as he turned towards the door. "At least until summer."

"Thank you, Jonathan. I'll remember."

But with Jonathan's cautions added to her original suspicions, she was beginning to suspect that she would need more than a friend, or even a lawyer, to deal with Lord Kayce.

She would need a husband.

CHAPTER TEN

THE NEXT MORNING Azalea again rose early. She had decided to make a regular habit of riding before breakfast, for she could tell that even in the few weeks she'd been living in London, her physical condition had deteriorated. In spite of her soreness yesterday, she had more of the energy she had always taken for granted back in Virginia.

She would not admit to herself that the hope of seeing Lord Glaedon played any part in this virtuous resolution. Still, she could not suppress the feeling that had buoyed her since yesterday morning. Surely he had shown something beyond simple courtesy towards her. What that was exactly, she didn't quite dare to speculate—not yet.

Her sore backside distracted her for most of the brief ride to the park, but as she neared the entrance, she finally allowed herself to consciously wonder whether Lord Glaedon would be there. Before she could summon the willpower to banish the fearful, hopeful, question, it was answered. He was waiting just outside the gates. If she had any doubts about whether he was expecting her, they were erased at once by his cheerful wave, along with his greeting.

"Miss Clayton! I was hoping you intended to repeat your morning ride, though I must admit I rather feared you would be too sore to do so." He grinned as she attempted to find a position in the saddle that would cause her less discomfort. "You have a new saddle, I see."

"Yes. I *am* a bit stiff, as you are obviously aware— and I think it most ungallant of you to mention it, my lord. But after being deprived of riding for so long, I fear it would take more than a passing ache to keep me from it!" She returned his grin, both delighted and relieved to find him not only present, but still amiably disposed towards her.

"I was counting on that, actually," he said. "I propose a brief trot this morning, followed by a lengthier stroll. That should set you up admirably and relieve your, ah, stiffness somewhat."

Azalea knew he was teasing her for downplaying her soreness, but found that she really didn't mind. "Very well, my lord," she said crisply, to conceal her conflicting emotions, and immediately sent Ginny into a brisk trot.

Lord Glaedon kept pace with her on his beautiful black and they rode, as yesterday, in silence for a few minutes. Before the horses could become winded, the earl pulled up and motioned for Azalea to do the same.

"I said brief, and I meant it," he explained to her questioning look. "Trust me. You still have the ride back, and I wouldn't wish you to be unable to dance at Lady Sunham's rout tonight."

"And how did you know..." Azalea stopped when she saw the amusement in his face. Of course he would have been invited. There were so few entertainments at this time of year that Lady Beauforth could not bear to forgo any of them—as he well knew. And he had told her to trust him. Did he mean more by that than it appeared?

"Thank you for your consideration, my lord," she concluded with a false sweetness that she sincerely hoped did not deceive him.

He pointedly ignored her comment and helped her to dismount. At the touch of his hand on hers, a tingle went through her. She could not bring herself to meet his eyes, so she had no idea whether he was likewise affected.

As her feet touched the ground, Azalea realized that even that very brief ride had affected her insulted muscles more than she would have believed—though she was careful not to let her expression betray as much to her companion. He seemed to read her thoughts, however, and pointedly accepted her thanks with a maddening "I-told-you-so" air.

After walking for a few moments, Azalea found both her soreness and her confusion over her physical response to Lord Glaedon easing somewhat. At the same time, her curiosity reasserted itself. When he broke the silence to suggest that she continue his instruction about the New World, she suddenly thought of a way to satisfy it, at least in part.

"Before I begin, my lord, perhaps it would be helpful if you could give me some idea of what you already know about America. That way I shall not run the risk of boring you by repeating information you are acquainted with."

She held her breath, half expecting either a set-down for her prying or another tirade on the shortcomings of her countrymen. Either would be a serious blow to her hopes. But she received neither. Instead, Lord Glaedon looked thoughtful.

"Several years ago I intended to learn quite a lot about your country," he said slowly, intently regarding a pair of wrens pecking hopefully at the frozen ground. "I read about its colonization and its rebellion against the king, and I have to admit, I rather admired the colonists for the stand they took. In many ways, their cause was just."

He rubbed the back of his neck with one hand. "When I set sail with my father six years ago, I was looking forward to seeing that vast country for myself and forming my own opinions of the land and its people. Our stay was to have been brief, but I had already half formed the idea of returning to make my fortune there if I liked what I saw. I was not then the heir, of course, but the younger son."

He glanced at her briefly, with a slight smile that made her heart pound. Surely he was about to mention their marriage now!

But he turned and fixed his gaze on the wrens again as he continued. "During the first week or two of the voyage, I spoke often with the captain—Taylor, I think his name was, or was it Whitten? I never can seem to remember. Anyway, I spoke often to him about his experiences in the colonies. He had some fascinating stories to tell. I was young enough then to become easily carried away by his tales of battling the elements and carving out one's own destiny. All too soon, however, I was given a chance to battle the elements myself—and to lose."

The earl seemed to forget Azalea's presence completely as he relived the frightful events on the ship. "A storm blew up suddenly. I remember the wind, the flapping sails, and Captain Taylor's assurance that it would be a brief blow. He sent my father and me below, but before I could reach the hatch, I was hit on the head by a falling spar."

He closed his eyes briefly. "The next thing I remember is being hauled aboard a different ship, half-dead, to be told by a crewman I didn't recognize that he and I were the only survivors of the wreckage. He was the one who always referred to the captain as Whitten. But I'm almost certain that the name was Taylor."

Christian's brow furrowed in an effort to recall exactly what had happened, and Azalea realized she was holding her breath. Slowly, she let it escape. She was beginning to understand.

"Of course, at the time, I couldn't even remember my own name," he went on, "and certainly no one else knew it. I didn't know where I was from or where I was bound, so when the captain of this ship, a merchantman heading for Jamaica, asked if I wanted to join his crew, I had no reason to refuse.

"That captain's name was Farris, of that I'm certain. I served aboard his ship for three months, and unfortunately, I can remember every grisly moment of it. Farris was a slaver, I discovered, and a ruthless one at that—if there is any other kind. No one dared to criticize his running of the ship. Twice, I recall, crewmen who spoke out against his treatment of the 'cargo' were flogged to death, then thrown overboard. I realized even then that I was playing the coward by saying nothing, but I assuaged my conscience with the conviction that dead heroes benefit no one."

Azalea pressed her lips tightly together. She wanted to reassure him, to comfort him, but was afraid that if she spoke he would recall her presence and stop his outpouring of memories. She wondered whether this might be the first time he had related them to anyone since his return.

Oblivious to her struggle, he continued. "In Jamaica, I was able to join the crew of another merchantman, this one Dutch, which didn't depend on human misery for its profits. I remained aboard the *Hyacinth* for nearly four years. Though my life there was far better than it had been aboard the slaver, I behaved as a common sailor—both aboard ship and in port. I knew no better, I suppose, but some of the things I did during those years..."

He stopped and swallowed before going on. "During that time my memory began to return in bits and flashes. One morning I awoke knowing, for the first time, who I was and where I lived. As soon as I could contrive it, I returned to England.

"In my absence, Herschel had gone to fight in America, against our grandmother's pleading. He apparently felt that it was his duty to represent the family on the battlefield, as I was not available to go. Word came only a month before my return that he'd been killed in Upper Canada, at the Battle of the Thames."

Though Azalea's eyes filled as she listened, his own remained dry. He spoke dispassionately, as though telling of events that had happened to someone else.

"I had already realized that my father must have perished in the shipwreck four years earlier. I was Earl of Glaedon, and had been for some months, though the title had erroneously passed to a cousin, as I was presumed dead. However, I had no difficulty proving my identity, and my title and inheritance were restored. Much happiness they have brought me." Sudden bitterness spilled over into his voice.

"One can make one's own happiness, don't you think?" asked Azalea softly, hoping to draw him out

of his melancholy mood. Quickly, she brushed her
tears away.

Her words seemed to bring Lord Glaedon back to
the present with a start. He stared at her for a moment
and then his gaze hardened.

"So you see, Miss Clayton, I have good reason to
detest Americans. Not only did they cause my brother's death and, inadvertently, my father's, but I have
seen the horrors of their abominable slave trade per-
sonally—the horrors 'innocent' colonists, like yourself, try so hard to ignore. Perhaps I know all that is
necessary about America, after all. Good day, Miss
Clayton." Turning on his heel, the earl walked quickly
back to his waiting horse and departed without a
backward glance.

Azalea stood as though rooted to the spot, staring
after his retreating form. His abrupt return to the hos-
tile manner that had marked their first meetings had
startled her, but she was ready to forgive him after
hearing his reasons.

What shocked her more was the certain knowledge
that he had never intended to deceive her. He was as
trustworthy as she had wanted to believe him. And
most disturbing of all was the fact that, in spite of everything, she still loved him with all her heart!

AZALEA HAD VERY LITTLE time to reflect on these unsettling discoveries, as she and Marilyn spent all of the
morning and much of the afternoon combing the various shops for just the right ribbons, gloves and other
accessories to set off the gowns they planned to wear to
Lady Sunham's that evening.

In spite of the distracting thoughts that would not be
dismissed, Azalea could not help enjoying their out-

ing. With a substantial amount of spending money in her reticule, she was free to indulge her tastes without regard to price, a luxury she feared she could become quite accustomed to, given half a chance.

She and Marilyn were dealing more pleasantly with one another than they had ever done, almost like the sisters Lady Beauforth enjoyed likening them to. But when her cousin mentioned that blue was Lord Glaedon's favourite colour, as she purchased a spray of artificial flowers in that hue, it cast a brief shadow over Azalea's enjoyment.

The comment served to remind her that she had come no closer to preventing the marriage that was due to take place in only two months' time. Lord Glaedon's sudden change in attitude toward her this morning made her hopes of a reconciliation, leading to a full disclosure, even less likely.

She had hoped to somehow win him away from Marilyn before attempting to explain about their marriage. Now it appeared doubtful that she would have that chance. But she would have to tell him soon, whatever his feelings towards her—especially now that she knew he was indeed ignorant of the true state of affairs. Too many people would be hurt if she remained silent.

THE GATHERING AT Lady Sunham's elegant Town house was noticeably smaller than the one at Lady Queesley's had been. Christmas was only two weeks away now, and even the most citified families were leaving daily for their country estates in order to spend the holidays in the traditional manner.

This was to be a musical evening, with a noted soprano engaged to delight the assembled guests, as well as a young Italian gentleman said to be worth listening to on the pianoforte. Dancing was to follow later.

As Lord Glaedon had implied that he would attend, Azalea discreetly scanned the room for him upon her arrival, but without success. She moved to take a seat next to Lady Dinsmore, wondering unhappily whether he had changed his mind in order to avoid encountering her. Could he possibly believe she would hold him to his promise of a dance after the way they had parted?

Azalea decided that it was just as well he was not here. They would only quarrel again, most likely. No, it would be better if they did not meet again until his temper had had time to cool. Then she might have a chance of arranging to speak with him privately.

Her thoughts were so busily engaged in convincing herself she was glad Lord Glaedon had chosen to stay away that she missed most of the soprano's performance.

"Not quite the quality we were promised, don't you agree?" The question was spoken so close to her ear that it made her start.

Glancing in some confusion at Lord Glaedon sitting behind her, and wondering how long he had been there, she replied rather at random that she had enjoyed the selection very much.

"Gammon," he whispered back. "I've been watching you, and you were hardly giving Signorina Devita your undivided attention. If you can tear yourself away from this riveting performance, I'd like to talk to you."

A few people in their immediate vicinity were glancing curiously at them by this time, and Azalea felt it would be wiser to accompany his lordship than to continue any discussion here. She rose and stepped past an elderly lady in purple crêpe with a murmured apology.

Out of the corner of her eye, Azalea saw Marilyn watching them, but decided she could not worry about that just now. She was struggling with the decision she had made earlier in the day—to tell Lord Glaedon the truth no matter what. Perhaps this would be an opportunity to do so. Her heart began beating uncomfortably fast.

As they left the room, she whispered, "After this morning, I had expected you would avoid me like the plague."

Lord Glaedon merely led her into the supper-room with a light hand on her elbow.

In point of fact, that was exactly what Christian had intended for about fifteen minutes after he left Miss Clayton in the Park. His emotions had been in such a turmoil that he could almost believe she had in fact bewitched him with her charming smile and those sparkling green eyes. She had betrayed him, somehow, into disclosing details of his past that he had deliberately buried two years ago. He had even momentarily blamed her for the sudden resurgence of grief he had felt at the double loss of his father and brother.

As his temper had cooled, however, he was able to sort through his conflicting feelings. In reality, he had confided in Miss Clayton simply because it seemed somehow the right thing to do. In just two days—two mornings, really—a closeness had sprung up between them that he found both comforting and alarming.

Talking to her seemed almost like talking to himself. He knew, somehow, that anything he told her would be kept in the strictest confidence. He trusted

her! That in itself was astonishing in a man who had
been cynical almost to the point of sourness since his
return to England two years ago.

What he felt went even beyond trust, however. There
was also that recurring feeling of familiarity. He had
known this girl before. He was now almost certain that
she had figured in the disturbing dreams that had
plagued him at intervals since the shipwreck.

Was fate drawing them together? While not a particularly religious man, Christian had actually taken to
prayer occasionally since his experience in hopes of
being imparted insight about—or simply relief from—
those dreams. Was this girl an answer to his prayer? He
felt as if he were on the edge of some blinding revelation, and he was unsure whether to stave it off or welcome it with open arms.

Miss Clayton attracted him on a far more basic level
as well. When he had first seen her in the Park this
morning, he had been seized by a wild desire to take her
in his arms. His brief anger had saved him from that
folly, at least.

After much thought, he had decided to return home
to his estates to search through his father's papers in
hopes of finding some clue about her. He wasn't sure
what he expected to discover, but he had an inexplica-
ble conviction that some answer would be revealed
there.

But first he needed to mend his fences with this most
extraordinary young lady. And what then? Not only
was he betrothed, but he shrank from the very idea of
thrusting himself, with his despicable past, on Miss
Clayton's sweet innocence. He did not pause to wonder why he'd had no similar reservations with regard to
Miss Beauforth.

"You wished to say something, my lord?" prompted Azalea, when Christian made no move to speak immediately.

"Yes, Miss Clayton," he responded, collecting his thoughts. "First, and most importantly, I humbly beg your forgiveness for my unpardonably rude behaviour this morning. Is it too much to hope that we may put the incident behind us?"

The mute appeal in his eyes caused Azalea's heart to dance. "I have forgotten it already, my lord," she said breathlessly, hoping he would not notice the flush she could feel mounting in her cheeks.

His sudden smile at her words was so dazzling that she felt almost faint, though whether from relief or some other emotion, she could not be sure.

"Secondly," the earl continued, "I wished to take leave of you, as I am going into the country tomorrow and will probably not return until after the first of the year. Family Christmas and all that. I did not want to depart with any ill will between us."

Azalea felt a surge of disappointment that he would be leaving, but the emotion was so overwhelmed by the joy imparted by his previous words that she could hardly feel depressed. But...she *must* tell him the truth before he left. By the time he returned, the wedding would be little more than a month away.

"I shall miss riding with you in the Park, my lord," she said, though she knew it must sound forward. But she would have to be more forward still if she was to stop him from marrying Marilyn. She would have to tell him that she was his wife. Desperately, she tried to form the words that would sound so unbelievable to him.

"I, too," replied Christian before she could speak. "I hope we may resume the practice when I return."

He felt a sudden resurgence of the temptation that had assailed him that morning, now stronger than ever. With her so near, his senses fairly swam at the thought of his lips on hers.

Azalea's eyes locked with his for an instant as she swayed ever so slightly forward, then were quickly veiled by those glorious lashes. "I—I hope so also." She looked back up at him then and spoke in a stronger tone. "Lord Glaedon, I—"

"Well!" Marilyn Beauforth's voice interrupted them.

Christian stepped hastily away from Azalea, for he'd been standing closer than was strictly proper. She looked guilty, too, cheeks suffused with colour.

"And what topic, pray tell, can be so fascinating that you two must steal away from that wonderful performance to discuss it?" his fiancée enquired in a shrill tone.

Not for the first time Christian wondered whether it was solely patriotism that had driven Herschel away from England before formally betrothing himself to Miss Beauforth. "I was merely apologizing to Miss Clayton, my dear," he replied smoothly. "In the past I have been less than cordial to your cousin, and I did not wish to leave London with any ill feeling on that score." That much was true, he told himself.

Marilyn's demeanour changed immediately. "How thoughtful of you, my lord, to attempt to overcome your very natural aversion to an American for my sake!" She simpered up at him in a way he found more irritating than usual.

"Yes, quite," he said shortly, torn between annoyance at her phrasing and guilt over what his thoughts had been a moment ago. He noticed that Azalea did not meet his eyes.

"Well, then! Shall we return for the remainder of the performance now?" Marilyn asked brightly.

"No, I fear I must prepare for my departure tomorrow. I came tonight so that I might take my leave. Pray give my regards to your mother, Miss Beauforth."

"I will. And now, if you will excuse me, I would prefer not to miss any more of the performance." Marilyn hurried away to resume her seat, which Christian had noticed earlier was quite near to that of Mr. Plummer.

"Good evening, Miss Clayton," he said to Azalea as she turned to follow her cousin. "I must admit that I scarcely regret missing the remainder of that soprano's offerings," he added lightly, wishing to see her smile once more. "I hope for your sake that the pianist is of better calibre."

She flashed him the smile he'd hoped for. "Thank you, my lord. I—" she glanced over her shoulder to where Marilyn had paused to wait for her "—I hope you have a safe journey and a pleasant holiday season," she said quickly, then hurried away.

Christian watched her thoughtfully for a moment before heading for the door. There was no denying that Miss Azalea Clayton attracted him, in more ways than he cared to admit. But it was an attraction he would have to subdue ruthlessly. He had entered into his betrothal with Miss Beauforth for the sake of his family's honour. If he were to cry off, or worse, to betray his promised wife, that would be more dishonourable than if he had never made the offer at all.

He still mourned his father and brother, but now, for the first time, he cursed the tangle they had left behind. Was his whole life to be lived fulfilling plans they had made? Scowling darkly, he left the house, too preoccupied with his thoughts to notice the thin, shadowy figure that ducked into a doorway as he approached his carriage.

Azalea returned thoughtfully to the music-room. Later, she could not have said whether the pianist lived up to Lord Glaedon's hopes or not, for she attended to his performance even less than she had to the soprano's.

She had failed in her intention to tell him the truth, but she could not manage to feel depressed as she thought over their brief conversation. Surely she had not imagined the warmth in his eyes as he had looked at her? Nor his coolness towards Marilyn.

Azalea felt badly for her cousin. While she no longer believed that Marilyn actually loved Lord Glaedon, she could not doubt that the proud young lady would be hurt when the truth came out. Marilyn, she'd come to realize, had as few close female friends as Azalea herself had. She had felt that the two of them were coming to terms, but this matter was likely to destroy their budding friendship entirely. Surely there must be a way to avoid that.

During the dancing and late supper that followed the recital, Azalea attempted to shake off her pensive mood. When she did manage to notice her surroundings somewhat, it was to realize that Jonathan seemed to be dividing his time fairly equally between herself and her cousin, though his manner with her could hardly be mistaken for anything but that of an old friend.

He appeared to be more smitten with Marilyn each time he saw her, and it was increasingly clear that his feelings were returned to some degree. Azalea allowed herself a small hope.

However, on the carriage ride home, Azalea's hope became fainter. It was clear that Marilyn had not forsworn Lord Glaedon and his wealth for the sake of the intriguing American—at least not yet.

"I still think it odd that Lord Glaedon should have felt it necessary to take particular leave of you, Cousin," she said. "It would have been more seemly had he asked me to convey his apology for him. How vexing that he could not stay for the dancing after all."

Azalea couldn't resist saying, "You seemed to have no lack of admirers, Marilyn. I noticed that Mr. Plummer enjoyed your company exceedingly this evening." She had the satisfaction of seeing her cousin start, then look noticeably guilty.

"He is a very good dancer, and his conversation is always interesting," was Miss Beauforth's only reply before she lapsed into silence.

Lady Beauforth, whom Azalea had assumed to be dozing in her corner of the carriage, sat up a little at her daughter's words and directed a penetrating gaze in her direction. Plainly, Azalea was not the only one who had noticed Marilyn's apparent preference for Mr. Plummer. She hoped that Lady Beauforth's silence on the matter meant that she did not find the discovery distressing.

For Azalea herself, it seemed the only possible solution to the problem of how she was to prevent Marilyn's marriage to Lord Glaedon without losing her friendship. If that preference could be encouraged to the point where Marilyn herself might cry off from their betrothal, then half of Azalea's problem would be solved.

On this happy thought, Azalea settled back in her seat to doze for the remainder of the drive home.

CHAPTER ELEVEN

THE NEXT MORNING Azalea slept late, partly due to her late night but also because she felt no particular inclination to ride. With Lord Glaedon gone from London, her virtuous plan of taking exercise in the Park every day seemed almost tedious. Thus, it was near noon when she and her cousins finally broke their fast, all together in the breakfast-parlour for a change.

They were just rising from the table when a footman delivered a large parcel for Azalea. It was from Lord Kayce. Distracted for a moment from her apathy, she rose to take the package to her bedchamber to open, but was forestalled by Lady Beauforth.

"Why, how curious!" her cousin exclaimed. "What do you suppose it is, Azalea?"

"I don't know, Cousin Alice, but we can certainly find out." She proceeded to remove the paper right there so that Lady Beauforth's curiosity might be assuaged immediately.

A moment later Azalea was startled by a flash of gold within the box and held up the gift for her cousins' inspection. It was a gown—but what a gown! Designed in the height of fashion, it was of a light, sheer material that seemed to have been spun of incredibly fine gold thread. Its overskirt of gossamer net was liberally sprinkled with tiny topazes, and several tiers of outrageously expensive gold lace graced the hem.

The three ladies gasped in unison. "Straight from Paris, without a doubt!" Lady Beauforth was the first to catch her breath. "My dear, you will look positively divine in it!"

"It should suit your colouring admirably," added Marilyn with more than a touch of envy in her voice.

"I—I've never seen such a fabric before." Azalea finally found her voice. "It doesn't seem quite real. Why should my uncle give me such a gown?" She was genuinely bewildered.

"Did he enclose a card?" asked Marilyn practically.

Azalea looked into the box. "Yes, here it is. And a matching fan, as well. Oh! He wishes me to wear it Friday night. It seems rather...extravagant for a private dinner party, though, don't you think?" She directed her question to Lady Beauforth.

"Oh, certainly you must wear it, my dear," that lady advised. "He obviously sent it for just that purpose— and why not? I should say it means that, as your new guardian, he intends to do well by you."

Azalea could well believe that Lord Kayce wished the world to think this, but it did not allay her uneasiness. During the past two days, she had nearly forgotten her worries about her uncle, so absorbed had she been by her other problem. Now her anxiety rushed back.

Still, as long as she could decipher his motives and plan her next move to counter his, she should be all right. But exactly what gambit was this dinner party a part of?

"Try it on, my dear," Lady Beauforth insisted, breaking into her thoughts. "Let us see if it fits, so that we can make any necessary alterations."

Nodding absently, Azalea replaced the gown carefully in its box and carried it upstairs.

"Why do you frown so, miss?" asked Junie curiously as Azalea gazed into the mirror a short time later. "Why, you look like a golden goddess in that gown! True, it's two or three inches too long, but that's easy enough to fix."

It was not the length that was bothering Azalea, however. The tissue-thin fabric clung to her figure seductively, even over the cotton chemise she had insisted on wearing underneath. The bright gold set off her colouring just as Marilyn had predicted, emphasizing the rich auburn of her hair and the creamy whiteness of her throat and bosom.

And that was the problem: entirely too much of her bosom was displayed. She was conscious of a sudden wish that Lord Glaedon could see her like this. If he had looked at her with admiration and warmth last night when she wore her demure blue silk, how might he react to her in this gown? Sternly, she pushed such indecent thoughts from her mind.

Since coming to London, Azalea had already managed to overcome modesty to the extent of wearing the evening gowns Lady Beauforth had deemed appropriate for a girl her age, though even some of those had seemed rather risqué to her less-than-sophisticated tastes. But this gown was positively obscene. Another half an inch and she would fall right out of it!

For some reason, it seemed that her uncle wanted her to project the image of a golden seductress, but she would not oblige him willingly. Azalea surveyed the gown thoughtfully for a moment.

"All right, Junie, help me out of this while I tell you what alterations will need to be made," she said. "Removing the bottom flounce should make it just the right length, but it seems a shame to waste so much of that beautiful lace, don't you think?''

Junie nodded. "I thought maybe an arrangement for your hair—" she began, but her mistress waved her to silence.

"No, I have a better idea," said Azalea. "I want you to work it into a ruffle for the neckline."

Junie looked doubtful. "Are you sure, miss? Them things really aren't in style anymore, you know, though I'll grant you, the top of this gown is a bit revealing, even by this year's standards."

"And much too revealing by mine," said Azalea decisively. "Fashionable or not, if my uncle wants to see me in this gown, it will be with ruffles above as well as below. Can you do it, do you think?"

"Oh, certainly, miss, as long as you're sure that is what you want."

"It is," Azalea stated firmly.

Gathering up the gown, Junie departed to make the desired changes.

TWO NIGHTS LATER, as Junie put the finishing touches to her hair, Azalea examined her reflection in the glass with far more satisfaction. The dress still clung to her body in a way that emphasized her curves, but the neckline met with her complete approval.

Junie had done a masterful job of sewing the gold lace from the bottom flounce around the top of the gown, making a ruffle that lined the front, shoulders and back, with an extra layer worked into the area just above her breasts. Azalea didn't see how anyone would guess the gown had not been originally designed this way, as the total effect was charmingly artistic. Perhaps she would create a new fashion.

Pulling on her long, fawn-coloured gloves and picking up the gold fan Lord Kayce had sent with the gown, Azalea rose to go.

"Junie, as always, you have done wonders with my hair. And I say again, if you should ever tire of being a ladies' maid, you can make your way quite well as a designer of gowns. Madame Clarisse herself could not have done better, I am certain."

Junie beamed with pleasure as her mistress left the room.

Before going out to Lord Kayce's carriage, which had just driven up, Azalea stepped into the parlour to take leave of her cousins. Marilyn's eyes widened as she took in the splendour of her country cousin's attire, and Lady Beauforth, after looking hard at the gown, exclaimed, "You're as lovely in that gown as I thought you'd be, my dear! But I thought... no, perhaps I was wrong. At any rate, you look charming."

It seemed but a few moments later that the coachman was helping her to descend from the carriage in front of Lord Kayce's imposing Town residence. Looking up at the uninviting façade, Azalea hoped it was his own acquisition rather than a family property and was conscious of renewed gratitude that he had never suggested she come to live with him here.

Gas lamps burned brightly on either side of the impressive entrance, but far from denoting hospitality, they merely served to illumine a particularly evil-looking gargoyle that leered down from over the front door. Azalea tried not to look at it as she mounted the steps.

The door opened as she reached it, and she was announced by a cadaverous-looking butler with a startlingly deep voice. As her uncle came forward to greet her, Azalea had a moment to notice that the interior of the house was scarcely more inviting than the exterior had been. The furnishings were undeniably expensive and even quite tasteful, but the gas lighting that Lord Kayce evidently preferred to candlelight threw everything into weird relief.

"My dear, I am so happy to welcome you to my home," said Kayce with a smile. "The guests have only just arrived, and I wish to introduce you to them, if you will accompany me."

Azalea thought he frowned quickly as he noticed her gown, but he had already turned away before she could be certain. She wondered why the other guests should be present already, since she was purportedly here to act as hostess, but followed her uncle without a word. They advanced into an elegant and expensively furnished drawing-room, also eerily gaslit, and three men of about her uncle's age rose to their feet.

"My niece and ward, Miss Azalea Clayton," announced Lord Kayce with a flourish. "My dear, allow me to present Mr. Fienton, Lord Drowling, and Lord Carfax," he said, indicating each gentleman in turn.

Azalea curtsied deeply, as was proper, but did not miss the speculation in their eyes. "I am honoured to make your acquaintance, my lords," she said politely in her soft, musical voice.

All three gentlemen stepped forward, but Lord Drowling was the quickest, eagerly seizing her hand to bestow a lingering kiss upon it. He was tall and coarsely handsome, with thick brown hair only slightly grey at the temples, and full, sensuous lips. His dark eyes burned as they met and held her own.

"The honour is all upon our side, I assure you, Miss Clayton," he said with a smile that was little less than a leer. "I had no idea the New World bred such rare and exotic flowers. Kayce is to be congratulated."

The suggestive tone in which this fulsome compliment was delivered, coupled with the man's frankly assessing gaze, made Azalea drop her eyes in confusion. The small amount of flirting she had done had not prepared her for this. When Lord Drowling showed no inclination to release her hand, despite a slight effort on her part to free it, she glanced somewhat desperately at her uncle.

Lord Kayce intervened smoothly. "Come, Drowling, you must not monopolize my niece tonight. She is here to act as hostess, and courtesy demands that she entertain you all equally."

Though she wondered about her uncle's meaning, Azalea was relieved that his words served to cause Lord Drowling to release her.

Mr. Fienton and Lord Carfax were now able to pay their respects. Both of them looked at her in a way that seemed calculated to unsettle her, though neither went quite so far as Drowling had done.

"When do you expect the other guests?" Azalea asked her uncle, devoutly hoping that there would be a few ladies among them.

"There are to be no other guests. I am sure I intimated to you that this was to be a small dinner party, so that you could meet a few of my closest...friends." His smile somehow failed to reassure her. "In fact, as we are all here, let us go in to dinner. My dear?"

Lord Kayce held out his arm and Azalea placed her fingers upon it, trying to stifle her misgivings. She was relieved, at any rate, that Lord Drowling was not to take her in to dinner, and hoped that he would not be seated by her at table.

This hope, at least, was answered, though by the time the second course was served, she thought that she might have preferred his conversation to his ogling, as he was placed directly across from her. She was seated at her uncle's right, with Mr. Fienton on her other side and Lord Carfax opposite him. They were in the smaller dining-room, as Lord Kayce had felt this more appropriate for such a small gathering.

Azalea barely participated in the conversation, feeling out of place in what seemed more like a business meeting than a dinner party. Mr. Fienton, a slight, mousy-looking man with fair hair and watery blue eyes, managed to engage her in conversation about America for a few minutes, but he seemed less interested in her replies than in her cleavage. She found his refusal to meet her eyes both irritating and disconcerting.

She still had not exchanged more than an initial greeting with Lord Carfax, but felt no inclination to further that acquaintance. He appeared to be the oldest of the group, probably well into his fifties, with heavy black brows and a cold, almost sinister directness to his gaze.

Whenever Azalea chanced to encounter his eyes, he regarded her with an intensity that disturbed her, though not in the same way as the knowing leer of Lord Drowling. She felt that Lord Carfax, rather, was trying to see inside her, to read her very thoughts and perhaps control them. She knew these to be mere fancies, but she could not quite dismiss them.

When Lord Glaedon sent admiring glances her way, she recalled, she had felt excited, even flattered. But the expressions of her uncle's friends made her feel soiled.

Thankfully, the meal ended at last, and Azalea began to cast about for some plausible excuse to leave early. As it happened, Lord Kayce himself provided her escape, saying that he was to meet a friend at White's that evening and would be obliged to turn them all out within the hour.

"But I have scarce had a chance to exchange two words with your charming niece, Kayce," protested Lord Drowling. "And I am sure my companions share my eagerness to know her better."

He stepped to her side as he spoke and allowed his fingertips to brush her upper arm, where it was bare between her glove and shoulder ruffle. It took all of Azalea's control not to shrink away from the man.

"Really, Kayce, Drowling is right. It is most inhospitable of you to end the evening so early," drawled Mr. Fienton in his high-pitched monotone. "Can't you send a note round to White's saying you've been detained?"

"I'm afraid not," replied their host. "But I'm certain you will have ample opportunity in future to speak with my niece, as she is permanently fixed in England and will remain in London at least through the Season."

"Might I offer you my escort home, ma'am?" Lord Carfax stepped forward as he spoke, his deep voice holding the same determined intensity as his gaze.

Before she could reply, her uncle answered for her with a smooth refusal, saying that he had already ar-

ranged to return his niece to her home on his way to
White's.

"If any of you would care to meet me there in, say,
two hours, we might have a game of cards or some
quiet conversation," he concluded. At these words, all
three gentlemen looked thoughtful and agreed to see
him later.

Azalea was so relieved that she need not endure being alone in a carriage with Lord Carfax that she
scarcely noticed this exchange.

Graciously taking leave of her uncle's guests at the
front entrance, she stepped into Lord Kayce's carriage
with a sigh that she hoped he did not hear. She had not
really expected to enjoy the evening, but it had been far
more uncomfortable than she had anticipated. Thank
heavens it was over!

Now that they were alone, she half expected Lord
Kayce to make some comment on her alterations to the
gown, but he did not. "What think you of my friends,
my dear?" he asked as the coachman whipped up the
horses. "They all seemed much taken with you."

"I am most flattered, of course, Uncle Simon," she
replied carefully, not wanting to offend him. "However, I was rather at a loss to understand why you
wished me to be there at all. No other ladies were present."

"Why, to present you to those most eligible gentlemen, of course," he replied silkily. "I said that your
future was my concern, did I not? Thus it falls to me to
find you a suitable husband."

With difficulty Azalea suppressed a gasp of dismay.
"I—I am sorry, Uncle Simon, if I gave you the impression that I wished for your help in that matter. It
is most unnecessary, I assure you."

"Nonsense, nonsense!" he said affably. "You do not wish to end up a spinster, I am certain. As I'm your guardian, it is plainly my responsibility to ensure that you make an advantageous marriage."

Azalea bit her lip. Did she dare tell her uncle the truth? She did not trust him a whit, but even he could scarcely have an existing marriage set aside for whatever ends he had in mind. Still, it seemed wrong to tell this man, whom she neither liked nor trusted, before telling Lord Glaedon himself. Besides, she had no idea just how ruthless Lord Kayce might be. Perhaps by telling him she might be putting Christian at some risk.

Making a quick decision, she said with assumed casualness, "That reminds me, Uncle, that I have not yet heard from Mr. Timmons on the matter of your guardianship of me. I believe I shall call on him Monday. I have certain other matters to discuss with him as well."

Lord Kayce darted a quick look at her. "What might . . . that is, of course, my dear. No doubt he will have the papers ready for your signature."

Just then, the carriage pulled up before Beauforth House and Kayce escorted Azalea to the door, though he declined to come inside. She heard the clatter of his departure with relief as she stepped into the house.

AZALEA WOULD NO DOUBT have felt less relieved had she been able to look in at White's later.

"Well, Kayce, I must admit you told no more than the truth when you described your new-found niece," said Lord Drowling, as he settled into a chair next to the baron. "If anything, you didn't do her justice. It would seem almost a waste to find a form and face like that on such an innocent, if one did not imagine the delights of instructing her. But I assume such a privilege won't come cheaply?''

"I think you know what I would want in exchange, Drowling. You have been holding that duel of my brother's over my head for more than twenty years."

"Ah, but it was such a, er, profitable investment for me, you see," replied Drowling with a smile. "Though I admit I had thought it's worth to be nearly exhausted until now. No doubt your dear niece would be most interested to learn how her father was deceived. Perhaps she would even be grateful enough to bestow her hand on me willingly."

Kayce snorted. "When she has every young buck in London panting after her? Not likely. No, if you want her, you must work through me. And do not forget that any son of hers would become my heir. But let us not be hasty. Here come Carfax and Fienton. I would like to hear what each of them has in mind, as well."

"With the charming Azalea to go to the highest bidder, I perceive," said Drowling, with a cynical twist to his smile. "That golden Aphrodite may well be worth what you ask. I shall think on it." Rising, the viscount nodded a greeting to the two approaching gentlemen and went in search of a game of whist.

FIRST THING MONDAY morning Azalea made good on her promise to call on Mr. Timmons. She had already decided to ask for her marriage proofs back, so that she would have them on hand when Lord Glaedon returned in a few weeks.

She still hoped that she could manage to convince him of the truth without them, but time was running out. Better to have the evidence in case she needed it.

She left Junie in the carriage and ascended confidently to the attorney's offices. Her confidence received a setback a moment later, however, when she
saw the sign on the door of Mr. Timmons's chambers:
Closed Until Further Notice.

Perplexed, she lingered in the empty hallway, biting
her lower lip. Could the lawyer have suddenly decided
to leave Town for the holidays? Surely he would have
sent a message, at least, as his work on her behalf was
by no means done.

Half-heartedly, she reached out to try the doorknob
and was surprised when it turned easily in her grasp.
She pushed the door open and gasped in astonishment
at the scene that greeted her.

The outer office had been far from immaculate before, but it was now in a state of complete chaos. Papers were everywhere, books lay open upon the floor
and one large wooden cabinet had been overturned and
broken. She stepped further into the room, torn between curiosity and a growing sense of misgiving.

Suddenly, Mr. Greene stood up from behind his
desk, where he had apparently taken cover at her entrance, causing her to start violently.

"Oh, Miss Clayton, it is you!" he exclaimed in obvious relief. "I thought they might have returned."

"Who?" asked Azalea, as soon as her heart resumed beating. She was still shaken, but determined to
find out what she could. "Whatever has happened
here? Where is Mr. Timmons?" She looked about her,
half expecting the lawyer to emerge from his inner office at the sound of her voice.

"He's laid up at home, senseless," replied Mr.
Greene, seemingly agitated out of his shyness by recent events.

"Senseless? What has happened to him? Is he injured?" asked Azalea in alarm, her concern for the old gentleman temporarily overshadowing her own problems.

"Set upon by footpads last night, miss, not two blocks from here," said Mr. Greene, shaking his head as if he still could not believe it. "They took what little money he had, and his keys, and beat him badly. Left him for dead, or so the Runners think."

"So the same footpads are the ones who did this, also, I presume," Azalea concluded, gesturing about the office. "What do you suppose they were after?" Her mind had already jumped to an ugly suspicion, but she had no intention of voicing it without any evidence to support it. At least not yet.

"After?" asked Mr. Greene in surprise. Apparently he had not yet thought that far into the matter. "Why, money, I suppose. What else?"

"Come, Mr. Greene, even a common footpad would hardly expect to find much money in a solicitor's office, and I rather doubt these were common footpads. It seems obvious to me that they attacked poor Mr. Timmons primarily for the keys to these rooms, and that they were looking for something specific here. Do not tell me that the Bow Street Runners had no similar theory?"

"No, miss," replied Mr. Greene, beginning to return to his usual flustered manner. "At least, I don't think so. No, no they couldn't have, for they didn't know the office had been ransacked. I just found out two hours ago when I came to put the sign on the door."

Perhaps to cover his embarrassment for not having thought of that obvious explanation himself, Mr.

Greene turned away to resume the thankless task of straightening up.

"They certainly must be told, and immediately," said Azalea decisively. "Will you do so, Mr. Greene, or shall I?"

The clerk gaped at her. "You, miss? Why ever would you want to involve yourself in this business? No, they will be back later today, and I shall tell them then—or, rather, show them. I'll hardly have the place cleaned up by then." He looked around hopelessly.

"Perhaps you should leave everything as it is until they've seen it," she suggested. Mr. Greene's face brightened noticeably, "Meanwhile, I don't suppose there is any chance you might know where Mr. Timmons kept certain documents I left with him?"

The clerk's face clouded again. "No, miss, I'm sorry. Nothing is in its proper place, as far as I have been able to tell, and Mr. Timmons's personal office is in worse shape than this one. That is where he kept the most important papers."

She had feared that would be the case. "Well, if you should find any papers connected with me, please send me a message or, better, the papers themselves," she said, but without much hope. Now what was she to do?

"Yes, miss, I'll certainly do that," promised Mr. Greene, appearing more optimistic than she was.

Thinking furiously, Azalea left the office. *Could* Kayce have been behind this? Had he somehow suspected her marriage to Lord Glaedon? That seemed unlikely, as the only person in London she had told was Mr. Timmons.

No, it seemed more probable that Kayce had been after the proofs of her identity if, in fact, he was responsible. Without those, she would have a difficult, if not impossible, time establishing any claim to her inheritance. Her uncle might be planning to declare her a fraud if she refused to go along with his plans. Of course, if he now had all the papers, he would know that marriage to one of his cronies was out of the question—wouldn't he? Still deep in thought, she descended to the carriage.

CHAPTER TWELVE

CHRISTMAS WAS NEARLY upon them. Azalea was glad that Lady Beauforth felt disposed to make little of the holiday season, since her own heart wasn't in it. She had called on Mr. Timmons at his home the previous afternoon, only to be told by his wife that the doctor had expressly forbidden visitors. Mrs. Timmons had agreed to convey a message as soon as her husband was on the mend, and Azalea tried to be satisfied with that.

Marilyn, however, was not nearly so willing to forgo Christmas festivities as her mother and Azalea seemed to be. At the breakfast table she bemoaned the scarcity of parties and routs in Town at this season, complaining that this was certain to be the dullest Christmas she had ever spent. Her mother's reluctant suggestion that they might go to their country estate for the holidays was quickly rejected.

"Maple Park is bound to be even duller than Town," Marilyn declared with a pretty pout. "If we could but give a party or, better, a ball of our own, it might serve to divert me."

"With Lord Glaedon in the country? People might think it odd, my dear. Besides, with Town so thin of company, who would we invite?"

Such discussions were diverted, however, by the arrival of a letter a short time later.

"Who is it from, my dearest?" asked Lady Beauforth, always eager for news of any kind.

"Mary Trentham," answered her daughter somewhat absently, as she was still perusing the contents of her letter. "Oh! She invites me to Alder House for the holidays! She mentions some of those to be present, and . . . oh, Mother, do say I may go! It will be ever so much more festive than staying here."

Marilyn's pout had been magically transformed into a radiant smile. Lady Beauforth could not be expected to deny her angel any treat that could bring her such happiness.

"Of course you must go, darling. It will be just the thing for you. It has been putting me about dreadfully to see you so in the doldrums. Do you suppose Miss Trentham could be prevailed upon to extend the invitation to include your cousin, as well?" she asked as an afterthought. She glanced guiltily at Azalea.

Marilyn looked distractedly at her in turn. "What? Oh. I suppose I could write to Mary, but there is so little time. . . ." It was obvious she had no thought to spare for her cousin just then.

"No, please, do not go to any such trouble," Azalea insisted. "I assure you that I have not the least desire to go. I shall be perfectly happy to stay here, catching up on my reading, which I have steadily neglected, and keeping dear Cousin Alice company through the holidays."

Her smile at Lady Beauforth during this last remark was perfectly genuine. Azalea did not wish to risk being away from London when Mr. Timmons recovered—or when Lord Glaedon returned.

Marilyn required no convincing whatsoever. "Well, then, since that is settled, I shall write at once to tell dear, dear Mary that I shall be there." She was out the breakfast-room door before she had finished speaking, and a moment later Azalea could hear her calling out to one of the footmen for a newly mended pen.

The rest of that day and the next passed in a whirl of preparation for Marilyn's visit. Azalea helped with enthusiasm, glad to have her cousin in such happy spirits for a change. Running out to the shops to find just the right shade of ribbon or a fan to go with the gowns being packed provided a welcome distraction to her own problems.

The night before her departure, Marilyn surprised Azalea by coming to her bedchamber. "Cousin, I have a favour to ask," she said with unwonted diffidence.

"Of course," exclaimed Azalea, warming to the welcome change in her cousin's manner. "How may I help you?"

Marilyn hesitated for a moment, then met her eyes with a rather sheepish smile. "Your gold dress—the one Lord Kayce gave you. Do you suppose . . . that is, could I borrow it for the house party?" she finished her request in a rush.

Struggling between amazement and amusement, Azalea was careful to let neither show on her face. She realized that it must be very difficult for Marilyn, who had always been accustomed to having everything she wished, to actually beg a favour of her country cousin. And lending clothes seemed so . . . so sisterly!

At this thought, Azalea smiled broadly. "Of course. I had no plans to wear it again any time soon."

She opened her clothes-press and removed the shimmering gold gown. As a matter of fact, after the evening she now associated with this dress, she had no intention of ever wearing it again.

"Feel free to make any necessary alterations," she said cheerfully. "I expect it will look better on you, anyway."

Marilyn thanked her graciously. "You don't think it will make me too...all one colour?" she asked suddenly, as she turned to leave the room.

"Oh, no!" Azalea assured her. "You'll look like spun gold, I'm certain."

Marilyn smiled. "Jonathan—your friend Mr. Plummer—once said something like that. I thought he might recall it if he saw me in this dress."

"Oh, is he to be there?" asked Azalea. Suddenly, Marilyn's careful preparations took on new meaning.

"Yes, but pray do not say anything to Mama about it. I—I wouldn't wish her to worry."

Azalea assured her that she saw no reason to mention the fact to Lady Beauforth. Thanking her again, Marilyn left to finally complete her packing.

The coach drew up to the door directly after breakfast the next day. Marilyn's maid and Tom, the head groom, were to accompany her, and her ladyship had managed to convince herself that her greatest treasure would be safe in their care. Still, Lady Beauforth could not suppress a tear or two at their parting, as this would be the first time in Marilyn's eighteen years that mother and daughter would be separated by any distance, even if it was to be for only a fortnight.

"Are you certain you don't wish to come, too?" Marilyn asked Azalea impulsively as she was turning to climb into the waiting coach.

Though extremely gratified, Azalea shook her head firmly. "No, I really would prefer to stay here, and Cousin Alice is rather counting on my company, I flatter myself. But thank you for asking."

Marilyn's smile was as genuine as her cousin's. "I shall see you in a fortnight, then. If anything interesting should occur in my absence, you must write to tell me all about it." With that, the door was closed and the coachman whipped up the team.

Azalea and Lady Beauforth were left standing by the railings. Azalea perceived her cousin's melancholy at once and quickly guided her back into the house, to divert her with a humorous tale she had overheard at one of the shops yesterday and saved for exactly this occasion.

YULETIDE PASSED as uneventfully as Marilyn had foretold. Virtually all of their acquaintances had taken advantage of the unusually good travelling conditions to visit family or friends in the country. Azalea, far from bemoaning the lack of diversion, welcomed this respite when she might read, write, ride and, most of all, think to her heart's content.

Christmas passed without any word from Mr. Timmons, and Azalea reluctantly realized that she would have to solve her problems without his assistance. And she must do it soon. Marilyn and Lord Glaedon's wedding loomed less than six weeks away.

It was always possible that Jonathan and Marilyn might come to some understanding while at Miss Trentham's house party, but she could not count on that. No, when Lord Glaedon returned to Town, she would do her best to *make* him remember.

Failing that, she must try to charm him away from her cousin. Without the marriage papers to back up her claim, it was the only solution she could think of.

One morning only a few days after Christmas, while Azalea was reading aloud to Lady Beauforth in the drawing-room, Lord Drowling was announced. Azalea tried to quell her instinctive dismay as Lady Beauforth rose to greet him effusively.

"Why, Lord Drowling! What an honour, to be sure! I suppose I may construe your call as a compliment to my dear Azalea?"

"Indeed, my lady. As she may have told you, I made her acquaintance at the home of her uncle two weeks ago. Since then, I have been unable to think of anything else. I am but this moment returned from my estates and wished to pay my respects immediately." Though he spoke to Lady Beauforth, his eyes caressed Azalea possessively as he spoke.

"How kind of you, my lord." Azalea kept her voice cool.

"Ah, kindness has nothing to do with it, my vision," he replied, seating himself in the chair closest to her. "My very sanity demanded that I come."

He seemed to devour her with his eyes, and Azalea felt her skin crawl. While his manner in front of Lady Beauforth was more restrained than it had been at Lord Kayce's house, Azalea was more than relieved that he kept his visit brief. After only ten minutes he took his leave with one last, lingering look that made her feel unclean.

Before she could convey her opinion of him to her cousin, however, Lady Beauforth began to express her admiration of his lordship's person, as well as his many and well-known worldly advantages.

"This is a greater conquest than you can realize, my dear," she concluded after a lengthy and glowing recital of Lord Drowling's assets. "I can tell you that I would have been more than pleased to welcome his attentions towards Marilyn, if he had ever shown the slightest inclination to bestow them. He's as rich as Croesus!''

She fanned herself rapidly before continuing. "But he has never been at all in the petticoat line. At least not with, well..." She tittered self-consciously, her florid cheeks pinkening.

Azalea understood quite well what her cousin had left unsaid, but she remained silent, not wishing to encourage Lady Beauforth in this flight of fancy.

"In point of truth," continued her cousin after a moment, "I never heard of him calling on *any* eligible girl before. I suppose it could be in deference to Lord Kayce, for I hear they are as thick as thieves."

A singularly apt analogy, Azalea thought.

"But even so, he seemed quite taken with you. Why did you not mention his presence at Kayce's dinner party before now?"

Azalea replied distractedly that she had not thought it of any importance, and thereafter excused herself, saying she wanted to finish writing a letter before nuncheon. She was wondering how she would be able to prevent any further attentions from Lord Drowling, since it was clear he would have Lady Beauforth's unqualified support. Cousin Alice would no doubt do all in her power to throw them together at every opportunity.

She prayed that Lord Glaedon would return to London soon.

THE EARL, MEANWHILE, was making the most of his time in the country, though not as his relations there had expected. Indeed, his grandmother insisted that his behaviour bordered on inhospitable.

Every moment that could be spared from his duties as host, Christian spent in his father's private library, going through musty old papers and letters, searching for the Lord only knew what.

When Lady Glaedon confronted him, demanding to know what could be so important that it caused him to neglect his guests, he merely replied that he had become curious about his father's youth and was endeavouring to learn more of his deceased parent through his letters.

The dowager pointed out that any personal letters he found were likely to have been written *to* the late earl rather than *by* him, but her grandson's attention had already wandered back to the pile of papers on the table before him. She gave it up for the time being and returned to their guests to compensate for their host's lack of attentiveness.

Christian's persistent research was yielding rewards, however. On leaving London nearly a fortnight before, his emotions had been a turmoil of guilt and longing. He was firm, though, in his intention of carefully examining his father's papers in the hopes of learning something—anything—about Miss Azalea Clayton.

He knew that the late earl had corresponded with the girl's grandfather regularly over the years, and it was to Reverend Simpson's letters that he directed his attention. There were more of these than he had expected, and what he was learning from their perusal surprised him even more.

Christian had known that the two men had served together in India. He found now that their friendship had begun years before that, when both his father and Gregory Simpson were mere boys at Eton.

Judging by the language in the letters, there was virtually nothing they did not confide to one another. Their separation, when Gregory left for America was felt keenly by both. These early letters gave Christian a great deal of insight into Azalea's heritage, at least on the maternal side.

Adele Simpson, Azalea's mother, had, by her fond father's account, been a spectacular beauty. Having appreciated what she bequeathed to her daughter in the way of looks, Christian saw no reason to doubt his word. Gregory lamented the fact that there were no young men even remotely worthy of his daughter in the small college town to which he had removed, and feared that she might become attached to some penniless student or, worse, a farmer's son.

Reverend Simpson, it appeared, had not quite embraced his new country's rejection of class distinctions.

Then Walter Clayton, eldest son and heir of Lord Kayce, had appeared on the scene. He and Adele were immediately drawn to one another, though she was only sixteen at the time. While he fully approved of such a connection, as well as the young man himself, Gregory was unwilling to allow his daughter to marry at so young an age. Finally, however, he had been persuaded to a formal betrothal.

Due to his father's illness, Walter had returned to England shortly thereafter, but had promised to return for Adele. Reading ahead two years, Christian found that Walter, by then the new Lord Kayce, had kept his promise; he and Adele were married in 1791.

Now, however, Walter elected to remain in America rather than take his new bride back to England as originally planned, leaving his estates in the hands of his younger brother. This development surprised Reverend Simpson, who hazarded a guess or two as to its cause. He did not openly question it, however, since he was grateful that his only child was not to be removed across the Atlantic.

Reading between the lines, Christian was able to infer that Kayce gradually became infected by the republican spirit of the newly liberated colonies, a turn of events of which his father-in-law did not entirely approve, it appeared.

Sporadic news of the couple occurred in the letters of the next few years, as the Claytons had resettled in the near-wilderness west of Richmond to try their fortunes. Two stillbirths were reported, then Azalea's birth in November of 1795. Gregory travelled west to see his new granddaughter in the spring of 1796 and sent a letter to the earl a few months later singing her praises.

Christian began to read the closely written pages more carefully from that point on, grateful that his father had chosen to retain all of his personal correspondence, though not according to any particular system. It had taken him several days to find and then chronologically order all of Reverend Simpson's letters.

Herschel's name, and his own, had been frequently mentioned, mainly in regard to enquiries after their health and activities. The third letter after the one detailing the remarkable cleverness and beauty of five-month-old Azalea, however, mentioned what was apparently a years-old dream of both men—to someday unite their families through the marriage of their offspring.

Gregory pointed out that, as Howard had been so disobliging as to marry much later in life than himself, that dream, if it were ever to be fulfilled, would have to be through his darling Azalea or some future daughter of Adele's. His tone was less than serious, but Christian was much struck by this revelation nonetheless.

There was to be no future daughter. When Azalea was barely two years old, Walter was killed by a fall while hunting, and Adele returned to Williamsburg with her baby daughter.

News of Azalea was now liberally strewn throughout every letter, and Christian read the accounts of her childhood escapades with an absorption he found hard to explain. So caught up in her history did he become that he was actually moved to tears at the account of Adele's death and her five-year-old daughter's uncomprehending grief.

Wiping his eyes, Christian glanced around the library, glad that his grandmother had not chosen this moment to remind him, yet again, of what was expected of the host at a family gathering.

As it happened, that perceptive lady had not believed for a moment in Christian's sudden acquisition of a passion for family history. She had discovered, through an investigation quickly and surreptitiously conducted during one of his brief absences from the library, that his attention seemed focused on a collection of letters from one Gregory Simpson of Williamsburg, Virginia.

Lady Glaedon's curiosity was thoroughly aroused but, as Christian himself seemed disinclined to be communicative, she had to content herself with supposition. For lack of a better confidante, she broached the subject to her daughter, Lady Constance Highton, one evening when they were alone.

"Connie, I've been meaning to ask you if you've noticed anything...odd...in Christian's manner since he arrived home."

Lady Constance, a handsome, middle-aged matron, considered carefully before answering. "Well, Mama, he has been quite as correct in his bearing towards me as ever, though I will admit I have seen less of him than usual this Christmas."

The dowager regarded her daughter with some impatience. She knew that Constance's understanding was not absolutely of the first order, but she felt a need to discuss her concerns with someone, and she was unwilling to share them with anyone less closely connected to Christian.

"I was not discussing his politeness, Connie," she continued carefully after a moment. "I meant that he has seemed rather...distracted of late."

"Oh! Yes, now that you mention it, I do remember that just this afternoon at nuncheon I had to speak to him twice before he would answer my question regarding the advisability of new draperies in my small salon at the London house. Mr. Highton favours cream, you see, but I have always felt that the blue and buff we have there now more appropriately reflect—"

"Yes, of course, Connie, we went over all that earlier, if you recall," the dowager broke in, forestalling yet another complete cataloguing of the furnishings of her daughter's small salon. "But we were discussing Christian. If I were to hazard a guess, I would say his manner almost resembles that of a young man in love. However, much as I have wished for just that, I fear there must be another explanation."

"But why? Miss Beauforth is quite lovely." Lady Constance frowned vaguely. "I must agree that if she has captured his heart, 'twould be no bad thing. But even if she has not, it is not quite the thing to be in love with one's spouse, anyway. No doubt they will deal perfectly well together."

"Yes, yes, you are right, of course." The dowager lapsed into discontented silence. Not even to Constance would she voice her suspicion that Christian's preoccupation had nothing whatsoever to do with Miss Beauforth. Nor the fact that she, herself, would be more pleased than dismayed if that proved to be true.

If he had truly fallen in love with someone else, she doubted she could bring herself to criticize his choice, if only Christian were happy. And she doubted he would ever be truly happy with Marilyn Beauforth. But would he cry off his betrothal, even for love? Not for the first time she mentally cursed that male code of honour with which all the men in her family had been afflicted, often to their detriment.

If her guess were correct, who might the lucky girl be? Could she possibly have some connection to those musty old letters from America? It seemed unlikely.

"Well," she said briskly, bringing her thoughts back to the present, "I suppose the most I can hope is that he will confide in me. Pray don't mention this conversation to Christian," she cautioned her daughter. "I am only guessing, after all, and it is certain that he would not appreciate any interference on our part."

Even as his grandmother and aunt discussed him, Christian was immersed in his self-appointed research once again. He had been charmed by Reverend Simpson's accounts of Azalea's early childhood antics as well as impressed by the evidence he offered of his

granddaughter's exceptional abilities. Christian began
to understand why the girl was so able to hold her own
in the few arguments they had had; her unusual intelligence had been augmented by an excellent education.

He read of her fascination with botany, which had
become evident by the time she was six years old and
seemed to be the child's way of retaining some contact
with her departed mother. Her other absorbing interest appeared to be horses, and he recalled with some
amusement the near-lecture she had given him on that
topic their first morning in the Park. They had even
more in common than he had ever realized.

Irresistibly, he remembered again her sweet curves,
her lustrous green eyes. He had tried to forget, but he
might as well have tried to stop his heart from beating.
The very thought of her, even after a fortnight's absence, still had the power to stir his blood.

Now more than ever he bitterly regretted his betrothal to Miss Beauforth, made for the sake of main-
taining the family honour.

Finally, only two letters remained. Christian had
forced himself to read all of them sequentially, although the temptation had been great to open the last
letter at the outset. It had been received by his father
only a month before their ill-fated voyage to the New
World.

Christian had already discovered that for some time
his father had taken a discreet interest in Azalea's
English inheritance and the Kayce estates, at her
grandfather's request. Some problems had apparently
arisen, and in the second-to-last letter Reverend Simpson implied strongly that Kayce was not to be trusted.
He also mentioned his own failing health, agreeing that

the "steps" Lord Glaedon had recommended might be necessary after all.

The letter concluded with a reference to "what would be best for the youngsters," which made Christian reach for the final envelope in hopes that this curious "problem" and his father's "solution" would be discussed more fully.

The last letter opened with the assurance that Simpson and his granddaughter would be honoured by a visit from Glaedon and his son, Christian, if the earl would only name the time. Reading further, Christian's interest turned to amazement as he realized what the purport of this visit was to be: no less than his own marriage to Azalea Clayton.

"I recommend that the young people be allowed to meet and form some sort of opinion of each other before any commitment be made," Simpson had written. "It is up to you whether you wish to discuss our plan with Christian in advance. Knowing Azalea as I do, it will probably be best on my part to wait until she has met your son, so as not to prejudice her against him at the outset. The girl has shown little inclination toward any young man as yet, but I suppose that is not to be wondered at, as she is barely thirteen at this writing."

It appeared obvious from the tone of this last letter that his father had earnestly desired this match. Christian had offered for Miss Beauforth thinking that his father would have wanted him to take up Herschel's betrothal. But it would seem the old earl had made plans for both his sons.

Earlier, Christian had cursed the very devotion to family honour and his father's memory that had led him to betroth himself to Miss Beauforth. It suddenly struck him now that it would be undutiful, as well as dishonourable, of him to disregard what amounted to his father's dying wish.

So where did that leave him? Honour bound to marry two different women? There could be no question where his inclination lay. Unfortunately, it was equally clear which course was the more honourable. He was already betrothed to Miss Beauforth.

Christian rose. It was high time he returned to London. He had a lot to sort out.

CHAPTER THIRTEEN

AS IT HAPPENED, several days passed before Christian was able to leave for Town. After directing Lawrence, his valet, to have everything ready for their immediate departure at his word, the earl went in search of the dowager in order to take his leave of her and to acquaint her with his plans.

He found his grandmother alone in the small parlour she habitually used as her private sitting-room. She had decorated it herself many years before, and it had since become her favourite retreat in the enormous, rambling manor house.

"Ma'am, I am off for London almost at once, but I wished to speak with you first," said the earl, striding purposefully into the room.

The dowager looked up calmly from her needle-work, apparently little perturbed by her grandson's tempestuous entrance. "Certainly, Christian. Pray have a seat." She gestured to the gilt chair opposite her.

Put off his stride by receiving none of the resistance to his abrupt departure that he had expected, Christian dropped into the chair and tugged at his collar, trying to decide how best to begin. Now that it came to the point of actually framing the words, he realized that his dilemma might sound vaguely absurd.

"You wished to tell me something?" Lady Glaedon prompted him.

"Yes! That is . . . you have expressed certain misgivings about my betrothal to Miss Beauforth, as I recall. I begin to think you may be right."

The dowager waited expectantly.

"In fact, I go to London to discover whether I can honourably extricate myself from it. If I cannot, I suppose I must marry her after all." A sudden depression seized him and he looked pleadingly at his grandmother.

"Not if you do not care for her," the dowager said placidly. "Your happiness has always been my foremost consideration, Chris, and I have been doubtful all along that Miss Beauforth would be likely to secure it. I am relieved you have come to your senses in time."

He shook his head disbelievingly, wondering if his grandmother had actually uttered those words or if he were merely hearing what he wished to. "There will be the devil of a scandal if I cry off, you realize," he said cautiously.

"That is neither here nor there," she replied, startling him again. "You had something else to tell me, did you not?" she prompted.

"You know me far too well, I see. Yes, there was something else."

"What is her name?"

Christian was beyond surprise now. "I did not realize that mind-reading was among your many talents, ma'am. Her name is Clayton. Miss Azalea Clayton. She is living in the Beauforth household, which makes the situation doubly awkward."

Now it was the dowager's turn to look surprised. "Clayton? But that is the Kayce family name, is it not? Lord Kayce has no daughter that I know of. Pray explain everything, Christian, from the beginning. Precisely who is this Miss Clayton, and why is she staying with Lady Beauforth?''

At that, Christian took a deep breath to organize his thoughts and proceeded to relate to his grandmother all that he knew of Azalea: her parents and grandparents, her history, and their few meetings, which had quickly grown into friendship and affection, at least on his part. Finally, he showed her the last letter from Reverend Simpson.

''If possible,'' he said, ''I should like to fulfill my father's final wish.''

''Very noble!'' said the dowager with barely concealed amusement at the conclusion of his story.

She had watched Christian's face closely during his recital and had a fair suspicion of what he had left unsaid. He was obviously head over ears in love with the girl, but she did not think he had yet admitted this to himself. He had instead convinced himself that it was his ''duty'' to his late father to offer for her—if he could extricate himself from his current betrothal, also entered into in the name of duty and honour.

Lady Glaedon doubted that such an approach would be likely to recommend his suit to the young lady in question, whatever her feelings towards Christian might be. Not if she had more sensibility than Miss Beauforth, which she must have if Christian had fallen in love with her.

''What do you intend to do, precisely?'' she asked. ''Hand her the letter and inform her that she owes it to her grandfather and your father to marry you?''

''Of course not!'' exclaimed Christian. ''I plan to... well, to continue our friendship and, eventually, explain things to her. She seems a level-headed girl and is sure to realize what a good catch I am." Christian grinned at his grandmother. "Am I not?"

"And what of Miss Beauforth?" she asked quietly, effectively removing all humour from his face.

"That is more difficult," he admitted. "I do not believe her heart is affected, but her pride and ambition assuredly are. Somehow I must convince her that she would not be happy wedded to me. If I could persuade her to cry off, it would be best for all concerned. 'Twill not be easy, however."

From what the dowager recalled of Miss Beauforth, her grandson's words were likely all too true. "My boy, you have a lot of work ahead of you, I can see. However, your 'plan' hardly requires you to rush off on the instant, offending your house guests and placing the burden of entertaining them on me."

This last was a shrewd stroke, for she knew that Christian would never intentionally shirk his responsibilities. It was rare that Lady Glaedon resorted to guilt to influence her grandson, but she felt that in this instance the stratagem was justified. A few days for thought might significantly enhance his chances for lasting happiness with this girl he had chosen.

Already she was delighted to see a resurgence of his old sense of humour and had no doubt that this Miss Clayton was the cause of it. The delay would also give the dowager a chance to do a little research of her own concerning the young lady involved.

"You are right, of course, Grandmother. I would be the most selfish of beasts to leave you to entertain a houseful of cousins—even if inviting them was your idea."

Christian was well aware that he was being manipulated, but he realized, now that the dowager had forced him to look ahead, that he indeed needed some time to think. He knew why the idea of fulfilling his father's wishes appealed so strongly to him—Azalea was all he had ever dreamed of in a woman, and more. But he had to consider how best to go about fulfilling those wishes.

There was also the sticky matter of his betrothal. And his grandmother was perfectly right. He knew very little about how to court a young lady like Azalea—look at the mess he had nearly made of things already with his prejudices. It would not surprise him if she never wanted to see him again.

"Very well," he continued after a brief pause. "I shall put off my departure until Thursday. I believe that between us we can manage to rid ourselves of our guests by then."

With this the dowager had to be content. She knew that young love could not be delayed for long, however good the reasons.

AZALEA SAT ALONE in the parlour, trying to keep her mind on the embroidery before her despite her growing fear that Lord Drowling might call at any moment. Lady Beauforth had plainly considered it likely. That was surely why she had gone out by herself, despite the chill drizzle, bidding Azalea to remain at home to receive any callers.

Ever more worrisome, Azalea had overheard her hostess telling Smythe that if her niece should have a gentleman caller while she was out, they were not to be disturbed. Clearly, Cousin Alice expected Lord Drowling not only to call, but to make a declaration in form.

She would refuse him, of course, but how might he react? And if the servants had been warned away, then there might be no one near enough to come to her assistance should he prove obdurate.

Perhaps he would not come at all, she thought, attempting to calm her frayed nerves. Certainly she had given him no encouragement yesterday when he had called. Perhaps he had realized by now that she had no interest in furthering their acquaintance. Somehow, though, she doubted whether that realization would weigh much with Lord Drowling.

A knocking at the front door brought her heart to her throat. *Don't be absurd,* she admonished herself. *He will scarcely ravish you right here in the front parlour!* So saying, she was able to present a calm front when the door opened a moment later so that Smythe could announce her caller.

"Lord Glaedon," he intoned.

Her relief, combined with the intense thrill she experienced at her first sight of him in three weeks, took her completely off guard. She was glad when the earl spoke first, giving her a chance to collect her suddenly scattered wits.

"Give you good day, Miss Clayton," he said cordially.

"Good—good day, my lord. I fear my cousins are from home just now. We...we were not aware that you were back in Town."

"I returned last night," Glaedon informed her, his smile warm. He seemed not at all put out that Marilyn was absent.

"I trust you enjoyed your stay in the country?" Azalea enquired politely, trying to calm the rapid beating of her heart.

"I found it most—informative," replied Glaedon with an enigmatic smile, "but I was unaccountably anxious to get back to London." There was no mistaking the significance of this remark, or the glance that accompanied it. "I missed you."

"And I you, my lord," replied Azalea somewhat breathlessly, scarcely daring to believe the evidence of her ears.

"Please, Miss Clayton, my name is Christian, and I make you free of it. And I've been dying to call you Azalea. May I?"

"Certainly, my... Christian, I mean." Azalea could feel a blush mounting her cheeks, and she hoped Lord Glaedon would not notice it.

"'My Christian.' I like that," he said teasingly, but with an underlying tenderness that caused her colour to deepen further.

"Oh, you know I did not mean..." she began, then stopped. "You are trying to embarrass me, I think," she finished severely.

"My apologies, Azalea," he replied, obviously savouring her name. "I won't let it happen again."

"I take leave to doubt that, but your apology is accepted." The warmth of her smile now matched his own.

Again Christian felt that strong pull of attraction to her. He had actually come to Beauforth House in hopes of seeing Miss Clayton again and to discover whether he had imagined her partiality to him. It was an unexpected boon to find her alone. And because of that privacy, he'd said more than he had intended—more than was probably wise. Sharply, he called himself to task.

Their conversation after that became general, focusing on stories of the Christmas just past, but the physical awareness between them remained. It was several minutes before Christian finally thought to ask about Miss Beauforth and her mother.

"Oh, Marilyn spent the holidays at Alder House with Mary Trentham, and has yet to return, though we expect her daily. Lady Beauforth has gone out to visit Lady Billingsley, but should return within the hour. She will be pleased to see you, I am sure."

"I shall pay my respects as soon as Miss Beauforth returns, of course," he promised.

He knew he should take his leave, but could not quite bring himself to go. Out of the corner of his eye, he saw that the parlour door was closed. Odd that the butler had shut it with only the two of them in here. Slowly, reluctantly, he rose.

Azalea rose with him, standing closer than was strictly necessary. "Will you not stay awhile longer?" she asked softly. "I—I have yet to answer all of your questions about Virginia."

Looking down at her, seeing her so near, Christian struggled to subdue a sudden blaze of desire. He had been trying to place his courtship of her on a more conventional footing—or as conventional as was possible, considering that he was engaged to marry her cousin. But now he wanted to sweep all the niceties aside, to gather her into his arms and kiss her thoroughly, explore her.... A shudder ran through him.

"My lord?" asked Azalea softly, noticing it. She had trembled at her own boldness in asking him to stay, but had been unwilling to give up this opportunity of getting to know him better—and of attempting to make him remember.

She had feared that her forwardness might give him a disgust of her, but the look in his eyes was not one of disgust, she was certain. When he remained silent, she reached up tentatively to touch his face, but he caught her hand in his before she could do so.

Her questions abruptly fled. Now she was startled and a little frightened by the naked hunger she saw in his expression.

His eyes locked with hers and she suddenly felt a warm stirring deep within her. Was this desire? She wanted it to stop; she wanted it to intensify. Trembling, she licked her lips, needing to say something, anything to break the spell.

Without warning, she was in his arms, his mouth hungrily on hers. After a shocked instant she responded, tasting his lips, his tongue, as he tasted hers. His hands roved greedily over her body, stroking her back, sliding up her stomach, cupping her breasts. Excitement flooded through her at his touch, shocking her in its intensity.

This, *this* was what she had wanted! This would bind her to him, and him to her. Surely it meant that he remembered.

Azalea returned his kisses eagerly. Her own hands began to move, tracing the strength of his jaw, twining through his hair. She felt more than heard a groan coming from deep within him. Suddenly, he swept her up in his arms and carried her to the sofa.

She knew she should stop him. Things were going faster than she had intended. But her will would not respond to her reason. Instead, reason itself was subverted to her surging emotions.

He is my husband, a voice argued within her. *It is perfectly natural that he should love me, and that I should allow it.*

Gently, he laid her on the plush upholstery. Kissing her again, he unfastened the top button of her gown. The second button was nestled between her breasts, and as he worked it loose, he allowed his fingers to wander across her bared flesh. Azalea felt scorched where he touched her. His lips blazed a trail of fire along the side of her throat.

He is my husband.

He had one hand inside her chemise now, stroking her breast, as the other worked on the next button. She leaned her head back, marvelling at the incredible sensations coursing through her.

It is perfectly natural . . .

He had opened her gown now, and her chemise, and brought his mouth lower, fastening on one breast. Azalea gasped. His tongue teased the nipple and her body responded enthusiastically.

. . . that he should love me . . .

The phrase echoed in her mind. Marilyn's face forced its way into her consciousness like a splash of cold sea water. Suddenly, she knew why this was wrong.

Christian felt the change in her at once. Her eager, fluid movements, which had been spurring him on, beyond rational thought, were suddenly stiff, mechanical. With an effort, he drew back.

"What is it?" His voice was still husky with passion. "Did I hurt you?"

"N-no." Her voice also quivered, but whether with desire or some other emotion, he couldn't tell. "It is only . . ." She dropped her eyes.

Sanity returned to him with a crash. What on earth had he done? "Oh, God, I'm sorry," he said. "I never meant..." He stood quickly and turned away, afraid that the mere sight of her, with her gown unbuttoned and her glorious auburn hair in delicious disorder, would tempt him beyond his precarious control. His body throbbed with his need for her.

Azalea thought she understood. He was disgusted with her, now that he was able to reflect on what she had allowed him to do. He was also doubtless frustrated, for she burned with thwarted longing herself, and she had once heard that it was far worse for a man.

"I—I didn't mean—" she began tentatively, but he cut off her words, his back still turned to her.

"No, I know you didn't." His voice was harsh. "I'd better go." Without looking at her again, he strode from the parlour.

Azalea rebuttoned her dress with trembling fingers, tears of shame and frustration burning at her eyelids. So much for her plan, she thought miserably. Instead of convincing him that she was his lawful wife, she had acted like the veriest strumpet! What must he think of her at this moment?

And how could she ever tell him the truth now? After this, he would no doubt see it as a desperate attempt to manipulate him into marriage. She had spoiled everything.

Smoothing her hair into some semblance of order and blinking back the threatening tears, she picked up her embroidery in trembling fingers, feeling nearly as bereft as she had when she first learned of Christian's supposed death at sea.

THE NEXT MORNING Azalea prepared for her habitual ride with grim determination. After yesterday she doubted that Lord Glaedon would be in the Park, knowing as he did that she rode there regularly. But if he were, she would somehow have to mend her fences with him. Although any future with him now seemed hopeless, she simply had to try.

Yesterday afternoon, amid the tumult of Marilyn's return from the country and her mother's raptures at having her home, Azalea had sent another query to Mr. Timmons, hoping against hope that the old barrister might be recovered enough by now to see her. The reply, again from his wife, was negative, though she imparted the information that her husband was gradually mending.

Azalea was to have no help from that quarter then, at least at present. No, if Lord Glaedon was to acknowledge her as his wife, it was up to her to achieve it. And achieve it she must.

In contrast to yesterday's drizzle, this was a beautiful, sparkling morning, warm for January, though still crisp enough to be invigorating. In spite of herself, Azalea felt her spirits rise as she and Ginny trotted in the direction of Hyde Park. If nothing else, a ride on such a lovely morning was bound to clear the cobwebs from her brain.

It was just as well that Lord Glaedon was unlikely to be there, she thought as she rode. Suddenly, she glanced ahead and saw him, apparently waiting for her at the Park entrance. Her heart skipped a beat.

"Well met, Miss Clayton!" he called as soon as she was within earshot. "I had hoped that you would not be able to resist riding on such a fine morning."

"I ride nearly every morning, my lord, fine or not," she replied, struggling to match his casual tone. He looked impossibly handsome, his hair gleaming nearly as black as Sultan's coat.

And he was here! Surely that must mean he did not hold her in contempt for what she had done yesterday? "You—you wished to ride with me, my lord?" she managed to say.

"Christian, remember?" he reminded her, making her cheeks grow warm. "Yes, I had to come, of course. I wished to apologize for my reprehensible conduct yesterday. Is it too much to hope that you will forgive me?"

Nervously, she glanced over her shoulder at the groom, who thankfully had dropped back well out of earshot. Further back, she saw a man on foot walking slowly towards them. Even as she watched, however, the man slipped behind a tree as though he did not wish to be seen. Curious, she thought. Was her uncle having her followed?

She dismissed it from her mind, however, and turned back to Christian, a tremulous smile playing about her lips.

Though he hid it well, Christian was exerting every ounce of control he possessed to maintain his light-hearted charade. He had come to the Park in hopes of seeing Miss Clayton again, to discover whether she had forgiven him for what he had tried to do.

He had planned this morning's meeting as a sort of test, and not only of his own control in her presence, he now realized. When he had seen her approaching, he'd been gripped by a sudden fear that she would turn and ride away, never wanting to see him again.

Certainly, he deserved it. He had never been in the habit of ruining innocents. But there was something about Miss Clayton that made him forget his rigid control, which he had worked so hard to maintain since resuming his place in Society. With her, he felt far more like the rough, debauched sailor he'd been before his memory had returned. She deserved better than that.

He took her hand and kissed her fingers without a word, but as their glances met, a world of meaning was exchanged. It was as though he asked a question with his eyes and she silently answered. She had forgiven him.

"Shall we ride, then?" he finally asked. In answer, she flicked her reins, sending Ginny into a brisk trot.

As they rode, they fell back into the easy conversation they had enjoyed yesterday, before the madness had taken them both. Slowly, Azalea felt her pulse returning to normal. Still, her troubles were not completely over, she remembered.

"Marilyn came home last night," she said casually when there was a brief lull in the conversation. To her relief, Christian did not seem unduly affected by the news.

"I trust she had an enjoyable visit in the country," was all he said.

In fact, Marilyn had been in such high spirits upon her return that Azalea had greater hopes than ever that she might be falling in love with Jonathan. She had spoken only vaguely of the other guests at the house party, and Azalea had noticed a certain sparkle in her cousin's eyes whenever Jonathan's name was mentioned.

"Yes, I believe she did," she replied.

She rode in silence for a moment, gathering her courage, then very deliberately said, "Do you know, I was just noticing how very similar your Sultan is to a stallion my grandfather owned back in Virginia."

"Indeed?" He regarded her with interest, though whether because her words struck some chord of memory or simply because the talk was of horses, she could not be sure.

"Yes. Even their names are similar. Our black stallion was named Spartan."

"You don't say!" Now he appeared almost startled. "Would you believe that is what I nearly named this fellow when I bought him last year? I finally settled on Sultan because of the Arabian in his lineage."

He went on to describe Sultan's parentage, but Azalea thought that he seemed rather distracted. Clearly he still did not remember everything, but it was a start.

Once or twice during their ride she glanced back to see whether the man she had noticed earlier was still following them, but saw no sign of him. Most likely it had been a stranger simply enjoying a walk in solitude, she thought with relief. But as she left the Park after parting cordially with Christian, a shadow detached itself from the Park gates and ambled off down the street after the earl.

Back at Beauforth House, Azalea felt more than satisfied with the results of her outing. She knew without a doubt that Christian cared for her, at least a little. And she had managed to prick his memory, she thought. In time it might return in its entirety.

All would soon be straightened out, she was sure of it. Smiling into the mirror as Junie pinned up her hair, she felt almost impatient to assume her rightful place as his wife, especially now that she'd had a taste of what joys that position might involve.

Azalea hummed softly to herself as she descended to breakfast. "Isn't it a lovely morning?" she asked her cousins brightly as she entered the dining-room. Walking to the sideboard, she helped herself to a generous portion of kippers and eggs.

"Did you go riding this morning?" asked Marilyn. She obviously considered her American cousin slightly deranged to have formed the habit of being abroad at the uncivilized hour of nine o'clock, or even earlier.

"Yes, I did," answered Azalea, taking her seat and picking up her fork. "And guess who I encountered in the Park?" She had decided that her cousins might need some preparation for what was to occur.

Neither answered, so she continued. "Lord Glaedon! He is returned to Town and promised to call, probably this afternoon." For obvious reasons she had said nothing of his visit yesterday.

Rather to her surprise, Marilyn frowned. "I did not know he was to return so soon. Still, it is flattering, I suppose, that he should wish to see me immediately."

It seemed obvious to Azalea that any pleasure her cousin felt at the news was due to her vanity, and not from any real romantic attachment to Lord Glaedon. Indeed, since her return she had spoken so incessantly of Jonathan Plummer that Azalea doubted there could be much room in her head—or heart—for any other man. Still, if events went as she hoped they would, it would be a blow to Marilyn's pride.

Lady Beauforth, meanwhile, was agreeing somewhat absently with her daughter's statement, being occupied with the Society news in the *Morning Post*, which she read religiously every day lest she fall behind in the current gossip. Suddenly, she let out a strangled yelp.

"Azalea, you sly creature! Here you are, to be most heartily congratulated, and you never said a word! How wealthy you will be! Wasn't I right when I told you not to discourage him?"

Her expressive face was wreathed in smiles, but Azalea was completely mystified. She chewed quickly and swallowed.

"I am afraid I do not understand you, ma'am," she said when she was able. "Do I collect that my name is mentioned in the paper?"

"Did you not know the announcement was to go in today? Well, then, I suppose I can forgive you for not having spoken. I shall assume you meant to tell us yourself before we saw it in print." Lady Beauforth still looked enormously pleased. "Here. Perhaps you would like to see the wording yourself. He must have called here yesterday after all, though you did not say so." She handed the paper across the table.

It took Azalea a moment to find the item that had caused her cousin such joy. A wild idea struck her, and her heart began to flutter. Surely, Christian wouldn't have... Then, halfway down the page, she found it: an announcement of the betrothal of Miss Azalea Clayton to George Bemler, Viscount Drowling.

CHAPTER FOURTEEN

AZALEA STARED at the paper for a full minute in disbelief, trying to understand how that particular combination of letters and words could have come there by accident. Surely this had to be an accident! Who would intentionally play such a cruel joke on her?

Kayce!

Meanwhile, Lady Beauforth was chattering on about the place in Society Azalea would have as Lady Drowling, the balls and routs she could give, and when the wedding would likely take place.

In near panic, Azalea interrupted her in midsentence. "Cousin Alice, you do not understand! There *is* no betrothal. Lord Drowling has not offered for me, and if he had, I most certainly would have refused. I cannot imagine how this announcement comes to be in the paper at all!"

That gave Lady Beauforth pause for a moment. Then she fastened her attention on what seemed to her the most significant part of Azalea's statement.

"Why ever would you refuse him, child? Drowling is one of the wealthiest men in England. Surely you cannot hope to do better, even as Kayce's ward."

A sudden thought seemed to strike her. "Perhaps that is the answer! Everyone knows that Kayce and Drowling are very close; perhaps he applied for your hand through your uncle—and very properly, too, I may add—and has been accepted. Certainly he should have spoken to you before any announcement was made, but if Kayce approves the match, then no real harm has been done.''

''No real harm!'' exclaimed Azalea indignantly. ''Ma'am, think what you are saying! All of London will believe me betrothed to Lord Drowling now, when I am no such thing!''

And what will Christian think when he sees this outrageous announcement? she wondered frantically.

''Please, Cousin Alice, promise not to discuss this with anyone, unless to deny it, until I have seen my uncle. If, as you say, he and Lord Drowling are responsible for this, then it seems to me it should be up to them to have a retraction printed.'' And in the afternoon papers, she hoped.

''A *retraction!* Oh, Azalea, my *dear,* how scandalous! Do you wish Society to think you a fickle young lady who accepts a man one day and rejects him the next? 'Twould ruin your reputation, I vow!'' Lady Beauforth groped for her smelling salts to underscore how shocking she found such an idea.

''Better my reputation than my life, ma'am,'' replied Azalea grimly. ''And I have accepted no one. Pray have the carriage sent round. I will call on my uncle at once, in hopes of straightening this out. Do cheer up, Cousin Alice! Perhaps it is merely some prank, after all.''

Lady Beauforth seemed not at all cheered by this idea, but Azalea had already left the room to fetch her pelisse and reticule.

''Shall I have the carriage sent round, Mama?'' asked Marilyn, who had remained uncharacteristically quiet throughout the exchange.

Lady Beauforth nodded gloomily. "We can only hope that Kayce will be able to bring the girl to her senses," she said.

TWENTY MINUTES LATER, Azalea presented herself at the door of Kayce's mansion to request an interview with her uncle. Her temper had cooled somewhat during the drive, and she now wondered whether the betrothal announcement might truly be a prank, perhaps by Drowling, rather than a plot by Kayce. In any event, she would know soon enough.

After leaving her to wait in the drawing-room some ten minutes, the skeletal butler returned to inform her that her uncle would see her in the back parlour, where he was at breakfast.

Looking about her as she followed the thin, black-clad back, Azalea was relieved to find that the mansion appeared considerably less eerie by daylight. In fact, the parlour she was shown into appeared almost cheerful. A measure of the high spirits she had possessed since her ride in the Park returned—until she encountered the cool, appraising expression in her uncle's eyes.

"Good morning, my dear," said Kayce without rising from the small table. His voice seemed pleasant enough.

But as soon as the manservant had bowed himself out of the room, he continued, "I fancy your presence here at such an unseasonable hour means that you have seen a morning paper. I rather expected that you would call."

"You know about it then?" Azalea's eyes narrowed, and anger began to well up in her again, along with a cold touch of fear. "You do not seem particu-

larly surprised or upset that someone would play such
a tasteless prank on us."

"Why should I be surprised or upset at the appearance of an announcement I wrote myself?" returned
Kayce with a thin smile. "I regret the shock this may
have caused you, but I thought it best not to delay the
announcement, when the wedding is to take place so
shortly."

His matter-of-fact tone put her off her stride for a
moment and she raised her hand to her head, overcome by a sudden feeling of unreality. "Wedding? But
there has been no betrothal!"

"Indeed there has, my dear," replied Kayce calmly.
"Drowling and I have come to a *most* satisfactory arrangement on the matter."

"Without my consent?" She was aghast. "I refuse
to have anything to do with this! I do not even like
Lord Drowling, and could not marry him if I did. I intend to send a retraction to the *Post* the moment I return home." Azalea's fear was forgotten in her
indignation at this blatant manipulation of her future.

Lord Kayce, however, appeared completely unruf-
fled. "The announcement has appeared in the other
papers as well, my dear—did you not see them? In any
event, no retraction will be printed. I am your legal
guardian, and you will marry whomever I think best
suited to the position. The contracts are already drawn
up. Pray try to accustom yourself to the idea. Drowling seems to think quite a lot of you, and may even
make you happy. He is not unskilled, by all accounts."

Irresistibly, Azalea was reminded of Christian's caresses yesterday, then thought of Drowling in his place.
A wave of revulsion swept through her.

"You can hardly force me to take the vows against my will, Uncle," she said in what she hoped was a reasonable tone. "I assure you that I cannot marry Lord Drowling."

"Certainly you can."

The utter confidence in his voice alarmed her. Perhaps he *had* been the one behind the attack on Mr. Timmons. Which meant he must have the marriage proofs—and had probably already destroyed them. Something of her dismay must have shown in her face, for her uncle again smiled thinly.

"I believe you begin to understand. I wouldn't bother trying to talk Drowling out of it either, if I were you. He stands to gain almost as much as I do from the match. He appears to desire you for other, ah, reasons as well. A most eager bridegroom, in fact. You should be flattered."

Azalea hesitated. It was still just possible that she was wrong. Perhaps Lord Kayce was yet unaware of her existing marriage. If that were the case, then bringing Christian's name into the argument at this point might do more harm than good. She bit her lip, trying to decide her best course.

Kayce's glance became impatient. He disliked having his morning routine disrupted, and though he had known this scene was inevitable, he felt that everything necessary had been said. Besides, there was something in the girl's face that reminded him all too forcibly of his brother, the one person who had exerted a measure of control over him in his youth.

"There is no more to be said," he told her abruptly. "I shall send for you in a few days to discuss the wedding." She was pointedly being dismissed.

"There is quite a lot more to be said, Uncle," replied Azalea determinedly, "but I suppose it can be said later."

Without waiting for the ghoulish butler to show her out, she left the house and re-entered the waiting carriage.

ONE GLANCE AT AZALEA'S face told Lady Beauforth that Lord Kayce had not been able to change his niece's mind. Looking as grim and determined as she had an hour ago, she proceeded directly to the library upon her return, not even pausing long enough to remove her pelisse.

Although her ladyship knew it would be wiser to say nothing to her young cousin while she was in this mood, her curiosity overcame her good judgement, as it so often did. Following her into the library, Lady Beauforth attempted to find out what had gone on.

"Well, my dear, what did your uncle have to say? Was the announcement a hoax, as you thought?"

"No, Cousin Alice, it was not," Azalea stated flatly. "In fact, this whole thing is entirely my uncle's doing, and he had the effrontery to tell me that I can do nothing about it. I mean to prove him wrong." As she spoke, she was purposefully pulling paper and pen out of the writing desk.

"What—what do you intend to do?" asked Lady Beauforth fearfully.

"I intend to send a retraction to the papers—all of them. If I do so immediately, it might make the afternoon editions."

Lady Beauforth made a last, despairing effort to talk Azalea out of such a disastrous course. "But, my dear, is it not possible that your uncle knows best in this matter? After all, Lord Drowling is a brilliant match, far above what you might have expected as a virtual unknown with only whatever dowry Lord Kayce sees fit to bestow. No doubt he has been very generous on your behalf to bring this about."

Azalea was already writing and made no reply.

Encouraged by her silence, Lady Beauforth continued. "Besides, it is not as though Lord Drowling were ugly, or so very old—why, many account him quite handsome, and he is but two or three years older than I. Pray try to accustom yourself to the match, my dear—it will save so much trouble and speculation if you do. And just *think* of the fun we shall have shopping for your trousseau! No doubt Lord Kayce will forward you a substantial sum for that purpose, as he is so set on the match."

At the happy thought, Lady Beauforth looked hopefully at the girl, certain that this last consideration would sway her. She was, after all, female.

Azalea, however, merely folded up the note she had written and addressed it. "Would you mind if I had one of your footmen take this round to the papers, Cousin Alice? I'd like to have it done as soon as possible."

Lady Beauforth's face fell. "Very well," she said heavily, and rang for the footman.

Abruptly contrite, Azalea rose to give her cousin a quick hug. "Please don't worry so. Trust me. This will all turn out for the best."

Lady Beauforth felt somewhat reassured by her young charge's confident tone. She had always acted intelligently before, after all, and perhaps, just perhaps, she really did know what she was doing.

Azalea, meanwhile, prayed that her words might prove true. In reality, she felt far less confident than she sounded. If Kayce had obtained the marriage documents, she might *not* be able to persuade him to call off this horrible wedding he planned.

As the fashionable hour for afternoon callers drew near, Azalea vacillated between hope and fear that Christian would come as he had promised. Would he have seen the announcement by now? How would he react? Would he be angry? Or even worse, what if he did not care?

She would have to tell him the truth about their marriage, she had decided, whether she'd prepared the ground well enough or not. With the marriage documents gone, he was her only hope for thwarting Kayce. But when, and where, was she to do so?

She intended to deny her betrothal to anyone who would listen, so there would be no need of privacy for that, at least. Surely Christian would listen to her explanation about the announcement; and, if not, there would be the retraction tomorrow to validate it, she comforted herself. As to the other—she would at least have to wait until they were alone for *that* explanation.

Did everyone read the Society columns, as Cousin Alice asserted? Surely not. Before today, Azalea herself had scarcely ever glanced at them, though of course she knew that she was not exactly a typical member of the London *haut ton*. At any rate, the majority of the fashionable world would not be in Town until April, and by then all of this would have been long settled. But how she wished that it were settled now.

Christian did not come.

Marilyn, at least, did not seem to notice. Jonathan arrived early and stayed for tea. He was to go to his grandfather's for a few days on the morrow, and clearly wished to spend as much time as possible with Marilyn before leaving. Lady Dinsmore called as well, fairly bubbling over with congratulations on her friend's betrothal. She, it appeared, did not neglect the social news.

"My dearest Azalea, I had no idea!" she exclaimed upon her arrival. "Did all of this occur while I was gone over Christmas? I would have liked to have been the first to congratulate you, but of that I despair."

"No fear, Barbara," said Azalea wryly. "You are indeed the first, not counting Cousin Alice, but I am afraid congratulations are somewhat out of order. You see, there is no actual betrothal, and I expect a retraction to be printed on the morrow."

Lady Dinsmore looked confused. "Do you mean it was a hoax? You are not betrothed to Lord Drowling after all?"

"Yes, a hoax," answered Azalea, having decided that this would be the easiest explanation. "Lord Drowling has not even offered for me, much less been accepted. So please, if you would be so kind, if you hear anyone else speaking of it, let them know it is all a misunderstanding."

Lady Dinsmore agreed good-naturedly, although she was still a little puzzled, and turned the talk to poor Empress Josephine's famed rose gardens at Malmaison.

"I vow, I am dying to see the new tea roses from China, which reportedly bloom nearly all year round—and the centifolias smell like a bit of heaven, I hear." Their conversation revolved about this and other botanical matters until Jonathan managed to break in several minutes later.

"What did I hear you saying about a 'misunderstanding' a few minutes ago, 'Zalea?" he asked with interest. "Did someone actually put a betrothal announcement in the paper as a joke? Pretty poor taste, if you ask me."

She quietly agreed, but tried to convey with her eyes that she wished to speak to him later. Unfortunately, Jonathan had already turned back to Marilyn and missed her unspoken plea.

At least he *is not ready to believe the worst of me,* Azalea thought, vaguely comforted in spite of Christian's absence.

Throughout the afternoon and evening, several notes of congratulation and good wishes were delivered to her, some accompanied by flowers, as well as a syrupy-sweet poem from Lord Chilton, declaring his heart to be broken.

Lady Beauforth had been right, it appeared, and Azalea began to realize what an awkward situation she had been placed in. When the *Gazette* was delivered that evening, she eagerly turned to the Society news. Another announcement of her fictitious betrothal appeared there, but no retraction.

She crushed the pages between her hands in frustration. Now she would no doubt have another round of congratulations to fend off.

Why hadn't Christian come to call?

THOUGH HE HAD ALREADY done so once that day, Christian decided to ride again before nuncheon. He had an extraordinary excess of energy, he found, and needed an outlet. As it was well past noon, the Park was more crowded than it was when he took his usual morning ride. He was forced to keep Sultan to a brisk trot, exchanging cheery greetings with acquaintances he encountered.

"Well met, Glaedon!" called Lord Chilton at one point, turning his roan gelding to trot alongside.

"Servant, Chilton," said Christian pleasantly to the older man. He had never particularly cared for the dandified marquess, but he felt in charity with the world today. "Splendid day for a ride."

"Indeed," agreed the nobleman. "It's been an unusually mild winter. Hope the spring shapes up as well. By the way, when do you tie the knot with the lovely Miss Beauforth?"

Christian frowned. He had no intention of allowing the fact that he meant to break off their betrothal to become gossip before he could speak to Miss Beauforth himself. "It's not quite settled yet," he said at last. "The lady is having second thoughts, I fear."

"Oh ho! The dashing American friend of her charming cousin must be to blame, I'll warrant. My heartfelt sympathies, Glaedon. Know just how you must feel."

"Do you indeed?" Christian spoke absently, eager to end the conversation so that he could be alone with his reminiscences of the day before.

"I certainly do. I had hopes of Miss Clayton myself, pearl beyond price that she is, but I find she is out of my reach. I am quite desolate, I assure you. Should you need someone with whom to drown your sorrows, I'm your man!" He executed a half bow from the saddle, one hand melodramatically over his heart.

"I'll keep that in mind," replied Chris shortly. "Good day, Chilton." He spurred Sultan down another path and was relieved when the marquess did not follow.

It appeared that Miss Beauforth's growing attachment to Jonathan Plummer was becoming common knowledge, which was all to the good for his purposes, Christian thought. But what had Chilton meant about Azalea? Had he made her an offer and been refused?

He smiled to himself at the thought, for though Chilton's fortune was no greater than his own, his title was. Christian had been right in his estimation that Azalea was no opportunist. The circumstance gave him reason to hope, as well.

A short time later, he returned to his Town house to change before paying his promised call at the Beauforth's.

"Have Cook put a sandwich together for me before I leave, Lawrence," he said to his valet. "I have quite an appetite today, I vow."

Sitting in the library with his feet propped on a stool, a roast-beef sandwich and a mug of ale at his elbow, Christian opened the morning paper, which he hadn't taken the time to read earlier. Munching thoughtfully, he digested the political news and took note of the current prices for sheep. He would have to mention to his steward that it might be a good time to purchase another flock.

Turning the page, he started to skim past the Society news, as he usually did, when a familiar name caught his eye. He went cold inside as he read the announcement of Miss Clayton's betrothal to Lord Drowling.

Suddenly, the roast beef tasted like ashes. He took a long swig of ale to clear his mouth.

Could it possibly be true? She had said nothing of it
this morning—nor yesterday, more to the point, when
he had nearly ravished her. She had never so much as
mentioned being acquainted with Drowling—a thoroughly unsavoury character, in Christian's opinion,
despite his wealth and standing in Society. It made no
sense.

Lord Chilton's words in the Park came back to him.
An avid follower of the current gossip, he must have
been referring to this very announcement, Christian
realized.

A black rage rose up in his throat, first at Drowling,
debauched rake that he was, then at Azalea. No opportunist, he had told himself. Drowling's fortune, he
knew, was many times greater than his own.

Unthinkingly, he untied the cravat he had so carefully knotted only a few minutes earlier. Until he'd had
a chance to collect himself, he didn't dare go to see her.
Rising, he rang for more ale.

THE NEXT MORNING, even before her ride, Azalea
opened the *Post* to see if her retraction had been
printed. It had not.

Riding did little to lift her spirits. Christian was not
in the Park, and the sky was overcast, threatening rain.
Though she felt chilled both in body and spirit, she refused to give up. With renewed purpose, she decided to
visit the news offices herself.

After forcing herself to eat a quick breakfast, she
summoned the coach and departed before her cousins
could appear to question her actions. They would not
approve, she knew—especially as she also intended to
call at Lord Glaedon's Town house before returning.

She went first to the *Morning Post,* since she knew beyond doubt that the announcement had appeared there and the retraction had not. The clerk who greeted her was polite, but very definite in his answers. No, the retraction had not been printed, and would not be unless it came from Lord Kayce himself. Those were his orders, and it was not for him or even his superiors to question a man in Kayce's position.

The clerk managed to imply, without actually saying so, that he considered her a flighty young woman who could not make up her mind and who would do best to let herself be guided by her elders. Furious, Azalea departed.

Her next stop was the office of the *Morning News,* where she met with the same story. Kayce had overlooked nothing, it seemed. She demanded to see someone in charge, and was shown into a smoke-filled office occupied by a very fat man with a thick cigar and a greasy black moustache. He did not bother to rise at her entrance.

"How might I help you, missie?" he enquired insolently.

Fighting down her revulsion and indignation, Azalea explained that her betrothal announcement had been submitted by Lord Kayce without her consent and that she wanted it retracted.

"There will be no marriage," she concluded reasonably, "so it would be wrong to lead your readers to expect one."

The man, who had not given her his name, laughed loudly. "If I only printed what was true, I'd be out of business before you could so much as blink, my girl! Lord Kayce said as how something like this might happen, and paid me well to deal with it his way. There'll be no retraction.''

Azalea turned on her heel and stalked out without another word.

There seemed no point in going on to the *Gazette*. Obviously, Kayce had these fine businessmen so cowed that they were afraid to do anything that might displease him.

She would have to deal with this problem at the source. She would inform her uncle of her existing marriage, and make it plain to him that she would go public with that news if he attempted to push her into this marriage. Once that was settled, she would go to Christian and tell him everything. She would *make* him believe her!

For the second time in two days, Azalea presented herself at Lord Kayce's front door, this time demanding to see her uncle rather than politely enquiring whether he were home.

Almost to her surprise, she was shown into his presence at once, this time in the larger salon where she had greeted his guests at that dreadful dinner party nearly a month before. Kayce rose, smiling broadly.

"My dear Azalea! What an unexpected delight!" he exclaimed in his most affected manner. Oddly, his delight seemed sincere.

"Your coming here like this has saved me more trouble than you can possibly imagine," he continued, with such apparent satisfaction that Azalea began to feel more than a little uneasy. "You see, I had been racking my brains for a pretext to get you here without arousing your suspicions or those of the Beauforths. I very much wanted to avoid a scene, and was not at all sure that you would oblige me in that."

He turned to his butler, who still hovered in the doorway. "Graves, pray send a footman to Lady Beauforth's to retrieve all of my niece's belongings, and to give her this message, informing her that Miss Clayton will be my... guest until her wedding takes place. He may take Lady Beauforth's carriage, which I imagine is outside."

The butler bowed and departed, and Kayce turned back to Azalea. "I think it best, my dear, considering your recent activities and certain discoveries I have made, to keep you—ah—safe here until Lord Drowling can claim his prize. So much more convenient for all concerned, don't you agree?"

CHAPTER FIFTEEN

CHRISTIAN RAPPED SMARTLY at the front door of Beauforth House, his brisk manner concealing the uneasiness he felt at being there. Last night, and again this morning, he had made a few discreet enquiries about Town, and even at one of the newspaper offices. He had been forced to the conclusion that Azalea's betrothal to Drowling was perfectly genuine, fully sanctioned by her guardian, Lord Kayce. He had come this afternoon only because it would have been cowardly not to.

He would put a good face on it, he was determined. But somehow he hoped to discover why Azalea, whom he had thought so different from the other young ladies of the ton, had agreed to such a match—and why she had concealed it from him.

"Lord Glaedon!" exclaimed Lady Beauforth in delight when he was announced. "Azalea told us you were returned to Town. We looked to see you before this, in fact. I trust you had a pleasant Christmas and left your grandmother in good health?"

Christian assented, nodding to his fiancée as he noted that Azalea was not present. "And I trust you enjoyed your house party, Miss Beauforth?" he asked pleasantly, though it cost him to maintain his smile.

"Oh! Yes," Marilyn replied, colouring slightly. "I had quite a lively time." She lapsed into silence, but almost before he could notice the change in her manner, her mother launched herself into the breach.

"You will have heard our happy news by now, I presume?" Lady Beauforth twittered. "Our little Azalea, to be a viscountess! And such a wealthy and personable man Lord Drowling is, to be sure!"

Gritting his teeth, Christian managed a nod. "Yes, I saw the announcement in the papers. I had hoped to convey my congratulations to her."

"Oh, I fear that will not be possible," replied Lady Beauforth with a nervous laugh. "She is gone to stay with her uncle until the wedding. He...we thought that more appropriate, as she is to be married from his house."

"The wedding is to be soon then?" Christian asked, startled. No date had been mentioned in the papers.

"Yes, well, you know how impetuous these young people are," replied Lady Beauforth, fluttering her fan.

Christian raised his brows. Drowling was five and forty if he was a day, he was certain. "Then your cousin is excited about her betrothal?" He had to ask.

Marilyn looked up quickly, but before she could say anything, her mother responded, with a brilliant smile, "Why, how can she not be? Lord Drowling is such a wonderful match, and so enamoured of her, too. I wish you could have seen how attentive he was when he called on her just after Christmas."

Christian stayed only the quarter hour that politeness required before rising to take his leave. Closing the door behind him with unnecessary force, he strode quickly away from the house, with no clear destination in mind.

What had he expected? Perhaps he had been hoping that Azalea would be there to throw herself into his arms, denying her betrothal and pledging him her undying love, he thought sarcastically.

For a moment he considered calling on her at Lord Kayce's house, but quickly decided against it. It would only be an added torment to him and, perhaps, an embarrassment to her.

He had thought she was different, but it seemed she was no better than any of the other debutantes, out for whatever they could get. Christian had never cared much for the refinements of Society, which too often concealed greed and avarice under a thin veneer of polished manners and polite conversation. Now, that whole artificial world actively disgusted him.

In Azalea, he thought he had finally found someone in tune with his feelings, someone he could trust. But he had been wrong. And that was what hurt the most—he had given his trust, his friendship, and it had been betrayed.

That thought suddenly determined his destination: he would go back to Glaedon Oaks, to the one person he knew he could still trust. His grandmother had always had a remarkable talent for putting things in proper perspective. Right now, he needed her help to do just that.

He turned abruptly, to walk decisively in the direction of his Town house to fetch his horse and a few belongings. As he did so, a ragged little man jumped out of his way with a muttered oath, then turned to follow him.

LADY GLAEDON WAS delighted, though surprised, to see her grandson again so soon. It was perfectly obvious from the constraint in his manner that something was wrong, but she trusted he would confide in her eventually. In fact, as he drifted aimlessly from one piece of estate business to another during his first day at home, she began to suspect that his primary reason for returning was to talk to her.

Several times when they were alone it seemed that Christian was on the verge of saying something to her, before changing his mind and lapsing again into a morose silence.

After a full day of waiting for her grandson to tell her what was troubling him, the dowager decided that some prompting was in order.

"You may as well go ahead and speak to me, Chris," she said bluntly after dinner that evening, when the two of them had retired to her ladyship's sitting-room. "We both know that you will eventually, and the wait is doing neither of us any good. In fact, just being around you in this mood has my nerves nearly as frazzled as yours plainly are."

Christian looked up sharply with a forbidding frown, then nodded ruefully. "I never could keep a secret from you, ma'am. You are perfectly right. I came here to ask your advice and to seek comfort, but my pride has kept me from doing so. Has it been so obvious?"

"To me, at any rate," replied the dowager. "I take it that your wooing of Miss Clayton has gone less than successfully?" She held her breath, hoping the question would not bring a storm down upon her head.

"Deuce take it, madam, *can* you read my mind?" exclaimed Christian in astonishment.

"When a young man leaves for Town determined to bring back a bride, then returns less than a week later without her, it hardly takes supernatural powers to deduce that his courtship has received a setback. Not a permanent one, I hope? I very much liked what you told me of the girl." And what she had discovered through her own brief research into Miss Clayton's family history, she added silently.

"Quite permanent, ma'am," replied Christian morosely. "And I fear the girl's character was not nearly so shining as I painted it."

He proceeded to tell the dowager of the announcement in the papers. "I was nearly certain that she cared for me." He decided against mention of the kisses that they had shared just three days ago in Lady Beauforth's parlour. "I was on the point of making her an offer, in fact. I had high hopes of extricating myself from Miss Beauforth, as she has lately shown an interest in someone else. Now I may as well marry her after all, I suppose."

The dowager grew thoughtful. She knew how headstrong her grandson could be if his pride or honour were pricked; and she was aware that much more than honour was at stake here.

"Did she give you no explanation? Why was her association with Drowling not generally known, if he were on the point of offering for her? Did you not press her for the details?"

"I had no chance. When I called, she had already left Lady Beauforth's to reside with her uncle. I saw no particular reason to call upon her there. Besides," he continued angrily, "I understand her motivation well enough. Drowling's fortune is great enough to make me seem a pauper in comparison—it is said that he owns a tenth of England! Mere affection, even were it genuine, could scarce compete with that." He lapsed back into sullen silence.

"So you never bothered to hear her side of the story," concluded the dowager drily. "Is it not possible that the betrothal was not her idea at all? Perhaps she was sent to stay with her uncle because she was resistant to the idea."

Christian's head came up at that, a glimmer of hope in his eyes. "Do you think it possible, ma'am?" Then the hope faded. "But Lady Beauforth made it quite clear that Azalea was pleased with the match. She told me that she had gone to her uncle because she was to be married from his house. And that is another thing. Azalea never even mentioned to me that she was Kayce's niece. I discovered that from her grandfather's letters."

"I can't say it's a relationship *I* would care to admit to," said the dowager tartly. "You say she herself never actually confirmed the betrothal to you?" she prodded, an ugly suspicion beginning to form in her mind.

He shook his head. "I never spoke to her after learning of it. But Lady Beauforth—"

"A shatter-brained female if ever there was one," said the dowager with a snort. "She would believe whatever Kayce wished her to, I have no doubt." She leaned forward, putting a hand on her grandson's knee. "Consider this. Perhaps there *is* a betrothal, but Miss Clayton had no hand in it."

It was Christian's turn to snort. "Azalea does not strike me as a young lady who would allow such meddling without a fight, Grandmother. She is not a particularly, ah, biddable girl."

"Precisely why her uncle might wish to have her where he can control her," exclaimed his grandmother triumphantly. "Kayce has been a scoundrel since boyhood, and hardly a man I would trust as guardian to an innocent young lady, be she his niece or not."

"Do you think she could actually be in some danger, ma'am?" Christian suddenly sat up straighter, apparently ready now to take up the role of White Knight.

"No *physical* danger, most likely," the dowager replied in a tone that deliberately implied other threats. "Was a wedding date mentioned in the paper?"

"No, but Lady Beauforth implied that it was to be soon."

"Then time may be running out for you to counter Drowling's claim on her."

"Whatever his claim, I won't allow her to be forced to marry against her will," vowed Christian, in a tone that boded ill for Lord Kayce. The dowager smiled to herself.

"Of course not, my dear," she said soothingly. "Now, if you would be so kind as to set up the table, I could fancy a game of piquet." She realized that her best course of action would be to let Christian mull over their conversation. She would be very surprised if he did not find some pressing reason to return to Town on the morrow.

Christian did indeed think over that conversation—many times, in fact—during a long and sleepless night. Could his grandmother's theory be correct? Might Kayce have forced Azalea into a betrothal against her will?

The dowager's carefully chosen words tormented him until, in the wee hours of the morning, he felt ready to race back to London at that very instant to assure himself of Azalea's safety. He burned to pro-

tect her with his name, to comfort her with his words,
his body....

The only thing that prevented him from leaving at
once was the possibility that the betrothal was genuine. What a fool he would look then! Still, by the time
he fell into a dreamless sleep just before dawn, he had
resolved to return directly after breakfast. Better to risk
looking like a lovesick idiot than to allow Azalea's
life—and his own—to be ruined by his own mistaken
pride and jealousy.

He acquainted the dowager with his intentions over
a late breakfast and was surprised at his grandmother's reaction. She seemed to have expected his decision.

"You must do whatever you think best, of course,
Christian," was all she said.

They were just rising from the table when an interruption occurred. Semple, the butler, entered with the
information that there was a "person" below request-
ing an interview with Lord Glaedon. Christian felt a
sudden certainty that it was Azalea herself, come to
explain everything and to beg for his protection against
her uncle.

"Is it a young lady, Semple?" he asked eagerly, already starting for the door.

"No, my lord, a man. And not very young," replied that worthy with a lack of expression that somehow conveyed his disapproval. "I would never have
admitted him, but he said that you would remember
him. He gave his name as Luke Sykes." He spoke the
syllables with distaste.

Christian experienced a sharp stab of disappointment. Just for a moment, he had been so sure... The
visitor's name meant nothing to him, in spite of his

message to the butler. Still, he would have to see him, he supposed.

"If you will excuse me for a moment, ma'am?"

The dowager, equally curious, nodded. "Let me know what it is about, Chris. I could do with some diversion."

When Christian saw the scarecrow figure that awaited him in the front parlour, he understood Semple's reservations. The man was short and wiry, with a shock of brownish hair and several day's growth of stubble on his chin. He was dressed in sailor's garb, little better than rags, and his bleary eyes and red nose proclaimed his fondness for drink. Christian was almost certain he had never seen him before, though there *was* something vaguely familiar about him.

The man rose eagerly at his entrance and stepped forward with a gap-toothed smile. "Thank ye, my lord, I knew ye wouldn't turn me away, after all the trouble I had to track ye down," the scruffy little man exclaimed in delight. He seemed to expect Christian to recognize him on sight.

"Mr.—ah—Sykes?" said the earl uncertainly. "You have some business with me, I collect?" A nasty suspicion began to form. Could this old sailor know him from his days aboard the *Angel* or the *Hyacinth* and have come to blackmail him?

Certainly, there were details about that time that he would not care to have come to light. More than anything right now, however, Christian begrudged the time—time he was losing in getting to Azalea. But he would have to hear the sailor out. Perhaps the man was no more than a common beggar, with some cleverly spun tale of woe.

"Ye don't remember me then, me lord?" the man asked, apparently disappointed. "I feared that were the case when ye went past me in Lunnon, day before yesterday. 'Twas the first time I got a good-enough look at ye to be sure of who ye was, and then ye went and left for the country straight off. Devil of a time I had gettin' here, too." He stroked the stubble on his chin. "I guess I *has* changed a bit, and not for the better, since ye see'd me last. But I thought certain ye'd not forget old Luke what saved yer life!"

"My life?" asked Christian sceptically. "And when might this have been?"

"Why, nigh on six years ago, me lord, out o' the wreck of the *Fortitude* afore we was picked up by that filthy slaver, Farris. Course, ye didn't know yer own name then, nor did I. 'Twas just by chance I found out who the lad was that I saved, and that just a couple o' months ago. I been trying to find ye ever since, hoping ye might see fit to reward old Luke for the little favour I done ye."

He had the earl's full attention now. The man certainly had some of the facts straight—but he could be anyone who had been aboard that slave ship. Christian said as much to the fellow.

"I suppose ye be right, me lord, seein's how ye don't remember me face. I didn't recognize yours right off, neither—I had to follow ye about Lunnon a bit, to be sure. But there must be some way to convince ye. Let's see—do ye remember how Captain Whitten of the *Fortitude* used to yank on his beard when he got riled? Thick red beard he had. No one on the *Angel*—what a name for a slaver, eh?—would know that. The captain was lost afore they ever found us." He watched Lord Glaedon expectantly.

"Whitten . . . The *Fortitude* . . . I do remember a red beard. But surely the captain's name was Taylor, and the ship the *Artemis*. I'm certain the captain who told me about the colonies was Taylor, and dark haired." Christian was becoming more confused instead of less.

"Aye, I remember back then ye kept saying something about a Captain Taylor. There weren't no Taylor, captain or crewman, aboard the *Fortitude,* that's certain. But ye say ye remember the beard. If so, ye must remember the storm, at least!"

At Glaedon's blank look, he continued. "We was two er three weeks out of Virginia, almost halfway to England, when it broke. It started with that dead calm under a funny-colour sky, then the thunder started rumbling, and almost afore we could batten down the hatches, the wind was on us! The chickens got swept overboard first thing, then we lost two crewmen—one was that tall, skinny fellow with the squeaky voice, do you recollect him?"

Christian nodded vaguely. He was thinking very hard, snippets of old nightmares swimming into focus and then retreating.

"Anyways, we ran afore that wind for two days, losing bits and pieces of the ship as we went. Finally, we was too bad hurt to stay afloat and started to go down. You and me and Jacob got into one of the boats, but Jacob got washed over by a wave, so then it was just you and me. Ye won't remember that part, though, 'cause ye was out cold—a spar knocked ye in the head, I think. Lucky for us, the wind died down a few hours later, but there weren't nothing left of the *Fortitude* that I could see. A couple days later the *Angel* picked us up. Ye was awake, but real dizzy. Neither of us hadn't had no water for prob'ly three days by then."

At this point Christian interrupted his narrative. "Wait, wait! I'm remembering all of this, I think. I certainly remember the chickens going over the side. But you said we were halfway to England? Don't you mean *from* England?"

Sykes looked at him strangely. "Ye never did remember it all, did ye? That must have been a worse knock on the head than I thought. No, we sailed out of port in Hampton, Virginia, in America. Not a real big town, but busy, and with plenty of amusements for sailors with time and a bit o' money on their hands. There was a big church tower in sight of the docks—red brick it was...."

Suddenly, Christian could see that church tower and the buildings surrounding it. He could hear the sound of the bell and...he could see another church, this one of grey stone. The day was bright, but the interior of the church was dim. There were only a few people in it: his father, the rector of the church performing the ceremony and, at his own side, a young girl with bright red curls under a lace veil.

With a suddenness that nearly sent him reeling, full memory returned—the remainder of his westward voyage, his meeting with thirteen-year-old Azalea, their marriage, everything. He sat down abruptly, trying to grasp it all.

Luke Sykes had stopped speaking, and was looking at the young nobleman before him in concern. "Be ye all right, me lord?" he asked tentatively. "Shall I fetch someone to bring ye some water or brandy, like?"

Christian looked at him dazedly. "I am fine, Mr. Sykes, perhaps for the first time in six years. You shall certainly have that reward—you have earned it twice over now!"

CHAPTER SIXTEEN

WITHIN THE HOUR, Christian set off for London at a pace a less skillful driver would never have attempted. He was determined to get to the bottom of the deception Azalea had been practising on him since her arrival in London.

Though *he* might have forgotten that they were married due to the injuries he had sustained in the shipwreck, *she* had no such excuse. Remembering certain looks and words she had sent his way, he knew it must have been on her mind from the first. Why hadn't she told him at once? He intended to find out.

Briefly, he had acquainted the dowager with all of the particulars of his suddenly recovered memory. She was at first astonished and then relieved. For the past two years she had been aware that something had been haunting Christian, and now she hoped that his ghosts could be laid to rest.

"Of course, you must speak to her at once, Chris," she agreed. "If she is indeed your countess, you must bring her here as soon as everything is settled. There must be records, if there was truly a wedding, which obviously there was," she continued quickly, encountering Christian's glance. "Those records may well be in America, I suppose." She had chuckled then. "This will be quite a setback for Kayce. I wish I could be there to see his face when you arrive!"

Christian could not help but feel that his grandmother was taking the situation a little too lightly, but he was at least relieved that she appeared more supportive than shocked. Somehow, he thought that she and his bride would deal very well together... if he didn't throttle Azalea first.

Now, he almost laughed at the anguish he had felt at "sullying" the innocent Azalea with his caresses. She was an innocent, there was no doubt of that, but to think that all along she had been his wife—and that she knew it perfectly well. Her lack of resistance was one more thing his full knowledge of the past explained. Well, he would show her boldness and more when he saw her next!

It was late afternoon when Christian pulled up in front of Beauforth House, where he meant to make enquiries before proceeding to Lord Kayce's. After a great deal of thought during the day's drive, he felt he now partially understood Azalea's reluctance to mention their marriage, when he himself had been so obviously unaware of it.

He had also rehashed each and every detail of their last conversation in the Park, and was now convinced that Azalea had not willingly entered into any betrothal. In only a few moments he would know for certain, he told himself, striding up to the front door.

"Is Miss Clayton in?" he asked the butler the moment the door opened.

"No, my lord," came the expected answer. "Shall I announce you to Lady Beauforth?" At the earl's curt nod, Smythe showed him into the front parlour with an expression suspiciously like relief on his normally passive face. "Perhaps now something will be done,"

Christian heard him mutter under his breath as he went
to make his lordship's presence known.

"Lord Glaedon!" exclaimed Lady Beauforth eagerly as she came into the parlour a few moments later,
her hands fluttering nervously. "One of the very people I was hoping to see! Perhaps you can offer me advice, for I am very nearly certain that something is not
quite right. But I was unsure what I could do about it
even if that were the case, for Kayce is her guardian,
after all. But maybe nothing is truly wrong, in which
case I would feel terribly foolish for interfering! I
would have asked Mr. Plummer, except he is out of
Town. But, of course, you understand." She dropped
into the chair closest to him and fanned herself vigorously.

"No, ma'am, I am afraid I do not understand at
all," said Christian more severely than he had intended. Lady Beauforth's disjointed manner had never
been more irritating. "When I was here last, if you recall, you told me that Miss Clayton was excited about
her upcoming nuptials. Are you now saying that she is
in some sort of trouble? What has Kayce done to her?"

"Well, nothing, so far as I know," said Lady Beauforth, twisting her fan in her hands. "She is staying
with him until the wedding, as I told you before, but I
fear that I did deceive you a bit on one point. She was
not at all pleased with the betrothal, I fear. At the time
I thought I was acting for the best, but now..."

"I think you had better tell me the whole, madam,"
said Christian, striving for patience he did not feel.
"Start with the betrothal announcement. You say that
it was not Azalea's idea?"

"Oh, no, she was most surprised, even angry, I fear,
that it had gone in. Apparently it was all her uncle's

doing, and I must admit it seemed odd at the time that he would not consult her first, even though Lord Drowling *is* such a good match. I do know that she sent retractions to all of the papers, but they never appeared in print. At least not in the *Post*, which is the only one I seem to find time to read."

Distractedly, she moved from the chair she'd been sitting in to the sofa, and motioned him to sit opposite. "And?" he prompted, seating himself on the edge of the chair indicated.

"Yes, I suppose that is neither here nor there. At any rate, on the morning of the day you last called, Azalea went out without telling anyone where she was going, and the next thing I knew I had received a message from Lord Kayce saying that in the interests of convenience, she would be staying with him until the wedding, which is apparently to take place much sooner than anyone told me about." Lady Beauforth paused to catch her breath.

"When?" snapped the earl. "When is the wedding taking place?"

"Why, as I just said, no one has told me anything. I've practically acted as a mother to the girl these few months past, too! I have sent a note around twice asking Azalea for particulars, and whether she wants my help in selecting her trousseau—her uncle is hardly the one she would prefer for that sort of help, I am certain—and all I have received in reply is a formal note from Kayce saying that poor Azalea is too busy at present to answer her correspondence. So, as I said at the first, I am beginning to worry, for it is not at all like her to ignore me. She has always been most considerate and sweet-tempered with me."

"Could Kayce be keeping her prisoner, do you think?" asked Christian sharply. Why had this shatter-brained female not done something the day Azalea disappeared?

"That is precisely what I am beginning to fear," answered Lady Beauforth worriedly. "At first, I thought that perhaps it was for her own good, as she kept declaring that she would never marry Drowling no matter what arrangements had been made. I thought she was merely being headstrong, as young people are wont, and that her uncle likely knew best. Such a good match, you understand, my lord! *Much* better than she could have hoped for in the ordinary way."

At Lord Glaedon's scowl, Lady Beauforth broke off uncertainly, before continuing in a slightly different vein.

"Anyway, the more I thought about it, the more wrong it seemed. Azalea really has become almost a daughter to me, and not for the world would I wish to see her truly unhappy in marriage. I fear her temperament is such that even great wealth may not compensate for her dislike of Lord Drowling. And so I would like your advice. Do you see any way that I might help poor Azalea? Without creating any sort of scandal, of course," she added hastily.

"Lady Beauforth, I believe you can leave this entirely to me. Was there any man of business—a solicitor, perhaps—with whom Azalea has consulted since her arrival in London?"

"Why, yes, a Mr. Timmons," replied Lady Beauforth in surprise. "Why?"

"Do you have his direction, by chance?" Lord Glaedon was becoming more impatient by the moment to be gone. He must not arrive too late!

"Well, I did at one time.... Ah! The coachman will know," said her ladyship, increasingly bewildered. "He drove her there more than once."

"Thank you, I'll speak to him on my way out. I shall be in touch with you on the matter shortly." Christian rose to depart.

At that moment, Marilyn hurried into the room. She was stunningly dressed in a powder blue gown that matched her eyes to perfection, but Christian scarcely noticed.

"Mother, Smythe told me ... Oh! You are still here! Good afternoon, my lord."

Christian nodded curtly, impatient to be gone. "Your servant, Miss Beauforth." He took a step towards the door, but Marilyn stopped him.

"Might—might I have a word with you, Lord Glaedon—in private?"

"Marilyn, Lord Glaedon is in something of a hurry just now, I'm afraid," put in Lady Beauforth, to Christian's relief. "Perhaps later—"

"But Jonathan will be back tomorrow, and I promised to speak to Lord Glaedon before then," protested Marilyn, earning a startled look from her mother and a frown from the earl. "And you have been from Town as well, my lord." She turned back to Christian accusingly.

He sighed and sat back down, realizing that he might as well get his unpleasant business with Miss Beauforth out of the way, as well.

Before he could speak, however, she hurried on, with a distracted glance at her mother. "It—it is about our betrothal, my lord. You see, I have thought much about it and I fear that—that we should not suit."

"Marilyn, my angel, have a care!" interjected Lady Beauforth, but her daughter shook her head.

"No, Mother, I am persuaded that I will not be happy as Lady Glaedon. You see, it is Jonathan that I love!" She turned apologetically to Christian, who was striving to conceal a smile. "I am so sorry to break your heart in this way, my lord, but I pray you can become reconciled to losing me. You would not wish me to marry you when I love another, would you?"

Manfully, Christian kept his expression serious. The fishlike opening and closing of Lady Beauforth's mouth did not make it any easier.

"Certainly I cannot hold you to our betrothal under the circumstances, Miss Beauforth. You may consider it at an end. And now, I really must be going." He nodded to both ladies and strode quickly from the room.

"He took it remarkably well," Marilyn commented after he had gone. "Doubtless he wished to leave before he could betray what he truly felt. Men do not care to express their sorrow publicly, I have noted."

Lady Beauforth finally found her voice. "My love, do you realize what you have just done?" she wailed. "You would have been a countess!"

"I have discovered that there is more to life than being a countess, Mother," replied Marilyn loftily. "I do feel badly for poor Glaedon, though. And after he came directly to see me first thing on returning to Town."

"Actually, my dear, I believe he came to speak to Azalea," returned Lady Beauforth somewhat distractedly, trying to sort out everything that had just occurred.

"Indeed?" asked Marilyn in surprise. "I thought...
Oh, well, no matter. What do you think of this dress,
Mother? Jonathan—er, Mr. Plummer—is due back
from his grandfather's estates tomorrow, and I thought
I would wear this when he comes to call." She pirou-
etted for her mother's evaluation.

"What? Oh, very nice, my love," said Lady Beauforth, scarcely looking at her. Oddly, she discovered
that Marilyn's broken betrothal did not upset her as
much as the thought of Azalea's possible danger. What
could Lord Glaedon possibly do for her? And would
he be in time?

AZALEA RAISED HERSELF on one elbow and shook her
head, trying to clear the fog from her brain. How much
time had passed since her uncle had imprisoned her in
this sumptuous bedroom?

She clearly remembered arriving at Kayce's Town
house, and that she had tried to leave after he informed her that she was to be his "guest" until the
wedding. Two footmen—fancy names, she thought,
for hired thugs—had blocked the front door, while
Kayce told her she had a choice between being carried
to her chamber and being escorted to it. She had chosen the latter only because open resistance would obviously do her no good, whereas a show of submission
might.

After a day spent in thoughtful solitude, she had
decided that there was only one sure way to avert her
uncle's plan. She must inform him of her marriage to
the Earl of Glaedon, much as she wanted to tell Christian first. If Kayce already knew of it, as she feared he
must, she would threaten to make it public. She felt,

however, that her words would carry more weight if she were to free herself first.

That night, after all was quiet in the house, she climbed down the tree outside her second-storey window. How she would love to see her uncle's face when he received her note from Lady Beauforth's in the morning, she thought.

But this hopeful scheme was not to be. Kayce had evidently been suspicious of his niece's uncharacteristic compliance and had posted a guard in the garden below her window. The man had seized her before her feet touched the ground and dragged her ignominiously back into the house through a rear entrance.

When called to the scene, Kayce had chuckled at her obvious chagrin and had ordered her window to be locked, leaving before she could gather her wits sufficiently to decide what she ought to tell him.

The next morning he had allowed her to descend and join him at breakfast, where he had conversed on general topics as though absolutely nothing were amiss. She had decided on stubborn silence rather than threats that might endanger Christian—she remembered the man she had seen following him—but her uncle had completely ignored her.

Finally, she had decided to devote herself to the excellent breakfast set before her on the rationale that if she were ever to make good her escape from this monster, she would need her strength.

Apparently, that had been a mistake.

She realized now that something in glass or plate must have contained a drug, for it was at that point that her memory failed. All she could recall after that were hazy images of being carried back to her bed, of being fed and ministered to at intervals by a large, grey-

haired woman with a deep voice, and of disjointed
sentences being spoken over her by Kayce and this
woman, who was presumably some sort of nurse. Now,
she tried to organize her confused thoughts, to remember anything that they had said, feeling vaguely
that it might be important—but she could not.

At that moment, Azalea heard voices outside her
chamber door and the rattle of a key in the lock. Hoping to discover something of use, she closed her eyes to
feign sleep. She heard two sets of footsteps enter the
room, one heavier than the other, and then detected a
glow against her closed eyelids. Presumably, the bedside lamp had been lit.

"Still sleeping, my lord," said the deep female voice
she remembered. "Shall I give her another dose to be
safe?" Before Azalea could begin to plan some way to
avoid swallowing the drug, Kayce's voice responded.

"No, I think not. We can hardly have an unconscious bride, after all. Check in on her periodically, and
when she begins to stir, give her just enough to keep her
quiet without putting her back to sleep. I have paid the
clergyman well, but he still might baulk if she were to
protest too violently during the ceremony. We certainly don't want any repetitions of those claims to a
previous marriage she was ranting about earlier, even
if they were mere fancies brought on by the drug. Report to me when she wakes."

"Yes, my lord," replied the woman, as Kayce's
footfalls receded.

Azalea forced herself to remain limp as the big
woman turned her body from side to side, washing her
and changing the cotton shift she wore.

She had told her uncle of her marriage? She had no
recollection of it. Had she mentioned Lord Glaedon

my name? Had her uncle obtained the marriage proofs, as she had feared? Or was he merely hiding that fact from this servant? She had no way of knowing.

The woman completed her ministrations and left, and Azalea cautiously opened her eyes again. The door and window were no doubt still locked, and she was not at all certain that she could walk yet, in any event. Experimentally, she tried to sit up in bed, and the room rocked crazily about her. No, even standing would be impossible for the present. She would try again later. In the meantime, she could at least think through her situation.

Why had Lady Beauforth not come to enquire about her? Of course, she very well might have, Azalea realized, and been fobbed off by some story of Kayce's. She would have to assume that there would be no help from that quarter. Lady Beauforth had always been strongly in favour of a match with Drowling anyway, and would hardly work to prevent it.

What about Marilyn then, or, better yet, Jonathan? She was positive that he would help her if she could somehow get word to him. But, then again, he would know no more of her situation than the Beauforths did—he might not even be in Town. Hadn't he been about to leave for his grandfather's estates the last time he called? Who else might possibly help her?

Involuntarily, her thoughts turned to Christian. If only she had gone to him and explained everything before coming here! He had called himself her friend, and had implied much, much more. And somehow Azalea knew that he would have no trouble dealing with Kayce and Drowling if he chose to do so.

But such fantasies were pointless. By now he would think that she had entered into a betrothal with

Drowling willingly, since that was doubtless what Lady Beauforth would tell people. Even if she were somehow to escape, what could she do? Go to him and tell him that she was his wife? Undoubtedly he would laugh and shut the door in her face. She could never bear that!

No, she would return to America, she decided. Even if her uncle somehow forced her to go through with this wedding—which would not be a true one, she consoled herself—they could hardly keep her under guard for the rest of her life. Somehow, she would eventually escape and make her way back, if not to Williamsburg, then at least to the New World, where no one would know of her humiliation here in England. If she could not have Christian's love, then she would take the secret of their marriage with her to the grave.

And that was another option, she suddenly realized. While her conscience recoiled at the sinful idea of suicide, a practical voice somewhere in her still-fuzzy mind told her that it would be infinitely preferable to a marriage with Drowling.

Thrusting that thought hastily aside, to be considered again only if no other solution presented itself, Azalea forced herself to prepare arguments that would convince the clergyman—even a well-paid clergyman—that a wedding ceremony could not take place.

By the time she again heard footsteps, she had composed a speech, to be delivered at the altar, if necessary, that she was nearly certain would free her, at least temporarily. She again pretended sleep, hoping to avoid another dose of whatever she had been given. Only if she were fully in control of her faculties would she be able to convince the clergyman not to perform the ceremony.

So far, her ruse appeared successful. The woman merely looked closely at Azalea and shook her gently by the shoulder before leaving the room.

It might have been two hours later when the door reopened. By now, Azalea had managed a brief walk about the room and was fairly certain that she had shaken off most of the effects of the drug. As before, she appeared to be sound asleep when her uncle and his henchwoman entered.

"Time grows short," said Kayce impatiently. "Surely she should be awake by now?"

"Aye, she should, my lord," replied the woman. "Mayhap we gave her a bit too much last time. She's smaller than anyone I've dosed before."

"Well, let's sit her up and see if we can bring her to. If possible, I'd like to have some conversation with her before the wedding."

Curiosity almost caused Azalea to open her eyes. What could Kayce wish to speak to her about? Should she try to convince him one last time, or would it be safer to pretend to be drugged until she could talk to the clergyman?

The beefy arm of her erstwhile nurse raised her into a sitting position while Kayce's footsteps receded across the room, then returned. Before Azalea could decide how to react, the decision was made for her—cold water was unexpectedly flung in her face.

She gasped and sputtered from the shock of it, her eyes flying open in astonishment.

"There!" said Kayce in evident satisfaction. "That was easy enough. Now, my dear, as soon as you have your wits about you, we must have a talk."

Azalea glared at him, forgetting in her anger that she should pretend to be still under the influence of the drug. "May I have a robe first?" she asked icily, glancing down at her wet cotton shift, which clung to her body in a most immodest manner.

Kayce nodded to the nurse, who brought Azalea's own velvet wrapper, apparently transported from Lady Beauforth's during her long sleep. Pulling it closely about her, she looked defiantly at her uncle.

"Well?" She knew she should try to placate Kayce somewhat if she were to talk him out of his plans, but she was simply too angry at the moment to care. "What do you need to say that necessitated waking me in such a manner?"

"You seem to be in complete possession of your senses," said Kayce, with a significant glance at the nurse. "Perhaps now you will tell me what your ravings about a previous marriage signified."

So he did not have the marriage papers! thought Azalea triumphantly. She thought she could see an easy way out of her predicament now.

"I had intended to inform you of it, dear Uncle, had you but given me a chance," she said with false sweetness. "I did, if you recall, tell you that a marriage with Lord Drowling was impossible, but you did not believe me."

Kayce's eyes narrowed. "And who is this alleged husband? Some American commoner whom you abandoned to seek your fortune—or rather, my fortune—in England? Is he here to step forward and claim you?" Disbelief showed openly in his face.

"Hardly that, Uncle," retorted Azalea, stung. "Lord Glaedon is no commoner, nor is he in America. And he *will* be here to claim me—in time to stop this ridiculous marriage you want so badly." She knew this last was a lie, but prayed that Kayce would believe it.

He did not.

"Yes, I knew about your partiality for Glaedon—your meetings in the Park have been reported to me. But my sources also tell me that he is presently in the country with his dear grandmama."

Kayce's features twisted with dislike; the dowager had given him more than one public set-down over the years.

"A pretty story, my dear, but most improbable. I fail to see why either of you should have desired a secret wedding. Where are the marriage papers? Why was there no announcement? And what of the small matter of his betrothal to your cousin, Miss Beauforth?"

Azalea's sudden confidence began to crumble. Without any proof, her story of a wedding in Williamsburg when she was but thirteen sounded absurd even to herself. The only person in England who could corroborate her tale was Mr. Timmons, and as far as she knew he was still bedridden.

At her silence, Kayce smiled unpleasantly. "I thought as much. No, my dear, it will take more than such a fable to change my plans. And I warn you—one word of this during the ceremony and I might have to arrange an unpleasant, ah, accident for young Glaedon."

He smiled as Azalea's eyes widened in horror. "I shall return for you shortly. Mrs. Melkin," he said, turning toward the nurse, "help her to dress."

The wedding gown Mrs. Melkin held up was beautiful, but did not serve to distract her a whit. Somehow, she must get out of this!

Since there was obviously no chance of overpowering the massive nurse, Azalea allowed herself to be fastened into the exquisite dress without a word, hoping that some opportunity for escape would present itself after she left the bedchamber.

True to his word, Kayce returned in less than an hour to escort her downstairs to a large room at the rear of the house—the dining-room, she realized, with the table removed and the chairs placed along one wall. Drowling was there, along with the skinny butler and a man she assumed was the clergyman. If anything, he appeared even less sympathetic than the others, she thought despairingly.

Drowling turned to smile at her, but there was more lust than affection in his glance. His look made her skin crawl, and Azalea suppressed a shudder, knowing that he would give up no more easily than her uncle would.

As if in a nightmare, she allowed Kayce to guide her to her place at Drowling's side.

Now? Should she deliver that carefully prepared speech? But what of Kayce's threat? Azalea had no doubt whatsoever that he was capable of carrying it out. She could not risk Christian's safety, or possibly his life, even to stop this travesty of a wedding.

Oh, Chris, where are you now? she moaned silently to herself.

AFTER DRIVING AT A reckless pace through the dark London streets, Christian finally drew to a halt a few doors down from Lord Kayce's Town house. He did not wish to call attention to his presence just yet. For the sake of Azalea's safety, he thought it might be wiser to discover all that he could before pounding down Kayce's front door.

Proceeding on foot, he went around to the rear of the house to check the stables, hoping to gain some useful information there. Sure enough, drawn up outside them was a handsome travelling carriage with a crest on the side that he recognized as Lord Drowling's. Here to visit his reluctant bride, was he?

Though not well-acquainted with the man, Christian had developed a dislike for Drowling after an occasion several months before when he had found him in a tavern forcing his attentions on a terrified young serving wench. The idea of that bully laying so much as a finger on Azalea made his blood boil.

Just then, a stable-lad came out of one of the stalls and stopped short when he saw a stranger, obviously one of the nobility, standing there. Plainly unsure of his responsibilities in this circumstance, he came forward hesitantly.

"How can I help you, guv'nor?" the boy asked in as deep a voice as he could muster.

"With information, my good man," answered Christian with a wink.

When the boy hesitated, he reached into his pocket and brought out a gold guinea. "This is yours, if you can help me," he said, flipping it expertly into the air and catching it again.

The lad's eyes gleamed as he watched the glinting coin. He was only an under stable-boy, and had never possessed so much money in his life as this liberal stranger was offering. Lord Kayce was not so generous that he commanded unswerving loyalty from his lower servants.

"What might you be wanting to know, milord?" asked the boy, suddenly respectful.

"Who is within with Lord Kayce right now?"

"Just the swell what owns this coach and the parson, milord," answered the boy eagerly, his eyes never leaving the guinea.

"No one else?" asked Christian sharply.

"Oh, there's the young lady, the master's cousin or niece or some such," replied the lad, "but she's been here since day before yesterday. I thought you just meant whose horses was here."

"Thank you. A parson, you said?" The boy nodded. "Does he come here often?"

The lad had to stifle a laugh. "Never before that I've see'd, milord. Lord Kayce ain't exactly the church-goin' type, if you take my meaning."

"I understand," said Glaedon. "Then what might he be doing here now?"

"Oh, I reckon he's to do the wedding, milord. The young lady be going to marry that swell as I mentioned. Harry, the groom, told me so."

Christian was already striding toward the house. "Thank you, my lad, you have earned this." He tossed the guinea over his shoulder and the boy caught it with a grin and stowed it in his pocket. It was by far the easiest money he had ever earned.

Walking softly now, Christian approached the kitchen entrance. No one seemed to be around, but he had no desire to raise the alarm prematurely. He peered into the scullery: empty. Closing the door silently behind him, he passed swiftly through the kitchens and into the passageway beyond, then stopped. He could hear voices behind the door on his left and pressed his ear to it, trying to make out the words.

CHAPTER SEVENTEEN

"MISS CLAYTON?" asked the acerbic clergyman with increasing annoyance.

Azalea knew she was supposed to be repeating his words at this point in the ceremony, but could not bring herself to speak, regardless of the threat Kayce held over Christian. Instead, she looked first pleadingly, then defiantly at her uncle. He could force her to stand here, but not to repeat wedding vows!

Kayce returned her look with a frown. "She does," he said firmly.

The harassed cleric looked from the defiant girl before him to the man who had paid him so well to perform this wedding. Really, this was most irregular! Still, for fifty pounds... "Very well," he said. "And do you, Lord Drowling—"

"I do not!" broke in Azalea, speaking just as firmly as her uncle had.

"A moment, please," said Kayce with deceptive pleasantness. He pulled his niece aside and beckoned to Mrs. Melkin, who had been standing unobtrusively in the background. "Must we drug you again, my dear? I had thought concern for young Glaedon would ensure your cooperation, but I am prepared to take other measures."

"What I told you is true, Uncle," said Azalea grimly. "Even if I say the vows, this marriage will not be legal. I swear it upon my life."

Kayce glanced over at Drowling, who was watching them with a mixture of curiosity and amusement. "If Glaedon were to die, then the point would be academic, would it not?" he asked in low tones.

Azalea gasped at his bald threat. "You would not!"

"My dear, you have no idea what is at stake here. There is very little I would not do to achieve my ends." Kayce watched her face shrewdly and nodded in satisfaction when he saw that she was finally defeated.

While Azalea was convinced that Christian would have no trouble besting Kayce, Drowling, or even both of them together in a fair fight, she knew that her uncle would never engage in one. What chance could even the bravest, most skilled man have against a paid assassin striking unexpectedly from behind?

Slowly, she resumed her place and the ceremony continued. As the clergyman droned on and on, she closed her eyes, praying for the miracle she knew was not to be. The service was nearly over.

"By the power vested in me—" the pastor was saying, when he was interrupted by a resounding crash from the other end of the room as the door to the kitchen slammed open.

"There will be no marriage!" proclaimed Lord Glaedon loudly, striding into the room and effectively halting the proceedings.

The clergyman's mouth dropped open. Even fifty pounds was surely not worth this kind of agitation to his nerves!

"Christian!" gasped Azalea thankfully, unable to believe that her desperate prayer had actually been answered. Then, seeing the look of fury on Kayce's face, she cried, "Watch out!"

Glaedon turned to face the older man, his anger at what he had tried to do to Azalea matching Kayce's fury at being thwarted. Almost without thinking, Christian felled Lord Kayce with a single blow from his fist before turning to face Drowling, who was advancing menacingly, having recovered from his surprise at the intrusion.

"By what right do you come bursting in here, Glaedon?" he demanded. "This is my wedding!"

"I think not, Drowling." Glaedon's voice was as cold and sharp as steel. "I am here by right of being the lawful husband of this lady. Do you care to name your second?"

Drowling's face became a study in astonishment. "Husband? Are you serious? Why was nothing said about this?" He looked accusingly at Kayce, who was struggling to rise, holding a handkerchief to his bleeding mouth.

"There is no proof!" shouted Kayce hoarsely. "The girl all but admitted it!"

"You are mistaken, Kayce," said Christian calmly. "I have the proof in my pocket. Your thugs did not do a thorough enough job on Mr. Timmons, I regret to tell you, and he is very much on the mend. He told me where the papers were hidden." At his words, Kayce paled visibly.

"By the way," Christian continued, "you may be interested to know that one of his assailants has been apprehended and has named you as his employer on this and one or two other occasions. I believe a magistrate is likely on his way here at this moment."

With a wild look, Kayce darted from the room.

Christian turned to Lord Drowling.

"'Twas all Kayce's idea, Glaedon," the viscount said, shrinking back from what he saw in the other man's eyes. "He thought that if I married into the family, I would remain silent about the trick he played on his brother Walter, back in '91."

"And what trick was that?"

"The duel he was goaded into fighting. He thought he'd killed his man, but it was all a sham. The pistols had been tampered with and the surgeon paid off. Walter fled the country, which was what Kayce wanted." He glanced at Azalea, who was regarding him incredulously, then back at Christian. "I never knew a thing about a previous marriage, though, I swear it!"

Christian regarded him coldly. "That may well be, but I cannot think you believed Miss Clayton amenable to the match. Get out of my sight, you piece of filth."

Drowling's life was infinitely dearer to him than his honour. He left.

"Just as well," said Christian, turning at last to Azalea. "I had no desire to flee the country myself just at present."

He opened his arms and she ran to him without a word.

During the short walk to Christian's waiting carriage, Azalea managed to find her voice. She was still shaking from the ordeal she had been through, as well as from the after-effects of the drug, but she felt it was imperative that she speak.

"I was never so happy to see anyone in my life, Christian," she began in a trembling voice, "but I don't understand—"

"Shh!" He laid a finger on her lips. "There will be time enough later for explanations. Right now, I intend to restore you to Lady Beauforth so that you can recover from this very disagreeable experience."

In fact, Azalea did feel unequal to any lengthy conversation, and it was obvious that a short one would never do. Since she had not yet had time to organize the chaos of her thoughts and emotions, she lapsed gratefully into silence.

Christian helped her into the carriage, where she nestled comfortably against him, to his complete satisfaction. By the time they reached the Beauforth mansion, she was sound asleep.

AZALEA AWOKE to find herself back in her own cozy green-and-gold chamber, the sunlight of early afternoon streaming through the half-open curtains. She smiled and stretched lazily, enveloped in a glorious sense of well-being. What a dream she'd had!

The door opened as she sat up to admit the ever-vigilant Junie, breakfast tray in hand.

"Good morning, miss—or, should I say, good afternoon. It's a treat to have you back with us, I must say! I trust you slept well?"

Full recollection flooded back, and Azalea's smile broadened. So it hadn't been a dream! "Marvellously, Junie, thank you," she said. "That breakfast smells delicious. I declare I am ravenous!"

"Cook thought you might be, so he fixed you up something special," said Junie, placing a tray bearing hot chocolate, creamed sole, ham and popovers for her mistress. "Ring when you want me, and I'll help you to dress."

A short while later, Azalea descended to the front parlour to find Lord Glaedon and Lady Beauforth deep in animated conversation. Seeing her in the doorway, Christian rose. She came forward hesitantly, looking from one to the other questioningly. Lady Beauforth spoke first.

"Oh, my dear, dear Azalea, it is wonderful to see you looking so refreshed! Christian has just been telling me the most extraordinary tale.... I vow, I don't know what to think! Are my wits addled, or is it true?"

Azalea glanced shyly at Christian, who smiled down at her in a way that made her heart skip a beat. "Yes, Cousin Alice, it is all true," she admitted. "I am sorry that you had to learn of it in this way. Pray believe I never meant to hurt you—or Marilyn! Especially when you have both been so good to me."

But Lady Beauforth was smiling, though she still looked thoroughly bemused. "Well, you *have* been the sly one! But there, I mustn't scold, for Christian here has been telling me why you never dropped a word about it before. And here was I in alt over the idea of a match with Drowling!"

Her ladyship dismissed that previous favourite with a flick of her fingers. "But we have many, many plans to make if this information is to be made public without a scandal! However, we can discuss that later. Christian tells me you were too tired last night for any talk, and, indeed, I believe him, for you could scarcely stand when he brought you home. So I'll leave you two alone for a few moments—not that it would be improper, I suppose, under the circumstances." She shook her head again. "But you must have quite a lot to say to each other. My, my, what an amazing turn of events...." Her voice trailing behind her, she bustled out of the room.

Christian led Azalea to the white-velvet sofa and seated himself next to her. She thought he had never looked so handsome, with his dark hair curling around his ears—curls she longed to touch. With him beside her, as she had feared he never would be again, a storm of emotion swept over her. But first, the explanations.

She met his eyes then, to discover that he had been regarding her intently.

"Can you ever forgive me?" they both asked abruptly, then laughed uncertainly.

"Christian, can you possibly understand why I said nothing to you at the start?" asked Azalea after a moment. His very nearness seemed to be affecting her ability to speak, or even to think.

"I think so," he answered with a gentle smile. "Are you certain you still wish to acknowledge me after the way I treated you?"

Azalea nodded silently, her eyes shining. "How did you find out? I know you didn't remember anything of your visit to Virginia. Do you now?"

"I remember everything." Christian told her about the old sailor who had visited him at the Oaks and how his memory had suddenly returned as a result.

"No wonder you seemed familiar to me from the first," he concluded, winding one of her auburn curls around his finger. "And to think that that familiarity was a part of what fascinated me about you when we first met—here in England."

He was openly laughing at himself now, and Azalea's last fear evaporated. Miraculously, Christian seemed to be again the carefree young man she remembered from Williamsburg rather than the moody stranger he had been in England.

Impishly, she reached up to touch the dark curl that had been intriguing her, and their eyes met again. Her breathing quickened as he bent his head towards hers.

His kiss, deep and passionate, brought back vivid memories of earlier caresses here in this very same room. She felt that she was being transported on a golden cloud to heavenly regions undreamed of.

As she responded eagerly, Christian was left with no doubt of the true state of her feelings—or desires.

"So where do we go from here?" he asked huskily at length. Before Azalea could answer, Lady Beauforth bustled back into the room.

"I have been thinking, my dears, and I have a plan to put before you. What would you say to another wedding ceremony, this time in St. George's, Hanover Square? That way we need say nothing about your having been married all this time, for you must realize that it will look excessively odd to everyone."

She gazed pleadingly at them. Azalea knew that her cousin really did want them happy and was delighted that they had reached an understanding, but that her horror of scandal could not be overcome.

"Dear Cousin Alice, what a lovely idea," said Azalea, rising to embrace her. "If Christian agrees, that is."

"On two conditions." Both ladies turned to look at him questioningly. "That it can be arranged within the month, and that we spend the intervening period at Glaedon Oaks. My grandmother has expressed a strong desire to meet my countess."

Azalea agreed readily and they all fell to discussing wedding plans. In the midst of arguing the merits of lilies over white roses, a topic Christian could not find as interesting as his bride apparently did, Marilyn and Jonathan walked in, flushed from a walk in the Park. Both looked extremely pleased with themselves.

"Might we make it a double ceremony?" asked Jonathan when all had been explained to them. Lady Beauforth, open-mouthed, looked at Marilyn, who nodded happily. "If you approve, that is, ma'am," he concluded more formally.

"Approve?" exclaimed Lady Beauforth. "My dear boy, you are already like one of the family. I am only surprised that you waited this long."

"There was the small matter of her previous commitment, if you recall," he reminded her. "In addition, I wanted to be sure of my prospects first. Lord Holte has made me his legal heir, as of yesterday, so I am now a man of substance both in England and America." He smiled fondly down at Marilyn.

"But we are to honeymoon in Virginia, as you promised," she reminded him.

"That I did," he returned. "Did you by chance plan on a wedding trip there as well?" he asked, turning to Azalea and Christian.

"No, I had something else in mind," replied Christian, grinning with delight at their news, "but I have yet to discuss it with my bride." He turned to Azalea. "Would you care to take a drive? My carriage is at the door."

She nodded, too happy to speak.

He took her firmly by the hand and led her outside to his waiting carriage. "Care to take a guess where we're going?" he asked. The intensity of the gaze he turned on her made her heart flip over.

"To the Park?" she asked shyly.

"No, to my Town house. It occurs to me that my countess might care to see the place, as she will have the managing of it shortly."

Azalea felt as if she were melting in the warmth of his regard. "Yes. Yes I would," she agreed.

On the way there, Christian told her about his arrival at Beauforth House the afternoon before and Marilyn's timely request. They chuckled together as they climbed down from the carriage, but when they stepped into the house, their laughter stilled. No servants were in evidence, by prior arrangement. Silently, hand in hand, they mounted the stairs.

Once in his own bedchamber, Christian closed the door softly and held out his arms. She came to him willingly, with no reservations. This was Christian, her husband—and he loved her.

"To think I was consumed by guilt for kissing my own wife," he said, echoing her thoughts. "Were you very angry?"

"Only that you stopped. I shall remember that time always, Christian." She smiled up at him, her heart in her eyes.

"I won't hold back this time," he warned her. "Prepare yourself for something even more memorable."

Azalea doubted that could be possible, but she soon found that she was wrong. Thoroughly, without any indication of haste, he kissed her, running his hands over her body. She returned his kiss passionately, the fire that he kindled within her suddenly bursting into roaring flame.

He chuckled deep in his throat as he sensed her response. She fumbled at his clothes, eager to have his skin against hers. What she had felt before was as nothing compared to the rage of desire that now had her in its grip.

Christian fastened his mouth on hers again and with eager hands began to strip away her gown. Azalea unhesitatingly responded to his ardour, opening to his kiss. She continued to fumble with his cravat, and in a moment had it undone. Her nimble fingers went on to the studs of his shirt, finally baring his chest even as he released her from the bodice of her gown. He ran his hands down her back, the sensation of her nipples against his bare chest nearly driving him mad.

Softly, wonderingly, Azalea's hands explored the contours of his torso, her fingers combing through the hair on his chest, sliding down the plane of his hard stomach. Christian untied the sash of her gown and slid the garment down past her hips until it lay in a shimmering heap at her feet. For a moment, he pulled back to feast his eyes upon her lush curves.

She did not cease her explorations, but slid one finger beneath the waistband of his breeches, which were now stretched tight over his straining arousal. Quickly, he helped her to unfasten them and a moment later stood as free of encumbrance as she.

Kissing her deeply again, he lowered himself onto the bed, drawing her with him, his whole length pressed against hers. This time there was no stiffening in her, no hesitancy, as he traced the curves and hollows of her body with his hands and then his mouth.

Azalea had never dreamed such sensations could exist. As his hands stroked and caressed, lower and lower, she arched her back to greet them. Heat pulsed between her thighs, spreading, licking over her until her whole body was aflame. Slowly, maddeningly, his fingers approached the source of the inferno.

She gasped as he fastened his mouth over one of her breasts, teasing and tantalizing the nipple with his tongue. At the same time, he inched his hand lower, into the curly tangle between her legs. One finger stroked the spot that had become the very centre of her being. Waves of pleasure and insatiable need washed over her. Without fully understanding why, she slid her hands around to his back to pull his lower body to hers.

Releasing her breast with a final, lingering kiss, he obliged her, allowing his hardness to slide up her thigh until it just rested against the fiery spot his finger had been massaging. Arching again, she pressed herself against him.

He moved from beside her to above, supporting himself on his arms, and slowly, gently rocked back and forth, barely grazing the place where her sensations were focused. Arching higher, she felt him slide inside her, into the void that cried out to be filled.

"Oh, Chris, yes!" she breathed.

He rocked faster, each movement now thrusting him deeper. Suddenly, she felt a sharp pain, a stretching, tearing sensation inside her, and then it was gone.

He had slowed for a moment, but now thrust with renewed vigour. Azalea wrapped her legs around his to pull him in further. Her ability to think was gone—her whole world was a kaleidoscope of emotions and senses. She rocked with his rhythm, her passions rising to a dizzying crescendo until they exploded in a rush of pleasure so intense that she cried out in ecstasy.

Christian thrust twice, thrice more, then arched his own back, shuddering, as he spent his own passion. Carefully, he lowered himself next to her, kissing her gently on the lips. She had been all that he had known

she would be, and more—far more. Still deep inside
her, cradling her to him, he felt that he could happily
remain here with her for the rest of his life. He had
never felt so complete.

But slowly, reality intruded. Loath as he was to
move, he knew that he had to get Azalea back to
Beauforth House if her reputation was not to be sunk
beyond repair—at least, if they were to go along with
Lady Beauforth's scheme.

"You realize that you will have to marry me now,"
he said softly, kissing a curl at her temple.

She looked up at him with those glorious green eyes
and smiled. "If I had known what being your wife entailed, I would have told you my first day in England," she breathed.

"Let that be your punishment," he said with a
tender grin. "You missed two months of pleasure for
your silence."

After another quiet moment of contentment, Azalea
asked him, "Didn't we come here to discuss our wedding trip?"

"Insatiable minx! That's not why I brought you here
at all."

"Cousin Alice will wonder at our being gone so
long," she prompted gently, though she had no desire
to leave.

"As you say. I had another setting in mind for my
surprise, anyway."

He would not answer her excited enquiries, but
helped her to dress, then held the door for her to pre-
cede him out of the suite and down to the waiting carriage.

"Chris, you are driving me to distraction," she declared as they pulled up before the Beauforth house.

"Only fair," he replied. "You've been doing that to me since the moment I met you."

Once inside, he did not take her back to the parlour as she had expected, but led her through the house and out into the deserted gardens behind. The sunlight made it cheerful despite the fact that only the conifers were green. They stopped under the rose bower, covered now with twisted grey canes awaiting the warmth of spring to bring them back to life.

"Happy as I am for your cousin and Mr. Plummer, I have no intention of sharing my wedding trip with them. It strikes me that we have a lot of catching up to do, old married couple that we are." His smile made her want to leap into his arms again. "But not necessarily in America."

She looked up at him questioningly.

"I thought we might tour the Continent," he said at last. "I hear the roses at Malmaison in June are well worth seeing."

Azalea gasped with delight at the prospect of having that botanist's dream fulfilled. How could he have known?

When she would have asked, he stopped her with a kiss at first gentle, then demanding.

"I made a promise nigh on seven years ago to make you happy," he murmured at length. "It is time I began to fulfil it, don't you think?"

ABOUT THE AUTHOR

English author Paula Marshall has had a varied life.
She began her career in a large library and ended
it as a senior academic in charge of history in a
polytechnic. She has travelled widely and appeared
on "University Challenge" and "Mastermind." She
has always wanted to write, and likes her novels
to be full of adventure and humour.

Paula, who has three grown children, has now
retired from academic life and spends most of her
time writing and travelling.

Books by Paula Marshall

HARLEQUIN REGENCY ROMANCE
 96—COUSIN HARRY
107—AN IMPROPER DUENNA

THE CYPRIAN'S SISTER
Paula Marshall

CHAPTER ONE

BEL PASSMORE was sorting papers in her late sister's pretty study, a thoughtful expression on her face. She had just read a letter written only three weeks ago, dated May 1st, 1818, a letter which bore out what the great banker Mr. Thomas Coutts had told her yesterday afternoon. The letter was still in her hand when there was a knock on the door, and she lifted her head to call, "A moment, Mrs. Hatch, and I will be with you."

The house she was in, also her late sister's, was a little jewel box, perfectly appointed, filled with treasures. Above the hearth a portrait by Thomas Phillips of that same sister, Mrs. Marianne St. George, apparently known in London as Marina, presided over the room. Marianne—no, Marina—looked enchanting, a remote, cool goddess; Pallas Athene, goddess of wisdom, rather than Venus, goddess of love, which Bel had just discovered that she had actually been.

Phillips had painted her at night in a grove of trees, a sickle moon showing through them—perhaps, improbably, he had seen her as a chaste Diana, because the Grecian robe she had worn, the jewel in the shape of a half-moon in her hair, and the tiny bow she was holding in one charming little hand, reinforced the notion of a chaste huntress.

Chaste! Bel gave a sharp laugh, and returned to her task, a task which she was determined to finish as soon as possible so that she might return to her own life, after deciding what she was to do with the remarkable fortune which Marianne's lawyers had told her that she had inherited, and which her visits to Thomas Coutts, of Coutts Bank, had confirmed in all its majestic details.

Three short weeks had been sufficient to change her life completely. Impossible to think that it was less than a month since she was living in the pretty village of Brangton in Lincolnshire, a parson's daughter, ignorant of anything but the banal round of pleasures and duties associated with a young and orphaned gentlewoman in the country.

Her life there with an elderly aunt in modest circumstances was made more easy because of the small income regularly sent to her by her widowed sister, living in London, who was happy to help out by remitting to Bel and Aunt Kaye a few modest pennies, as she had put it, when her husband had died, leaving her, she had said, everything.

Bel remembered Marianne's visits—she had to think of her as Marianne; Marina was someone whom Bel had never known. She had arrived, modestly dressed in her decent black, handkerchief to her eyes every time she had mentioned the late Henry St. George's name; later, still modest, clothing good, but inexpensive, eyes downcast, visiting old friends, saying that she could not return to Brangton, all her social life was now centred in London.

Aunt Kaye had suggested to Marianne recently when Bel was reaching the age of eighteen that Marianne might like to take Bel back to London with her, introduce her to Marianne's wide circle of friends, perhaps find her a husband with a modest if useful income, since there were few for Bel to marry in Brangton.

Marianne had looked at Bel, charming in a white muslin dress that was dated by London standards, wearing a straw hat with a wide brim, a sash of pale green silk wound round the crown, enhancing the combination of red-gold hair, ivory complexion and brilliant green eyes, with dark arching brows, which were beginning to make Bel a beauty after whom every eye would turn to look—especially as the face was matched with a figure of stunning perfection and grace.

But it was the look of perfect innocence, of candid, unaware charm which gave Bel her greatest distinction and which had made Marianne draw in her breath a little. "Oh, no," she had said vaguely, "I think that Bel is formed for country living—her very name, the one we use, fits her so much more than a Londonised Anne Isabella would. She must marry some good little country gentleman, not some bored townee. Besides, town would ruin those delicate looks."

Aunt Kaye, Bel thought, remembering this conversation, not many months old, was no fool, even if innocent of the great world.

"But you do not object to living among bored townees, Marianne," she had said. "Indeed, your own looks have improved since you left Brangton, not deteriorated."

"Ah, but I am not Bel," Marianne had replied incontrovertibly, "and I can best help Bel by providing her with a good dowry to take with her to her husband, and by your letting it be known that I intend to do so—*that* should serve to encourage gentlemen to come calling, who might be deterred by thinking that

Bel is nothing but a poor parson's undowered daughter."

"Oh," Bel had said, "do I really want to marry someone who might not offer for me if he thought that I had only a little to bring him?"

"You have virtually nothing to bring to him without my help, so we must use our common sense and my money," Marianne had replied, she who usually behaved as though common sense were a virtue she might have heard of, but rarely practised, so airily unworldly had she seemed, "when it comes to marriage and the setting up of establishments. Even the most virtuous and loving of men would expect his wife to bring something with her to their wedding day; such a consideration would do him no discredit—quite the reverse. No, Bel must marry here, I insist."

Well, Bel thought grimly, consigning yet another document to the fire, I now know why Marianne did not wish me to join her in London, and where all the money came from for the last ten years, to keep me in modest comfort, her in luxury, and enable her to leave me a fortune on her untimely death—and what am I to do about the fortune? For after all I am a parson's daughter, and a virtuous one.

But Marianne was a parson's daughter, too, said a tiny voice in her head, and that did not stop her from following the way of life which has enabled us all to live in luxury, instead of being little better than paupers since Papa died six years ago.

"I must think," she said aloud, on her knees on the hearthrug, then thought, when Marianne visited us, she was so vague and gentle, almost otherworldly, so very much the parson's elder daughter that we assumed that she led a quiet life in London, full of good works and virtue; we were perhaps a little surprised that she did not remarry, to have someone to shelter her from the harsh realities of life.

The harsh realities of life! And what a joke that was. She remembered the letter arriving from the lawyers, to tell her that Marianne was dead, had died of a fulminating illness of the stomach, quite suddenly, after being in perfect health, and that Bel was her sole heir, and it was to be expected that she would visit London to settle "your sister's considerable estate."

That had been the first puzzle, "considerable estate." Marianne had always said that her fortune, which her husband had left her, was modest, had sighed that she could only dower Bel with a few thousands, and the papers for that, which had not been completed before her death, were waiting for her, Bel had learned when she reached London, her signature not now needed, since she had inherited all.

Bel had gone to London, leaving Aunt Kaye behind—that lady's rheumatics were troubling her more than usual—taking with her only her elderly maid, Lottie, as a dragon to repel boarders, as Marianne had said of her guardianship of Bel on her last visit—a piece of London slang, not too polite, she had added on Aunt Kaye raising her eyebrows a little.

The first surprise had been Marianne's home, in Stanhope Street, near the Park, now named after the Prince Regent. Bel had expected something small and modest, not the splendour of the house in a row which was obviously occupied by upper gentry, if not to say minor members of the nobility—a house near by, she discovered, had been occupied by Viscount Granville and his family.

The next surprise was the luxury of the furnishings, more splendid than anything Bel had ever seen before, paintings, tapestries, china, silver, bibelots, the three bedrooms also perfectly appointed, the small study so elegant, with its break-front bookcases, Buhl desk, cabinets of cameos and porcelains; the whole place reeked of wealth.

The two servants left—the rest had been discharged after Marianne's death—were a housekeeper and a maid of all work. The housekeeper was as close-mouthed as Lottie, and the little servant girl was the same—even Lottie complained that their conversation with her was limited to yes, no, and perhaps.

At first, nothing seemed untoward, except that, on seeing her immediate neighbours when leaving the house to visit the solicitors, Bel had bowed to them, a man and a woman, and they had both turned their backs on her. Perhaps, she thought, that was London manners, and then she remembered that when she had visited the church on the following Sunday, and those same neighbours had been there, the whole congregation had stared at her when she entered, and again when she left, and although the parson had greeted her his reception of her had been cool, and the whole thing had left an odd taste in her mouth.

And then the solicitors, Fancourt and Hirst. *That* had been most disturbing. On giving her name to a man in a kind of sentry box at a very grand office in Lincoln's Inn, he had stared at her in the most frank manner, almost insolent, waved her in with a quill, and, although she could not fault the grave gentlemen who had interviewed her and had informed her of the stunning size of her sister's bequest, there had been something distinctly odd about their manner.

Finally, all the papers signed and she having been given the address of Coutts Bank which she needed to visit to sign still further papers to take possession of her sister's account there, one of the two men, the younger one, had leaned forward and asked her, almost a grin on his face, "I must enquire, madam, do you intend to keep on the business?"

"The business?" she had faltered, her wits, she thought afterwards, a little addled by the shock of her sister's sudden death, and the magnitude of what she had inherited. "Pray, what business is that?" For she had not seen any evidence of a business in Stanhope Street, was only aware that Marianne had lived on what her wealthy husband had left her.

"Oh, come..." began Mr. Hirst, to have a detaining hand put on his arm by the older man, Mr. Fancourt, who said, very courteously, "We must leave Miss Passmore to her grief, my dear Hirst. Time enough for her to think of other matters later," and he bowed her out, both of them going through the polite rituals demanded in such circumstances.

Other matters? What could he mean? Bel thought. Happily her meeting with Mr. Thomas Coutts was not so mysterious, that gentleman being a model of polite regret for her grief and congratulation on her great good fortune.

But even he looked at her keenly, enquired after her country circumstances, and then said, quietly, "I expect that you will be going through your sister's papers when you return to Stanhope Street. It is of all things essential that you do so speedily. If..." and he hesitated "...if, after doing so, you feel that you require...assistance...pray do not hesitate to call on me."

Bel took the puzzle home with her, for it to be resolved when she opened Marianne's desk, and began to look through her papers. Mr. Coutts had given her a letter from Marianne, which she read before she did so. The letter was also baffling, and she read it twice, in some wonder.

Dear Bel

If you are reading this, I shall have died suddenly, without ever having told you my true circumstances which have enabled me to leave you what I hope is a more than modest competency. You will find some of the answers in the letters and papers in my desk, but the real meat of the matter is to be found in a secret cupboard behind the books on the second shelf in the right-hand hearth alcove in my study. It is for you to do what you wish with what you find. The cupboard is well hidden, but if you place a firm finger on the exact middle of the central panel and push it will open and you will find there—what you will find.

It was obvious to Bel that Marianne did not wish to put anything on paper, even in a letter reposing in Coutts Bank!

Having opened the desk, to find pigeonholes stuffed with letters and papers, most of them apparently innocuous, if a little cryptic, she moved to the alcove, removed the books on the second shelf and did as her sister bid—to discover a cupboard, crammed with documents, two ledgers, plus a small cedarwood box.

Bel removed everything from the cupboard, and began to read through them, with mounting incredulity and a face which flushed hotter and hotter with every passing word.

Brutally and briefly she learned that her apparently modest sister had been a courtesan, a Cyprian, of the first stare. Far from having married the man whom she had met when a companion in London, Henry St. George, she had been seduced by him, and then deserted, but left with a small apartment and a lump sum, both parting presents, his letter said, "to one who has pleased me, but from whom my marriage now debars me."

Bel read the first page of Marianne's ledger.

I was not deterred by this betrayal—seeing that it was the second which I suffered—his refusal to marry me after ruining me being the first. For I decided that with the money I had saved, and what he gave me on parting, I would set myself up as a Cyprian of the first water, my talents seeming to lie that way, and offering me a better living than being a governess or companion ever could. From then on, I concentrated on milking men of their money, as they have milked me of virtue and reputation. Marina St. George, I called myself—the second name to punish *him,* and the first because it carried no taint for the family I felt compelled to support. If you ever read this, dear Bel, forgive me.

The ledgers and the letters proved that Marianne had carried out her intent by virtue of her sexual accomplishment and her business brain—for not only had she charged high rates and accepted magnificent presents from a select band of wealthy and titled lovers, but she had also lent money at extortionate rates of interest to those less wealthy, and furthermore, to Bel's fascinated horror, she had blackmailed many of the great men who had enjoyed her favours secretly while preserving their reputation to the world, by threatening to expose them, if not further recompensed.

Although they had not known the full extent of Marianne's career, her neighbours had certainly known that she was a courtesan, thus explaining their behaviour to Bel and that of her lawyers, as well as Mr. Coutts's offer of help should she feel that she needed it. He had rightly seen Bel as the chaste and innocent girl she was—so like Marianne as she had been before she left to become the companion to a lady of wealthy family in Bruton Street.

The cedarwood box contained love-letters from a person of such high standing that Bel consigned them to the fire without reading other than the first—but it was apparent that Marianne had also acquired a fair fortune from him—and he had commissioned the Phillips portrait and presented it to her.

Oh, yes, Marianne's fortune was fully explained.

The other ledger detailed her income and its sources, and the documents consisted of the incriminating letters of her powerful lovers, who seemed impelled, thought Bel critically, to immortalise their folly on paper, unaware that each was only one of many whom Marianne was remorselessly persecuting.

What now exercised Bel was whether she should accept a fortune made by such methods at all. Was it right, was it proper, that she, a virtuous young person of good family, the daughter of a parson, the greatgranddaughter, through her mother, of an Earl, should live on such ill-gotten gains, not only the fruits of vice, but of blackmail and usury? Would it not, perhaps, be better to give the whole lot to a home for fallen women, leaving herself and Aunt Kaye a pittance to live on? Would such an act be quixotic, rather than virtuous? She could not tell. Oh, dear, she thought, can Marianne's dreadful example be infecting me?

She had taken the puzzle to Mr. Coutts, confirmed from him that Marianne had indeed been a courtesan of the first rate—the most famous in London when she had so unfortunately died, he said, who was able to pick and choose her lovers. He was not at all surprised by the fortune which she had amassed.

"Your sister's understanding was excellent," he had said. "Unlike many young women in her condition, she did not waste the—er—fruits of her labour. She consulted me frequently on financial matters, made many wise investments, and I see no reason why you should refuse your unexpected good fortune."

Well, that was as may be, Bel had thought, but she had listened to him carefully when he had told her that if she proposed to retire to the country again, as she had informed him she would, then it might be advisable to go through Marianne's papers and dispose of most of them.

It was this advice that she was busy carrying out when she heard a violent knocking at the door. The letter which she was examining was from a young man infatuated with Marianne, to whom she had lent several thousand pounds at an extortionate rate of interest, and he was begging further time to pay, having already paid over a sum in interest larger than the principal! It was apparent that Marianne had been a skilful usurer as well as a whore. Bel felt quite faint at the thought, remembering her sister's delicate charm and apparent innocence.

She kept the housekeeper waiting while she bundled the ledgers and most of the documents back into the cupboard, rapidly replacing the books, finally calling, "Come in," to repeated impatient bangings.

Mrs. Hatch, the grim-faced woman whom Bel suspected of being Marianne's watchdog, said, "Lord Francis Carey to see you, madam, if you are At Home."

And who the devil was Lord Francis Carey? thought Bel rapidly, seeing that his name had not been on any of the documents she had read, nor was he listed in Marianne's business ledger, so crammed with the names of the rich and the powerful; but, before she could ask, Mrs. Hatch was brushed to one side and a large gentleman entered, saying impatiently, "I have no time to waste, madam, even though I am sure that your day is free for all the folly you may care to carry out," and pushing Mrs. Hatch, protesting, through the door and out of the room, he shut it behind him, and turned to Bel, to say grimly, "And now, madam, let us come to terms, and quickly. From what I have heard of you, you are not backward in demanding your pound of flesh, so let us get down to it, at once, and no skimble-skamble, if you please, for I know exactly what you are, and am not to be bought off by anything you can offer—either your person, or your promises!"

CHAPTER TWO

WHAT BEL SAW at first glance was the hardest, haughtiest man's face which she had ever encountered. A pair of grey eyes, as cold as a wintry sea, were set beneath thin arched eyebrows in a face as imperious as an eagle's. The mouth was as firm and cruel as a mantrap's jaws, and his blue-black hair was cut fashionably short, adding to an almost imperial presence.

He was slightly over six feet tall, his body was beautifully proportioned, and he held himself as though he knew it. He possessed broad shoulders, a deep chest, a narrow waist and hips, with long legs ending in the inevitably perfect boots of a youngish gentleman of high fashion. She judged him to be in his early thirties.

He moved towards her with a superb arrogance, the habit of command so strong in him that it seemed as though everyone else was put on earth to be his servant and to carry out his orders.

Bel hated him on sight. His face, his body and his clothes were all anathema to her. And to address her as he did! He deserved, and would get, no quarter.

"To what," she enquired, her voice poisonously sweet, "do I owe the honour of your visit, sir?"

"No honour is intended, madam," he replied, and his voice was acid, corrosive, vitriol to shrivel her and all that she stood for. "I can assure you of that."

"Oh, then," said Bel, voice still so sweet it was nauseating, cloying, "to what do I owe the pleasure?" She would not be put down by insult, not at all. It was plain to her that he had mistaken her for Marianne, and she did not intend to enlighten him—yet.

"No pleasure either, madam," he said grimly. "I must insist that I take no pleasure in consorting with such a one as you. Only the direst necessity would bring me to this—house." And the look he cast on the pretty room would have had it bursting into flames, so fierce was it.

"Oh, that is of all things the most convenient," responded Bel, who was discovering in herself a fund of nastiness which she had not been aware that she possessed, but by all the gods of legend he deserved every unpleasant word which she flung back at him, "seeing that I feel the same about you, sir, which makes us quits."

The fine eyebrows drew together and rose alarmingly, the mouth thinned even further. "I have no wish to be quits with you, madam, no wish to know you at all... other than for a quite obvious and brief purpose..."

"Nor I to honour or to... pleasure, you, sir," Bel threw at him when he paused a little for breath, "and it would satisfy me greatly if you quit my house on the instant. My only regret is that I possess no footmen to drive you from my presence. Pray leave at once!"

He made no effort to leave, merely said, through his excellent teeth, "I had not heard that you were impudent, madam; on the contrary, I was told that you dripped honey. I see that, as usual, rumour lied."

Bel might remain outwardly cool, but she was seething inside. How dared he? Oh, how dared he? To say that he wanted her only for one purpose, and that briefly—in direst necessity, indeed! For Bel was not so innocent that she had not caught the insult.

"Come to the point, sir, I beg of you. Philosophic discussion on the nature or otherwise of my conversational powers is a digression I do not wish to encourage—unless, of course, we move on to the nature of *your* manners towards a lady—or rather the lack of them!"

"Lady, Mrs. Marina St. George? Lady? What lady seduces a very young man, and then gets him into her financial toils—with blackmail threatened? A whore, madam, a very whore. By God, were I not a man of some honour I would take you on the instant, unrecompensed, as your payment for criminal conduct. Be grateful that I neither do that, nor send for the Runners."

"All this puffery, sir," riposted Bel contemptuously, "directed towards the wrong quarter. I fear you are a little behindhand. I am not Mrs. St. George. You may observe—it cannot have escaped your notice, so eagle-eyed as you are—that I am wearing black. I am, sir, her younger sister, up from the country."

Lord Francis stared at her contemptuously, took in the whole enchanting picture—the ivory skin, green eyes, red-gold curls, enhanced, not diminished by the depth of her mourning black.

"Oh, madam, I thought by the colour and cut that it had been one of Marina's conceits! Up from the country, you say? I assume that you have been practising there the profession which your sister so successfully followed in the town! No matter, I will deal with you instead. By the state of this room you are settling your sister's affairs. You may settle this one—with me.''

''I will settle with my principal, sir, since I gather that you are not he,'' Bel flung at him, white to the lips, the temper, signalled by her red hair, so strong in her that she wished that she were a man, to call him out, or ''plant a facer on him'', as Garth, the vicar's son with whom she had played as a child, had gravely informed her, when he had been wild with a schoolboy's ambition to be a bruiser of quality.

''Indeed you will not. The young fool could not protect himself against your late sister, and since you seem, by your tongue, to be an even greater scorpion than she was, it is my duty, if not my pleasure, to see you off.''

See her off! By God—for Bel's internal language was growing more unladylike by the minute—she would see *him* off, if it were the last thing she did.

Tactics! Tactics! What served her on the chessboard might, inexperienced as she was, serve her in life.

She sank down into her chair, clasped her forehead with her left hand, picked up her quill with her right, spoke in faltering accents, quite unlike her recent fiery speech.

''Forgive me, sir,'' she achieved. ''I am quite overset, my sister's sudden death, the long journey here, the lawyers, and now...this...'' And she heaved a dramatic sigh.

Lord Francis, a man not to be easily caught by anyone, as all London could have informed Bel, stared suspiciously at this transformation, not softened at all by the tear-drenched green eyes which were now raised towards him.

"Oh, we are singing a different tune now, madam, are we? What brought this about—the threat of the Runners, or a sudden access of common sense?"

"Neither, sir. The knowledge that...shouting at each other will not bring us to a conclusion, and I am anxious that this transaction of which you speak should be concluded. If you will please give me the name of the young man of whom you speak, and explain your relationship to him."

Francis Carey, a man who temporised with nobody, was certainly not prepared to be temporised with by a whore on the make, as he judged Bel to be, but he decided that if madam's opposition had collapsed so dramatically she was either engaged in tricking him, or had given way before his own intransigence. That being so, he decided to finish by being as brutally frank as he had begun.

"My nephew, madam, Mark—Marcus—Carey, Viscount Tawstock, who, I admit is the veriest fool, having been over-indulged by a stupid mother—" Did Lord Francis Carey like nobody? was Bel's immediate and uncharitable thought, masked by a heaving bosom, showing for the first time a maidenly distress which she did not actually feel "—came upon the Town last year, and among other follies became embroiled with your *sister*—" he almost spat the word at her "—conceived that he was passionately in love with her, proposed to make her Viscountess Tawstock, save the mark, and was foolish enough not only to write her a proposal of marriage but to borrow money from her, having thrown away his allowance on the gaming tables."

He paused for breath, and about time too, thought Bel, busy deciding what to do next—for the letter relating to the money borrowed by Marcus Carey was the one which she had been reading when his uncle arrived, and somewhere in Marianne's secret store she was sure his letter of proposal—useless now—existed.

No matter; Lord Francis had obviously come here, not knowing of Marianne's death—and where had he been, not to know that?—to frighten Marianne away, and was still, not knowing that she, Bel, was no threat, trying to warn Bel off, presumably frightened that she would continue with Lord Tawstock what Marianne had begun.

For one delirious moment she contemplated "going into the business", and doing so. Her own strong sense of rectitude, her revulsion for the life which poor Marianne had apparently perforce chosen stifled the unworthy thought at birth. But this arrogant monster deserved to be taught a lesson, and somehow she would teach him one.

She fumbled among the papers on the desk, although well aware that the relevant letter was placed immediately before her. No matter; let him think her disorganised, scatter-brained. She appeared to find it at last, waved it distractedly at him. "Forgive me, sir, I am not *au fait* with such matters. I am not sure whether in inheriting my sister's estate I have inherited the right to the monies owing to her—but whether that be so or not," she added hastily, seeing him about to open his mouth, "I am sure that you would not wish to see these papers, or the love-letters and proposal which he made to my sister, published to the world as an example of his folly." And that, your haughty lordship, is a pretty threat to make, is it not? She continued rapidly again, "That being so, I am prepared to return all the papers to you in return for some service which *you* might do *me*—but I am a little exercised as to the nature of the payment.''

She stopped, smiling sweetly at him through her tears, aware that for the first time she had wrong-footed him.

''You are?'' he said glacially, but against his will suddenly fascinated by the sheer impudence of the young woman opposite him.

''Yes,'' replied Bel, outwardly appearing to recover from her recent distress, and inwardly beginning to enjoy herself. Where, she thought, was all this coming from? From what hidden depths was this dreadfully devious behaviour emerging?

''You see, reading over Marina's papers, and being aware, by hearsay, of course, that to be a . . . Cyprian of the first stare is very difficult from offering such a . . . service in the countryside, I need a little advice if I am to carry on poor Marina's . . . business . . . successfully. Who better than to perform such a service for me, by tutoring me, as it were, than such a one as you, so obviously *au fait* with everything as you are? And then you could have your nephew's . . . indiscretions back, and we shall all be happy, not least yourself, having performed such a pleasant and trifling service to gain your ends. Your patronage would help to en-sure my success.'' And she fluttered her eyelashes at him, quaking inside at her wicked daring, for his face had grown still, and slightly flushed as he took in what she was saying.

''By God, madam, are you proposing that I should be your pander?''

''No, indeed, not at all,'' replied Bel, obviously prettily agitated at the very thought. ''Just the one service, small indeed, which you might . . . perform for me. And after all, you cannot pretend that gentlemen hesitate to recommend pleasing...ladybirds...to their friends. I have been instructed quite otherwise. That is all that is necessary for you to gain what you want. Our intercourse would then be at an end...unless, of course, you wished to be a regular client. I might allow a discount for *that*."

Bel had the delight of seeing him rendered almost tongue-tied by her insolence. What she did not understand was that a pair of green eyes, red hair and a superb figure, allied to a ready wit, were beginning to work their magic on even such a hardened specimen as Francis Carey, who had long told himself that women, virtuous or loose, played no part in his life.

Desire roared through him, so suddenly and unexpectedly that he almost gasped. This...lightskirt, so fresh and seemingly virginal, had roused in him passions he had long thought extinct.

If he were honest, from the moment he had first seen her, so unlike the brass-faced creature of his imaginings, she had aroused the strangest stirrings in him. As a result of the effect the lovely eyes, the smiling mouth, the air of virtue—denied to some extent by her ready repartee with its hint of forbidden knowledge—had had on him he had become immensely taken with her, which to some extent explained the coarse cynicism with which he had spoken to her, in an attempt to deny her attractions.

Oh, no, he had no wish to be tempted by a woman again, particularly by a deceptive little bit of muslin working her practised tricks on him!

But tempted he was. His hands curled by his sides; if he had answered her immediately his voice would have been thick with long-suppressed desire—no, lust, it must be simple lust which gripped him, the result of long continence. And now that continence was at risk, and he had the most overpowering wish to take her into his arms, to make love to her until that charming face was soft with fulfilled passion beneath him…. He must be going mad to think such thoughts, but yes, improbably, he was going to consent to what she had suggested.

He told himself sternly that he was merely doing so to dig young Marcus out of the pit into which he had been pushed by that hellcat her sister—but that was not the truth—he knew better than that, and, worst of all, he was so roused that he wanted her now, this very minute, on the carpet even, no time to wait. He savagely bit the inside of his mouth, to feel it fill with blood, anything to assuage the actual physical pain he was feeling. And now she was speaking again, mocking him.

"Silent, sir? You were voluble enough a moment ago."

"Your impudence serves to silence me, madam, and I also need to consider your proposition."

"Do not take too long," Bel could not resist taunting him, her tone a trifle pert, but none the worse for that, she thought. "The post awaits. Mr. Leigh Hunt might like this prime piece of scandal for his news-sheet—another member of the aristocracy to expose."

Francis Carey did not know which he wanted to do more—strike her, or push her against the wall to take his pleasure. His normally restrained behaviour, so long practised, that it had become a habit, saved him.

She was speaking again. "I own that I am not too sure how exactly to converse with those of the first flight. By your own grasp of language you seem to be well enough informed to instruct me in that a little, too."

Francis found his voice at last. "Conversation, madam? You wish me to instruct you in conversation also?"

"By all means. I understand that these days lively repartee, as well as...expertise...elsewhere, is much in demand among the gentlemen who will be my...clients. I know I can supply the main part of the business, but conversation...of *that* I am not so sure."

Francis succeeded in curling his lip, and achieving normal-sounding speech, something of a feat in the state to which he had been reduced. "Oh, I would not have thought, madam, that you would have any difficulty in that department, on the evidence of our *conversazione* so far," and then before she could answer him, "as to your proposition, madam, yes, I find it...agreeable to me. I am willing to...tutor you. At once would be...most pleasing to me. Fortunately I am at a loose end at the moment—I am usually a busy man. I take it that the house is in readiness for...visitors; we could set to straight away."

This was not at all to Bel's taste. She had no intention of allowing this arrogant brute to as much as touch her, and in her inexperience did not know the degree to which she had stirred him—almost dangerously.

"Oh, no," she said sadly, bringing a fine lace handkerchief into play, "not so near in time to my discovery of my sister's death. It would be improper, as you would surely agree—"

Not so improper, thought Francis, savagely, as leaving me in the state to which you have reduced me, but compelled to nod, since speech seemed suddenly beyond him again, as the houri's luminous green eyes did their work on him.

"No, you must allow me a week to recover. I need at least that . . . to do myself justice."

You need nothing, was his unspoken reply, for I am the one to do myself justice, and that I could do on the instant, but decency . . . yet where was decency in all this? For she had bought him, not he her, by the promise of Marcus's incriminating papers in exchange for his body—for that was what their bargain amounted to.

Bel peeped at him over her handkerchief, and was not too innocent to understand that Lord Francis was in a fine pelter over something—surely the man could wait a week to sample her? No, she decided, ten days, time for her to arrange to get clear away, for she had no intention of keeping any bargain which she might make with him. He, and every other fine gentleman who had enjoyed her sister, and the other unfortunate women who sold their bodies for money, could pay for his lust. That she wronged Lord Francis a little she was not to know, and in the mood she was in the knowledge would have made no difference to her.

"Ten days," she said, and then dropped her face into her handkerchief, sobbing, and the sobs were not all counterfeit, for she found that she was suddenly weeping for the lost sister whom she had never really known. "Ten days; you can give me that, surely."

Francis wanted to give her nothing, but the thought of the double gain—Marcus's papers, and the enjoyment of the woman before him—spurred him on. He nodded, reluctantly.

"Ah," breathed Bel, putting down the handkerchief and picking up the quill pen again, "we have a bargain, I see. Your nephew's papers in exchange for my...instruction at your hands,'' and she began to write, affecting a die-away air that had him all the more hot for her, every expression on her vital face beginning to affect him strangely.

"Allow me to make a note." And she continued to write nonsense on the paper before her, anything to keep him hanging on in suspense, since it was plain that he had changed dramatically from the violently aggressive man who had forced his way into Marina's study.

Common sense suddenly hit Francis hard over the head, stifling the demanding pangs of desire which he suddenly understood had been rendering him foolish. Why he did not know, but something in her posture, some hint of mockery affected him. With one bound he was over by the desk, and had wrenched the paper on which she was writing from her.

He read it, stared at it, then, "Three blind mice," he read, "written in a fine scholarly hand—an educated whore, by God." Rage mixed with lust, a totally delightful but potent sensation, had him in its thrall. "Why, you bitch, what games are you playing with me?"

His aspect was suddenly so frightening that Bel quailed. She realised that she was going too far, did not want to be raped in Marianne's study, for now she could see what the poet called "the lineaments of desire" plainly written on his face. Half of her was triumphant at the sight—oh, yes, he wanted Bel Passmore, did he not, but he would never get her, that was for sure—and the other half was fearful at what she might have provoked.

"No games," she said. "I was merely writing to...
keep myself steady."

"And if I take you at your word, madam, then you
will not cheat me?"

"No," replied Bel, and this was not, she told herself, truly a lie, although she had no intention of keeping any rendezvous with him, neither did she ever
intend to use Marcus Carey's indiscretions on paper, or
his borrowing of money from Marianne against him or
his uncle.

"So," said Francis, much against his will, though his
will, for once, was weak, "I shall be here on the first of
June at three o'clock of the afternoon, at your wish,
madam, and afterwards you will give me everything on
paper pertaining to Marcus Carey, Viscount Tawstock, and his debts will be cancelled."

Bel crossed her fingers under the desk, met his eyes
with her own, greenly limpid, and thinking, God forgive me, said, "Yes, a bargain."

"Good." He turned on his heel, gave her one last
searing look, threw at her, "*Auf Wiedersehen,* madam, until we meet again," and was gone through the
door, leaving Bel to fall forward, drained, across the
desk, only for her, a moment later, to sit up smartly
again.

Well, one thing was sure. There was no question of
her giving up Marianne's wealth now; she would live on
it in comfort if only to put out her tongue at every
member of the male sex who saw fit to exploit women,
and damn them all, and that self-righteous monster
Lord Francis Carey the most of all. Self-righteous!
Why, the brute could hardly wait to get his hands on
her. Another hypocrite unveiled.

What a pity she could not see his face when he arrived to find her gone!

FRANCIS CAREY, that man of discretion, probity and, as Bel Passmore had immediately seen, damned arrogance, arrived back at Hathersage House just off the Strand, where his older half-brother, Jack, paralysed and dumb these last three years since a riding accident, still lived, leaving his unsatisfactory wife Louisa to try to check the unwelcome excesses of her son Marcus, who had gone to the dogs the moment he had achieved the age of twenty-one and been relieved of his uncle's guardianship.

The Carey family, or rather the senior members of it, comprising the paralysed Marquis of Hathersage, his wife and only child, were as poor as church mice; ironically, the only wealthy member of the family was Francis himself, the late Marquis's child by his third wife, whose vast estates had been settled at the time of her marriage on any male child she might bear.

This unusual turn of circumstances was fortunate, for the Marquis, almost in his dotage, had been so set on marrying her that he had agreed to these unequal terms, with the result that Francis's inheritance had not been swallowed up on the gaming tables where his father had spent the last years of his life disposing of his once great wealth—which he had wrongly assumed to be bottomless.

To Marcus's resentment of his uncle as guardian was added his further resentment of his uncle as the wealthy man which he was not.

He was in the big shabby drawing-room, standing over his weeping mother, when Francis came in to tell her that she need not worry overmuch, he had come to an agreement with Marina St. George's sister and heiress, and Marcus's name was saved.

Marcus was not grateful. "What the devil's all this, sir?" he exclaimed rudely. "Who gave you leave to deal with my debts? The whore is dead, and can persecute me no longer, nor her doxy of a sister either."

Francis winced: when another used the language with which he had recently abused the St. George's sister, he disliked the ugly sound of it.

"You are mistaken, sir," he replied stiffly. "The woman was in a position to do you a mischief. You were not to be found, and your mother was agitated on your behalf, so I attempted to bring the sister off. I think that I have succeeded, but of course I do not expect gratitude."

"No, indeed," said Marcus unpleasantly. "Interfering again, I see. What was the sister like?" he enquired eagerly, more concerned with that than with his new safety from scandal and ridicule, his uncle noted with disgust.

"What you might expect," said Francis, lying through his teeth. He had, unexpectedly, no wish for his nephew to be chasing Miss... He suddenly realised that, for all his cleverness, he had no idea of the name of Marina St. George's sister!

Marcus flung away. For all that he was not so many years younger than his uncle, who was the child of his grandfather's old age, he seemed a boy beside him, his mother thought dismally, remembering what Francis had been at Marcus's age. But then Francis had probably been born old and steady and high-handed, although his high-handedness had usefully saved Mark from more than one scrape. She always called him

Mark, so much warmer than cold, classical Marcus, she thought.

Francis was a little worried that the name of the houri whom he was to bed in ten days' time was unknown to him. But what of that? Meanwhile Louisa moaned and sighed at him, bade Mark thank his uncle, advised him to be more like Francis, at which Marcus glowered at his uncle and flung out of the room—to the devil, his uncle supposed wryly, unaware that that same monster of truth and probity whose praises his mother was singing was glumly contemplating the acres of time which would have to pass before he saw the St. George's sister again!

As in the pretty study where he had met her, he thought once more that he was taking leave of his senses. He was in England for only a few weeks, having come over from the Paris Embassy, where he was stationed as an attaché, for some instructions relating to the parlous state of Europe in the aftermath of the Napoleonic wars.

Everything seemed to be going wrong at once, he decided, both publicly and privately. How could he be in such a damned taking over a pretty little Cyprian who would always sell herself to the highest bidder; and why could he not work his unwonted state of passionate arousal off on any piece of muslin in a nighthouse, or in a private love-nest?

But he knew that he couldn't. Fastidious to a degree, he was only too well aware that after years of Puritanical abstinence the lure of a green-eyed, red-haired witch with a provoking smile and tongue had been too much for him. Oh, well, he would probably feel better in the morning, would have returned to his senses, be his usual self, might even reconsider the bargain, except that in some strange way honour seemed to be involved in that, too.

Not only could he not let Marcus down, but he had pledged his word to her, and what a joke that was— honour to a courtesan!

But he felt no better in the morning, nor the following morning, or any other morning afterwards, and while he was sitting in committee-rooms, talking with grave, black-coated gentlemen about what was happening in Spain, Italy, passing on his unsatisfactory master's messages, being deferred to by some, given orders by others, a pair of bewitching green eyes haunted him.

And on the final day, a sunny one, June the first, "the Glorious First of June," that great sea battle, he remembered—naturally so, because he had been an officer in the navy in the late wars—he dressed himself as carefully as a green boy going to meet his love, instead of a seasoned man preparing to bed a damned cheating whore, a phrase he used to mock at his own unlikely passion.

Driving to Stanhope Street, he doffed his hat at passers-by whom he knew, mentally rehearsed what he would say and do when he was with her, burning to see her, to hold her in his arms, to...do all the unspeakable things with her which he had not done to a woman for years, and finally drove down the street in a swelter of desire to the St. Georges' house—to stare at drawn blinds, shuttered windows, and a board outside, advertising that the house was for sale!

He threw the reins to his tiger, Cassius, a nickname given to him in jest because of his lean and hungry look, like Shakespeare's murderer of the same name in *Julius Caesar*, and half ran to the front door, to bang

the knocker on the door in a tattoo sufficient to wake
the dead.

A well-dressed fellow emerged from the next house
to stare at him, since no one answered, and a strange
slow rage, quite unlike any he had ever experienced
before, began to consume him.

He hailed the fellow imperiously, to receive an
equally imperious stare in return. "I see that the house
is for sale," he managed, with reasonable equanimity.
"Do I infer from that that the occupants have left?"

The fellow's stare grew lubricious. "Why, sir," he
began, "if you have business with the new doxy, you
will be disappointed, I fear," and then stopped dead in
gasping fright as Francis leaned over the railings to
seize him by his stock with such force that he was half
strangled.

"And damn you, sir," said Francis in a deadly
whisper, "give me a straight answer, a yes or no; I want
no damned moral sermons from strangers who do not
know my business." And he released the man just
enough to allow him to croak from his half-ruined
throat.

"Pardon me, sir, but they all departed forty-eight
hours agone, in a hired coach, and the furniture went
after them, but where they went I have no knowledge,
nor any wish to know. Too happy to see them go, and
their gentlemen friends with them."

Gone! Francis suddenly had total recall of that
mocking, mischievous face, and knew that she, who-
ever she was, had never had the slightest intention of
honouring the unlovely bargain which she had made
with him.

The rage which swept over him, as he stood there,
frustrated, was of an order which he had never expe-

rienced before. He loosened his grip on the man, said savagely, "Stay a moment, until I give you leave to go," and stared at the blank windows. He did not even know her name, nor where she came from, nor how to find her. Her lawyers, her bankers, the real name of Marina St. George—he was sure that it was a pseudonym—were alike unknown to him.

He only knew that in his baffled desire he felt murderous enough to kill her for the trick she had played on him, and that if he ever met her again he would make madam pay for what she had done after a fashion she would never forget.

Hell knew no fury like a woman scorned, said the old proverb, but what of the scorned man? What pity did that man stand in? What flames of frustration consumed him? And why should he feel such insensate anger towards a woman with whom he had only spoken for a few short minutes?

He turned towards the man he had cowed with his ferocity. "Do you know by what name the woman who came to live here after Mrs. St. George's death passed?"

The man was pleased to thwart him. "Indeed no, sir." He smirked. "I am happy to inform you that I have, and had, no wish to have truck with any such creatures!"

"Then damn you for a mealy-mouthed, canting swine, who probably takes his pleasure in alleys," replied Francis savagely, nothing gentlemanly left in his make-up, he thought dismally when he finally returned to Hathersage House. He seemed lost to decency and proper conduct, he who was usually known for the correctitude of his behaviour and his keen sense of honour. The red-headed witch had deprived him of both.

But she had forgotten something in her desire to humiliate Francis Carey, to leave him in a cold stew of frustrated lust. The bill of sale on the house gave him the name of the agent who was selling it, and who would be aware of the owner's identity, and he drove there at speed to trace the bitch who had cheated him so vilely.

To find a dead end; for the house had been placed on the market in the name of Coutts, the banker, and Francis knew full well that were he to visit Thomas Coutts, whom he knew quite well, indeed banked with, that gentleman would tell him nothing, if such were the instructions of his client.

And so it proved. Mr. Coutts welcomed Lord Francis, served him sherry and biscuits, asked after his career, but on Francis's enquiring about the property in Stanhope Street which the banking house had placed on the market Mr. Coutts had regretfully shaken his head, and told him that his client had demanded strict confidentiality. He could tell my lord nothing. Another dead end: the witch had disappeared into the obscurity from whence she had emerged.

Of course, if he had ever met Marina St. George, so that he had known at once that it was not her to whom he was talking when he had thrust his way into the study, then things might, just might, have been different.

He told Marcus later that he was probably safe, and would hear nothing more of his letters or his debts, for he judged, correctly, that the vanishing lightskirt had been so careful of her name and her circumstances because she wished to disappear completely, probably to set herself up elsewhere, trap fools, and laugh at them behind her hand when she had succeeded in duping and frustrating them.

But oh, my dear madam, he promised her that night, as he made ready for bed, his whole body one mass of frustrated and unfulfillable desire, if ever I meet you again, then beware, for revenge is sweet, and it shall be slow and long!

CHAPTER THREE

"Now, MY DEAR BEL," said Lady Almeria Harley to her best friend, Mrs. Bel Merrick, that charming red-headed widow whom every eligible male who lived in or visited Lulsgate Spa had tried to woo or win at some time or other in the two years which she had lived there, "you are not to make faces at me. It is time that you were married again. A pretty woman needs her own establishment, a good husband, and a brood of handsome children. If Henry Venn is not good enough for you, then there are half a dozen delightful fellows who would be only too happy to take you in matrimony."

"No doubt," retorted Bel, smiling and holding up the pretty little baby's gown she was busy sewing, "but I dare swear that when you came to marry it was not one of a half-dozen or so delightful fellows, but your own dear Philip Harley whom you chose to accept. I promise you that when I find someone who means to me what Philip so obviously does to you I will snap him up on the instant, but until then I shall remain a widow. After all, I am still not yet twenty-one, and would like to enjoy my single state a little longer, seeing—" crossing her fingers surreptitiously as she spoke "—that I enjoyed it for so short a time before I was married."

Bel marvelled once again at her own powers of deceit. Sometimes her own duplicity, her powers of invention, frightened her, but she always felt the need to protect herself. After she had fled London, leaving behind, with the help of Thomas Coutts, no clue to her identity, she had returned briefly to Brangton with a faithful and silent Lottie, having pensioned off Mrs. Hatch and given the little maid enough for a dowry, to find Aunt Kaye rapidly failing.

She never told her of what Marianne had become, and had sworn Lottie to secrecy, so that Aunt Kaye had died happy to the knowledge that dear sweet Marianne had left Bel enough to set her up for life. Bel had then decided that that life was not to be passed in Brangton—where she might be traced—but that she would retire to Lulsgate Spa in Leicestershire, where she knew that a varied and rich society obtained, where she might find a new and happy circle of friends, and a place of her own.

Being a supposed widow conferred respectability, and Lottie was sworn to secrecy over that; she was a hard-headed, silent woman who needed no telling why. After she had arrived in Lulsgate Bel had hired a companion, Mrs. Broughton, to give her respectability, a quiet, vague, rather silly woman, if kind, who accepted that Bel had been married off young to a rich old man, who had soon died, and that Bel, having no relatives, had chosen to settle at Lulsgate in search of company, and—who knew?—a second husband, Bel had said to anyone who cared to listen, smiling sweetly as she spoke.

Lady Almeria Harley was the wife of the vicar of St. Helen's church, set in the centre of Lulsgate, its beautiful vicarage beside it, so that Bel, looking out of the drawing-room window, could see the church's thirteenth-century spire, with its truncated top, known as the Little Stump to the locals, because it was not so impressive as the Stump at Boston in Lincolnshire.

Opposite to the church were the Baths, which Bel could not quite see, although they were visible from the small house which she had bought, the Willows. Small was perhaps the wrong word for it, it being so much larger than anything Bel had ever lived in before she had inherited Marianne's fortune.

"I am quite serious," said Lady Almeria suddenly, after fifteen minutes' companionable silence, removing a row of pins from her mouth in order to speak without swallowing them. "I do admit that there is no one whom I could wholeheartedly recommend to you, but I am sure that one day soon I shall be able to matchmake with a good heart—seeing that you will not wear Henry Venn."

The look she gave Bel on saying this was for some reason vaguely conspiratorial, as though she had something up her sleeve, Bel thought, and then forgot her thought.

The Reverend Mr. Henry Venn was the curate of St. Helen's, who looked after the Lady Chapel at Morewood. He was moderately wealthy in his own right. "I own," said Bel serious now, "that I am quite attracted to Henry, in a lukewarm way, you understand, but if I take Henry then I have to take his mama, and *that* thought I cannot stomach. Besides, his sense of humour is deficient, and I should be sure to say so many things at which they would both look sideways!"

Almeria's charming laugh rang out. Bel's ever-ready sense of humour was one of the things Almeria liked about Bel, coupled with Bel's good heart and industry. She had recently been made, despite her youth, the leader and the organiser of the church's sewing circle, "So reliable, Bel," being the usual comment, so that when old Mrs. Harper went to her last rest no one, not even the old tabbies, as Almeria irreverently called them, who were the church's mainstay, had objected to Bel's replacing her.

Tact as well as charm and humour typified Bel, Almeria thought once more, watching her friend, and she thought that she knew a man who might appreciate her, and she hoped to introduce Bel to him one day soon, but until that day arrived she would continue to tease Bel about suitors, for she knew that despite her charm Bel was sufficiently hard-headed not to accept anyone for the sake of it.

"The town is filling up with visitors," commented Almeria, watching the procession of fashionably dressed people walk by the vicarage windows. "August usually brings the most, the London season being almost over. Philip says that although he prefers Lulsgate empty they bring much needed money into the town and give occupation to many. How many shops would Lulsgate support if there were no visitors? he says. Think of the sempstresses and milliners who would have no work without them, to say nothing of the lodging-house keepers, and those who rent their homes out for the summer, to pay for their few weeks at Brighton, or in London in June."

Both women were silent. For all the wealth which Lulsgate contained, they were well aware of the poverty which the ending of the wars had brought, and that Morewood, once a pretty agricultural village, was now a small town of frameworker knitters, made desperately poor by the depression and the coming of the new machines, which produced more cloth but needed so many fewer workers to manage them.

It was those thrown out of work for whom Almeria and Bel were making baby clothes, and there were times when Bel, visiting Morewood, thought, And what should I be doing, with Aunt Kaye's small annuity disappearing with her death, and a pittance of my own, if Marianne's wealth had not saved me from penury?

In an effort to banish sad recollections she said, determinedly bright, "And last night I finished *The Nun of Torelli*; are not you going to ask me what I thought of it?" and the face she showed Almeria was full of amusement, none of her true thoughts visible.

"Well, since you ask," began Almeria, her own lively face responding to Bel's promptings, "yes, what did you make of it?"

"Such a strange nun." Bel held the little garment, now finished, up again to admire it as she spoke. "Not that I know any nuns, you understand, but I should be astonished to discover that they passed their time running around underground crypts, spending the night alone with handsome young mercenary captains, and being rescued from pirates at sea; all that was missing was a burning windmill, a beggar who turned out to be a prince—oh, and a little common sense on everyone's part, in which case, of course, there would have been no story!"

"Of course," Almeria was delighted to have Bel's wit in full flow again; she had sensed a quietness, almost a reserve lately in Bel's manner. She was not to know that Bel had recently been having second thoughts about her many deceptions because, since the flowering of her friendship with Almeria, she had come to hate deceiving her.

"What Bel needs," she said later to her husband after dinner, Bel having left earlier in the afternoon, "is a husband, someone to love her, to do for her what you do for me."

Philip Harley poured himself a glass of wine. He was an orthodox churchman, not by any means an Evangelical, and did not see the need to deny himself the small luxuries of life, a little wine being one of them.

"I'm sure she has had, and will have, offers," he said gently. Sometimes, he thought, his Almeria was a little impetuous and needed guidance—discreet, of course.

"Oh, offers," said Almeria; "there is no one in Lulsgate good enough for her. No, I was thinking of someone else."

The telepathy of happily married couples informed Philip of her meaning. He put his wineglass down carefully, said slowly, "No, Almeria, better not try to interfere if it is Francis whom you are thinking of, if you have invited him here to throw Bel at him, or him at Bel. He is not a man to play with."

Almeria rose, put her arms around his neck. "Now, Philip, you are not to scold me, but they are made for each other. He ought to marry again, and a woman with Bel's wit and fire, to say nothing of her looks, would be ideal for him. No milk-and-water miss would do for Francis; *he* would not want her, and *she* would not stand up to him."

Philip disengaged himself gently and gave her a loving kiss. "I don't like matchmaking at the best of times, and I don't think you really know your half-brother. He is not to be manipulated; nor, I think, is Bel.''

''Oh,'' said Almeria sorrowfully, ''now you wrong me. I have no intention of manipulating them. I merely intend to have him here, introduce them, give them the opportunity to see how well they suit. Beneath all that severity Francis is, I am sure, a man who needs the softer passions, however much he tries to deny it. He is at a loose end at the moment since being seconded from the Paris Embassy to work at the Foreign Office. I have not told Bel that he is coming, nor him that I have a pretty widow waiting for him. Give me credit for some delicacy of thought. I simply hope that they will find one another.''

Philip thought of Lord Francis Carey, that rather grim man, sighed, and wondered. He did not doubt Almeria's delicacy, but she was planning to throw two people together, and experience—for he was rather older than his wife—had told him how little that sometimes answered; but he decided to say nothing further—better so.

BEL KNEW that Almeria's half-brother was coming to stay in Lulsgate. Almeria had let it slip one afternoon at the subscription library, or rather, she had overheard Almeria telling Mrs. Phipps so. She had expected Almeria to say something to her of the visit, they were so close, but no, and Bel, who was not over-curious about other people's lives and doings, because she had no wish for them to be over-curious about hers, had forgotten the matter completely until she had met Almeria in the milliner's that morning.

She was trying on an enchanting poke bonnet, but did not like the gaudy red flowers decorating it, and

was discussing having them replaced by blue cornflowers with Mrs. Thwaites, who made and sold them,
when Almeria came rushing in, all aglow.

"Oh, Bel, there you are. I just missed catching you
before you left home. Mrs. Broughton told me that you
were coming here—I haven't a moment to breathe, my
brother arrived late last night, earlier than expected,
and I am giving a little supper party this evening for my
most intimate friends to meet him. Do say you will
come, I beg of you."

"Of course." Almeria's impulsiveness amused Bel as
it did Almeria's husband, being so unlike the calm face
which Bel had presented to the world since Marianne's
death. "I shall be delighted. Do I dress?"

"Indeed," said Almeria, and, remembering Philip's injunctions against matchmaking, added, "I shall
expect all my friends to be looking their best. Wear
your delightful bluey-green gauze," she could not help
adding; "it goes so well with your eyes and hair—and
now forgive me, I must rush. Between being a parson's wife and a great hostess, no time to breathe," and
she was gone.

Typical of Almeria not to inform me of her brother's name, thought Bel, amused. She knew from
something once said that Almeria's maiden name had
been Freville, and assumed that her brother was the
Hon something Freville, Almeria's father having been
an earl.

What she did not know was that Almeria's father
had died young, Almeria's mother had married again,
and was the Marquis of Hathersage's second wife, but
had died in childbirth nine months after the wedding,
and that Almeria's brother was a half-brother with a
different name. Had she known the brother's name,

she would have run screaming from the milliner's, but, happy in her apparently secure world, she ordered the cornflowers for her bonnet, walked on to the mercer's where she bought some book muslin for a dinner dress, and went happily home to care for her garden, talk to Mrs. Broughton, enjoy a light luncheon, and play the pianoforte while Mrs. Broughton did her canvas work, to such a complacent Eden had she finally come.

"Now, Francis," said his half-sister severely, much as she had done to Bel Merrick a few days earlier, "you are not to make faces. Quite proper for you to do the pretty to all my friends immediately and at one go. No time wasted, and you will be at ins with everyone, and have time to decide who will do, and who will not do."

"Useless to argue with you, I know, my dear Almy," said Francis lazily; he was draped over an armchair too small for him. "You are the most managing creature I know, beneath all the piff-paff. I wonder how you stand it, Philip. No, on second thoughts I do not; such wonderful powers of execution must make for a well-run establishment, if nothing else. You are putting on weight, I see, and do not look like a managed man."

"Oh, we manage one another," said Philip truthfully, "and there is a lot in what Almeria says."

"And do I dress?" enquired Francis, still lazy, unconsciously echoing Bel Merrick.

"Of course," said Almeria affectionately, "Everyone will expect you to be the epitome of London polish, seeing that you are who and what you are."

Francis laughed. He was always at ease with Almeria, and if he could find a woman like her, he decided, he might change his mind and marry again. He looked merrily across at his brother-in-law, raised one eyebrow at him. "Now why," he drawled, "do I gain the impression that Almy has some ulterior motive in inviting me here? That she is determined that I shall find a Lady Francis in one of the pretty young heiresses or buxom widows who frequent Lulsgate in its high season?"

"Oh, come, little brother," riposted Almeria, not a whit put out that, as usual, Francis had caught her at her games, "you flatter yourself—" to have him riposte,

"Not at all, and 'little brother'? Why, you are not so many years older than I am, and half my size. Do you wish me to dish the English language altogether by calling you big sister?"

"You may call me what you like," said Almeria, leaning over and kissing his cheek, "provided only that you stay as easy as you are with all my friends when they arrive tonight, and do not come the high-handed grandee with them!"

"Agreed," he said, catching at her hand and pressing it, "and tell me also, Philip, why you should be so lucky as to catch one of the few truly agreeable females in the world for a wife!"

DRESSING FOR Lady Almeria's little supper, which would probably not be little at all, Bel found herself wondering what the brother would be like. Like Almeria, she hoped, brown and jolly, of amiable appearance; or would he possess wintry grey eyes, a hard face and a superb body?

She blinked with annoyance as Lottie eased the seagreen gown over her head. Would she never get that monster Lord Francis Carey out of her head? How was it that, whenever she read of a man in a novel, or thought of one whom she might like to come calling, he always seemed to look exactly like the brute who had insulted her so?

Why, even the mercenary captain in that ridiculous farrago *The Nun of Torelli* had in her imagination taken on the appearance of the noble ruffian whom she had cheated so neatly. She could forget him for weeks and then he would start walking through her dreams again. Damn the man, and damn the circumstances in which she had met him. Well, she was unlikely ever to meet him again, and perhaps she ought to start thinking of Henry Venn as a possible husband—and why should the odious Francis Carey make her think of marriage, for goodness' sake? *He* certainly had not seemed to be a marrying man—far from it!

She set in her hair the half-moon jewel which Marianne had been wearing in the Phillips portrait, and placed a small pearl necklace round her neck, pearl drops in her ears, and a pearl ring on her finger. They were all that she had kept of Marianne's jewellery; the rest had, with the help of Mr. Thomas Coutts, been sold, and the proceeds wisely invested.

Kid slippers on her feet, a cobweb of a shawl and a tiny fan of chicken feather, dyed sea-green, completed her toilette. There, that should please Almeria, convince her that Bel Merrick just might be husband-hunting. Mrs. Broughton had cried off, so Lottie would escort her there, and would take her home—she was to help in the kitchens, having begun her career in them, and was not too proud to revive it occasionally, for the Harleys' cook-housekeeper was her best friend, and the two old women helped one another out when Bel or Almeria entertained.

The company was almost completely assembled in Almeria's drawing-room when she arrived, to be smothered in an embrace before Almeria held her off to examine her. "Oh, famous, my dear. You should be gracing Town with your looks and presence. You know everyone here, I think, except of course, the guest of honour."

She led Bel across the room, bowing and acknowledging her many Lulsgate friends, towards the hearth, where a group of people stood talking together. Philip was standing before the empty fire-grate, speaking to a tall dark-haired man who had his back to the room, and was bending to listen to what Mrs. Robey was saying. Mrs. Robey was a lady on the make with a daughter to marry off and the daughter was standing shy and embarrassed before the London polish of Almeria's brother, Bel supposed.

"Oh, do forgive me for interrupting," said Almeria gaily, tapping the tall dark-haired man on his arm, "but, Francis, I do so wish you to meet my dear young friend, Mrs. Bel Merrick, who as I have already informed you quite brightens all my days for me."

With a muttered, "Pray excuse me," to Philip and to Mrs. Robey the tall man turned to give Bel his full attention, and, his having done so, they stood staring at one another.

Oh, dear God, thought Bel frantically, how can you play such a dreadful trick on me? For the face of Almeria's brother was that of Lord Francis Carey, and she saw his expression change immediately from one of polite amiability to one of an almost unholy glee as he, too, recognised the lady to whom Almeria had so blithely introduced him!

CHAPTER FOUR

HIS FACE CHANGED again, so quickly that the stunned Bel almost thought that she had imagined what she had seen, and he was bowing over the hand she was offering to him.

"Delighted to meet you, madam," he said smoothly, straightening up, so that she could see the mockery in his hard grey eyes, "absolutely delighted," and the ring of sincerity in his voice also delighted Almeria, who was innocently unaware of how two-edged, if not to say two-faced, his declaration was. "My sister has been telling me that she has many charming friends in Lulsgate, and from the manner in which she has introduced us it is plain that you are one of the most favoured. You will not take it amiss if I inform you that I am determined to know more, much more of you—will seek by every means to improve our acquaintance." And his eyes were devouring her, taking in every line of her body, even more curved and desirable, he noted, than it had been two years ago. How wrong he had been to delay coming to Lulsgate Spa!

Bel had thought that she would not be able to speak, had feared that he might unmask her immediately, like a villain in a melodrama, and declare, Ho, there, this woman is a fraud, a Cyprian like her late notorious sister of whom you have all heard.

But no such thing, and she had no time to think, simply to murmur graciously, and her cool tones astonished her, "I am always pleased, sir, to meet a valued relative of my dear friend, Lady Almeria Harley. I hope you will enjoy your stay in Lulsgate, Lord Francis."

Bel was trying to take her hand back, but he would not let go of it, raised it to kiss it again, said, his eyes hard on her, "Now that I have met you, my dear Mrs. Merrick, I know that I shall enjoy my stay immensely. You cannot conceive of the pleasure it affords me to meet such a charming person as yourself. And now, forgive me, I must tear myself away, return to Mrs. Robey. I was informing her of the delights of the London season just passed, and of the coming trial of Queen Caroline; such a pity that virtue and beauty are not always allied, don't you think? Yes, I see that you agree with me. Let us speak again soon."

Oh, she would die, thought Bel, as each sentence he uttered carried a double meaning to taunt her, causing one vast blush to overcome her whole body, so that she thought that everyone in the room must be staring at her.

But no such thing to that, either. Even Almeria, who had been half listening to what had passed, seemed to have seen or heard nothing untoward; was pleased, indeed, that on the face of it Francis seemed to have been attracted to her dearest friend and protégée.

"What a splendid fellow he is," she said fondly to Bel, when Francis had returned to the group by the fire. "I knew he would like you, and I was not wrong; he seemed quite struck. And he has a genius for saying and doing the right thing; I had no fear that you would not like him." She seemed oblivious of Bel's unnatural silence, so pleased was she that her innocent little plot seemed to be working.

"I have placed him next to you at supper," she murmured, "so that you may further your acquaintanceship with him. I am determined that my best friend and my dear brother shall also be friends. He has been a lonely man recently, and I am trying to repair that—where better than Lulsgate Spa for him to recover his old spirits?"

Where, indeed? thought Bel sardonically. I am sure that he will recover his spirits completely in returning the disfavour I did him, with interest, if I read that haughty face aright, but aloud she said, "Oh, he seemed quite charming, if a little too polished for Lulsgate. London polish, I presume."

"Oh, and Paris, too," said Almeria enthusiastically, "and Bright really must announce supper now. The party is all assembled, and food is the cement of conviviality, Philip always says—to say nothing of drink for the gentlemen."

So there was Francis Carey taking her in to supper, whom she had last thought of as standing on the pavement at Stanhope Street, staring at the empty house and the "For Sale" notice, knowing that his prey had escaped him—only to find her, by fortunate accident, two years later, enthroned in respectability in Lulsgate Spa.

He was, she now had time to notice, magnificently turned out in the almost black that fine gentlemen were now wont to wear. Only his waistcoat, embroidered with yellow roses, spoilt the chaste perfection of his *tout ensemble*. He was a dandy almost, his stock a work of art, like the rest of him.

How could she have dreamed of him, seen him as the hero of *The Nun of Torelli* or any other piece of nonsense? And how could she ever have thought that she would be walking in to supper with him, her hand on his arm, feeling the living, breathing man, warm beside her, so very much in the flesh—making her uncomfortably aware of her own flesh, feeling naked almost, although she was wearing a considerably more chaste turn-out than most women had chosen to appear in?

So why, she thought crossly, did she have the impression, once he had touched her, that all her clothes had fallen off? Neither Mr. Henry Venn's nor any other gentleman's touch had ever had such an effect on her before.

Did he know? She had the uncomfortable impression that he did, and once they were at table he turned to her with the utmost solicitude to ask her whether she was comfortable, and whether she needed water immediately. "You appear a touch pale, madam. Are you sure that you are feeling quite well? Is there anything I might be permitted to do for you, any trifling service you would care for me to perform?"

"Not at all," retorted Bel, almost shrewishly, she feared. "I am in the first stare of health," thinking, Oh, how dare he? Someone would surely notice; such two-edged comments could hardly escape detection.

But no, Almeria, not far from them, leaned forward to say, "Commendable of you, Francis, to care for Bel's welfare."

"Bel," he murmured, before he turned to speak to Mrs. Robey on his right. "Charming, quite charming, nearly as much so as... Marina. And Mrs. Do I take it, dear Mrs. Merrick, that you are a widow, so young as you are?''

She must say something, she who was usually so charmingly free with her opinions, was noted for her repartee, her acute wit.

"Indeed, sir. I was married young to a much older gentleman, who unfortunately died soon after our marriage.''

He leaned forward to say, very softly, so that no one could hear him, "Oh, indeed, I understand you completely. Of his exertions, I suppose.''

Bel was in agony. Not only from embarrassment as to what he might say next, but quite dreadfully his last comment had made her want to laugh. She was trapped, but would not be put down, said loudly, "No, you mistake quite. Of putrid water, which brought on palpitations, other more dreadful symptoms, and death. Oh, my poor Augustus! Yes, now I do feel overset.''

There: if that did not hold him, nothing would. "Forgive me,'' he said to Mrs. Robey, who might think him unmannerly if he attended to Mrs. Merrick too constantly, "but I fear that Mrs. Merrick is not after all on her highest ropes,'' and he called to Bright for a little brandy, to add to Mrs. Merrick's water glass, as a restorative, he announced gravely.

Bel found everyone looking at her, with varying degrees of sympathy. Henry Venn, who was temperance-minded, said a little reprovingly, "Are you sure, Lord Francis, that it is wise to ply Mrs. Merrick with drink?'' to which Francis, busy pouring Bel an extremely liberal dose of brandy from the bottle which he had firmly taken from Bright's hands, replied,

"I am persuaded that brandy, and brandy alone, will restore Mrs. Merrick to the charming state which she was in on her arrival here. I do hope, Mrs. Merrick," he said as he handed her her glass, "that nothing that I have said or done has brought on this fit of... discomfiture."

"Not at all," said Bel, drinking her brandy and water, and aware of every guest's eye on her. "May I assure you that nothing you could say or do would ever overset me—quite the contrary."

His pleasant smile at this was one of genuine admiration, and he chose to favour Mrs. Robey with his conversation, after Bel had assured Almeria that her malaise was passing.

"It was only that I thought suddenly of my poor late husband, Augustus," she explained shyly to Almeria and the table, "and I was distressed all over again. He loved such occasions as these."

"And bravo to you, my dear Mrs. Merrick," she heard Francis murmur in her ear when the third covers arrived. "Such *savoir-faire*, in one so young, but then, I forgot, so... experienced, too."

"Thank you," was Bel's response. "I know exactly the value to place on any praise which I receive from you."

Francis could not help but admire her. A houri, a lightskirt, passing as virtuous, deceiving his sister and the polite world she might be—but what spirit, what sheer cold-blooded courage, to defy him so coolly when he was doing everything to provoke her into indiscretion.

Oh, she was going to pay for her cavalier treatment of him two years ago, but before he enjoyed her in bed, where she belonged, he was going to enjoy her everywhere else, too, with the world watching. What a pity virtue had not been included in her many attributes!

"And was there a Mr. Merrick?" he enquired again in a tone so low that no one else could hear.

"How can you doubt it, sir?" was all she chose to say.

"Oh, easily, easily. You have packed a great deal of living into a short time, my dear Mrs. Merrick, since Lady Almeria informed me, just before I escorted you into supper, that you have been living in Lulsgate for almost exactly two years. I calculate on that basis that after your London adventure you must have met, married and buried your late husband in less than six weeks."

"You forget, I might have met and married him before—" Bel paused. She did not wish to say anything incriminating, even in the low tones of the supper table, with everyone else conversing freely with their neighbours. Fortunately for her, young Amabel Robey had Henry Venn fully occupied.

"Before? Before what, madam? I am agog."

"Which is what Mrs. Robey will be if you do not attend to her a little more," responded Bel smartly. "I am not obliged to tell you the story of my life over the supper plates."

"A great pity, that," he said lazily, "since I am sure it would be of the utmost interest. Another time perhaps."

Oh, damn him, thought Bel, he has the most dreadful effect on my internal language, and he is as light-footed as a . . . as a . . . She could not think what he was as light-footed as, resolved to turn her attention to Henry, who was worriedly asking her whether she felt any effects from the brandy, all of which she had drunk without even noticing that she had done so!

"None at all," she said severely, thinking how soft Henry looked after she had been inspecting Francis Carey's hard face. Was he soft all over? Was Francis Carey hard all over?

Oh, dear, it must be the brandy causing all these improper thoughts, and she tried to concentrate on Henry's tedious conversation about the next bazaar which was being held in the vicarage grounds, weather permitting, to raise money for the fallen women of Morewood, there being presumably none in Lulsgate, since the fallen women there plied a good trade among the summer visitors and did not need financial help.

If it were not the brandy which was upsetting her, thought Bel, it must be the frightful effect of sitting next to Francis Carey, who now turned his attentions to her again, and was asking her solemnly where she lived, for he would like to pay a call on her on the morrow to ascertain whether her malaise was chronic, or merely passing.

"Merely passing," said Bel firmly. "Not worthy of a call."

"You must allow me to be the best judge of that," announced Francis soulfully, his eyes wicked. "Besides, think how pleased Almeria would be if we enlarged our acquaintanceship. Oh, yes, I do wish to enlarge my acquaintanceship with you, dear Mrs. Merrick. I wish to see so much more of you; you cannot imagine how much more I wish to see of you."

Bel could not help it. Wrong and wicked it might be of her, and oh, how she disliked him, saying all these dreadful things to her, but his appalling jokes were too good not to laugh at. She could really be no lady, she decided, between a bout of frantic giggles, and her efforts with a handkerchief to pass it off as a mere consequence of eating something which disagreed with her a little.

Scarlet in the face, she allowed Francis to pat her on the back, heard Henry say, "Most unlike you, dear Mrs. Merrick, to be so distressed, and twice in a night, too." The tactless fool, she thought indignantly, and, fortunately for Bel and everyone, Lady Almeria rose to her feet and led the ladies out of the room to leave the gentlemen to drink their port, while the ladies sat over the tea-board, settling Bel in a chair and anxiously asking her whether she was quite recovered.

"Oh, indeed," responded Bel, giving for her what was almost a simper, "I believe it was the August heat which affected me."

"How unfortunate for you," said Mrs. Robey, ever one to improve the shining hour. "Now my dear Amabel is never affected by the heat, are you, my love?"

"No, Mama," replied that young lady meekly, but before her mama could gather any congratulatory smiles on her hardihood she added, unluckily, "You know it is the cold which oversets me. Why, do you not remember, Mama, only last winter...?"

"And that will be quite enough of that," announced her mama. "May I say what a fine finished gentleman your good brother seems to be, Lady Almeria? One is astonished that he is not married yet. Where are all the ladies' eyes? I ask myself."

One would be astonished if such a haughty creature were to have been snared and married, thought Bel naughtily, and surprising for dear kind Almeria to have such a brother as he is. And then she recollected; half-brother only, of course. That must explain all.

Almeria poured Bel more tea and said warmly, "You and Francis appeared to be getting on famously. I am so pleased; I felt sure that you would be kindred spirits. He has such a taste for reading as you do, and his wit would sort with yours."

Bel nearly choked over her tea on thinking of the conversation in which she and Francis Carey had indulged over supper, so different from Almeria's kind imaginings.

Mrs. Venn, who considered that Mrs. Bel Merrick usually had far too much attention paid to her—enough to turn such a young person's head, and she didn't want dear Henry marrying her, by no means—said loudly, "My dear Henry has a pretty wit too, but then he does not possess a title and ten thousand a year, so admiration for *his* wit goes abegging. I consider that Lulsgate has as much to offer in *that* line as any London salon."

Bel winced over her tea at this none too veiled insult aimed at Francis and Almeria, and thought again that so long as his mama would be part of his future household there was no question of her accepting poor Henry.

Lady Almeria, though, treated Mrs. Venn as though she were some gnat buzzing about—making somewhat of a noise, but not really doing any harm.

"Oh, Francis rarely puts on airs," she said cheerfully, "and as for wit, one can hardly claim that Lulsgate is awash with it, dear Mrs. Venn, though it does you credit to think so. Local patriotism is always a virtue, I think."

Dear, good Almeria, thought Bel with a rush of affection, so perfectly formed to be a satisfactory parson's wife, quite unlike myself with my dreadful wish not to be put down, and my equally dreadful ability both to catch *double entendres* as well as to create them. What sort of man am I fit to be the wife of? I wonder. Francis Carey, I suppose, since he seems to be as disgracefully improper in his conduct and speech as I am in mine.

This untoward thought shocked her so dreadfully that she sat there with her mouth open. How could she even think such a thing? Why, she hated the monster, did she not? He thought her a lightskirt and worse, showed her no respect—no, not a whit—might be going to tell Almeria at any moment that she was not fit for decent society—indeed, she could not imagine why he had not had a private word to that effect with her already... and here she was, mooning about being his *wife*. Not only light in the head, but fit for Bedlam.

She had just consigned herself to a dank cell, and a bed of straw, with Almeria visiting her once a sennight, when her fevered imagination was soothed a little by the entry of the gentlemen, which if it did nothing else would put a stop to the inane conversation to which Lulsgate ladies, left on their own, were prone.

Bel had been brought up by an eccentric papa who had educated her as though she were a boy, and Aunt Kaye had been such a learned lady that she even knew Greek—which was the reason, she had once said sadly, that she had never married. In her long-ago youth she had been a pet of the great Dr. Johnson himself, so that gushings about sweetly pretty bonnets and the unsatisfactory nature of servants had not come Bel's way until she had been settled in Lulsgate. Part of her attraction to Lady Almeria, and Almeria's to her, was because they were both rather out of the common run of women in their interests.

The gentlemen were all a little flushed, except for the two men of cloth, Philip and Henry, and the look on Lord Francis's face, Bel saw with a sinking heart, was even more devilish than the one he had worn at dinner. He was making straight for her, too, and she could feel Mrs. Robey, and all the other women with pretty young daughters, bridling at his partiality for a widow. He finally arrived by her side, said softly, "You will allow, Mrs. Merrick," and pulled up a chair to sit by her. "Perhaps you could persuade Almeria that a fresh pot of tea would serve to satisfy your humble servant's thirst."

Your humble servant, indeed, thought Bel—what next? But she did as she was so politely bid. Almeria rang for more tea, and while he waited for it Francis Carey proceeded to tease Mrs. Bel Merrick under the guise of paying her the most servile court.

Oh, if she had known she was going to pay for it in this coin, Bel thought, she would have turned him out of Marianne's home, not tried to punish him for his insolence to her.

"You have relations in Lulsgate, I collect, Mrs. Merrick, to cause you to settle here?"

"No, sir, not at all," was her stiff reply. "I have, unfortunately, virtually no close relatives since my aunt died."

"No? Your husband had relatives here, then?"

Bel had always understood that it was grossly impolite to quiz people so closely on such matters, but perhaps, like many grandees, Lord Francis made his own manners.

"My husband had few relatives, sir, and none in Lulsgate. The reputation of the place attracted me."

"Now there you do surprise me," he said, bending forward confidentially, and fixing her with his hard grey eyes. "I would have thought Lulsgate far too dull a town to attract such a high-stepper as yourself, and as to having no, or few, relations, I can hardly tell whether that would be a convenience or an inconvenience. It would depend on the relatives, one supposes. Some, as I am sure you are aware, might even be grossly inconvenient."

"Since I have so few," she parried spiritedly, "it is difficult for me to tell. Now I do believe that you have a few inconvenient relatives yourself, or so I had heard, given to making unfortunate acquaintances, with unfortunate results."

Lord Francis, accepting a cup of tea from his sister, who was up in the boughs with delight at the apparent sight of Bel and Francis on such splendid terms, chuckled drily at this, took a sip of his tea, shuddered. "Too hot." He put it down, leaned forward again, and said, most intimately, "Are you threatening me, Mrs. Merrick? Most unwise." And from the killing look he fixed on Bel, Almeria was certain that her dream of wedding bells might yet come about.

"Threaten you?" said Bel innocently. "Now how should I do that?"

She had no idea how the wicked spirit which was beginning to inform all her conversation with him had begun to alter her whole appearance. The slight flush on her ivory face, the sparkle in her eye, the charmingly satiric twist to her mouth was beginning to affect the man opposite to her in the most untoward fashion.

Francis Carey had begun his campaign against her with the decision that he would harden his heart against the harpy he judged her to be. He would desire her, lustfully, would feel nothing for her, but see her as a body to be won.

Alas, with every word which passed between them, his desire for her as a woman, rather than as an object to satisfy him sexually, grew the more.

Oh, he wanted the revenge he had promised himself if he were ever fortunate enough to find her again, but more and more that revenge was beginning to take a different form from the one he had first contemplated. For he wanted her to respond to him in every way—yes, every way. He had for a moment considered exposing her to his sister once her supper guests had gone, but now he had decided that he would enjoy himself more in this dull backwater by taking on this mermaid at her own game, and beating her.

He had, after losing her, enquired of Marina St. George and her reputation, but this woman was St. George's best, he was sure. He had not heard that the great Marina was remarkably witty, but her sister certainly was. And clever enough to pass as an innocent, for he was quite sure from what Philip Harley had told him of her, in answer to his apparently idle questions, that she was not plying her trade in Lulsgate.

Presumably with what she had earned herself, and had inherited from her sister, she had acquired a fortune of a size large enough to keep her in comfort, for the time being, at least. He was also certain that the late Mr. Merrick was a convenient invention, to confer an aura of respectability on her which she might not otherwise have possessed. Oh, he was going to enjoy himself in Lulsgate, that was certain!

Bel could almost feel his thoughts, apparently respectful though his face was, for she read his body—and his eyes—and both were disrespectful after the subtlest fashion. How do I know such things? she thought, a little shocked at herself, for this was not the first occasion on which she had read men and women correctly, divining their real thoughts rather than their spoken ones. Had Marianne been able to do it? Was *that* why she had been such a great courtesan?

She avoided pursuing the matter further, and said swiftly to him, "If you continue to direct your whole attention to me, sir, you may create criticism of yourself as well as of me, and I am sure that you do not wish that to occur, for Almeria's and Philip's sake, if not your own."

Francis almost whistled. By God, she was shrewd as well, and recalled him to the proprieties. He rose, said to her, "Oh, madam, you presume to teach me manners, such a highly qualified dominie as you are, but you are right. Provincial life is different from London life, and I must remember that. I will call on you tomorrow, madam, and we shall carry our acquaintanceship further; you may depend on that."

It was a threat, Bel knew, but she had driven him from her successfully and could breathe again. If that were so, however, why did she feel so desolate at the monster's going?

She watched him walk away, with an air of such consequence and purpose that he dimmed every other man in the room. She was not yet aware that she performed the same disservice for all the women in the room—but Francis knew, as he knew of his own talents—and he looked forward to the future.

CHAPTER FIVE

BEL WAITED FOR Lord Francis Carey to call on her with a flutter of excitement gripping her in the oddest fashion. It seemed to be centred at the base of her stomach, and yet be able to spread at times to other, more embarrassing parts of her body. Mixed with this was a combination of fear and exhilaration. She feared to see him—but panted to see him.

The pleasantly dull tenor of her life in Lulsgate Spa, a dullness which had wrapped her round and comforted her since Marianne's death, had disappeared, presumably for as long as Francis Carey made his home with his sister. What surprised her most of all was that the fear that she might encounter him again, now that she had encountered him, had turned into something quite different, and infinitely complex.

She looked around her pleasant drawing-room, that haven of quiet which she had built for herself over two years. The little desk in the corner had come from Marianne's study, as had a large armchair; the rest was the pleasantly shabby furniture from her father's home at Brangton, even down to some of the religious tomes which sat in an alcove of bookshelves by the hearth, mixed in with more frivolous works like *The Spectra of Castle Ashdown* and *Emily Wray: A Sad History*—the last so unintentionally amusing that Almeria and she had laughed themselves into crying when reading it, so unlikely was Emily with her fictional trials.

Well, she was not Emily, whose one response to trouble was to faint upon the spot—Francis Carey would soon find *that* out; but all the same unease became the most powerful of her feelings as the day crawled by without him appearing. Oh, drat the man, why could he not get it over with?

For his part, Francis was in no hurry. Let the bitch wait; do her good to suffer, was his savagely uncharitable thought as he made a slow toilette and ate a late breakfast in his sister's breakfast-room, as pleasantly shabby in its own way as Bel's home.

Then he read a two-day-old *Times*, savouring the thought of Mrs. Bel Merrick—he still did not know what her maiden name was—maiden name, a good joke that, he thought sardonically—waiting anxiously for him, perhaps even shedding a few tears. He laughed at himself and put down *The Times*. Bel Merrick, shed tears? Another joke, remembering the proudly defiant face which she had worn two years ago, and again last night when he had confronted her and mocked her during supper and after.

Like Bel, he had the feeling that life was going to be far from dull before he had madam beneath him, and it was certainly not going to be dull then, not at all. Strange that for the first time in years he was hot for a woman, and that woman a . . . Cyprian, a creature he had always avoided in the past. Well, he thought sardonically, Shakespeare was right again. "We know what we are, but we know not what we may be."

He pulled out his watch as Almeria came in, a child clutching at her skirts, watching him around them; his nephew, Frank, named after him.

"Hello, old fellow," he said gently, putting out a hand so that Almeria might set the shy child on his knee, where he played happily with his uncle's watch. "I thought," he offered Almeria casually over the top of Frank's head, "that I might pay your pretty little widow a visit."

He was interested to see how Almeria brightened on hearing Bel spoken of. She had sunk into a chair opposite to him. She was wearing an apron, he noted, and was a far cry from the somewhat empty-headed but perfectly dressed beauty who had taken the London season by storm before accepting Philip Harley, the poorest of her many suitors, whom she had married against everyone's wishes and forebodings that it would not last.

They had not known how strong-minded and loving Almeria was. "I am jam-making later on," she said. "Cook is getting old, needs a helping hand and I do not like being idle while others work. Oh, Francis, I should not say so—Philip would say that I was interfering—but I am so happy that you and Bel appear to be at ins. She is the dearest friend I have ever had, despite the difference in our ages. Her mind is so good. You will ask her to join us on our trip to Beacon Hill tomorrow, will you not? She would enjoy a jaunt there in your curricle, always providing the weather is fine."

Francis had the grace to feel a little ashamed, would have liked to say, perhaps, Her mind is the only *good* thing about her, but refrained, showing Frank how the watch opened, and even revealing its workings. Frank loved the little wheels he saw, and said so.

"I remember," said Francis, amused at the small boy's solemn scrutiny, "how when I was Frank's age poor Jack showed me his watch, and how it delighted me," which was a way of avoiding discussion of Bel Merrick, he knew, and served to divert Almeria.

"Jack grows no better, then," she said quietly.

"Not at all, and never will." Francis was short. "And more's the pity. He is a good fellow, and both his wife and son needed the guiding hand he would be giving them—particularly Marcus, who is more outrageous than ever. When he heard I was to visit you, he talked a little wildly of coming here himself—with some of his more disreputable friends, I suppose. Said he would not put you to the trouble of giving him a room, would go to the White Peacock."

"Nice to see him at all," said Almeria, who loved Marcus for all his harum-scarum ways, she not knowing the worst of him.

"And now I must be going." Francis retrieved his watch from his nephew, put him gently down. He was so surprisingly good and patient with children, thought Almeria regretfully, he really ought to have some of his own. All his haughty pride disappeared when he was with them.

Francis was not thinking of children as he strolled through Lulsgate Spa, noting the Baths, the Assembly Rooms, a small classically fronted building with a vague stone god standing in front of it. Vague, because no one knew who the god was supposed to be. The less reputable but still charming house where a private club in which one might game was established—public gaming houses being forbidden by law—also interested him, and he promised himself a visit—in the intervals between persecuting Mrs. Merrick, that was.

Her own house, built early in the eighteenth century, was small by the standards of the vicarage and some others, he noted, but obviously perfectly kept, which was not surprising, as she was so perfectly kept herself, he thought with a somewhat savage grin at the pun. He knew that his savagery, if contained, was never far from the surface, and he thought—nay, hoped— that the hint of it, plus a hint of wildness which he thought he detected in the St. George's sister, would give salt to their encounters. To his horror he found his breath shortening at the very thought. No, he must at all times be in control; one slip and the tigress would have him, and not the other way about.

The conceit amused him. Two tigers prowling, the one around the other. His fists clenched a little. How had the tigress convinced Almeria that she was only a pussycat?

No matter; he stared at the knocker in the shape of a grinning imp before rattling it sharply, and then standing back, to be admired in all his London finery by a passing group, who rightly identified him as a gentleman of consequence, come to grace Lulsgate Spa.

BEL WAS IN A FINE old taking when she heard the knocker go. She was stitching at her canvas work, a charming design of yellow roses, to be a cushion cover to enhance her battered old sofa. It had been Mrs. Broughton's turn to read aloud, and she was sitting in front of the garden window, reading not an improving work—Mrs. Broughton had no mind for improving works, nor talent for reading them aloud—but a charming piece of froth entitled *Lady Caroline's Secret*.

Mrs. Broughton, who was a woman of sound common sense when not reading sentimental novels, was so distressed by Lady Caroline's ridiculous secret, and the absurd lengths to which she went to keep it, that she could barely restrain her sobs as she read of them. Bel could hardly restrain her laughter. Having a few real secrets of her own, she could not take Lady Caroline seriously, but could scarcely inform Mrs. Broughton of that interesting fact.

The sound of the knocker, while distressing her in one way, saved her face in another. She really must pass poor Caroline on to Almeria—she would enjoy her for sure—but in the meantime here undoubtedly was the monster come to attack her.

She compelled herself to sit still, to yawn a little even, one graceful hand before her mouth as the maid of all work came in.

"Gemmun to see you, mum. Are you in?" A pair of phrases which it had taken Lottie a week to teach her, so shy was she.

"Indeed, pray admit him. He did not give his name?"

"It was Lord Francis something, I think, mum."

"Oh, how too delightful!" exclaimed Mrs. Broughton, who was always impressed by a lord. "So flattering of him to visit us so soon!" She put down *Lady Caroline's Secret*. Real life suddenly attracted her more.

Both women rose to meet him. He was as splendid as ever, Bel noted, his tailcoat today a deep charcoal and his trousers charcoal also, but of a lighter hue. By his expression, one of power contained, he was out for blood, and, if so, she was ready to meet him, supported as she was by the presence of Mrs. Broughton.

"Charge, Chester, charge! On, Stanley, on," she thought in the words of Sir Walter Scott, only to remember the next bit of the quotation, "Were the last words of Marmion." Well, they were not going to be *her* last words, by no means, and the small defiant smile which her face bore as she thought this was noted by her enemy.

So, madam was prepared to fight, was she? Good!

"Ladies," he said, bowing, "pray be seated. I am come to renew a friendship, newly made. Delighted to see you both again. In good health—industrious too, I see." His sardonic gaze encompassed Bel's tapestry.

Bel and Mrs. Broughton made suitable noises in answer to this, his splendour and address, Bel noticed wryly, quite overcoming Mrs. Broughton: she obviously thought him one of the Minerva Press's heroes come to life.

"I am not always the industrious one," she answered, happy to find something innocuous of which to speak. "Today it is Mrs. Broughton's turn to read to me. We were just palpitating together over the happy accident that the hooded stranger Lady Caroline met on a glacier high in the Swiss Alps turned out to be her true father, whom she had never before met. You may imagine the affecting scenes which followed, almost melting the snow and ice in which they were set!"

If Bel could not prevent her wicked spirit from displaying itself, even to this odious nobleman whom she had decided she could not abide, then Francis Carey could not help giving a delighted crack of laughter at this piece of satire.

"Oh, now I see how you won Almeria over!" he exclaimed. "By sharing her delight in reading such novels, but equally her appreciation of their many absurdities."

Won Almeria over! He made her sound a worse plotter than dastardly Guido Frontini, Lady Caroline's villainous pursuer; but her reply to him was gentle.

"Quite so, and you, I had not thought you to be a devotee of the Gothic novel, Lord Francis. Blue books and red boxes are more in your line, surely?"

Better and better, thought Francis. It will be a pleasure to overcome such a learned doxy. Madam has received a good education, somehow, somewhere. It will be an equal pleasure, perhaps, to discover how.

Aloud he said smoothly, "Blue books and red boxes are sometimes so exquisitely boring, Mrs. Merrick, that relaxation is required—and then I was wont to raid Almeria's bookshelves, and the habit still endures. One cannot be constantly austere in one's reading. Even the great Dr. Johnson once wrote a novel."

"Oh, *Rasselas*," said Bel carelessly, as much to inform Mrs. Broughton, who looked a little surprised at this news, as to display her own learning, although the delightfully sardonic quirk of Lord Francis's right eyebrow served to inform her that he was perfectly aware of that learning. "But hardly in the line of the Minerva Press. Where are the Italian Alps, the ruined castles...the heroine disputing with the climate in quite the wrong turn-out?"

Mrs. Broughton was vaguely distressed. "I thought," she said tremulously, "that you enjoyed what I was reading to you, dear Bel. Perhaps you would prefer something a little more serious in the future," and she looked with regret at poor Lady Caroline, now face-down on an occasional table.

Bel's "Not at all, I find them most enjoyable," was followed by Francis's comment, meant particularly for her.

"Better she disputed with the climate, madam, than with the hero. Heroes and heroines should never be at odds. Unlike their real-life counterparts, where odds are more common than evens—as you, I know, are well aware."

Oh, dear, he is at it again, Bel thought. Not only will it be difficult for me to keep a straight face if he goes on, but I shall find myself responding to him in the same coin, and perhaps even Mrs. Broughton will notice what we are doing.

"Oh, real life and novels are always different, Lord Francis," she explained, as one to an idiot, "since in them everything is resolved at the end, and that is rarely true in life, there being no end there, except the obvious one which we shall not mention."

"No, indeed," he replied instantly. "Happy to learn that you understand that. It will make matters between us so much easier if we know where we stand. You agree to that, I hope?"

"In that, if nothing else, we are in agreement," she answered smartly. "Plain speaking is always better. A little more of it and Lady Caroline would not be in such a pelter."

"You really wish it?" he said, eyes wicked. "Plain speaking? Would you wish some informed plain speaking from me, Mrs. Merrick? That would remove misunderstanding, I am sure, but would it be wise?"

Oh, damn him, damn him. She knew now why he was a diplomat, so rapid in his responses, so pointed in them, but the poison disguised so neatly beneath the sugar.

Fortunately for Bel, Mrs. Broughton was as charmingly and blindly amiable as she was kind and useful as a companion and watchdog, literal-minded to a fault, and she saw nothing untoward in the veiled exchanges going on between her mistress and her visitor. On the contrary, she thought how splendidly well they were doing together, and after a few more exchanges of a like nature she thought to further Bel's interests by saying eagerly, "You are interested in gardens, Lord Francis? I saw your eyes wander to the view outside. Perhaps you would like dear Bel to show you around hers; it is a little gem, and all due to her exertions. She makes a delightful sight, potting plants, I do assure you."

"Oh, you need not assure me, Mrs. Broughton. I can quite imagine it—seeing that Mrs. Merrick is a delightful sight at all times, and all...places." And his dreadful eyes caressed her. "I should be delighted to have such an...experienced guide to lay the delights of her...garden before me."

Bel privately damned Mrs. Broughton. She had absolutely no wish to be alone with Lord Francis, either in a garden or anywhere else, where his conversation would, no doubt, become even more pointed; but there was, in politeness, nothing for it.

She rose and said resignedly, "If you really wish to study the delights of nature, Lord Francis, then I will be your guide," and led the way through the open doors—to Purgatory, doubtless—where else?

Bel's garden was large enough to have pleasant flower-beds in the new informal style which was becoming popular, a small glass-house and, through an archway, a kitchen garden with a south-facing wall. James, her gardener, who came in several days a

week—she shared him with other like-minded ladies—
provided salad stuffs, vegetables, and fruit from the
cordons on the warm wall.

They strolled at first among the flowers in full view
of a beaming Mrs. Broughton, who could already hear
wedding bells as she watched them engaged in apparently amiable conversation. Had she been nearer, she
would have retreated in shocked dismay.

At first, all was proper, Lord Francis saying nothing but um and ah as Bel gave him a short lecture on
her plants, showering him with Latin names and eru-
dite horticultural information. If his expression was
even more sardonic than usual, his haughtiness a little
more in evidence, they were shielded from Mrs.
Broughton by the fact that his head was bent to gaze,
apparently admiringly, at Bel.

He had to confess that she made the most charming
picture. She was clad in a simple cream dress of fine
muslin with a faint amber stripe running through it.
The collar was chastely high; in fact the whole of Bel's
turn-out apparently sought to convince the beholder of
its wearer's extreme sense of virtue. Even the red-gold
curls, which he remembered as riotous in London, had
been carefully confined, and the luminous green eyes
were modestly veiled, and did not flash fire until he
became too provoking.

Francis decided to be provoking.

He was admiring a small goldfish pond, and Bel had
begun a short lecture on the care and feeding of fish,
designed less to inform him than to keep him from
speaking, when he leaned forward, took her by the
arm, and said gently, "You make a most damnably
desirable spectacle, my dear Mrs. Merrick. Allow me
to desire it in a little more privacy." He led her firmly

towards the archway into the kitchen garden, away from Mrs. Broughton's interested eyes, where they would be quite alone.

"So," said Bel, who had been hoping that he might have changed his mind about her after seeing her with his sister and in the chaste confines of her home, "by your language—for you would not speak so to a lady—you still consider me a . . . lightskirt."

"Oh, come," he mocked. "Plain speaking, you said. We both know exactly what you are, and for the moment it is our little secret." He was still walking her towards the kitchen garden, adding, "I must confess that if it gives me greater access to you I prefer early plums and late lettuces to goldfish—though had you a mermaid in your pond I would have admired that. But the only mermaid in Lulsgate Spa at the moment is your good self, whose company I propose to enjoy until the weather changes."

He released her, but not before he had turned her towards him. "To enjoy the view more easily," he informed her with lazy hauteur.

Bel stepped even further away from him; to her horror she found that his lightest touch had the most disastrous effect on her, and the sight of him so near to her was even worse. She supposed that it was fear which was causing her to tremble and her whole body to ache, not yet knowing that quite another emotion was affecting her.

He smiled and narrowed the distance between them again, his grey eyes glittering. Bel's breathing shortened still more, but she could not retreat further; she would end up inside the row of lettuces if she did.

"Why are you here?" she enquired hoarsely. "What is the true purpose of your visit?"

"Ah, so we arrive at the meat of the matter, madam, no prevarications. It may have escaped your memory, but we had a bargain, my dear Mrs. Merrick."

"A bargain?" Bel kept her voice steady with difficulty.

"Yes, my dear houri. A bargain, freely offered by you, not by me. I was to... instruct you, you remember, in exchange for certain papers. I am here to... fulfil that bargain."

"I did not mean—" she began, heart thudding. Fear of him, she was beginning to realise, mixed with a most dreadful desire, so that she was almost mesmerised by the sound of his voice, a beautiful one, exquisitely modulated, used to command and also to enchant, although Bel was not aware that he had done little enchanting with it of recent years.

"You 'did not mean'? Of course you *meant*. You meant to make a fool of me, leaving me staring at a deserted house like gaby. No, I will teach you, slowly, not to make bargains which you do not intend to keep, and I hope to enjoy that charming body, usually reserved for those who pay you well—without paying you anything."

Bel licked her lips, tried to pull her wits into some sort of order, for this was worse than she had feared, and said, "You could gain your revenge so easily. Why have you not informed your sister—oh, not of the truth, but what you mistakenly think is the truth?"

"Tell her who and what you are, you mean? The courtesan with a blackmailer and usurer for a sister, she using her charms in bed to cheat and deceive as you used them out of bed to cheat me, with promises you never intended to keep?"

His lip curled; he was enjoying the distress he could tell she was suffering beneath her brave front.

"Yes," said Bel, suddenly fierce, showing spirit. "One sentence is all that is needed; why not say it?"

"Because I wish to enjoy myself...and you. You humiliated me, madam, and I have carried the memory around with me for the last two years. Oh, sometimes I forgot, and then at the most inopportune moment I would remember; see you again, mocking me. Oh, you roused me, dear Mrs. Merrick, as you well know, held me off with promises, sobbing about your sister's death. I should have remembered how truly hard-hearted courtesans are. Now I shall make promises to you which *I* intend to keep. When I think fit I shall tell my sister exactly what I have discovered you are, a lightskirt who plies for hire most viciously; but when and where I choose to do that, and how long I shall take, I shall not tell you...you must live in delightful anticipation...as I did."

"And which of us is the more vicious, sir, tell me that? No, you cannot do this. You do not know...you are cruel, so cruel."

"Yes, I am cruel, rightly so." And he laughed grimly. "And what is it that I do not know? Pray tell me. I need to know everything about you, as I intend to make you keep the bargain you made with me—eventually—lest you betray poor Marcus, as your sister did."

"I am not what you think," Bel offered sturdily. "I am quite innocent, not a Cyprian at all."

Lord Francis looked her up and down, and she followed suit by so scanning him. He was delighted at the sight, for winning a spiritless whore would have been no pleasure. The cool perfection of that lovely face,

framed in its light curls—some of which had escaped
from the severe style in which she had bound her hair—
the careful and tasteful toilette—all presented to the
world a model of apparent virtue.

"Oh, you are exactly what I think you are—" and
his lip curled "—a whited sepulchre, a worm on the
rose of this small town, not because you are a whore,
no, not at all, but because you pretend to be what you
are not. You are dishonest, madam."

"And you are vile," retorted Bel, "to conduct a
vendetta. Yes, you are vile even were I the creature you
think I am, doubly vile because I am innocent. Oh, you
are like all men, to despise what all men use and pay
for. You flaunt yourself as virtuous, walk where you
please, remain respected, while condemning those with
whom you take your pleasure to be unconsidered out-
casts."

"I repeat: your trade is not what I protest, but the
dishonesty with which you plied it—and your pretence
of virtue."

"No pretence," flashed Bel, and suddenly was
steady, a rock, her own fists clenched as she had seen
his were—and why was that? "I will not consent to
this. It is war, sir, war, with no quarter. I will give you
nothing."

"On the contrary, by the time that all is over you will
give me everything, beg me to take it, and I will debate
whether I wish to do so."

Oh, but she was gallant, and his fists were clenched
because were he to do what he so desperately wished he
would be upon her, to compel her at once to give him
what he so dearly wanted. He must make her beg, if
only to stop himself from doing so!

"Come," he said—he could not prevent himself—
"a foretaste," and before she could stop him she was
in his arms and he was kissing her, and she was responding, madly, wildly, against all sense, all reason,
until, remembering where they were, with Mrs.
Broughton perhaps beginning to wonder what they
were doing, he pushed her away.

"No dishonesty there on my part. You know why I
want you—and you, were you practising your usual
arts—or were you being honest too?"

He held out his arm, and perforce she took it, so that
when they came into view again he was passing on to
her his sister's invitation to the picnic on Beacon Hill,
"and Mrs. Broughton, of course," he finished, giving
that lady a gallant bow which had her admiring him all
over again. "I look forward to seeing you both; I shall
call for you at eleven of the clock." For he had told Bel
he would brook no denial, and she dared not offend
him, lest he tell Almeria her secret straight away.

"So charming, so gracious," gushed Mrs. Broughton when he had taken his leave. "If only all fine gentlemen were like him!"

And thank God that they are not, was Bel's response to that, but so steady was she, so much herself,
that nothing of her distress showed.

One art she was rapidly learning was that of con-
summate self-control, and she thanked Lord Francis
for that, if nothing else.

CHAPTER SIX

As HE WALKED BACK to the vicarage, Francis Carey's thoughts were a strange mixture of an almost savage pleasure, frustrated desire and, astonishingly enough for such an arrogant, self-assured man, a feeling which was almost shame.

Nonsense, he told himself firmly, she deserves all that I care to hand out to her; but he was almost relieved when he reached the Harleys' to discover such a brouhaha that it was enough to drive Bel Merrick temporarily out of his head.

Little Frank ran to meet him, pulling at his hand, three-year-old Caroline toddling behind. Frank was holding a miniature wooden horse, and Caroline was dragging a new rag doll behind her. "Oh, Uncle Francis!" exclaimed his nephew. "Ain't it jolly, Cousin Mark has come, with presents; now we shall have some famous times!" for heedless Cousin Mark was quite naturally a roaring favourite with equally heedless small fry.

Francis lifted little Frank up, walked into the drawing-room to discover Marcus sitting there, as carelessly turned out as ever, hair and stock awry, drinking port while Philip Harley drank water, and Almeria was exclaiming, "No, really!" and, "Never say so, Mark!" at every other sentence.

"Oh, there you are, Uncle," cried Marcus, as though the last time the two had met they had parted as bosom bows, and not, as usual, at daggers drawn over Marcus's ever-growing debts. "I'm sure that you'll be pleased to hear that I have decided to come and retrench in the countryside, leaving Town to improve my financial situation as well as my health. I am at the White Peacock with a couple of friends, have no mind to add to poor Almeria's expenses," he said, ignoring the fact that he had already added to them, since Almeria had just asked him to bring his friends along to dinner.

"I have been asking whether there are any pretty young girls here, with good competences," he rattled on gaily. "The pretty part is essential, the competence would be an added virtue. Almeria informs me that, while there is no one here to rival Miss Coutts in terms of the available tin, there are some quite decent belles, including of all things a pretty young widow with more than a competence, but she's saying hands off to that—reserved for you, I gather."

Now why should that careless reference to Bel Merrick make Francis clench his fists and want to strike his inoffensive nephew? For it was Bel whom he did not want to be exploited, he oddly discovered, not Marcus whom he felt should need protection!

He stared coldly at his nephew. Did this idle lounger really resemble himself? He supposed he did. They both possessed the same grey eyes, dark hair, and somewhat straight mouth. But where Francis was severe, Marcus was slack; where Francis looked like a grave Roman senator of the old school on a coin, Marcus rather resembled a dissolute young Roman emperor in the last days of that Empire's decline. Not that

Marcus was vicious, Francis decided wearily, simply idle and stupid, the spoiled son of a silly mother.

"And who are these friends you are inflicting on us?" he enquired sternly.

"Oh, jolly good fellows both," said Marcus rapidly, knowing quite well that his uncle was bound to dislike them. "Rhys Howell, lately a captain in the Lifeguards, and Fred Carnaby—you know Fred, he was in the Diplomatic himself until recently."

"As well I know," remarked Francis glacially, "until he was sent home for drunkenness and mislaying important dispatches. Hardly the sort of friend to bring here."

"Well, too late now," said Marcus cheerfully. "Invitation already gone out."

"And Howell, so-called captain," pursued Francis determinedly—like a confounded dog with a juicy bone, thought his nephew irreverently. "I have heard nothing good of him. A man is known by the company he keeps, Marcus, and your company is not nice."

"You have forgotten what it is to be young, sir."

"Oh, come, Mark," interjected Almeria, trying to keep the peace. "Thirty-four is hardly old, and you are already twenty-four yourself. Francis is right to wish you to settle down."

"I'll make a promise," said Marcus earnestly, who had made many promises before, and never kept one of them. "If I find a splendid young woman here, I promise to pop the question and settle down myself—in Lulsgate Spa, perhaps! Will that do, sir?"

Francis regarded him with distaste. Perhaps he ought to throw him to Bel Merrick; it was all the young fool deserved. Question was, did she deserve him? And what an odd question that was to ask himself, he thought crossly.

"And I am to meet the pretty widow and some of the Lulsgate belles soon," continued Mark, "for Almeria has asked us all to accompany her on the trip to Beacon Hill tomorrow, and fortunate it is that I have brought my curricle with me. If I fall on my knees and say, Pretty please, Almeria, my angel, may I escort the charming young widow..."

"No," said Francis coldly, before Almeria could answer Marcus, "you may not, for I have already asked her to accompany me, and you are not a safe enough whip to escort any young woman. Confine yourself to conveying your disreputable friends about Leicestershire. Their loss, should you overturn the curricle and them, would not be felt by their relatives or by society." He turned to his half-sister. "If you will excuse me, I will leave you to change for dinner."

"And what's the matter with him?" exclaimed Marcus frankly when his uncle had left them. "What burr sits under his saddle? Pretty widow not coming up to scratch? More chance for me, then. Think I'll change myself." And he left whistling a cheerful tune, the words of which were not known to Almeria, and just as well, thought Philip, giving his wife an absent kiss as she rolled her eyes at him, not knowing which gave her the vapours most, silly young Marcus, or his unbending uncle.

One reason for wanting Francis to marry Bel was that she might take some of the starch out of him—but it would not do to say so!

BEL, WAITING FOR Francis to arrive the next morning, was quite unaware that the plot was thickening as yet more actors arrived on the scene. Mrs. Broughton beside her was all of a delighted flutter. Francis had said that he would come for them in the Harleys' carriage, and Bel would then be transferred to his curricle, the Harleys' coachman taking over the responsibility of the carriage in which Mrs. Broughton would sit with the Harley family. Henry Venn was driving his mother and Mrs. Robey in their carriage, and several other equipages of varying age and fashionability would make up the party.

Fortunately the day was fine, and even if Bel's spirits were a little low at the prospect of being persecuted by a haughty nobleman all day, the other prospect of a picnic and a stroll in good countryside could still attract. She would not allow him to destroy the pleasure which she had come to feel in living at Lulsgate Spa.

But he behaved himself perfectly when he arrived, handed Mrs. Broughton in, and later out of, the carriage in fine style, and confided in them both that his and Almeria's nephew, Marcus Carey, Viscount Tawstock, had arrived with friends, and would be accompanying them on their jaunt.

Marcus Carey, the young fool who had proposed to Marianne and to whom she had been lending money! And what would *his* friends be like?

They were all assembled in Almeria's drawing-room, congratulating themselves on the fineness of the weather. Francis's hand was firmly on Bel's arm when he led her in, as though she might be about to desert him again at any moment, and she knew at once which of the three men whom she had never seen before was Marcus, the blurred likeness to Francis was so strong.

Marcus's candid appreciation of her when he was introduced did a little to mollify the spirits which Francis's treatment had wounded.

"Why, you dog, Uncle, is that what brought you to Lulsgate?" And he bent over Bel's hand with as much gallantry as he could muster, straightening up to stare at her in admiration, adding, "We have not met before, I know, but I have the feeling, almost, that we have. You have a sister, perhaps? You certainly possess the look of someone I have known, but I should never have forgotten that divine shade of red-gold hair!"

Bel could almost feel Francis's sardonic and mocking stare at Marcus's artless words. She was well aware that, although she had not greatly resembled Marianne in looks, there had been an indefinable resemblance between them—something in the expression, perhaps?—and that Marcus had seen it!

She judged it politic merely to smile; anything she said would be a lie, and, worse, might hang her later— and then she was being introduced to two men whom she instinctively knew were Marcus's toad-eaters, mere hangers-on whom only Marcus's presence there could have brought into the vicarage.

Fred Carnaby was nothing, but, unworldly though she was, she disliked Captain Rhys Howell on sight— and did not know why. He was handsome in an easy, obvious fashion, quite unlike Francis's severe and harsh haughtiness, and his manner was as warm and soothing as Francis's was abrasive. He held her hand a trifle too long, smiled a little too easily, and she decided that she disliked soft blue eyes and curly blond hair. Besides, by his manner, she thought, Captain

Howell was a deal too fond of himself, and did not need anyone else to be fond of him.

But she was all courtesy, and when Francis had handed her into his curricle, a beautiful thing, picked out in chocolate and cream, drawn by two matched chestnuts, and they were starting off towards Beacon Hill, he said coolly to her as he manoeuvred her through the light traffic of Lulsgate's main street, "A lady of great discretion, I see. First to be such a diplomat when Marcus committed his unintended gaffe, and then your reception of the dubious captain—I must congratulate you. Such *savoir-faire.* A pity that you did not choose to settle in London; you could have gone much further than your sister, been a great man's public ladybird, the queen of the *demimonde,* no less."

"Am I supposed to be flattered by that?" said Bel curtly. "Your compliment is as dubious as the captain's."

"Keep on remembering what you are is my advice," was his only reply, "for, resourceful though you are, I hardly think you carry enough armament to keep the captain in order. And now shall we declare a truce? I have a mind to enjoy my day in the sun." The look he gave her as he said this was so warm and caressing that it altered his whole face, transforming it so that Bel had a powerful and sad wish that she could have met him in different circumstances, and then their whole intercourse could have been different, too.

She shook herself mentally, and said coolly, "If you wish. I have no desire to distress Almeria, who is goodness itself, and Philip also deserves consideration, to say nothing of the children."

This last sentence gave her a pang. She dearly loved little Frank and Caroline, who in return loved Aunt

Bel, and the pang grew worse as she suddenly thought
that this renewed meeting with Lord Francis Carey
might yet mean that she would have to fly Lulsgate and
give up the happy life which she had created for herself.

"Good," said Francis, and then applied himself to
driving, for the roads around Lulsgate were not good,
and this part of Leicestershire, near Charnwood For-
est, was a little hilly. "For we are not so far from the
Pennines, after all," he remarked, smartly negotiating
a difficult corner.

"I suppose you are what they call a whip," offered
Bel, who had, much against her will, been admiring the
whole athletic picture which he presented.

"After a fashion," he returned lazily. "I have no
pretence to being a name in any way. My life has been
too busy for me to indulge myself in following fashion's dictates—I have never wanted to rival a coachman on the road or a pugilist in the ring. They are the
pursuits of men without occupation. Merely to do ordinary things well is an aim worth following."

Bel was suddenly determined to know more of him.
"And your occupation—what was, or is that?"

"At the moment," he returned, "I am a diplomat of
sorts. I was at the Paris Embassy, but I have been recalled to act in an advisory capacity at the Foreign Office, a duty which is neither here nor there, and if that
is what I am doomed to then I shall seek other duties.
I suppose I ought to sit for Parliament at the next elec-
tion and find my future there. The idea does not particularly attract."

"And you have always been a diplomat?" Bel was
curious. Something about his athleticism, the habit of

command strong in his voice, had suggested quite otherwise.

"Oh, I see why you, and she, were so successful," he remarked, breaching their truce a little. "This gentle interest in a man's affairs, flattering as well as soothing. No," he said hastily, seeing her expression grow stormy, "I will answer you. I was in the navy, until there was no ship for me—was seconded to the admiralty, and from thence, by degrees, ended up in my present position."

"The navy!" exclaimed Bel. It explained so much about him. His cold certainty—she could imagine him commanding a crew of recalcitrant sailors, quelling them with a look. "Did you see action in any of the great battles in the recent wars?" Her voice was as eager as a boy's. "Lord Nelson was quite my favourite hero. I used to dream of running away to sea and being a midshipman!"

"And a deuced hard life you would have found it," he said, giving her a surprised glance on hearing this unlikely revelation. "I was at Trafalgar, and allow me to tell you that sea battles are most unpleasant things, not romantic at all. You are better reading of them with Almeria, rather than taking part."

"All the interesting doings in life are reserved for the male sex," remarked Bel, a little aggrieved, "such as being a sailor, driving a curricle, or a thousand other things. We are left with such milk-and-water occupations as sewing and tatting, no comparison at all!"

"But so much safer," riposted Francis, using his whip to touch his horses lightly to make them turn more tightly than they wished. "One rarely ends up with one's head removed by a cannon-ball while making baby-clothes."

Bel could not help giving a fat chuckle at this. She had a vision of herself and Almeria sitting decorously in the vicarage drawing-room, dodging bullets, balls and grenades. Could one dodge them? She thought not. They "arrived", one supposed, willy-nilly. She remarked so to Francis, who, rapidly looking sideways at her, registered a pang at the sight of her vivid face.

"Indeed, you are perceptive to understand that—there is no avoiding them—and I may add that driving a curricle is not the easiest thing in life. There are daring ladies who do, although most confine themselves to perch, or ladies' phaetons."

Bel had a vision of herself, seated behind a pair of milk-white unicorns—for if one were using one's imagination one could surely imagine that—driving a curricle whose body was silver gilt, rubies set in the wheels, and the harness gold cord, and all the metal connected with it silver and gold, too.

Her face took on such an expression of pure happiness that Francis, despite himself, was touched. How did she do it? He had met many ladybirds, and not one of them could assume that look of enchanting innocence.

The day pleased Bel as well; the sun was at its kindest, golden and warm, with the faintest hint of mist in the distance taming the summer's heat. The greenery which surrounded them had achieved its final perfection before it began to fall into a golden or dull-ochre decay, the grasses becoming straw, losing their lushness.

Beacon Hill now lay before them. They were not to mount in their various carriages to the top, but to draw up on a flattish meadow at its base. Last of all to be wheeled into position was to be the landau which contained the cold collation and the servants who would prepare and lay it out for them, once their masters had taken their pleasure, either by sitting in the shade or strolling up to the top to look out across the countryside towards Cold Ashby in Northamptonshire where the previous beacon to herald the Armada's coming had been lit, or northwards to the next.

"Stirring days, were they not?" remarked Bel to Francis, after his tiger had handed her down, and he had taken her arm, most proprietorially, she noticed. Anyone watching them would have assumed that Lord Francis Carey was indeed smitten by the widow's charms.

"And fortunate that the great Elizabeth and her sea captains won," was Francis's answer, "seeing that if they had not done so we should hardly be jaunting here—or might be speaking Spanish at the very least."

"Only think," said Bel, "it would have been in the Channel that you won your spurs—if naval captains win spurs—and not Trafalgar, if you had lived then."

"Spurs are for knights," said Francis, "of whom I am not one, not sailors." And was that a reminder of their true situation? thought Bel, but she determinedly made nothing of it, particularly when little Frank, happy to be free again, came running to his uncle.

"You will give me a ride in your curricle one day, will you not, Uncle Frank?" he exclaimed. "Perhaps you would let me sit on Aunt Bel's knee? She is quite my favourite aunt," he went on, "even if she is not a true one—a friend-aunt, Mama says. Perhaps—" and he screwed his eyes up at his daring "—you would make her a real aunt, and then I could have her all the time. Oh," he said sadly, "Mama told me not to say that to

you, Uncle Francis, and now I have forgot—but,''
brightening, ''I am sure you do not mind,'' and he ran
off again, his legs itching, his mama later said, after
being confined in the carriage during their longish
journey.

Bel, all blushes at the little boy's artless remarks,
hardly dared to look at Francis, particularly when he
remarked drily, ''You have won one male animal of the
Carey family over, Mrs. Bel Merrick, that is plain to
see.''

Pricked, she could not help retorting, ''Oh, indeed?
I thought, by your behaviour, that I had won two. One
hardly pursues with such determination those to whom
we are indifferent!''

Where all this was coming from Bel did not know.
Ever since she had first met him, two years ago, she had
begun to change from the milk-and-water creature who
had gone to London and who had nearly been extin-
guished by the revelation of Marianne's career. The
speed of change had slowed down during her time at
Lulsgate, but since Francis had arrived so dramatically in her life again its pace had increased equally
dramatically. There was something about him to which
she responded, and whether that would have been so if
she had met him as the respectable unknowing young
lady she had once been she had no means of knowing.
She only knew that in order to cope with him at all she
needed all her wits about her, and those wits were
sharpened every time she met him.

Marcus was approaching, Miss Robey on his arm,
and Captain Howell with another pretty young thing
on his—Kate Thomson, a manufacturer's daughter,
visiting Lulsgate with her clergywoman aunt, and part
of Almeria's circle in consequence, the clergywoman's

late husband having been Philip's tutor at Oxford. And a less suitable partner than Captain Howell for a virtuous young woman Bel could not think of, but she assumed that Marcus had done the introductions and Almeria was helpless before them.

"Ah, Carey," murmured Captain Howell, "you had a good journey here, the roads not too tricky for a good whip?" And he waved a negligent hand at his own rather showy phaeton. "And now for a walk to see the panorama—I am assured by the ladies that it is worth subjecting oneself to the sun and the insects to enjoy it. We shall shortly find out."

Even his most innocuous remarks, thought Bel, appeared disagreeable when offered with such oily knowingness. She could almost feel Francis stiffen when addressed so familiarly by such a toad-eater, but there was nothing for it, and it was really, thought Bel unkindly, a little amusing to think that for once the great Francis Carey was being put down, even if she had to thank such a cad for doing so!

Almost as though he had divined her thoughts, Francis gave her arm a little pressure, similar, Bel thought, to that which he applied with his whip to his horses, saying, "Shall we find our own way to the top, Mrs. Merrick? Will Mrs. Broughton allow you out of her sight? Surely in such a public view, with such a large party, I may be allowed to escort a young gentlewoman without adverse comment."

Even as he spoke, Mrs. Broughton walked towards them, fanning herself, her face already scarlet; being somewhat plump, she felt the heat of the day more than a little.

"You will forgive me if I do not accompany you both, but I wish to rest; the sun afflicts me, and I may help Lady Almeria with the collation. She needs to oversee it, she says, and I am to bid you to be back not later than two. The servants have placed the wine bottles in the stream, and the sandwiches will be greasy if you delay overlong. You may tell me of the view when you return, Bel. Philip, who has already set out, has promised to sketch it for me."

Matchmaking, matchmaking, thought Bel of Mrs. Broughton and dear Almeria both; if only you knew the truth! Almeria—Frank and Caroline running about her—waved her hand to them and made shooing motions in the direction of the path up the hill. Henry Venn, a disconsolate look on his face, his mother by his side, proprietorial as usual, was apparently about to escort the Harley children to the top, in default of being allowed Bel.

"I like my niece and nephew," remarked Francis, as they set off, "but feeling as I do they would be distinctly *de trop.* I shall endeavour to make up for my defection later. Almeria has packed a cricket bat and ball so that we may have some lively entertainment when we have recovered from luncheon, or nuncheon—I am not sure what one calls what one consumes at two in the afternoon, in the open."

"A new word is needed, perhaps," suggested Bel, as they began their upward march after Marcus and his companions, who could be heard laughing and talking together, Kate and Miss Robey not finding Captain Howell and his witticisms as unlikeable as Bel did. She was aware that, since discovering what Marianne had become, her knowledge of the world had increased so greatly that she could never again be so young and innocent as they were.

Curiously, the knowledge did not depress her. Young women ought not to be kept in the same state as fools, she decided, and this redoubled her intention not to be cowed by Lord Francis Carey. Not that he was doing much cowing of her at the moment, and when they reached the top of the hill, where Captain Howell was pretending to look for ash from the beacon—after over two hundred years!—she noted that Francis was careful to keep her away from Marcus and his friends— whether this was for her protection, or theirs, she could not decide.

In deference to the ladies, the whole party—a large one, for others beside the Harleys' immediate friends and relatives had come along—now sat for a moment. Parasols were opened, and Bel's, a frivolous lemon-coloured specimen, to match her loose gown, served to protect Francis as well as herself. They sat at a little distance from the others, and he pointed out to her the various landmarks around them, and in the warmth of post-noon Bel felt delightfully sleepy and relaxed, muttering um and ah at him, rather as he had done yesterday when she had been telling him of the plants and the fish.

"Why do I gain the impression that *you* are funning *me?*" he said, the loose expression coming oddly from him—his speech was usually precise, devoid of the slang which Marcus and Captain Howell used so freely, making the young women about them giggle and titter, with cries of "Never say so!", "You are teasing me!", and "Who would have thought it, sir?"

"Funning you? Never!" replied Bel calmly as though she were discussing parliamentary matters with him. "No such thing. I would not dare. Perfect respect is what you always demand and are invariably given, I am sure."

"Said like that," he returned lazily, "it can only mean that you are offering me perfect disrespect, secure in the knowledge that, here, no condign punishment can immediately follow. Take care. My memory is long and payment will be required—later."

The grey eyes mocking her were no longer cold, his face, usually so set and stern, soft; whatever else, there was no doubt that Francis Carey was enjoying himself, and, had Bel but known, was doing so after a fashion which he had not felt for years. The only flaw, he considered, in the delightful sensation that being with her was producing was the knowledge that consummation of it might take a little time.

Oh, the siren that she was! She need do nothing, but nothing, to engage and trap him. She had captured him from the moment he had walked into the study at Stanhope Street, had merely needed to look at him and he was lost. Oh, the pity of it that she was what she was. To have paid court to her properly, enjoyed her wit, beauty and fire in due form, *that* would have been something. And yet was not this sparring even more delightful with its undertones of the forbidden and the wicked carried on as it was in the presence of those who had no, or little, suspicion of what was going on in front of them?

If Bel were truthful, and had been informed of how Francis felt, she would have been compelled to admit that she shared much of his feelings. The spice which their unwilling conspiracy gave to all their encounters was having its effect on her—there must be more of Marianne in me than I thought being her response as he helped her to her feet, and with one last look at the splendid view beneath them, they set off for lunch, the last to leave.

"Come, we will follow a different path from the others. I don't want company," commanded Francis, and, taking her hand, he led her down a secluded track, shaded by some scrub. Once well into it, out of view of the rest, he turned, took her parasol from her unresisting hand to place it on the ground, and before Bel could prevent him—did she want to prevent him?—took her in his arms, saying, "First payment for me, Mrs. Bel Merrick, a foretaste of what is to come," and began to plunder her mouth.

Untried, unkissed, never before even touched by a man, Bel felt her senses reel. Beforehand she would have quailed at the thought of such an intimate caress as his mouth teased her own mouth open and his tongue met hers, causing such a roaring wave of sensation to pass over her that her knees sagged and she almost fell against him.

She should be shocked, revolted; she had not asked for this, did not want it, no, never—but yes, oh, yes, this was delightful. When his palm cupped her right breast, stroking it through the light muslin, his thumb finding her nipple and doing dreadful things to it, so that this time the sensation produced had her gasping aloud, his mouth having progressed to the creamy skin below her slender neck, almost to the shadow of the cleft between her breasts, Bel said aloud before she could stop herself, "Yes, oh, yes," so that he withdrew, laughing, saying,

"The first plea of many from you, madam, I trust," and the mockery in his voice rendered her wild—with rage now, not with passion.

"No," she panted, "no, not at all, you are quite mistook. Yes, you must stop was what I meant."

"Not, No, you must go on?" he riposted, eyebrows wickedly raised. "I am sorry I may not pleasure you further now, but we risk comment. Later, perhaps, we may continue where we left off."

"No, never!" raged Bel. "I should not have come with you at all. I shall ask Almeria for protection. You are not to treat me so cavalierly. I do not deserve it."

"But you wanted it as much as I did. Never say that you did not. A most willing encounter, by my faith. It augurs well for our future dalliance. Come." And he picked up her parasol. "Open it again, not to shield us from the sun, but the rest of the world from the spectacle of a well-roused woman. You look delectable, madam, but ripe for bedding at the moment."

Oh, horrors! Bel knew the truth of what he was saying. Her whole body had become slack, relaxed, her mouth, even, had become almost slumbrous. She wanted more. Her body was on fire, not from the heat of the day, but from the heat of him.

This would never do. She opened the parasol and looked away, suddenly almost in tears at her body's betrayal of her. However much she thought that the cold mind ruled, once exposed to the fires of passion the body had taken its own wilful way. She could no longer deceive herself. She desired Lord Francis Carey most desperately, but if she could not have him in honour she was determined not to have him at all. He could not win his disgraceful campaign, however powerful the broadsides he fired at her.

This unintended nautical metaphor restored Bel's self-command and her ready humour. How apt it was to think so of a sailor. Did Lord Francis have a girl in

every port? she wondered, and, thinking so, the face
she showed him was one of Bel restored. Humour had
replaced erotic passion, and he marvelled at her self-
command. A mistress, a very mistress of the amorous
arts, to recover so quickly. She was wasted living a pure
life in Lulsgate; such art, such self-command would
compel a fortune in London—and all to be enjoyed for
nothing by Francis Carey—when he was ready.

Nonsense. He was ready now, but the open meadow
was before them, cloths were spread on the grass, the
food was waiting, the wine already being drunk, the
ladies' lemonade being poured from glass pitchers. He
handed Bel down, saying lazily in response to Almeria's slightly raised brows at their latecoming, "I was
enchanted by the view, persuaded Mrs. Merrick to remain while I took my fill of it and beg pardon for dil-
atoriness."

But the view which Francis Carey had been enjoying was that of Bel Merrick's enchanting profile, and
for the life of him he could not have told his half-sister
what he had seen from the top of Beacon Hill!

CHAPTER SEVEN

EATING IN THE OPEN, delightful though it sounded in prospect, for she had never engaged in it before, was not so remarkably pleasant as Bel had thought it would be. True, the food tasted delicious in the open air; it was the other aspects of picnicking which were not so attractive.

First of all there were the wasps and flies, which were attracted by the food; secondly there was the difficulty of eating gracefully without making one's fingers unpleasantly sticky, or ruining one's gown; and finally the position was not so comfortable as one might have expected.

She said so to Francis, who was busy eating a chicken wing, and saving his glass of sparkling white wine from overturning on the ground.

"Alfresco meals sound delightful in novels," she informed him, "but are not so remarkably pleasant as I thought they would be."

"Exactly so," was his reply to that. "Boring though it might sound, I always think food best eaten at a good table. One's cravat," he said, rescuing a portion of chicken from his own perfectly tied butterfly fall, "takes less wear and tear."

Pleased to agree with him over something, Bel, who had recovered from the inward confusion after the encounter on the hill, began to listen to the conversation of the others. Inevitably, the news being what it was, the company had begun to discuss the delightfully scandalous business of the Bill of Pains and Penalties, instigated by her husband, King George IV, against Queen Caroline, the wife he loathed, accusing her of low behaviour culminating in repeated acts of adultery.

Discussion over this interesting event, sure to provide gossip for months, centred not on the question of the Queen's innocence, but on political grounds, those Tories favouring the king being adamant on the Bill's passing, and those Whigs who wished to see the King and the Government embarrassed wishing to see it fall.

The liveliness of the gossip was assisted by the fact that Marcus, Fred Carnaby and George Hargrove, another amiable but light-minded youth, had removed all the young unmarried girls, once lunch was over, to the other end of the green, and were playing childish games with them, leaving the seasoned men and women to gossip at will, Bel, as a widow being included in the number.

Even Mrs. Venn, that austere matron, was not averse to joining in, wagging her high dressed head, her coiffure a relic of her long-lost youth, deploring everybody, King, Queen and lords.

"And is the poor creature truly innocent, do you think?" asked Almeria of her brother. She could never bear to think ill of anyone.

"Hardly," was Francis's dry response to that. He normally avoided joining in with such idle gossip, but the Queen's trial was more than that, it was politics, and who knew what might happen? Some doomsters had even suggested that the King's unpopularity might result in revolution, if the mob grew too restive. "No-one, not even those who support her, think that. I was at a dinner party, seated near Viscount Granville, George Canning's friend and adviser, and his comment was that the Bill indicting her would not pass the Lords, there not being sufficient evidence. He felt the majority would be for her, not on the grounds of her unpopularity, but of his. The answer to 'Is she bad?' is 'He is as bad.' Guilt and innocence, he indicated, do not enter into it, and I fear that he is right. All the same, his friend George Canning fled to the Continent when the Bill was to reach the Lords, for fear that his relationship with the Queen might cause him damage, even though it was years ago."

Captain Howell, not loath to show his own acquaintanceship with society gossip, commented, "One wonders that Granville himself did not fly the country, since the Princess of Wales, as she was then, was one of his many conquests."

"Ah, but Granville does not wish to be Prime Minister one day, and Canning does," returned Francis unarguably, "and he is now quite reformed—which Mr. Canning is not."

He did not add that it was reported that Lord Granville's clever wife had commented that if the qualification of the members of the House of Lords entitled to judge the Queen was that they had not had an affair with her then the House would be remarkably empty when the Bill designed to judge her was brought in!

Almeria said, "One would like to believe her innocent. It is not right that vice should occupy the throne itself," and then thought sadly that if that were so, then the Queen's husband, George IV, ought to consider abdicating.

"Yes," said Francis, sanctimoniously for him. "Vice should never flourish; one wishes to see it gain the punishment it deserves. You agree with me, I am sure, Mrs. Merrick?" he added, turning to Bel, who sat beside him, a little wary of this conversation, waiting for some two-edged comment from him, and sure enough here it came.

She would not be daunted, not she. "Oh, I do so agree with you," she said. "The wages of sin, as the Bible says, are cruel, and none of us, however high in rank, should be exempt from them. Although if there is an element of revenge in the King's pursuit of his poor Queen then I must add that I deplore that, too. A most unworthy sentiment, revenge." That should hold you a little, she thought.

But no. "Bravo," said Francis, "a most Christian sentiment and exactly what I would have expected from you, Mrs. Merrick, so absolutely does it sort with your character as I have come to know it," and this was said with such apparent sincerity that not only Almeria but others thought how partial Lord Francis was growing towards the pretty widow.

Henry Venn, indeed, ground his teeth, seeing beauty and a modest fortune slipping from him; Captain Howell, still with the wineglass in his hand, sipped from it thoughtfully and turned inscrutable eyes on the subject of Lord Francis's apparent admiration.

The Reverend Mr. Philip Harley, that saintly but shrewd man, was the only person who did not quite take Francis Carey's apparent compliment to Mrs. Merrick at its full face value. But he said nothing, being wise as well as perceptive. Instead, tiring of this lubricious gossip about a woman whom he considered to be as unfortunate as she was ill-advised, he said gently, "You suggested a game of cricket, Francis, to entertain Frank as well as the ladies. Enough time has passed since lunch to enable us to perform without difficulty."

"Then we must round up Marcus and the rest," drawled Captain Howell, rising from his recumbent position on the grass, to give him his due, thought Bel, as ready to join in childish games as the less sophisticated of the party. The servants were to be pressed in, the coachman being a useful bowler for the Lulsgate team, and the audience was to consist of the ladies, and little Caroline, young Frank being allowed to field under the eyes of his papa and uncle.

Somewhat to Bel's surprise, that haughty gentleman, Francis Carey, joined in as enthusiastically as anyone else, taking off his beautiful cravat, his tight, fashionable coat, and rolling up his shirtsleeves. She had not thought it of him, but Almeria, seeing her surprise, said, "Oh, dear Francis excels at all sports and pastimes. He is a fine shot, and although he does not care for it Philip says he was a good pugilist—only practises it now to keep himself in trim."

In trim he certainly was, thought Bel. Losing a little of his outer clothing had served to reveal what a splendid body he possessed, emphasising its strength and its masculinity. Soft, self-indulgent Marcus looked almost effeminate beside his uncle. He, too, shed his coat and stock, and gave Bel his dazzling smile; she had to admit that he possessed his own charm, even if it were different from his uncle's, as he said, "You will cheer for me, will you not? Francis must not be the only one of us here to gain your approval."

"Bravely said," remarked Rhys Howell, who had come up to them while Marcus was talking. "Lord

Francis must not be allowed to monopolise the only real charmer in Lulsgate Spa. You will allow me to call on you one afternoon, Mrs. Merrick, will you not? I mean to further my acquaintance with you, to both our advantages, I hope.''

Was she mistaken—Bel hoped she was—but was there something a little two-edged in this remark of Captain Howell's; or was her doubtful association with Francis Carey beginning to colour every word said to her by anybody—however innocent they meant those words to be?

Bel shivered a little, bright though the sunshine was, but forgot her malaise in watching the men enjoy themselves. All boys again, was her reaction, as it was Almeria's.

"Difficult to think how serious Philip is and how severe Francis is," she said to Bel, "when one sees them at play. I do believe all men remain boys at heart."

Bel could not but agree with her. They were seated at some distance from the one stump at which the bowler was aiming, and she joined in the cheering when someone was out, or scored a good run by dashing towards Almeria's parasol, set upright in the ground instead of another wicket, there not being enough players to justify two batsmen at once, Philip said.

When Francis came to the wicket, the fun began. Almeria had been correct to describe him as adept at all sports, and despite herself Bel rose from her seat, the more easily to see him perform. Frank was jumping up and down, shouting "Huzza!" every time his uncle lashed the ball into the distance.

"Bravo!" he shouted, after one splendid shot had sent the ball into the undergrowth and the fielders had spent some time looking for it, and the next ball Francis treated with even more disdain, striking it high into the air, towards the bevy of applauding women.

Bel never knew why she did it, but as the ball reached the top of its flight and began to arc towards her the memory of jolly days in Brangton with Garth were on her. She had purposely worn a dress whose skirts would not confine her, whose hem was unfashionably well clear of the ground, showing, as Francis had already noted, a pretty pair of ankles, and so she began to run towards the spot where the ball would land.

And then, as it was almost upon her, she saw that she would have to throw herself forward to catch it, and to catch Francis out was suddenly the most important thing in the world, so she launched herself forward, caught it, held it high, and then landed flat on her face, all the wind knocked out of her body, but the ball safely clear of the ground and Francis dismissed.

The only person not nonplussed by her extraordinary action was Francis himself. He flung down his bat and ran towards where she lay prone in the grass, unmoving, his face white. He threw himself down on his knees beside her, and why should it matter to him that Bel Merrick was not hurt? But all the same, before anyone else could arrive to help, he was assisting her, saying hoarsely, "You have taken no harm?"

"No, none," said Bel faintly, still holding tightly to the ball, "and I have dismissed you, have I not?"

They were face to face, closer than they had ever been except for the brief embrace on the hill. So close that Bel could smell the warm masculine scent of him, the scent of a man engaged in powerful exertion, touched with a little fear for her safety, a smell uniquely that of Francis Carey; while he was equally aware of

the unique flowery scent of Bel Merrick, and, all unknowing, his face was soft with love and concern for
her.

Bel later thought that had they not been interrupted
there might have been the beginning of healing between them. But then the world, in the shape of Captain Howell, was on them.

"Madam not damaged, eh, Carey?" he said, his face
hard and knowing. "A splendid catch, that, Mrs.
Merrick; should be a cricketer yourself. Bound and
determined to get him out, were you?"

Their moment was over. Francis's face resumed its
normal haughty aspect, and Bel's a look of slight
withdrawal.

All in all Mrs. Bel Merrick was quite the heroine of
the afternoon, particularly so far as the gentlemen were
concerned. The ladies, especially the younger ones,
were not so sure. The pretty widow had stolen their
thunder again.

"Oh, famous," cried Frank, jumping up and down
on the spot while Bel was tenderly carried by Francis to
where Almeria gently straightened her dishevelled ap-
pearance, removed the dry grass from her hair, and
generally restored her to her usual state of calm order.
"That's the very first time any one has ever got Uncle
Francis out when we've played cricket, and it was Aunt
Bel who caught him! Would you like a go with the bat,
Aunt Bel? Oh, do have a go with the bat—and then
Uncle Francis can try to catch you!"

Everyone laughed at the little boy's enthusiasm, not
least Uncle Francis and Aunt Bel, who laughingly declined, saying, "I have had quite enough excitement for
one afternoon, dear Frank, without putting myself in
the way of allowing your uncle to gain his revenge.

Another time, perhaps," and she hardly dared to look at him while she spoke, helped a little by his nephew who flung his arms around her and tried to climb on her knee, disputing the favour with Caroline, who wished to offer Bel her new rag doll to play with.

"Pray, children, allow your aunt to rest," instructed Almeria; "she has had quite enough excitement for one afternoon," amusing Bel a little, for she felt tremendously invigorated, if not to say uplifted, after giving haughty Francis his come-uppance—except that she could not forget the expression on his face when he had come to rescue her—so strange and gentle, almost loving.

Well, enough of that, she thought briskly, amused to note that Francis was so proprietorial with her, glaring at Rhys Howell when he tried to comfort her by saying, "A fine opportunity for you to take Lulsgate waters tomorrow, to restore yourself, Mrs. Merrick. I understand that they are full of that rare stuff, sodium chloride."

"Very rare," snorted Francis, almost forgetting himself by being openly uncivil to a man he detested, "seeing that sodium chloride is nothing but common salt—and would hardly restore Mrs. Merrick to anything—other than giving her what I am sure she does not wish—a monstrous thirst!"

Captain Howell did not glare back, but said, rather wittily and pointedly, Bel thought—this was suddenly not Francis's day—"Well, Carey—" and she could almost feel Francis grind his teeth at this unwanted familiarity "—since the nobility and gentry see fit to rush to Brighton to bathe in and drink the salt sea-water there, it would not come amiss for Mrs. Merrick to do the same, perhaps. Do I hope to see you there tomorrow, madam?" he queried. "We could take the waters together; overfeeding in Town has rendered me a little bilious."

Bel did not care for him at all—there was something false in his obsequiousness to her—but Francis Carey needed to be taught a lesson; that he could not dictate to Mrs. Bel Merrick whom she should meet, and how she should conduct herself. So she smiled sweetly at Captain Howell, fluttering her eyelashes after a fashion she usually avoided, and said softly, "Should I feel sufficiently up to an excursion to the Baths tomorrow, Captain Howell, you will be sure to see me in the Pump Room, and, if so, I shall be pleased to take the waters with you."

She hoped that this would end the matter. The cricket match resumed again, for a short time only; the afternoon drawing on towards evening, and a late dinner beckoning, the party regretfully assembled for home, all the picnic stuff and cricketing paraphernalia having been packed. Francis, on his sister's instructions, came forward to escort her home, Captain Howell being fobbed off with lesser attractions.

He said nothing until she was safely tucked in; for some reason both he and Almeria thinking that a young woman who had engaged in such minimal exertion as running to catch a ball and then falling over needed the utmost in tender, loving care—to the degree that they thought fit to muffle her in a blanket on such a warm day!

Bel was something in agreement with Cassius, whose sardonic expression before he hoisted himself on to his small seat behind them both told her what he thought of the coddling of such fine ladies as herself.

Coddling did not stop there. Having started off once more, Francis remarked in his most lordly voice, not so loud as the one he used on the quarter-deck to be sure, but full of the same command, "You would be wise to have as little as possible to do with Captain Howell, Mrs. Merrick. I tell you so for your own good. His reputation, particularly with women, is deplorable."

"Oh!" Bel almost gasped; she was not to be lectured on proper behaviour by a man whose declared intent to her was so determinedly improper. "For a man whose stated intentions towards myself are so dishonourable, I find such an . . . objurgation insufferable indeed. Am I to suppose that to be . . . deplorable to me is reserved strictly for you? Such hypocrisy! What would your poor sister say if she knew of the lengths to which you are going to reserve my ruin for yourself? Why should you care what Captain Howell does with and to me?"

She was well aware that Cassius was probably listening to every word she uttered, ears flapping, for she had not attempted to keep her voice down, but she did not care about that, not she! Nor apparently did Francis.

A look of fury crossed his haughty face; the hand holding his whip upright—they were driving along an easy stretch of road, his horses needing little direction—was shaking a little.

"Rant on, madam," he said at last. "I thought that perhaps you were a little nice in choosing those on whom you conferred your favours—or so you have suggested. I see that I was wrong—paddle in the mud with Captain Howell if you will; it is probably no more than I should have expected. I thought to help you."

"Paddle in the mud! Thought to help me!" Bel was running out of exclamation marks. "The public spaces of the Pump Room are not exactly muddy! And as to your notion of helping me—well, words fail me!"

"I cannot say that I have ever noticed any such phenomenon," said Francis through his teeth. "On the contrary, a longer-tongued shrew I have seldom encountered. You lack gratitude, madam. Stupid of me, I know, but I was only speaking for your own good." He knew perfectly well that in the light of what he had promised to do to her he must sound ridiculous, but the mere idea of Rhys Howell, or any other man, laying a finger on Bel Merrick made him feel quite ill, and as for all the men she had...entertained before he had met her, well, he could have killed the lot of them...slowly.

The very last thing he had expected had happened to him. Standing there, his bat in his hand, watching her run to catch the cricket ball he had launched into the air, her beautiful face alight with joy, seeing her fall, had produced in him the most astonishing sensation. Inconveniently, against all reason, he knew that he had fallen hopelessly and desperately in love with a Cyprian of Cyprians, a woman whom, as he had seen this very day, men had only to look at to want. Henry Venn, young Marcus and his silly friends, Rhys Howell and the rest of them, married and single, had all walked around her, their tongues hanging out, panting at the sight of her, and he was no better—no, much worse—than the rest.

How could such a thing have happened to him?

Oh, he must possess madam, and soon, to anaesthetise himself, to cool this terrible fever which he now knew had been burning him up since he had first seen her two years ago. *That* was the reason for his rage against her. But worse even than that was the dreadful thought that to have her in his arms might not assuage his desire, but would merely serve to inflame him the more! For he hated every man who spoke to her, not simply the dubious semi-criminal he suspected Howell to be.

A mistress of the erotic arts, sitting beside him in his curricle, arguing with him wittily and unanswerably, refusing to be put down, robbing him of honour and common sense—how could he deal with her? He could go to his sister, tell her the truth about her friend, destroy her socially and for good—and make Almeria and all her family unhappy into the bargain. He told himself that he could not do it, because it would deprive him of the revenge which he had promised himself he would have if he ever encountered the sweet cheat again, but there was more to it than that.

He was drowning in love's cross-currents, for astonishingly he did not want to ruin her in *that* way, if he did in the other. Indeed, he hardly knew what he did want.

Why could she not have been chaste, so that he could have gone on his knees to her, instead of wanting her on her knees before him, to ask her to be—what? His wife? The second wife whom he had vowed he would never take, so determined was he to be faithful to the memory of his dear, lost Cassie.

His dear, lost Cassie! For the first time in years he had ceased to think of her; ever since he had first met Bel Merrick her poor shade had grown thinner and thinner; the years had done their work on him, and the boy who had loved and married and lost her was as dead as Cassie.

No! He would not be caught by madam; he had made his intent known, and by God he would have her, and on his terms.

The silence between them stretched on and on. Francis's eyes were on the road, Bel's on her hands, now lax in her lap, now gripped together, for, like Francis, the terrible trammels of love were netting her about; she was a fish or a bird, caught in the meshes, unable to move in any direction. And, also like him, she hardly knew what to think, feel or do.

She told herself that she hated him, but knew that she lied, or rather knew that love and hate were now so inextricably blended that the power of decision had almost gone from her. As in the moment she had caught the cricket ball and had held it aloft she had felt regret for catching him, mixed with her triumph, so now she hardly knew where detestation ended and obsession began.

Oh, why could she not have met him in Lulsgate for the first time, been introduced to him as Miss Anne Isabella Passmore, the Reverend Mr. Caius Passmore's virtuous daughter, on whom he could have smiled, with and to whom he would have spoken honourably, so that he would have been gentle with her, not reproached her in fierce despite?

They were entering Lulsgate again, passing the first new houses, and the even newer half-finished ones lining the road, tribute to the developing wealth of this part of Leicestershire. They were passing the Baths, reaching her home, he was setting her down, Mrs. Broughton was being conducted home, too, and the day, so fraught with incident, was over. Lottie was coming out to greet her, exclaiming, "Oh, Miss Bel, what have you done to your bonnet?" and Francis was bowing over her hand, saying in a low and stifled voice, "I had forgot the truce I proclaimed; pray forgive me."

She replied, wearily, because although so little had happened on the way home she felt as though she had lived through years of emotion, "And, I, too, forgot myself, Lord Francis. I thank you for the journey and," she could not help herself, "for the cricket. I had not played it for years, and found it strangely satisfying to catch a ball again."

His strong face lightened at that, filled with somewhat unexpected humour as she lanced the tension which had lain between them. "Oh, yes, you triumphed mightily, did you not? One act only, all afternoon, and you are immortalised in Lulsgate's annals. Allow me, if you would, to escort you to the Assembly Ball tomorrow evening," and before she could reply he bowed over her offered hand as courteously as though they were what they appeared to be; a lady of spotless reputation and her loving cavalier—living for a moment, thought Bel, in the world of make-believe.

CHAPTER EIGHT

LULSGATE SOCIETY called the next morning, either in their own person, or sending a footman, to ask whether Mrs. Bel Merrick was fully recovered from her exertions of the previous afternoon.

Bel's amusement that such a mild event as her catching a cricket ball and falling over had caused such paroxysms of excitement was tempered by the thought that life in Lulsgate Spa was so tame that it needed only for a lady to be a little unladylike and take the consequences to send everyone into such regal fantods!

Only she knew what really lay behind her own respectable façade—that she was the sister of one of London's most notorious courtesans, and was being persecuted by a man whom everyone in Lulsgate Spa thought was her dearest admirer.

She had decided to take Captain Howell up on his suggestion that she join him during the morning in the Pump Room, and was debating whether to ask Mrs. Broughton to go with her, that lady being truly overset after a day in the open and eating and drinking too much in the fresh air.

She lay wheezing on a sofa, and it was Bel who was tending her, rather than the other way round, when the knocker on the front door sounded, and the maid came in to tell her that Lady Almeria Harley was calling.

"Oh, I see you are in splendid fettle!" kind Almeria exclaimed when she entered, and then, remorsefully, to Mrs. Broughton, "I see that you, and not Bel, have been rendered *hors de combat* as the result of yesterday's adventures. You must not sit in the sun again, dear madam. Not wise, not wise at all. Have you taken Epsom Salts? I am persuaded that they are the very thing for the bilious."

"Epsom, and every other variety of salts, my dear," replied Bel briskly; "however, nothing but rest will answer, I fear."

"I came to offer to escort you to the Pump Room, dear Bel," offered Almeria, looking dubiously at Mrs. Broughton. "Shall you feel happy at leaving your companion?"

"Oh, pray, do not consider me," said Mrs. Broughton faintly. "Dear Bel needs restoring, too. A cup or so of Lulsgate water will set her up for the day."

Bel privately thought not. She thought Lulsgate water vastly overrated, but did not care to say so. Everyone in Lulsgate was convinced that drinking very salty liquid was a recipe for perfect health, long life, and a good complexion.

Mrs. Broughton was, indeed, asking Bel to bring her a bottle back—"seeing that I have not the energy to go there to drink it in its proper surroundings. And you will change my book for me at the subscription library, will you not, dear Bel? Although I fear that you will not find anything to equal *Lady Caroline's Secret*; that was not only sweetly pretty, but exciting, too. So sad, poor Lady Caroline, but to marry dear Belfiori in the end, that was the best thing of all! I could not have endured it if he had continued to think the worst of her because she dared not tell him her secret."

Bel wondered what unkind god in the Pantheon was arranging matters so that everything said and done these days seemed to cast its shadow on her own unfortunate condition. What Belfiori would spring from what trapdoor to rescue her from Francis's vengeance? And perhaps from Captain Howell—there was something in his manner to her which she did not like—and now she was being fanciful.

"Dear Mrs. Broughton," said Almeria affectionately, as they left the house. "I sometimes wonder whether you are her companion rather than the other way round. She is so easily overset and needs so much shepherding. It is you who wait on her, fetch and carry her library books, correct her tatting. You are a good soul, Mrs. Bel Merrick, and Philip agrees with that verdict, I must tell you. He was praising you at dinner last night to Francis, almost as though he thought Francis needed to be told what a good creature you are, when he can see so for himself.

"Shall we go to the library first, and find something we can both enjoy, and which Mrs. Broughton will cry over? Secrets, indeed! Real life contains very few, thank goodness, and Lulsgate Spa is not the place where people have them. Goodness and virtue may be dull, but think, my love, how appalling it would be to nurse a guilty secret. I am sure that I could not sleep if I did!"

This lengthy speech did not end until both women were safely inside the library and checking through the bookshelves, Bel reflecting sardonically that those like Lady Almeria who were born into wealth, position and security could have little idea of how the rest of the world fared, so easily could she deny what lay all around her, for Bel was certain that others besides herself would not care for their entire life to be exposed to public view.

Filippo's Tower was finally decided on as a suitable book to comfort Mrs. Broughton by making her flesh creep and her eyes drip salt tears, and which would serve to sustain her through her malaise; and then their destination was the Pump Room.

"I tried to persuade Francis to come with me," remarked Almeria reflectively, "but he says that an old sea-dog friend of his has settled near here, and that he proposed to visit him. He said that not even Lulsgate water could reconcile him to meeting Captain Howell for two days in succession!"

And I really do not want to meet him either, thought Bel. He makes me shiver, and I do not know why. He is not ill-looking after all, and although his manner is a little oily it is no more so than that of many other self-consequential men.

They finally entered the Rotunda, with its high glass dome, classical archways and statues of various gods and goddesses disposed in niches around the walls. The well was in the centre of the large room, and a series of spouts in the shape of shells were set in its high sides from which water flowed, to run into a low trough, be conducted away, or be caught in suitable receptacles to be drunk by those, like Bel, who might find it health-giving—not that Bel really thought any such thing.

Beyond them were the big double doors through which visitors who wished to bathe in the life-giving waters took their way. Bel had once surrendered to her doctor's wishes and gone there, but the springs which fed the baths contained a great deal of sulphur as well as salt, and she found them distasteful. She concluded that she was not at Lulsgate for its waters, whether sulphur-laden or not.

Fortunately for Bel, Captain Howell was not alone. He and Marcus and other young bloods were standing in a corner of the room, quizzing the passers-by, and laughing openly at some of the old men and women who chose to frequent the Pump Room, often daily. They were discussing the evening's dance at the Assembly Rooms—they were held twice weekly.

Entry to the Rooms was by a large subscription to keep out riff-raff, and, although Lulsgate had no powerful Master of Ceremonies to rule the spa as Beau Nash had once done at Bath, the MC who ran the Assembly Rooms, Mr. Courtney, organised the events staged there very strictly, so that Lulsgate should not deteriorate socially, as some spas had done, losing their attraction for wealthy visitors and depriving the growing town of money.

Bel and Almeria both accepted glasses of Lulsgate water, Almeria being greeted by one of the churchwarden's wives with demands to discuss the decoration of the church when Harvest Festival time arrived, and, offering Bel a smile of apology, Almeria was led away, leaving Bel to drink her water alone.

Rhys Howell must have had eyes in the back of his head, Bel thought crossly, for the moment Almeria was swept away he came over to greet Bel, and bowed extravagantly to her. "Come, you must not be solitary, Mrs. Merrick, when there are those who wish to entertain you." And he escorted her towards some armchairs in the corner of the room, near to his cronies— he was one of those men who always attracted a small court around them—made up of victims as well as toadies of someone who they mistakenly thought was a man in the first stare of fashion.

"You are in looks today, madam," he proclaimed. "I am happy to inform you, Mrs. Merrick, that you show no signs of yesterday's exertions. You hardly need the restorative properties of the water you are drinking."

More compliments followed until Marcus, restless, said, rudely, Bel thought, "You are as bad as Uncle Francis, Howell—and that is saying something—for monopolising Mrs. Merrick. Allow me to entertain her for a little." And he pushed Howell to one side, and sat in the next armchair to Bel.

"Have you lived here long, madam?" was his opening gambit. "I would have thought Lulsgate a dull spot for such a charmer as yourself to grace for long. Were you ever in London?"

"A short visit, once only," replied Bel, determined not to lie more than she need.

"Forgive me for quizzing you—" Captain Howell was taking the conversation over from Marcus Tawstock, whom he undoubtedly had in his toils "—but you did not go into society, I collect."

"No," was Bel's short answer. She *did* object to his quizzing her, would much have preferred to speak with artless young Marcus, but could not say so.

"I thought not," he said, offering her his wolfish smile. "I should have been certain to have remembered you, so distinctive as you are, but I have been out of England these last few years—on business—and thought I might have missed you then."

Bel gave him an ambiguous smile, which she also offered to his next remark. "You intend to vegetate here, madam, not grace London with your...inimitable presence? One wonders why." And again Bel did not like the expression he assumed when he had finished speaking.

"I enjoy country living," was her short reply.

"Oh, indeed, so do I. For a short time, that is. And, of course, you gather useful admirers round you here, as you would in Town, do you not?"

Bel was suddenly certain that this conversation was, on his part, by no means innocent. She shivered a little, and was grateful when Mark intervened again.

"You are an inconsiderate devil, are you not, Howell? You knew that I wished to converse with Mrs. Merrick, and here you are again, cutting me out. I particularly wished to ask her whether she would allow me to escort her to the Assembly Ball this evening, and since you will not leave us alone you compel me to ask her publicly, for if I leave you with her much longer, you are sure to be there before me."

"Oh, indeed," said Captain Howell and favoured Bel with his vulpine stare this time—she thought that perhaps with that tinge of red in his hair he was more fox than wolf—"I shall ask her now, seeing that you were more concerned to reprimand me than to make your offer directly to her. Tell him, my dear Mrs. Merrick, that you would much prefer me as a partner— seasoned men are always preferable to raw boys, as I am sure you are well aware."

There was something so brutally suggestive in his manner of speech to her, so unpleasantly coarse, that Bel was sure he was offering her a double meaning— suggesting that she was a courtesan, or very knowing, at the least. She would much prefer Marcus, and began to falter, her usual calm on the verge of breaking down, as Captain Howell plainly saw, so that he said, quite softly, "It would be wise, I think, Mrs. Merrick, to accept my offer for tonight's Assembly, rather than Mark's here." And this time his smile was almost a leer.

"Forgive me, Howell," announced a new voice in the conversation glacially, "but Mrs. Merrick will be attending this evening's Assembly with me. I was beforehand, although you have not given her time to say so."

It was Francis Carey, turned out completely à point, not for a cross-country journey as his half-sister had suggested, but wearing Town clothes of the most exquisite perfection.

"So you say, Carey," said Rhys Howell smoothly. "But Mrs. Merrick has mentioned nothing of this. He seeks to pre-empt you unfairly, does he not, dear madam? Pray tell him either that you have changed your mind or that he took your consent for granted!"

"Oh!" Bel was suddenly quite outraged by the behaviour of all three men, for Marcus, unseen by either Francis or Captain Howell, was mouthing something at her and pointing to himself, while Francis and the captain faced one another like a pair of mad dogs disputing a particularly juicy bone. And what was Francis doing here, anyway? Why was he not, as Almeria had said, jaunting about Leicestershire, rather than rushing here to tease her again?

She could think of nothing better to say than to ask him that!

"What are you doing here, Lord Francis? Almeria said that you were paying duty calls about Leicestershire."

"I changed my mind," he announced curtly. "And, for your sake, a good thing too. I will not have you throw me over to go with another man."

"Mrs. Merrick does not confirm that she agreed to attend with you," Rhys Howell began. "I think you, must be mistook—"

"No," snorted Francis. "It is you who are mistook, Howell. In decency you had better retire."

"Oh," cried Bel, suddenly beside herself at all this, and stamping her foot. "I have not agreed to attend with anyone yet. You are both intolerable, Lord Francis for taking my agreement yesterday as read, without waiting for an answer, you to persist, Captain Howell, so mannerlessly, and as for Marcus, making faces at me behind you both. With such examples before him as the pair of you, I am not surprised at *his* conduct. No—" as both men opened their mouths again "—I shall be going with…with…Mr. Henry Venn," for poor Henry had been besieging her for weeks to attend with him, and now she would inform him that she would be his partner this evening if he wished.

She had not the slightest wish to go anywhere with Henry, with or without his mother, for she was sure that Mrs. Venn would attach herself to them this evening, but she was suddenly so enraged with both of them, and the attention which this altercation was causing, as their voices grew louder and louder, that she wanted nothing from either of them!

Both men suddenly realised that there was nothing left to fight for, and both said together, "Then you will do me the honour of allowing me to wait on you this afternoon," to which she replied shortly,

"Indeed no. I never receive on Wednesday afternoon. I have other duties to attend to, other matters to occupy me."

Both men, unknown to each other and to Bel, were immediately struck with the same thought.

Other matters to which to attend! What could they be? Could it be that madam was still plying her trade in Lulsgate, discreetly, of course, but keeping in practice and earning a little money on the side? Both opened their mouths to try to make other arrangements. Francis's fury with both Bel and Captain Howell made him behave most uncharacteristically, as he later told himself dismally, Mrs. Bel Merrick having such a devastating effect on his manners as well as his morals, but Bel was before them again.

"If you are trying to make an appointment with me," she said crossly, "you must both call at my door and take your chances, and that goes for you too, Lord Tawstock," she added, seeing Marcus look hopeful at the prospect of cutting out his seniors. "And now you will excuse me. I must return to Mrs. Broughton with her latest novel, and you, Lord Francis, will proffer my excuses to your sister for not returning with her, but I feel the need for something stronger than Lulsgate waters to restore me."

She was completely unaware that slightly flushed, her face animated, she had never looked so desirable, so that both men before her were in the grip of the strongest desire to enjoy the little widow whether she would or no.

Fortunately unknowing, Bel bowed and retired, anger lending grace to her carriage, elegance to her walk and fire to her eyes, so that every head in the room turned to see her go.

Well! she thought on emerging into the street again. If I had thought to ensure for myself a quiet life by coming to Lulsgate, I certainly made the biggest mistake of my life. What with Francis promising me ravishment and surrender in the distant future, and Captain Howell uttering veiled threats in the present, it seems that I must have all my wits about me or I shall be sunk with all hands by Lord Francis and be charged to destruction by Captain Howell. A plague on you both, gentlemen. But, oh, dear, she knew that that sentiment did not apply to Lord Francis Carey, however much it did to Captain Rhys Howell!

CHAPTER NINE

"So," said Lady Almeria to her half-brother, "you changed your mind about your day's activities."

"Yes." Francis was brief. He had no mind to explain to Almeria that he, who had dismissed women to the edge of his life, had been so haunted by Bel Merrick that he had been unable to leave Lulsgate Spa that morning knowing that she was likely to meet that ineffable swine Rhys Howell at the Pump Room.

Even Almeria, less so her husband, was surprised when, over luncheon, a cold collation as usual, Francis remarked, apparently idly, "I understand from Mrs. Merrick that she never receives on Wednesday afternoons, is otherwise engaged. With you on parish matters, I suppose."

Almeria, as well as Philip, looked at him sharply. "I really don't know, Francis. I only know that Bel is never available on Wednesday and Friday afternoon, and it has not occurred to me to question her on her activities. I know that everyone in Lulsgate likes to think that they know what everyone else is doing, but it is a cast of mind which I deplore."

Nothing more to say on that, then! was Francis's glum internal comment. Nothing for it but to set Cassius to watching her, an ignoble act of which he was ashamed, but then his whole conduct lately had become shameful, and he shuddered a little at what Almeria might think if she knew, not only the truth about Bel, but how he was virtually trying to blackmail her into his bed—for he had to acknowledge that his actions justified no other description.

Luncheon passed without further discussion of Bel Merrick, Philip contenting himself with discussing local matters, and commenting on the latest news in *The Times* about Queen Caroline and matters European, being determined to pick Francis's good brains while he was staying with them.

Only, when Francis had excused himself, ostensibly to change into riding clothes, but actually to brief Cassius—who had performed several such missions for him in Paris on behalf of some diplomatic subtleties—Philip looked up at his wife and said quietly, "A private word with you, my dear."

Almeria's expression showed her surprise when in response to her nod he said, "Tell me, my dear, you know him well. Do not you think that there is something a little odd about Francis's interest in Mrs. Merrick?"

"Odd?" repeated Almeria. "Well, only in the sense that it is as long as I can remember since Francis showed an interest in any woman."

"I think there is more to it than that," observed Philip thoughtfully. "I may be mistaken, but there is something in his speech and manner to her which is—to me, at least—a little strange, not at all like his usual conduct towards women."

"I cannot say," answered Almeria, "that I have noticed anything untoward—and why should there be? Bel is a dear, sweet girl, and that should gain her nothing but approbation from Francis, surely."

"Exactly so," said Philip mysteriously, and decided to let the matter drop. He did wonder why his brother-in-law had bolted so rapidly from the room after asking pointed questions about Bel Merrick, and also wondered what he was doing now.

What Francis was doing was briefing Cassius, that close-mouthed Mercury, the messenger whom Francis could trust, who would never gossip, however bribed or tempted, because Francis had saved him from ruin and transportation some ten years ago, and he had served him devotedly ever since.

"Watch the house," Francis concluded, "and if Mrs. Merrick leaves it follow her discreetly, find out where she goes, and then come and report to me immediately."

Cassius nodded, saying aloud as he set off on his mission, "And what's got in to you, cully? Never seen you so hot after a skirt afore. Not to say that this one ain't a prime piece of meat—and if you think she's a lightskirt, which I suspects as you do, then you're fit for Bedlam, sir, though I'll not tell you so!"

Francis, unaware of his judgemental servant's thoughts, decided to change, then rest a little in Philip's study until Cassius should return, hopefully with some useful information. Could Bel Merrick really be plying her trade in Lulsgate Spa? And if she were, why should it trouble him?

BEL SET off on her usual Wednesday afternoon errand seemingly unaware that Cassius was on her tail. She had, he noted, no one with her, was plainly dressed in dove-grey and walked briskly along. She carried a covered basket, and took the road out of Lulsgate in the direction of that small and poverty-stricken village, Morewood, where the long depression after the late wars, coupled with the new machinery, had virtually destroyed the livelihood of the framework knitters there, so many fewer men being needed to operate the new machines, which were also capable of knitting much wider and longer pieces of cloth—a fact which still further depressed the wages of those fortunate enough to be employed to work them, whose old standard of living had been destroyed.

Occasionally some of those who had no work intruded into Lulsgate, their ragged children behind them, to try to beg from rich visitors to the spa, but the constables officiously ordered them back to their "proper dwellings" and told them not to annoy their betters.

Well, thought Cassius sardonically, if m'lord thought madam was after trade, which Cassius suspected he did, then she was visiting an odd place to find it; and when Bel finally reached her destination he gave a long whistle before investigating further. The smile on his face as he hurried back to report was even more sardonic than it usually was, and the report he finally made to Francis more cryptic than it need have been—for Cassius was not averse to teasing the master who had saved him, but who he sometimes thought was too high-nosed for his own good!

Morewood! She was visiting Morewood! What the devil was she doing there? The sketchy report which Cassius had made had told Francis only that Bel had visited a small house on the further side of the little village, and that Cassius had no idea what she was doing there or to whom the house belonged, not liking to ask questions and draw attention to himself.

Francis had driven through Morewood once, and the place had depressed him. It contained a few good homes, the whole village being given over to cottages with long windows in their upper rooms, the typical sign of framework knitters' homes, their machines always kept on the upper floors. The air of poverty saddened him, as it did Philip Harley, who tried, through Henry Venn, who looked after the Chapel of Ease there, to alleviate the villagers' dreadful conditions. To small avail, for the villagers had turned away from the established church and favoured a Methodist ministry whose chapel was a tin tabernacle, very unlike the graceful Gothic building for which Henry Venn was responsible.

He decided to take his curricle to Morewood and reconnoitre—the word sounded better than spying, somehow—which, after all, was what he was doing, but all in a good cause, he told himself sanctimoniously. But what good cause was that? The cause of Francis Carey's insatiable curiosity about everything which concerned Bel Merrick, of course.

The journey to Morewood, a silently gleeful Cassius up behind him, was soon accomplished, and just outside the village he left the curricle and the tiger concealed in a side-lane and began to walk briskly to where Cassius had told him Bel had made for.

The little house was modest enough—surely not a worthwhile customer there—and he stopped a sullen old man to ask him to whom it belonged, and his jaw dropped when the man said, "Gideon Birch, the Methodee minister, o' course. Everyone knows that!"

The minister? What the devil was Bel Merrick doing with a Methodist minister? He stared at the little house, and then, on an impulse, hearing voices, he walked down the lane by the side of the house, to stare over a hedge at the garden from whence the voices—and now childish laughter—were coming.

There was nothing for it. That grandee, Lord Francis Carey, the pride of the Corps Diplomatique, was reduced to standing tiptoe in a lane and peering over a hedge. Worse was to come, for what he saw shamed him.

Sitting on the lawn, a group of small children facing her, was Bel Merrick. The children, of all ages from five to about twelve, so far as he could judge, were equipped with slates and pencils, and an impromptu spelling bee was in progress. The laughter was because as each child correctly spelt the name of an animal Bel was drawing it on the slate before her and showing it to them.

And while he stood there, fascinated, she drew an animal and then asked a small child in the front row to tell her its name, and spell it for her. Something strange seemed to happen, something passed from him to her, for as the child finished Bel turned her head slowly, to see him watching her.

A tide of colour washed over her face. She looked defiantly at him, said loudly, "Children, we have a visitor. Pray join us, Lord Francis, seeing that you have tracked me down. I could do with an assistant."

Francis had never, in his whole life, felt so miserably helpless and ashamed. He shook his head, disembodied, he knew, the rest of him hidden by the hedge, only for her to cry, "Never say you are shy, sir, nor that you have no feeling for these little ones. You have a duty to *me* now, having followed me here; pray fulfil it. There is a gate a little further on by which you may enter." And now it was her look which challenged him, so that he shrugged; nothing for it. He could not retreat like whipped cur—which was, astonishingly, how he felt, there was such a world of difference between what he had thought she was doing and what she was actually doing!

Bel felt indignation roaring through her, for how dared he spy on her, and follow her, especially after this morning? So that when she rose to meet him her face was brighter than ever, with a mixture of anger and scorn.

"Come, sir. You must meet my pupils. They are some of the poor children who have no work to go to. You do know that these little ones work long hours, and shame on us that we allow it. They need to learn to read and to write, and there is no school here, no dame to teach them, nor could their parents pay to keep one, so Mr. Birch, the minister here, whom I met some few months ago, accepted my offer to teach these little ones, he having no aptitude for the task and having so many other duties."

Francis tried to revive his scorn by assuming that Mr. Gideon Birch was some handsome young fellow of the artisan class turned preacher who might have some attraction for Mrs. Bel Merrick, she presumably having come from that class of persons herself, but he despised himself for the thought, and sat on a white-painted wooden garden seat—"where," said Bel, scornfully, "you may remain if you do not disturb us."

The lesson continued, Bel, watching him, occasionally asking him a question, to include him in the lesson. One of the children read a small passage from the Bible, the story of Joseph, and then Bel asked them questions about it, as Francis remembered his governess similarly questioning him, long ago, in the schoolroom at the top of Tawstock House, something which he had long forgotten.

Outwardly calm, Bel was in turmoil. What business did he have to track her here? Could there be nothing left to herself, nothing private? For she had not even told Almeria of this. In her middle teens she had run, at her late papa's suggestion, such little classes for the poor children of Brangton, but Lulsgate, rich, important and comfortable, did not need such amenities. Accidentally meeting Gideon Birch, she had discovered the need in Morewood for such help as she could give, and had offered to give it.

The little meeting ended, as Mr. Birch always wished it, with all the class reciting the Lord's Prayer, heads bent, hands held together, and then the children filed out, the little boys bowing to Bel, and the little girls curtsying, and before they left through the gate, they extended, at Bel's instructions, the same politeness to Francis.

"And now, sir," she said, turning to him, "why are you here?"

He had the grace to look awkward, she thought, and said, "I was annoyed—I know that it was wrong of me—when you said that you were not at home this afternoon. I...was determined to find out what you were doing."

"And now you have found out," said Bel, almost contemptuously, thinking that for the first time the initiative in their meetings had passed from him to her. "I think that you should leave, don't you? Unless you feel that there is some edict you might like to pass to prevent me from lightening these children's lives a little." Here, in this quiet garden, where she could see Gideon Birch through his kitchen window preparing to come outside, there was no place for his aristocratic scorn.

"Now you are being unfair," he protested, watching an old man leave the house and come towards them, carrying a tray on which stood a pitcher of lemonade and three glasses. "I can have no conceivable objection to the errand of mercy on which you are engaged."

"No?" said Bel fiercely. "I thought that you might protest that my presence might pollute them," but, suddenly hearing Mr. Birch approach them, she said more coolly, "I think that I ought to introduce you to Mr. Birch, even if I cannot explain your presence here to him, since I have no inkling of the reason for it myself."

Mr. Birch had placed his tray on a small wooden table, painted to match the bench. Francis rose as he did so, and bowed, saying—and it was all that he could think of in his very real distress and embarrassment, "I have come to escort Mrs. Merrick home," after Bel had performed the necessary introductions.

No virile young suitor, Mr. Gideon Birch, but an elderly man with a warm, concerned face, who said, "You will do me the honour, my lord, of taking a glass of my sister's good lemonade with us. She is unfortunately absent, so cannot welcome you. I am happy to learn that Mrs. Merrick will have an escort today. I am never easy that she comes alone, although I understand why she does. She does us a great kindness in offering services to us, free of charge, especially as she is not a member of our church, although I am one of those Methodists who likes to think of himself as still part of the Church of England's fold, as John Wesley was."

Bel noted that Francis was rapidly recovering his *savoir-faire* and spoke interestedly and informedly to Mr. Birch, so that the gentleman thought what a gracious person he was, unlike many of the mighty whom Mr. Birch had so far encountered.

"So," said Francis, "you were an Oxford man yourself before you heard George Whitfield preach and were converted."

"Yes," said Mr. Birch mildly. "I was offered a preferment in South Yorkshire, whence my family is sprung, but once I had been converted, had endured my private encounter on the road to Damascus, there was nothing for it, I had to follow my Master's call. Besides, there are many to succour the rich, few the poor. They need the Lord more in places like Morewood than in Lulsgate Spa."

"Well spoken," said Francis, now the grandee who could accommodate himself to any society, and plainly both interesting and pleasing the old man by displaying his knowledge without flaunting it, as Bel noticed.

She realised again, as she had often done before, that men were quite different when not with women, spoke differently, and had a range of interests rarely displayed in social intercourse. Whether she was glad or sorry at this she did not know, only that it was true, and wondered why so few women seemed to realise that it was so.

She was aware of Francis's eyes on her, answered a question of Mr. Birch's, drank his excellent lemonade, and promised to be back on Friday to take the class again.

She made her adieus to the old man, picked up her plain bonnet, and put it on, and tied its ribbons, retrieved her parasol and the empty basket which Mr. Birch had brought from the house.

"Mrs. Merrick," he informed Francis, "always brings us some excellent cake. She says that it is surplus to her wants, would be thrown away if we did not accept it, but I suspect by its excellence that that is her way of bribing us not to refuse it, not letting us seem to sponge upon her kindness. She is a true friend—does good by stealth. I trust sir, that you will not reveal to others what you have discovered."

"Indeed not," Francis replied, sincerity in his voice, "if that is what you both wish."

"I would not discommode her, sir," said Mr. Birch, "for there are those who would not be pleased at what she does, and would gossip unpleasantly of it, and I am happy to learn that you are prepared to be discreet, will be careful to consider her interests," and the old eyes on Francis were shrewd. "We may meet again sometime, sir, I hope. It is a long time since I was privileged to talk with a person as informed as yourself."

They all bowed their farewells, Mr. Birch retaining the formal manners of the eighteenth-century days when he had been a young scholar at Magdalen, Oxford.

"So," said Francis, a little heavily, Bel thought, on their leaving the pleasant garden, "I owe you an apology, Mrs. Merrick."

"For what you thought of me," returned Bel shrewdly, "or for following me?"

"Both," said Francis, "and I think you must agree that I could not possibly have guessed what you are doing. You will not hold it against me, and refuse a ride home?"

Bel looked about for his curricle, noting that when he added, "I have it down a side-street, Cassius attending," he had the grace to blush.

"Diplomatic treachery at work, I see," she commented sardonically. "Was it Cassius who followed me? I am sure that it was not yourself!"

Francis chose to ignore this, saying instead as they rounded the corner to see Cassius staring at them, a knowing expression on his wrinkled face, "I shall say nothing of this to Almeria and Philip, for had you wished them to know I am sure you would have told them. I do not think they would be displeased, you know."

"Perhaps not," said Bel a little curtly as Francis helped her up, Cassius attending to the horses, "but I have no wish for gossip, as Mr. Birch says, and you must know as well as I do that the Methodist connection is not well seen, even if the Countess of Huntingdon has established a connexion of her own. But I am not a countess, and my patronage would not be so honoured as hers, by no means."

They were off, Bel's now empty basket on her knee, both of them unwontedly silent. Francis was wondering again about the strange nature of the courtesan he was driving home, and Bel was wondering about him. He had behaved so simply and properly to old Mr. Birch; could it ever be that he might behave so to herself?

CHAPTER TEN

HENRY VENN, unable to believe his luck, did take Bel to the ball at the Assembly Rooms, and of course Bel was right: his mother did accompany them. Captain Howell and Marcus also claimed her for dances, but not Francis Carey.

Francis, in the oddest state of mind it had been his misfortune to suffer after the afternoon's contretemps—for that was the only way he could interpret it truthfully—could not bring himself to see Bel Merrick in public until he had recovered his usual haughty equanimity—if he could ever regain it, that was!

He hardly knew how he felt, and could not have believed the confusion of mind which he found himself in. If anyone had told him a month ago that he would be in a mad frenzy of desire for a ladybird, was refusing to slake it by buying her, was not sure that he was other than in love with her, and was determined to have her in love with him, desperately and beyond reason, he would have called them a liar.

Seeing her in the garden with the children and later with Mr. Birch had brought a new dimension to their relationship. What a paradox she was! He supposed that he should not be surprised to find that a loose woman was a practical and practising Christian, but he was.

Bel, for her part, was surprised to discover how sorry she was that Francis was absent. Whatever the reason, when he walked into a room she felt that he brought passion and vitality in with him, never mind that he despised her. All the other men she met seemed third-rate beside him.

"So, you have taken pity on poor Henry, then," Almeria said to her in the interval between dances when Bel was alone. Henry had gone to fetch her a cooling drink, and his mama was busily engaged with three other mature matrons, destroying the reputations of any who incurred their displeasure, in the intervals of playing a game of whist in a small room opening into the ballroom itself.

"Francis refused to come," she continued. "He sent you his compliments, and hoped to attend, but said he was weary, needed an early night. Although what," she added, "he can have been doing in Lulsgate to weary him neither Philip nor I can think. London never seems to tire him so."

"The country air this afternoon too strong for him?" said Bel, cryptically if a little naughtily.

"Perhaps," said Almeria doubtfully. "He did take a drive this afternoon—I believe he gave you a lift at the end of it; he seemed *distrait* when he returned." She hesitated. "He was a little as he was when his wife died. I feel that perhaps it would be right of me to inform you of his sad story. I know that he will never tell you, and Philip would say I was interfering, but I think that you ought to know; it explains him so much."

She fell silent, and Bel said nothing. Francis was, or rather had been, married! She wondered what had happened, and her heart beat rapidly as she waited for Almeria to continue.

"He was only nineteen when he married his child-hood sweetheart, Cassie—Cassandra Poyntz, Sir Charles Poyntz's daughter. They were so in love, and Francis was not a bit as he is now—a little forbidding, I must admit. He was so happy and jolly, rather like a more responsible Marcus. He was in the navy, as I suppose you know. They only had five happy months together, then Francis had to go to sea and left Cassie in Portsmouth; she was two months pregnant. He was on HMS Circe, which was sunk in action; he was transferred to another ship going to a West Indies station, and, what with one thing and another, instead of being back with her in a few months to be there when the baby was born it was a year before he saw Portsmouth again.

"And when he reached home she was five months dead, and the baby too. She was a little thing, very sweet and gentle, and the birth was something like poor Princess Charlotte's and the outcome was the same. Mother and child both dead. Poor Francis. You can imagine what it did to him. He quite changed. Jack, our brother, said he grew up in an hour, and that it was a pity it was so quick, for he refused all consolation, would never speak of her, and took occupation and duty for his wife, would hardly look at a woman—indeed, he has spoken to and shown more interest in you than in all the other women in his life since Cassie died put together."

Almeria fell silent; she had promised Philip that she would not interfere, but she had felt that Bel should know the truth about her half-brother.

Oh, poor Francis, what a terrible story! was Bel's immediate and pitying reaction. It gave him no right to treat her as he did, but she could understand why he would never give his heart away again, seeing what had happened to him when he had done so before—everything gone in an instant when he had been looking forward to wife and child both.

She grew quiet, thoughtful, and when Henry returned, the bright sparkle of her early evening manner had gone, so much so that on Henry's showing his displeasure at Captain Howell for coming to claim her for their dance she dismissed it as absently as she did his further criticism of the raffish captain, as he termed him, after he had returned her. In the same *distrait* fashion she had agreed to Rhys Howell's insistence that he visit her the following day.

That night, lying in bed, she thought over her relationship with Francis, and bitterly regretted the anger which had seized her when he had burst in that first day, and the reckless deceit with which she had cheated him. She was compelled to admit that her own conduct had helped to provoke him into believing that she shared her sister's profession, and that at no time had she given him any reason to think otherwise than that she was a courtesan, too.

Well, in the words of her old governess, she thought ruefully, you have made your bed, Bel, and must lie on it, and then her usual bright wit conquered her ridiculous self-pity, as she added the gloss. And you must try to prevent Francis Carey from lying on it, too. Unless he offers you a wedding-ring, that is. And, thinking of him, she let sleep take her into a land where regrets and hopes were transformed into other symbols and she was running through a wood, tears streaming down her face, looking for something—what?—and, panting, woke to the realisation that, treat her as he might, it was Francis Carey, so sadly bereaved, for whom she was weeping. Or was it herself?

BEL HAD NO DESIRE whatsoever to entertain Rhys Howell. She felt an instinctive distrust of him and all his works, and was sorry to see what a firm friend he was of silly young Marcus's; for all her youth, she had discovered that she possessed the power to read people aright. She wondered if Marianne had shared it, and wondered further it if helped to make her so successful.

She waited for the sound of the knocker all morning, quite distracted, causing Mrs. Broughton to say mildly, "You are hardly yourself today, my dear. I do hope that you are not sickening for something."

"No," said Bel rapidly, and to stop further comment picked up *Filippo's Tower* and said, "Pray allow me to read to you, madam," only for Mrs. Broughton to look at her, scandalised, and remark, "In the morning, my dear?" for she had been brought up in a household where novels were allowed to be read provided only that they were indulged in in the afternoon, when all one's duties were done.

"Oh, yes," sighed Bel, and picked up the little nightdress she was working, and began to hem industriously, an occupation which had one drawback—she had the time to think both of Captain Howell's unwanted visit, and of Francis Carey's being either cold and haughty, or unwontedly amorous—both expressions seemingly reserved for Mrs. Bel Merrick!

The doorknocker duly reverberated through the house. Mrs. Broughton looked up from her plain sewing—canvas work, like novels, being reserved for the afternoon, and said hopefully, "I do hope that that is dear Lord Francis come a-calling. I do declare I am quite in love with the man. Oh, to be twenty-five again!''

But it was, as Bel expected, Captain Howell, whom the maid announced, and Captain Howell who came in, his black cane with its ivory top in his hand, his clothes just that little bit too fashionable. Indeed, in another world, of which Bel knew nothing, he was known as "Flash Howell" and valued accordingly.

"Ladies." He was all good manners this morning: he put down his hat and his cane beside the chair which he was offered, made small talk for a moment, and then said, almost carelessly, leaning forward to give Bel the full benefit of his smile, "My dear Mrs. Merrick, I wonder if you would allow me to have a few words alone with you? I have some private messages for you, from your sister, which she has asked me to deliver, concerning your family. You will forgive us, madam, will you not?" he said, turning his doubtful charm on Mrs. Broughton.

"My sister?" queried Bel, trying to keep her voice steady. She had had but the one, Marianne, also known as Marina St. George, and to hear Captain Howell speak of sister and messages filled her with nameless dread.

"Your dear sister Marianne," said Rhys Howell sweetly. "You have but one, I believe."

Had was the proper tense, thought Bel distractedly, but looked at Mrs. Broughton—if Rhys Howell proposed to speak to her of Marianne—and how had he tracked her here, and how did he know that she was Marianne's sister?—she had no wish for Mrs. Broughton to be present.

"No matter." Mrs. Broughton smiled, determined to love every gentleman who seemed to possess a *tendre* for dear Bel. "I will take a turn in the garden. I see our neighbour is there; we may discuss the prospect of a good plum crop together. Plum tart is a favourite delicacy of mine," and she drifted through the glass doors to the garden.

"What an obliging soul," remarked Rhys Howell, looking after her, an unpleasant leer on his face.

"My sister, you said," offered Bel, desperate to get this over with, an indelicate expression used by her maid Lottie for anything from taking physic to listening to a tedious sermon in church.

"Ah, yes, your sister," drawled the captain. "Dear Mrs. Marina St. George, such a high flyer; you may imagine how I felt when I came back from urgent business on the Continent to discover her unexpectedly dead, her sister inherited, the house sold. I was desolate. We were partners, she and I. I cannot for the world understand how she came to forget me in her will. Why, she owed her start in her...way of life to me, and an apt pupil she certainly was."

He paused. "You were about to say something, *Mrs.* Merrick?" and he trod hard on the word Mrs., his expression sardonic.

Bel would not be put off by his odious mixture of innuendo and familiarity.

"Mrs. Marina St. George?" she began. "I know of no such person."

"Oh, come, my love," said Captain Howell, closing one eye in a wink so lubricious that Bel shuddered before it. "No need to try to flim-flam me, my dear Miss Passmore. A useful invention, Mr. Merrick, I am sure. You share your dead sister's wit and inventiveness; we should be splendid partners, you and I. Clergymen's daughters make the best whores, should they decide to go to the bad, and your sister went to the bad most spectacularly. Now you, you could rival her—you have managed to preserve a delicacy and innocence which are quite remarkable."

"You have lost me," said, Bel, rising. "I ask you to leave. I have no idea of what you speak."

"Won't do, you know," leered Captain Howell confidentially, putting a hand familiarly on Bel's knee. "Father the Reverend Mr. Caius Passmore, sister the late and talented Marina, servant named Lottie, who was close-mouthed for a woman, but felt compelled to write to her great-nephew, upon whom she dotes, where you are and what you were doing.... You see I speak no lie; your sister and I were so close she told me everything of you. Now what, I wonder, would that upright gentleman Lord Francis Carey think if informed that the virtuous little widow was the sister of the fair Marina, and probably a dab hand at the game herself? Wouldn't like him to know, would you—eh, would you?" And his voice rose menacingly.

Bel had a desperate desire to laugh, seeing that Lord Francis also shared the delusion of her lack of virtue with Captain Howell, and would not be in the least surprised at whatever Captain Howell chose to tell him.

"And the aristocratic sister, and the parson husband—what would they think of their pious home's being a haven for such as yourself, my dear? Worth something to keep me quiet, do you think? That is if you don't want to resume Marina's partnership with me, eh?" His wink grew more grotesque by the minute.

Had Marianne really been this low rogue's partner, thought Bel, and did it matter if she had? In the here and now he was perfectly able to ruin her socially and financially, and would have no scruple about doing either.

She rose, deciding to put on a brass face and deny everything. "I am still at a loss," she replied, her voice freezing, "and I ask you to leave immediately. I am not accustomed to being insulted in my own home."

Captain Howell put his finger by his nose. "Oh, I'm patient, sweet, patient. I mean to stay in this dull backwater awhile longer, and you, you'll go nowhere, for you've nowhere to go. I shall remind you of my wishes, madam, until reckoning day, when you'll either give me what your sister morally owed me, or I shall tell Lulsgate Spa of the serpent in their bed of flowers. Until then, madam, *adieu.*"

He picked up his hat and cane, walked to the door, bowed mockingly and added, "Allow me to congratulate you, madam. I do believe that you are as cool a piece as the great Marina herself, and you deserve his haughty lordship as a prize, yes, you do. But beware, madam, beware. I know these high-nosed gentlemen. Should he discover who and what you are..." and he wagged his head commiseratingly at her "...*that* would be an interesting day, a most interesting day. Till we meet again, madam, for meet we most assuredly shall—to do good business together, I hope—you must not keep all the rewards to yourself!"

CHAPTER ELEVEN

BEL HARDLY KNEW whether to laugh or to cry: to laugh at Captain Howell's notion of the shock which Lord Francis Carey would receive over the knowledge that Bel's sister was Marina St. George, or to cry over the fact that two men now knew her secret—and the second a malignant creature who would not hesitate to harm her in any way he could in order to get some, or all, of Marina's fortune for himself.

And there was no one whom she could tell or to whom she could turn for advice or help. She was quite alone, and the strange thought struck her that the vile way in which Captain Howell had spoken to her, not only the manner of his speech, but the way in which he had looked at her, held his body, revealed how different a man Francis Carey was from the unpleasant captain, even though he despised her for being, as he thought, a courtesan.

Bel even realised that in other circumstances she might have gone to Francis for help and protection, something which was now impossible.

Pondering this, she heard the knocker go again, and voices in the hall. The door opened and the little maid stood there, only to be swept aside by Francis, his face ablaze, saying, "I must see Mrs. Merrick, and at once."

Bel wanted no more scandal, and said coolly, feeling that she had exchanged one tormentor only to gain another, "Yes, you may see me, Lord Francis," so that the little maid bobbed at her and departed. She turned to him, lifted her brows and, still cool, said, "Well, sir, what brings you here in such a pelter that you have forgotten your breeding?"

Francis made no response to this last. Lip curling, he said, "So, you have been entertaining the captain alone? Remarkable, seeing what a pother you made over walking with me in the garden with Mrs. Broughton playing nearby dragon!"

"It is no business of yours...." began Bel, only to have him fling at her,

"It is not only your reputation for which you should have a care, madam, but your safety which you should also consider. The man is, I am certain—nay, I have reason to know—little more than a common criminal. He left the Lifeguards under the most dubious circumstances, was forced to flee England because he cheated his criminal associates, performed the same unwise act in France, and was compelled to return— which is why he is here, rather than London, to escape vengeance, one presumes—and you, madam, see fit to entertain him alone!"

He ran out of breath, and about time too, thought Bel, the courage with which she always faced life strong in her as he moved towards her. She had been standing by the glass doors when he entered, about to rejoin Mrs. Broughton, whom she could see, head bobbing, talking with their neighbour—about plum tart probably! This prosaic thought, against all the suppressed violence which had been going on in her quiet drawing-room, made her want to giggle.

Francis saw the smile blossom on her face, misinterpreted it, and said furiously, "A joke, madam? You think Rhys Howell's unsavoury reputation a joke!"

"I am wondering," said Bel, her heart hammering, "why, knowing this of him, you do nothing about it. The man should be before the Justices, surely, if half of what you say of him is true."

"Oh, indeed," he almost snarled. "I should have known that your light-footed wit would have you firing broadsides at me. Well, let me tell you, my legal-minded lady, that I have no evidence of this to satisfy a court, but, being in France when he was, and at the Embassy, I knew a deal more than I should about such...persons, even if little enough to do anything about it, except to be wary, and warn my friends."

"Your friends!" Bel's contemptuous snort of laughter would have graced a Drury Lane melodrama. "Am I, then, to count myself one of their number? You surprise me, sir. I thought that I was only fit to be thrown on a bed and ravished, or tied to the cart's tail as a common whore to be whipped!"

"Oh." Poor Francis was breathless. Armoured with rage at both men who were in their different fashions blackmailing her, Bel had never looked so lovely. Her luminous green eyes flashed fire; even her red curls seemed springier; the tender mouth quivered voluptuously; her whole beautiful body, although she did not know this, seemed to be straining against the light muslin dress she wore. It was enough to drive any red-blooded male mad with desire. Francis Carey felt a very red-blooded male indeed. "I come to warn you, help you, madam, since you seem to need it, and what reward do I receive? A lawyer in skirts, instructing me of my duty."

He was almost upon her, and a dreadful mirth, akin to hysteria, Bel knew, began to inform her. She dodged away from him, into the room—she dared not let him pursue her outside, for fear that the anger which consumed him might cause him to be unwise before Mrs. Broughton and reveal all, which would never do.

In her haste to remove him from the revealing window she caught against the little occasional table on which her workbox stood and knocked it over, the child's nightdress and the contents of the box cascading across the floor, pins, reels of cotton, her thimble, crochet hooks and all the paraphernalia which accompanied a lady's sewing spread out between them.

To Bel's surprise this minor disaster seemed infinitely more important than all the dreadful threats which the two men in her life had thrown at her.

"Oh, no," she wailed, "now look what you have made me do!" and she fell plump on her knees on the carpet, grieving over each pin and hook as though she were recovering the treasure of Midas.

Francis was nearly as fevered as she was. Jealousy, desire and frustration held him in thrall, and the sight of her on her knees on the carpet, lovely face distressed, overset him further.

To his own subsequent astonishment—what could have got into him to behave so uncharacteristically?—he found himself on his knees before her, to the ruin of his breeches, his boots and his common sense, none of them assisted by the violence which he was doing to them. "Oh, no," he crooned, clumsily trying to pick up pins, "do not grieve," and then, as she stared at him astonished, the little nightgown in her hands, a crystal teardrop running down one damask cheek, he was going mad, wanting to write poetry—to a whore, yes, a whore, but what did that matter? He put up his hands to clasp her face in them, saying tenderly, "Oh, do not cry, I beg of you, do not cry, pray let me kiss that tear away," and before she could stop him he licked up the salty pearl and began to suit his actions to his words.

He had forgotten that he had promised himself that she would be on her knees begging him, not the other way round, but no matter. While Bel...

While Bel what? She should be thrusting him away, telling him to take his mouth where it was wanted, but each delicate moth-like kiss made it harder and harder for her to do any such thing. She was so near to him that she could see that his eyes were not a pure grey but had little black flecks in them, like granite. Could granite melt? It seemed to be doing so.

She gave a little moan, dropped the nightgown among the scattered pins and needles, and gently, very gently, as he lifted his mouth from her eyes to transfer it to her mouth, she kissed him back—and then sanity prevailed.

Mrs. Broughton might come in, and she hated him, did she not? He thought her a whore and would shortly, if she were not careful, be treating her as one, here on the carpet, among the pins and needles; and what would Mrs. Broughton think? For his hands had left her face and were beginning to pull her dress down. So she pushed him away before her body could betray her, and sprang to her feet, to leave him among the needles and pins; it was all that he deserved.

"Oh, you are all the same," she raged at him. "Show a little weakness, and you are all over us. And how can you, with all that you have said to me, be in the least surprised that I should wish to favour Captain Howell? If all diplomats are such muddled thinkers as you are—and naval captains, too," she flung in for good measure, "no wonder it took us so long to win the war, and to win allies, such mad heedlessness as you show, with Mrs. Broughton in the garden and likely to interrupt you at your work any minute. Shame on you!"

Francis, still on his knees, stared up at her. Paradise so near, and now so far away. He wanted to pull her to the carpet, but Mrs. Broughton's name was like cold water to him, whereas the sight of the angry Bel served only to rouse him further. He ached, yes, he did, and damn his treacherous body which had now overtaken the cold mind which had ruled it for so long, and mastered it quite, so that Bel Merrick walked through his days as well as his dreams.

And that came, he tried to tell himself sternly, from over-continence; Marcus was right, he should have indulged himself more, pleasured a few bits of muslin, and then this one bit of muslin would not inflame him so.

Useless talk—it was Bel Merrick he wanted and none else, and now she must know it, the witch, and would tantalise him the more, if he knew women.

He rose, conscious that for once all his haughty pride had fled from him—and she had done that, with one tear: one damned tear, and he was undone.

"You wrong me," he began, and what a stupid thing to say—could he think of nothing better? "I had meant to console you merely, but you do not seem to need consolation."

"Oh!" exclaimed Bel. "Consolation! I am not so green as to think that *that* was what you were about. Unless you were consoling yourself, that is!" She was rather proud of that last statement; it was quite fit to be one of La Rochefoucauld's witty *Maxims,* she thought.

Francis said, through his teeth, "You are pleased to reproach me, madam. Believe me, you cannot reproach me more than I reproach myself."

"For failing in your fell design to ravish me, presumably," flashed Bel, on whom adversity seemed to be bestowing the gift of tongues. "I cannot believe that you are feeling ashamed of so accosting me—*again!*" And her eyes flashed fire and ice.

That usually resourceful nobleman Francis Carey had no answer to this. He had never found himself in such a position before, and had certainly no experience to call on to advise him. God help me, he thought, if I were the womaniser she must think me, I should know what to do—unknowingly in the same case as Bel, who was as innocent as he was!

They stared at one another, each crediting the other with a past as lurid as it was imaginary, and each so strongly attracted to the other that they were compelled to call the emotion they were mutually experiencing hate, for they dared not admit that it was love.

"I think that you had better leave, at once, sir," declaimed Bel, all dignity, rivalling Mrs. Siddons in her best dramatic fit.

He replied humbly, for him, "You will remember a little what I said of Captain—"

"Oh, this is brave, sir, brave," Bel retorted more in the line of Dorothy Jordan expressing grief at a wanton social misunderstanding than Siddons as Herodias about to demand John the Baptist's head on a platter.

Francis walked to the door, head high, past Bel, also head high, both principals congratulating themselves firmly on their recovered self-command, both painfully aware that in their recent passage they had given themselves away completely.

To think that I could find myself in love with such a haughty peacock who thinks all women are fair game, raged Bel inwardly, as Francis reproached himself for falling for a lightskirt, and then behaving towards her like a bullyboy whom Captain Howell might despise.

"Oh!" Bel let out a long breath, sank into a chair, as Mrs. Broughton finally arrived, to prattle vaguely of plum tart, Lord Francis missed, *Filippo's Tower,* the changing weather, and how delightfully well Bel looked.

"All this social junketing must agree with you, my dear. You never looked so when we led a quiet life. You bloom, you positively bloom, I do declare!"

LORD FRANCIS CAREY was not blooming. Furious with himself for his loss of self-control—or was it that this loss of self-control had not gone far enough?—he strode down the main street of Lulsgate Spa, cutting everyone right, left and centre in his determination to reach his nephew and warn him of the captain. A letter which he had sent to London had brought him a reply, giving him further, worse information about the man—hence his visit to Bel, and his anger at seeing Howell visit her, apparently in her confidence.

He strode into the taproom at the White Peacock unaware that his expression was thunderous, and whether his rage was directed at himself, Marcus, Captain Howell or Bel Merrick he did not know.

Marcus was seated at one of the tables, a tankard in front of him, smoking a clay pipe, an experiment he was beginning to regret. There was no sign of his usual court of hangers-on. He looked up in mild surprise as his uncle entered.

"Didn't know you favoured this sort of entertainment, sir," he offered almost reproachfully.

"I don't." And Marcus could not help noticing that, saying this, his uncle was even more glacial than usual. Oh, Hades, another sermon, he thought glumly, and prepared to be lectured again. What was it this time? He did not have long to wait to find out.

"I am glad to find you alone," began Francis, refusing the chair which Marcus pointed out to him. "Thank you, no, I have no intention of staying. I have come to warn you that Captain Howell is not a fit person for someone of your station and expectations of whom to make a friend, never mind a boon companion," he continued, his temper not helped by Marcus's eyes beginning to roll heavenwards.

"I know what I am no longer your guardian—"

He got no further for Marcus said petulantly, "Amen, to that, sir, and, that being so, I am in no mind to be lectured by you. Rhys Howell is no better and no worse than a hundred others in society, and I find him amusing."

"Then your taste is deplorable." Francis was not prepared to give way on this. "I must warn you not to play cards with him. I know that you frequent the tables at Gaunt's Club on Bridge Street, and it has come to my attention that you have already lost large sums to him; you must be aware that you cannot afford to do so."

"Win some, lose some." Marcus yawned aggravatingly. "I won last week, he wins this week, next week the luck will turn again. All square at the end, Uncle, the odds see to that."

"They do if all the players are honest—" began Francis, only to be interrupted again.

"Oh, damn that for a tale, sir, begging your pardon," said Marcus. "No reason to think Rhys other than straight. Sing another tune, sir, this one's flat."

Francis could think of no tune which he could sing that would please anyone he knew. Even Almeria and Philip were looking at him a little sideways these days, especially Philip, and as for Bel Merrick...so it was not surprising that Marcus was recalcitrant—he should have expected nothing else.

"Very well," he said, preparing to leave. "I have done my best to warn you, but if you refuse to listen..." And he shrugged his shoulders. "I would have thought that the man's character shone on his face—that, and the fact that he has come to Lulsgate at all."

"He came because I did," returned Marcus impudently. "Is it so very strange, Uncle, that someone likes me, does not spend his time dooming at me like some messenger fellow in that damned dull Greek stuff they forced down my throat at Oxford?"

Francis turned and stared at his nephew, wondering how his clever brother Jack could have spawned such an ass. "If you had listened to that damned dull stuff more carefully," was his cold reply, "you would have discovered that fools in them got short shrift for their folly. I leave you to Captain Howell. You deserve one another."

And I was no more successful with Marcus than I was with Bel Merrick, he thought, but at least she was intelligent in her waywardness, whereas Marcus... All that he possesses to recommend him is a pretty face and a willingness to be cozened.

LISTENING TO Mrs. Broughton read *Filippo's Tower* to her did absolutely nothing to restore Bel to her normal tranquil state of mind. The determined silliness of Bianca dei Franceschini's every response to the predicament in which she found herself roused her, for once, to tears rather than laughter.

How could she be so stupid as to take refuge with vile Federigo Orsini and fly the noble and improbably virtuous Rafaello degli Uberti? Real people did not behave like that, not at all. Why, even she, inexperienced as she was, could recognise Captain Howell for the villain which Lord Francis had confirmed him to be.

Her anger with Francis Carey was not for pointing out to her what she already knew, but because he seemed to think that he was the only one allowed to prey on Bel Merrick! Not that she saw Francis Carey as wicked; no Federigo Orsini he—that role was reserved for Rhys Howell. It was merely that he was morally blind when it came to reading Bel Merrick. And that was partly her fault, was it not? That blind moment of temper in Stanhope Street had unleashed all this on her.

Not that she could blame Rhys Howell's villainy on Francis Carey, since the captain would presumably have tracked her down even if Francis Carey had never existed, and she was now caught in two nets, not one, with no idea how to extricate herself from either.

But one way or another, she promised herself, I will. And how inconvenient life was, that real people were not hopelessly virtuous like Rafaello, but more of a mixture, like Francis; and presumably, then, even Rhys Howell was not as completely villainous as Federigo Orsini was, even though he might be so towards herself and Marcus....

Bel gave up, allowed Mrs. Broughton's soothing tones to pour over her, like treacle from a jar, and when that lady put the book down, sighing, "Oh, how delightful, even better than *Lady Caroline's Secret*," Bel did not scream at her. Oh, what bosh you talk, madam. You know as well as I do how ridiculously improbable all that we read to each other is. For it passed over her in a wave, or even as a revelation, like one being smitten by God, as Mr. Birch would have said, that Mrs. Broughton and all those who read the Minerva Press's productions were seeking refuge in them from the intolerable demands of a world in which Mrs. Broughton, if not employed by Bel, would have slowly starved to death in genteel poverty.

To live in a world where right always triumphed and virtue was its own reward—but also gained a fair share of the world's goods as well—must always be not only soothing to the nerves but an aid to sleep; and happiness achieved that way felt no different from happiness achieved in any other.

Bel could not help smiling to herself as she thought this. I am truly a parson's daughter, she decided, to moralise and think such things, and I don't believe, although pray God I shall never be put to it to find out, that I could ever have followed Marianne's way of life.

And then, again, revelation struck. But suppose I had been tempted by Francis, without the cushion of Marianne's ill-gotten wealth behind me; how would I have behaved then? For face it, Bel, if he desires you, as he plainly does, then you desire him, and if that were a way out of poverty and misery, what then, Bel Merrick, what then?

CHAPTER TWELVE

OF COURSE, life had to slow down a little, Bel thought; it could not go on in the same hectic fashion that it had done since first Francis Carey and then Rhys Howell had arrived in Lulsgate Spa.

Neither of them made a move in the strange three-cornered game she was playing with them—or they were playing with her. The somnolent peace which had prevailed in Lulsgate during the two years in which she had lived there resumed; it was as though nothing had happened, or would ever happen.

Bel attended the St. Helen's sewing circle, arranged the flowers in the church, took her daily walk, visited Lady Almeria and Philip, spoke coolly to Lord Francis when she met him, bowed distantly to Captain Howell—she could not afford to cut him—joked a little with Marcus, finished *Filippo's Tower*, took out *The Hermit of San Severino*—the hermit being someone who vaguely resembled Francis Carey, all haughty pride, straight mouth and hard grey eyes, as well as his overbearing rectitude towards everyone except the heroine.

The heroine was not a bit like Bel; true, she was virtuous, but she had no spirit at all, allowed the Hermit to walk all over her, scorning her, although she was so determinedly proper that she was only fit for a saint.

Bel was quite out of patience with her. She really ought to give the Hermit what for, as Garth used to say.

Coming out of her little class at Morewood one day, the late August rain pelting down, she found Francis Carey waiting for her at Mr. Birch's gate, a large green umbrella in his hand. This unromantic sight amused her—was this part of his strategy to bring her to her knees before him? If so it seemed a strange one.

"You will allow me to drive you home, I trust? It is really not at all wise for you to walk through this downpour. You will catch a cold."

What could Bel say? She could not bring herself to send him away when he had been standing in the rain waiting for her. She could see Mr. Birch hovering in his little bow window; he had expressed his distress that she should be going home without proper protection. "You will be soaked before you get very far."

Bel could not make out the expression on Mr. Birch's face as Francis held the umbrella over her head and walked her to the curricle, Cassius, his withered face impassive, water dripping off his little top hat, standing behind.

"Poor Cassius," she said. "He will be soaked through by the time we reach Lulsgate."

"His fault," said Francis curtly. "He insisted on coming. I told him that he was not needed. He said that he was always needed." His expression lightened a little. "I could not make out who Cassius thought needed the chaperon, you or me."

"Oh, you!" exclaimed Bel, relieved that matters were light between them. "He does not heed me, I am sure. He is protecting you from me."

Francis knew this not to be true. He had been aware ever since they had reached Lulsgate that both Cassius and his man, Walters, disapproved of him and his dealings with Bel. Cassius had said to him, indeed—and how he knew of Francis's belief as to Bel's lack of reputation Francis could not imagine, "You're wrong, you know, *sir*—" and the "sir" was insulting. "She's a good woman, Mrs. Bel Merrick, none better," and then had turned his back on his master.

"I," Francis had said frostily to the turned back, "am not interested in your opinions about any woman, good or bad."

Cassius had muttered something rude under his breath, and when ordered to fetch the cattle, and see them properly harnessed, had announced that he would be up, "whatever."

Francis rarely pulled rank with his servants. They and he usually knew exactly how they stood with one another. "A hard man, but fair," was Cassius's usual description of him to the staff in the houses which they visited. Faced with this act of mutiny, he said coldly, "You will do as I order you, man. For God's sake, who is the master here?"

Cassius, already donning his hat and its red and white cockade, Francis's colours, said, "You'll do without me, then, for good, sir," and turned steady eyes on his master.

Francis drew in his breath and readied himself to use his best quarterdeck voice, designed to make Satan on his throne quail, but something in the unflinching gaze Cassius turned on him stopped him.

"I do believe," he said, face and voice incredulous, "that you are constituting yourself her protector when I drive her in the curricle."

"She needs one, then?" returned Cassius, giving no ground at all. "You wish me to leave your service, *sir?*"

Francis cursed beneath his breath. He had no mind to lose Cassius, and why that should be was another mystery. The little man always went his own way, and this was not the first time such an act of insubordination had occurred.

"Get up, then, damn you," he finished. "You may have the privilege of being soaked to the skin, and if you take a rheum do not expect me to nurse you, or give you sympathy!"

Cassius rolled his eyes heavenwards, did as he was bid, and all the way to Mr. Birch's home and back again Francis could feel his beady eyes boring into his back.

"You have thought of what I told you of Captain Howell?" And then, seeing Bel's face flush with anger, he added hastily, "I have reason to believe that Marcus has begun to lose large sums of money at Gaunt's gaming house to the captain and his dubious friends. Howell allowed him to win when he first came here—a common trick to catch pigeons and pluck them, and now Marcus sits about waiting for his luck to turn, which it never will."

He did not know why he was telling Bel this—except to reinforce his warnings about Howell, and when she said, "Have you spoken to your sister of this?" he replied wearily, "Yes, and he will take no note of her warnings, either. The trouble is, the man comes from a reasonably good family, and Marcus is innocent enough to think that that alone is a guarantee of his good behaviour. But Howell tarnished his good name and reputation long ago, although that has never prevented him from ending up with some young fool in tow."

Bel thought for a moment. She was genuinely sorry for Almeria's sake that Marcus was being so stupid, but could not help saying, "When we first met, you were of the opinion that I was about to pluck the pigeon myself. Does this confidence mean that you have changed your mind?"

"Only to the extent," he said kindly, but with his usual air of effortless superiority, "that I do not think that Marcus is now your target—not rich enough, I think."

"Oh," said Bel, exasperated, "then who, pray, is my target? I should like to be enlightened. I hate to think that I am working in the dark."

Overhearing this, Cassius gave a series of strangled coughs, like a small horse neighing.

"Myself, of course," said Francis, pulling back on the reins to indicate that they were to stop, Bel's front door being reached. "Richer, more of a prize; not such a good title perhaps, but better than you might have hoped to achieve. Not that marriage is necessarily your—"

At this point what he was about to say was drowned by a coughing fit from the dripping Cassius, so noisy that Bel turned, said sympathetically, "Oh, poor Cassius. How heartless of you, Lord Francis, to drag him out in such weather, without any means of protection. You must see that he has a hot lemon drink with rum in it when he goes in."

Francis turned to stare at Cassius, and said glumly, "His fault entirely if he dies of a rain-induced fever. He insisted on riding behind, in defiance of my orders. I have to say that it is bad enough to be bullied by my tiger, without my would-be doxy putting her oar in, and requiring me to nurse my servant, instead of the other way about."

"You have not been sitting in the rain, inadequately clothed," replied Bel incontrovertibly, "so the question of his nursing you does not arise."

"No more," said Francis wrathfully. "I insist, Cassius, that you hand Mrs. Merrick down before she orders me to carry you to bed. I do believe the pair of you are hatching some damned conspiracy against me." And then, seeing Bel's laughing naughty face at having provoked him to lose his temper, "Why, madam, do I understand that you are roasting me? Has your impudence no limits? I should marry you off to my tiger here as a suitable punishment for the pair of you." Then, on hearing the tiger's coughing laughter as he prepared to hand Bel down, he was seized—again—with the most dreadful desire to do her a mischief—the sort of mischief which involved removing her clothes and...and...

Francis thought that he was going mad. He pushed Cassius to one side, took Bel by the arm, and half ran down her little front garden to her own door, and regardless of watchers, said goodbye, or rather kissed her goodbye, tipping her face up to do so.

The kiss, contrary to usage, began fiercely and ended gently, and Bel said, eyes wicked as he straightened up, "You had best hurry, Francis, or Cassius will drown."

"Oh, you witch, Bel, you witch," he replied with a half-sob. "What is it that you do to a man? When I am with you, all sense, all honour flies away from me."

"I?" said Bel innocently. "I do nothing, Francis. And while you are about it you have provided Mrs. Venn with enough ammunition to aim at us for the rest of the season. If you have no care for your reputation, Francis, you might consider mine. I know that you think I do not possess one—but Lulsgate is my home, and so far I have led a spotless life. Should she say anything, I will inform her that she was mistook—you were removing a smut from my eye. Her sight is notoriously bad."

"And you, my dear doxy," said Francis, delighted at her quick wit, "are as devious as you are desirable. You are right to remind me not to be over-fierce with you publicly. I have no mind to ruin you—yet; but if you smile at me like that I shall not answer for the consequences," and he bent towards her again.

"Cassius," said Bel firmly, and pushed him towards the gate, where Cassius stood patiently, holding the horses, his eye on his master. "He thinks that you need protecting from me, in which of course he is quite wrong, the reverse being true."

But you, my dear Mrs. Bel Merrick, thought Francis, striding back to his curricle, do not have the right of that, for, improbably, Cassius has constituted himself your protector!

"BEL," SAID LADY ALMERIA carefully as they sat side by side in the Harleys' drawing-room, working busily away, waiting for the rest of Lulsgate Spa's sewing circle to arrive, "a word to the wise. Mrs. Venn is a little of a viper for gossip, as I'm sure that you are aware, so it would be better not to give her occasion to circulate any." She fell silent again, staring at her hem stitching.

Bel knew at once that Mrs. Venn had been busily spreading the news of Francis Carey's public and stolen kiss around Lulsgate, that some kind person had gleefully relayed the gossip to the vicar's wife after such a fashion that Almeria felt that she had to counsel a young friend.

The sturdy independence which lay behind her decorative appearance reared its head; she bit her thread in two and said quietly, "Perhaps such advice ought to be offered to your brother rather than myself, the man usually taking the lead in such matters. I think I know to what Mrs. Venn referred, and she was quite mistook." She was astonished at how easily the lie flowed from her lips, but she was not about to be destroyed by a combination of Francis's folly and Mrs. Venn's jealousy of herself as a possible wife for her son—self-preservation was the order of the day. "Francis gave me a lift home the other afternoon. He saw me to the door where he removed a smut from my eye for me. Doubtless Mrs. Venn, in her enthusiasm to spread gossip around Lulsgate, misinterpreted what she saw."

"Oh, dear." Almeria coloured to her hairline, looked distressed, and put down her sewing. "I should have thought before I...I should have known you both better, but I only wished to help you; you are after all so young, and Mrs. Broughton..." She almost began to stammer, and Bel felt remorse that her lie should overset poor Almeria, but she had not asked for the kiss, or, rather, she *might* have done so, but never in such a public place. She knew that Francis had lost control for a moment, but could hardly tell his sister so.

She put out a hand to Almeria, the younger woman comforting the older one—there were times recently when Bel felt that she was ninety—and murmured gently, "Do not distress yourself; you were right to counsel me if you thought that I was being indiscreet. I promise you, my dear friend, that I know how to treat your brother—or any other man for that matter. Trust me."

Almeria's face changed again. "Oh, dear Bel," she said, "you are so alone, with no relatives to whom you may turn for advice, and, although you have always behaved with the most perfect discretion, as a woman you are vulnerable, and as your friend I would always wish to help you. Forgive me if I have hurt you by believing a falsehood."

Bel, from being cool, a little distant, was herself again, charmingly impulsive, even if her impulses were controlled. She rose, kissed Almeria on the cheek and went to stand before the window, looking out across the garden, which backed on to Bel's own, tears filling her eyes, hating herself for the lie and at having caused Almeria distress by telling it.

Oh, Francis, she thought, if only we could have met after a proper fashion, introduced at a ball or in a drawing-room where the strong attraction we feel for one another could have taken its due course. Or if only I *had* been a lightskirt, so that we could have taken our pleasure together, heedless of consequences. As it is, we are trapped in a situation nearly as fraught as those of the novels I take home for Mrs. Broughton, and with no easy way out, no author to wave a magic wand and bring all to a happy conclusion.

She resumed her seat, for she could hear the others arriving, and when they came in, Mrs. Venn among them, she was her normal self again. Bel was not to know that when Francis entered the vicarage drawing-room later that day, telling Almeria that he would not be in for dinner, he intended to spend the evening at Gaunt's gaming club, she said quietly to him, something which Bel had said having struck home, "Francis, a word with you." She was a little fearful at his reaction to what she was about to say, for he was a formidable man, and no mistake. "Lulsgate Spa is a small place, and gossip abounds, some of it not nice. I know that you seem attracted to my good friend, Mrs. Bel Merrick, and I trust you to do nothing which would hurt her, or destroy her standing here."

Francis stood stock-still, rigid. What could he say? Like Bel, he was reduced to a lie. He could not reply, The woman is not what you think, and, being what she is, has no reputation to destroy, and sooner or later I intend to take my long-deferred pleasure with her, and damn the consequences!

To his horror, shame ran through him. He tossed the gloves he was holding on to an occasional table, and, like Bel, walked to the window, but saw nothing. Through numb lips he said, "I will never do anything to hurt a lady, Almy dear, you may be sure of that."

He hated himself for the equivocation. What a weaselling declaration! Bel Merrick being far from a lady, he might treat her as he pleased, but his half-sister would take his statement at its face value.

Like Bel, he wished that things had been different. He could, he knew, solve his problems by leaving Lulsgate Spa, forgetting her, but he could not. He was in her toils; what had begun as simple revenge had become something much more complex—he wanted Bel Merrick, most desperately, all of her, and he wanted her to come to him; he would not go to her, he would not, never.

Thinking so, he turned. "Any more good advice, my dear?" And, although he did not know it, the face he showed her was hard, inimical, the face of a man staring down an enemy.

Almeria was horrified. Philip had warned her against meddling. She had meddled, and—what had she done?

"Oh, do forgive me," she stammered, "I had not meant..."

Like Bel, he leaned forward, his face softening a little, to kiss her on the cheek. "I know," he said. "But the road to hell is paved with good intentions—and there is a limit to what vicars' wives may or can do."

It was a rebuke, Almeria knew, and one more proof of Philip's wisdom. She would not meddle with Bel and Francis again, and she would listen to her husband's quiet advice in future—in the present she must learn to live with the knowledge that something more than simple mutual attraction lay between her friend and her brother.

GAUNT'S GAMING CLUB was, as usual, well patronised: husbands, fathers, brothers and lovers were busy enjoying themselves. Francis looked around for Marcus and his low friends when he entered, but there was no sign of them. There were a few persons present whose acquaintance he had made in Lulsgate, including an old friend from his boyhood days, George Stamper, now a fat squire with a fat wife whom he had deserted for the night, having met Francis earlier in the day and offered to introduce him to Gaunt's.

"Good to get away from the women," he sighed. "See you had the common sense not to marry, Frank." He had no knowledge of Francis's short marriage to Cassie, and Francis did not choose to enlighten him. He agreed to make up a four for whist with two cronies of George's, and looked around Gaunt's while introductions were being made.

It was quite a reasonable gaming hell, as hells went, and if one had to gamble outside one's home, seeing that it could only be done in clubs in private these days, Francis supposed that Gaunt's was as good a place as any.

The room he was in was respectable enough, although there was another down a short corridor, George told him, where there were girls and "other possibilities"—to do with the girls, presumably. Francis wondered, briefly, if Marcus was already there, but the "other place" did not open until nine of the clock, and it was now only seven.

Along one wall a huge sideboard ran, on which were set out plates of excellent food, which came free once the heavy entrance fee had been paid. On a small table stood a large silver wine cooler, full of bottles of good white wine; red wine stood on a shelf beneath the table, and rows of glasses were stored in a cupboard whose doors were perpetually open.

The four men about to play whist ate and drank first. Francis attracted a good deal of attention. A member of a distinguished noble family, he was something of a pasha in this company, and his very air of cool indifference to others added to the impression of effortless superiority which he always gave off.

Even George Stamper was affected by it, and sought to dispel the unease it created in him by clapping Francis on the back and behaving as though they had been uninterrupted boon companions in the sixteen years since they had last seen one another.

Eating over, they carried their wineglasses and a plate of ratafia biscuits to their table and began to play. Francis's luck was as good as his skill; his attention was not on the game, however, but on the door, and it was almost with a sense of relief that he saw Rhys Howell enter.

Marcus did not, at first, appear to be with him. But, suddenly, in the small group which comprised Howell's raffish court, and which followed him in, Francis suddenly saw his nephew being held erect by two knowing rogues. Marcus was half-cut already, his face flushed, and as he walked or rather staggered to the table where hazard was being played it was evident that he was a pigeon ripe for the plucking.

Rage with Howell, coupled with annoyance at Marcus for being such a weak young fool consumed Francis, but little of it showed. He kept an unobtrusive eye on the goings-on at the hazard table, and became convinced that Howell and the man who ran the table were in collusion, and that Marcus was their joint victim. Marcus was playing against Howell, and Francis could hear the rattle of the dice box behind him, and Marcus's blurred voice cursing as luck constantly favoured Howell.

"Dammit, Howell, the devil's in the dice that I do so badly," floated across the room towards Francis as the round of whist ended.

"Excuse me, gentlemen," said Francis, rising, his face hard and angry. He pushed the money he had won into the centre of the table. "I fear that I must leave you, and you may share what I have won between you as a recompense for spoiling your game, but I have a duty to perform."

He turned towards the hazard table, where Marcus, face purple, was sprawled in his chair, peering angrily at a smiling Rhys Howell, who was plainly sober. The whole scene was reminiscent of a print from a sequence rightly called *The Rake's Progress*, showing the young fool of an heir being despoiled by his hangers-on.

On impulse Francis picked up a bottle of wine and a glass as he passed the wine table on his way towards Marcus. He ignored Rhys Howell, who stared at him insolently, saying, "Want to throw a main, Carey? Thought you was only interested in old lady's games like whist, haw, haw!"

"Marcus," said Francis, not quite in his quarter-deck voice, but near it. "Time to go home, I think. You're hardly up to hazard or any other game in that state."

Marcus peered at him owlishly and muttered, "Death's head at the feast again, Uncle, are you? Want to stay until the luck changes. You go home to bed if you want...."

One more drink, thought Francis dispassionately, might have him unconscious, judging by his appearance. He disliked Howell intensely, but did not want an open fight with him; however, behind Francis's back, Howell was saying in a jeering voice, "Man's of age, Carey. Can do as he pleases. Not yours to run any more."

Francis decided on another ploy. He poured a bumper of what he suddenly saw was port, not a light red wine, from the bottle he was holding, and held it out invitingly to his nephew.

"Come on, old fellow," he almost crooned. "I'm not such a bad chap after all. Drink a toast with me. No heeltaps, and God bless Queen Caroline, and all who sail in her."

This was so uncharacteristic that Marcus took the proffered glass with a crack of laughter, and throwing his head back drank the lot down, watching his uncle swallow his share from the bottle.

Francis's own draught was smaller than any of the spectators realised, and as Marcus, the drink safely down him, shuddered and fell forward, his eyes rolling, and purple face turning ashen, Francis, praying that he had not overdone things, caught him, and swung his nephew over his shoulder, head on one side, legs on the other.

Even Rhys Howell, he thought, could hardly complain at his removing a victim who was now dead drunk; but he underestimated the captain.

One hand plucking at Francis's sleeve as he manoeuvred his way to the door, he hissed for the room to hear, "Damn you, Carey. You did that deliberately. He owes me this game."

Francis, enraged at the hand on his arm, and Howell's unwanted familiarity, swung round to face the man who was robbing and exploiting his nephew.

"Oh," he said, his face ferocious, the face of the man who had boarded French warships, pistol in one hand, cutlass in the other, "you mean that you wanted him drunk enough to fleece, but not so drunk that he was unconscious and you couldn't ruin him?"

Everyone in the room heard the insult. A deathly quiet fell. Howell's face turned black with fury, and Francis, who had broken his own rule of not provoking trouble, was so buoyed up by anger that he hardly cared what he said or did.

"Satisfaction!" cried Howell. "I'll have satisfaction from you for that, damn you, Carey. No fine gentleman insults me with impunity."

"No?" said Francis through his teeth. "Well, let me inform you that I have no need to prove my courage, and I have no intention of fighting such as yourself. Rummage through the gutter if you want a fight, but don't come near me."

"You'll pay for this. I swear you'll pay for this, Carey."

"By God," said Francis, swinging around again, treating Marcus's dead weight as though it did not exist. "Call me Carey in that familiar way once more, and I *will* kill you. Now be quiet, and let me get this young fool home to his aunt's. Tell the White Peacock he'll not be returning there. My man will call for his traps tomorrow."

He was out of the door and in the street, his companions holding back the raving Howell, Francis's late whist partners staring after him.

"Well," said George Stamper, happy at this interesting diversion which had lightened the drab domesticity of Lulsgate Spa. "I heard that Frank Carey had turned into a tiger when he went into the navy, but this beats all. That feller," he said, pointing at Howell, "ought to be glad Frank won't fight him. A devil with pistol or swords, they say. A man would be a fool to provoke him."

Which was the general epitaph agreed to by those present as the evening now settled back into its usual calm, and George Stamper treated himself to one of the girls in "the other place" as a reward for having introduced Frank Carey to Gaunt's gaming club, and given the company there a rare treat.

"OH, BEL," wailed Almeria to her friend, "we have never had such goings-on in Lulsgate in all the years we have lived here. So quiet and, yes, dull. And it is all Francis's fault—and he is usually so proper. First of all he excites éveryone just by being here—Lulsgate is not used to such fine gentlemen—and then Mrs. Venn accused you and him of kissing in public, and now this to-do over Francis, Marcus and Captain Howell at Gaunt's! You have heard about it?''

Yes, Bel had heard about it, as who had not?

''I suppose it has all been exaggerated—like the kiss,'' Bel offered, and she was devious enough to laugh at her own duplicity—for the kiss had been true, and doubtless Francis had done all that gossip said he had in Gaunt's—not less.

''I cannot think what has got into Francis. There is a look about him which I have never seen before. It is as though—'' and Almeria hesitated, but she had to speak to *someone* ''—as though he is sowing all the wild oats he never sowed in youth. Not that he is chasing women, not at all, he seems interested only in yourself, but otherwise, I mean. Do I know what I mean?'' Almeria finished distractedly.

Bel knew only too well what had got into Francis Carey. It was Bel Merrick, and the fact that she was refusing him herself. It had got into her, too, and was affecting everything she said and did, especially since, being virtuous, although Francis thought that she was not, she could not offer him herself. Of course, being a woman, she had learned self-control in a hard school; but Francis, she suspected, was a passionate man who had held his emotions on a tight rein for so long that now that he was sorely tempted and unable to do anything to satisfy himself his passion was taking its revenge by provoking him into unwise action elsewhere.

But she could hardly tell Almeria that, simply said gently, ''I suppose that Francis thought it was the only way to protect Marcus—who really does seem to need protecting."

"Hush," said Almeria feverishly, not wanting to be thought to be interfering again, but if she did not talk to Bel about all this she would burst. "Here they come, quarrelling as usual."

They were sitting in a little open-fronted summer-house, set at an angle to the path, so that they could hear the men's approach, but not see them, as Francis and Marcus were equally unaware of their presence. It was plain that they were, as Almeria had said, quarrelling.

"I tell you, I won't be kept in leading strings, Uncle." Marcus's voice was petulant. "You had no right to do what you did. Rhys told me that you deliberately gave me that drink to push me over the edge. A fine way to go on."

"It was necessary," Francis said coldly, one difficulty in arguing with him, Marcus found, being that Francis rarely lost his temper, which made his recent conduct the more baffling, "quite necessary, if you were not to be fleeced by the cheating toad-eater you call friend. I would prefer that you stay here, at the vicarage, and not return to the Peacock."

"You cannot stop me...." began Marcus, and then hesitated, on Bel's giving a giant cough to warn them they were overheard. "Oh. Excuse me, Aunt Almeria, Mrs. Merrick, I did not see that you were there." And he gave them both an embarrassed bow.

Francis also bowed, the marks of anger plain on his face. Anger conferred even more power on him, thought Bel, fascinated. She had a sudden dreadful wish that she had seen Francis in Gaunt's, Marcus, dead drunk and incapable over his shoulder, insulting

Captain Howell, his face on fire, power radiating from him, she was sure. It certainly made a change for him to be insulting someone other than Bel Merrick!

But how strong he was, how impressive! She had another vision of him, jumping on to the deck of a ship in battle, waving a pistol—or would it be a sword?—magnificent in anger against the French.

Almeria, desperate to mend matters, said nervously, avoiding looking at Francis, "I could not help overhearing what you were saying, Marcus. I do beg of you to stay here. Philip and I would like it of all things—so much better for you than an inn."

This emollient request had a stronger effect on Marcus than Francis's stern orders. It was hard for him to be rude to kind Almeria.

"I am imposing on you, I know," he began.

Almeria responded rapidly, "Not at all. Philip was saying that you really ought to be with us, one of the family as you are. You could put your groom up at the Peacock, for we haven't really room for him here."

She thought ruefully that since that passage with Francis she had rarely quoted her husband so often, and even he had noticed that her usual cheerful and managing habits had changed lately.

Marcus looked at the two women, said doubtfully, "Well, if you really say so, then I will, but you are to turn me out if I become a burden, mind."

"Good," said Almeria, regaining a little of her normal cheerfulness. "Now you may take me for a walk into Lulsgate to visit the mercer and then the apothecary, and Bel, my dear, perhaps Francis might like to visit your shrubbery for a turn there; there is an entrance at the back through our dividing fence, Francis." And this, she thought, would give Francis a chance to recover a little of his normal self in Bel's company—and did not know how much she was deluding herself.

She and Marcus set off down the path away from them, leaving Bel and Francis face to face.

"You heard my sister," he said. "The least that you can do is entertain me as she wishes. Now how I might wish you to entertain me is, of course, a little different. But lead on, my dear Mrs. Merrick, pray do. Of all things I wish you to provide me with enjoyment in your shrubbery."

"Oh!" gasped Bel, thinking how right Almeria was. The devil was in Francis these days. One eyebrow cocked at her, his head bent in mock-humility, his arm held towards her with exaggerated and mocking courtesy; safe in the knowledge that none could overhear them, he felt free to indulge in his passion for her.

Last night he had woken up in a fever of desire, his whole body roused, her image in his mind; and now, seeing her, only the strongest exercise of self-control was preventing him from falling on her at once. He wondered how private the shrubbery really was, and how long it would take Almeria and Marcus to do Almeria's few errands.

There was nothing for it, thought Bel exasperatedly. Almeria was sure to ask him of the shrubbery and would think it odd to learn that Bel had refused him his treat. His treat? Inspecting the shrubbery, a treat? Bel suspected that Francis's notions of what a treat in the shrubbery was did not encompass a mere oohing and aahing and recital of Latin names, and admiring the gloss on the leaves and the state of the few blossoms.

Oh, no, it would be the gloss on Bel Merrick and *her* state which would engage him, she was sure, and as she led the way she prattled as lightly as she could of the difficulties of the true gardener she was in restoring a garden which the previous owner had neglected.

Talking so, she felt Francis bend down and deposit a kiss on her sun-warmed neck, and she said crossly, "Now you are to stop that at once, sir. I cannot properly explain the garden if you carry on so."

They were by now through the opening in the fence, always left there so that Bel and Almeria could visit one another freely, and were standing on a secluded path, surrounded by plants of all sizes and shapes, overlooked by nothing, as secret a place as even Francis Carey might wish to find himself in with his prey.

"I have not," murmured Francis, "the slightest wish to have the garden explained to me. Gardens are made for other purposes than botanising, and it is those purposes which I wish to explore."

"Almeria," said Bel severely, "told me to show you the shrubbery, and that is what I am about to do." They had reached a cross path where an old wooden bench, painted green, stood, where they would, Bel knew despairingly, be even more secluded.

Even the shade was green, and here everything was quiet, the scents of late August were all about them, the summer visibly beginning to die. Francis said, still gentle, although at what cost to himself only he knew, "Pray, let us sit, my dear Mrs. Merrick. I wish to be at one with nature—in every way known to man."

And that is what I am afraid of, thought Bel, but allowed him to seat her gently, hoping perhaps that what he was saying might be more aggressive than what he might be about to do, and so it proved—at first, that was.

"Now I wonder why you are in such a pother, my dear doxy?" he said, leaning back and surveying her enchanting face and form lazily. "Can it be that you are a trifle hopeful that dallying in gardens might be productive in other ways than gathering flowers, fruit and vegetables?" And he picked up her hand and kissed it.

Bel pulled it away furiously. "You are not to call me that, sir."

"No? But that is what you are, is it not? A doxy, and dear to me, for the moment at any rate."

She rose to leave him, crying, "I have shown you the shrubbery, and so you may tell Almeria."

He caught at her to detain her, saying, "But I wish to see so much more than the garden," and, using his strength, pulled her on to the bench again, took her in his arms and began to kiss her, gently at first, and then more and more passionately.

Bel began by fighting him off—or trying to, but as his kisses began to stir her, so that his arousal fuelled hers, she found herself drowning in the strangest sensations, quite unlike any she had experienced before.

They involved her whole body, not just her mouth, and then, when his kisses travelled down her neck, found the cleft between her breasts, and he began to caress her there, she threw her head back so that without her meaning to not only did she give him a better access to her body, but she was able to gasp her pleasure the more easily.

Reason had fled, and she felt that she could deny him nothing. Worse, her hands were beginning to caress him, and when he lifted his head for a moment she began to kiss him in the most wanton manner.

He had stopped kissing her only to give himself easier means to pull her dress down, as he had done on Beacon Hill, and this time she did not stop him, and he did not stop either, so that he was now stroking and kissing her breasts, taking them into his mouth, so that the sensations which he produced in her were so violent that Bel thought she was about to dissolve.

She writhed beneath him, and he gave a soft laugh, and now, lifting her slightly, he began to pull her skirts up, his right hand travelling up her leg, beyond the garter on her stocking, to stroke the soft inside of her thigh—and she was not stopping him, no, not at all. She wanted him there, wanted the hand to travel further still, so strongly did she ache for him; shamefully she wanted all of him there—not just his hand—there, where no man had ever been.

Oh, madam is ready for me, thought Francis exultantly; she is as on fire for me as I am for her, and she is as sweet as I had thought her—sweeter—and it is she, Bel, I desire and none other, no one else will do. Then he remembered his vow that she should plead for him, and not he for her, and now, so wet and wanton was she, so far gone, that surely this, too, he would have.

"Feel me, Bel, feel me," he said hoarsely. "Feel how I need you," and he took her hand and pressed it against his naked chest where she had unbuttoned his shirt, so that she could feel the fever which gripped him. "And you, I can tell how much you need me. Say it, Bel, say it; say, Francis, pleasure me, please, beg me to do so, and then we may be in heaven together."

As before, his voice broke the spell. In agony as she was, body trembling, on the very edge of a spasm of pleasure so strong that it would consume her quite, wanting most desperately the man in whose arms she lay, some strong core of integrity so powerful that it willed her to refuse to be used by him as an instrument of revenge when she wanted to be an instrument of love asserted itself.

"No, Francis! No! Never! I will not be used to despite, to prove what you think of me is true. I will not plead. You must plead for me, and in honour, not take me here as you might the doxy you call me, to boast later of how you had me—without payment."

And the last phrase was the cruellest thing that she could think of to say to him, and as he pulled away, face blind and soft with desire, she added, "Such a man of honour as you are, to save your nephew one day, and then despoil me another."

The pride which ruled him, even at the last fence of all, was strong in him. Believing her to be otherwise than she was, he had told himself that he could not love a whore, but every fibre in his body told him that he did. That it was not, as he wished, mere lust which moved him, but that, against all reason, he loved Bel Merrick—and did not wish to hurt her.

And, that being so, he could not do what many another in his case might have done, and that was to take her as she lay before him, whether she consented or no, since, she having consented so far, a man might do as he pleased with the whore with whom he lay.

He could not resist saying as he sat up, and allowed her to free herself from his grasp, "Not honest of you, madam, to progress so far, so willingly, and then refuse me at the last gasp of all."

How to say, I am not experienced, did not know how quickly we should arrive at such a pass that my very virginity was on the point of being willingly lost? Had you not spoken, reminded me of how matters really stand between us—that I love, and that you only desire—then I would have been lost in an instant, no better than poor Marianne—indeed worse, for she was betrayed by a man who she thought loved her, whereas I—I know perfectly well that that is not so.

Instead Bel lowered her head, said numbly, "I am sorry. I was carried away."

Francis stared at her. "Carried away! You cannot expect me to believe *that?*"

"Believe what you please," she returned. "And now you have had what you came for, or most of it, and you may safely tell Almeria that you have seen the shrubbery, without the necessity of lying."

Bel was straightening herself, repairing the ravages of passion as she spoke, and Francis was feeling the worst pangs of passion die within him, the physical pain which refusal had produced abating a little.

"You will excuse me," she said, on the verge of tears, not wishing to shed them before him. "I must go. You know the way back, I believe."

Francis had one final parting shot for her like a crippled ship able to fore one last ball at the enemy. "Oh, yes, my dear doxy, I know the way back; you have made me take it so often now." And the smile he gave her as he left was rueful, not reproachful, no enmity in it.

And Bel? She knew now beyond a doubt that blindly, inconveniently, what she felt for Francis was love, and that what had begun in light-hearted mockery of him at Stanhope Street was ending on quite a different note in Lulsgate Spa.

CHAPTER THIRTEEN

LULSGATE SPA had not known such a season for years. Bumbling along in its quiet middle-class way, few great ones visiting it, it was a haven for minor gentry and tradesmen; the aristocracy, the upper gentry, the flash coves and Cyprians of the *demimonde* usually passed it by. But in 1820 all were present and sensation followed sensation.

Marcus provided the next delightful bit of gossip. Living at the vicarage, he could not drink and ruffle as he had done, and, being sober most of the time, he suddenly, as Francis had hoped he might do, saw through Rhys Howell and his cheating ways.

Smoking was not allowed by Almeria, and his boon companions stank of smoke as well as drink, which he came to find distasteful. Clear-eyed physically, Marcus became so mentally, and one evening at Gaunt's it was Marcus who challenged the captain over his honesty at dice and cards, and not his uncle.

According to rumour, high words followed, and Marcus, imitating Francis, declined to give the captain satisfaction. "You have had enough of my tin," he had declared, "and in future I shall play cards at the Assembly Rooms."

"Go there, then," roared Rhys, and swore at him, seeing his pigeon fly away, and funds running low. "Shuffle the pasteboards with the tabby-cats and dowagers. Bound and determined to turn parson yourself, are you? Having a genuine one for an uncle and a defrocked monk for another not enough for you?''

Marcus ignored the insults and, said sturdily, ''No need to shout at me, Rhys. I shan't change my mind. Uncle Francis was right about you, dammit.''

There was nothing Rhys Howell could do. The damage was already partly done. To be proven a cheat at cards or dice would brand him pariah for life, and he had no mind for that. Best to let it go, accuse the young fool of being light in the attic, trying to excuse his own bad luck and less skill by attacking another's honesty and reputation.

Of course, there was always Mrs. Bel Merrick to fall back on, for others were declining to play in any game in which he was taking part. Lulsgate was slowly growing too hot to hold him, but he did not wish to leave yet. He felt safe in such a backwater, thought that his enemies from London and Paris might find it hard to track him down and harm him there.

Bel was sitting in her drawing-room when the doorknocker rattled and a man's voice was heard. Mrs. Broughton, reading yet another romance, *The Curse of the Comparini* this time, looked up hopefully, and said, ''Lord Francis?''

Bel shook her head; it was a week since Francis had nearly had his way with her in the shrubbery, and they had met only in public, and both of them had been glacially proper, so much so that Almeria had sighed at the sight. Oh, dear, yet another chance for Francis to make a happy marriage seemed to be disappearing. What could have happened? Ever since she had asked

Bel to show him around her shrubbery an arctic frost seemed to have descended on both of them.

She had always thought shrubberies were places where romantic interludes took place. Obviously Bel's had had no such effect on her and Francis. It was not that they were not speaking at all, but they were going on as though they were both ninety.

To Mrs. Broughton's dismay, Bel was right, it was Captain Howell who was announced, and she did not like him—not the person to pursue dear Bel at all. She had seen the captain's eye on her mistress, and had interpreted his interest wrongly.

Not completely so, for, having an eye for a pretty woman, Rhys Howell not only wanted a good share of Bel Merrick's fortune, he also had an eye to her body as well. Now if she possessed half Marina's possibilities . . . why, they would both be in clover.

"Your servant, ladies." And he gave them his best bow, which did not mollify Mrs. Broughton. She would rather have read *The Curse of the Comparini* than entertain the captain.

Bel rang for the tea-board; it was not long since they had dined, and she assumed that the captain had dined, too. They made unexceptional small talk, and Mrs. Broughton looked longingly at the clock.

Her salvation came early, and Howell's intention to rid them of her presence was so boredly naked that Bel feared even Mrs. Broughton might notice how thin his excuse was. "I have further private news for you," he said bluntly, raising his eyebrows at the unwanted companion, so that Bel was compelled, flushing slightly, to indicate that she should leave.

Fortunately, for all her vague ways Mrs. Broughton was discretion itself; she never gossiped, but she must be beginning to ask herself what unlikely bond existed between Bel Merrick and Rhys Howell, that he should be bringing Bel private messages!

"You grow bold," said Bel severely. "Even Mrs. Broughton will notice your cavalier manner to me and wonder at it."

"Oh, as to that," said the captain carelessly and beginning to roam round the room, picking up ornaments and staring at them, inspecting the bookshelves as though he were a bailiff pricing goods for distraint, "you have the remedy in your own hands, my dear. Either hand over the dibs in large quantities, or join forces with me to our mutual advantage. I am surprised that you should wish to remain in this dull hole."

Bel went on to the attack, that being the best form of defence.

"And I am surprised, sir, that you should wish to stay here, or should come here at all. The pickings must be small, compared to what you might hope to gain in London."

"As clever as you are beautiful," he remarked with a derisive bow. "But you are a little off the mark. You are providing me with one reason—or rather, Marina's small fortune which you inherited, and your own person, more remarkable than I had dared to hope. I could make you Marina's best, you know. And also it suits me to be here at the moment."

Bel knew nothing of the criminal underworld, but prolonged reading of the novels which Mrs. Broughton loved had given her some insight into the nether side of life. "London too hot for you?" she enquired politely.

He was across the room in one fell stride and had gathered her into his arms.

"Come, you bitch, are you lying to me as well as to the rest of the world? Are you still in touch with your London cullies, that you know such a thing?" And, pressing his lips roughly to hers, he forced a brutal kiss on her, so that Bel's senses reeled, not with the erotic passion which Francis's touch produced, but with the utmost revulsion.

If she had ever feared that any man's touch might stir her sexually, Rhys Howell had shown her in a moment that that fear had no basis.

As he forced her mouth open, she allowed him to do so, in order that she might bite hard on his invading tongue.

He reeled back with a curse, clapping his hand to his bleeding mouth.

"Damn you for the hellcat you are! I was right about you, I see. All that parade of virtue a mockery. I've a mind to proclaim what you are to the world from the steps of the Butter Cross."

"And what a mistake that would be," said Bel, heady with a feeling of sweet victory, even if it were to be temporary and unwise. "For you would undoubtedly ruin me—at the expense of the possibility of gaining anything for yourself."

The hard eyes which surveyed her were full of an unwilling admiration.

"By God, you're the shrewdest piece it's been my good fortune to meet. You remind me not to let passion rule reason. Now, madam, let us come to terms. If you wish to leave here with reputation intact, you must be seen to go with me willingly, for I have a mind to take you and your fortune both. My bed and my future assured at one go. With me to run you, there is no telling where we might end. No, do not turn away." For

Bel, sickened, had thrown out a hand, and walked to the fireplace, where, hands on the mantelpiece, she bent her head, staring at a hearth filled with flowers. "No, I would not ruin you. Better, I would marry you. Thus I would gain everything—and you lose nothing. Refuse me, and you lose everything."

What to do? Frantic, Bel stared blindly at the flowers. There must be something. She would not agree to this, she would not. If all else failed she would let him destroy her reputation rather than agree to such a bargain. But could she not, somehow, cheat him of both alternatives which he presented to her? The spirit, the courage with which she had so far triumphed over everything in her short life was strong in her still.

She would appear to agree with him. By what he said he did not intend to leave Lulsgate Spa yet, and it was to his long-term advantage to have her retain her reputation, if only that he might sell her more profitably in the end—for Bel had no doubt of his intentions. Ever since she had learned what Marianne had done, had read her letters, the letters of her lovers, examined her books, she had known of the harsher side of life usually concealed from young gentlewomen like herself. She had no illusions at all, none.

Yes, she would appear to give way—and then would scheme an escape—even if giving way meant that she would have to endure Rhys Howell's hateful company.

She swung around to face him. His handkerchief was at his mouth, the eyes on her were inimical, baleful. She drew a deep breath, summoned up all her arts. He had said that she was Marina's best. She would be Marina's best.

"Yes," she said. "Yes, I will do what you want; I have no alternative, it appears."

His whole face changed, became darkly triumphant. He strode towards her, to assault her again, no doubt. Bel put her hands on his chest to push him away as he reached her.

"No," she said. "No. Most unwise. If you wish to take me away, my reputation intact, to be your wife, then you must court me in proper form, so that all will be deceived. No liberties, no hints or innuendoes. You are struck dumb by my virtue, sir. My apparent innocence is what you are after, is it not? Preserve that by your manner to me. Go slowly at first, and even after; a modest admiration will deceive all."

He stepped back, and his face was full of an unwanted admiration for her. "I was right," he breathed. "By God, we shall rule the world together, you and I. Between us there is nothing that we might not do. It was an unholy parsonage which spawned you and Marina, to be sure." He made her a grinning, derisive bow. "It shall be as you so wisely advise. I don't want that damned canting swine of an aristocrat after me over you, as he charged at me to deprive me of his thick-headed nephew."

He took her hand and kissed it with the greatest solemnity, though winking as he straightened up. "You will do me the honour, my dear Mrs. Merrick, of taking the air in my phaeton this late afternoon, will you not? I have a mind to drive a little beyond Morewood. One of the grooms from the inn will be my tiger, to retain propriety's demands. You see how well I know the manners of the world which I intend we shall despoil."

He released her hand, strolled to the door. "Until five of the clock, madam. Oh, I know that we shall enjoy working together."

He was gone. Bel sank into an armchair, her head in her hands. She had gained herself a reprieve—but for how long? And at what a cost. What would Francis Carey think, when he saw her at such ins with Captain Howell, but that she was exactly what he thought her to be?

The faint hope that somehow she could convince him of her purity and that they could begin their relationship all over again on a better footing had been destroyed forever this afternoon. And Lady Almeria and Philip—what would they think of her, to consort with such a creature as the captain was? Would it not be better to have done, let him destroy her, rather than have them all despise her——?

She jumped to her feet. No! This way, she might yet escape him. The other way, she was doomed forever. Any hope that she might yet have Francis in honour would be gone forever—and she knew one thing, and one thing only. What she felt for Francis Carey was so strong, so powerful, that she would do anything to have him hers, to try to ensure that what she felt for him he would feel for her.

Meantime she must appear in public with Howell, and then this evening she was to sup at the Harleys'— and she could only imagine what would happen then. Best not to; best to take each moment as it came, and trust that the God who presided over all might yet spare Bel Merrick.

So, ANOTHER SPLENDID piece of gossip for everyone to chew over. Mrs. Bel Merrick, that virtuous widow, pillar of the church, best friend of Lady Almeria Harley, a lady to her fingertips, was seen riding down Lulsgate Spa's main street in Captain Rhys Howell's flashy phaeton, with only a groom from the Peacock to act as chaperon!

And naturally, thought Bel despairingly, the first person whom they passed was Lord Francis, driving his curricle, who gave them both the coldest stare a man could, before cutting them stone-dead in full view of half of what Lulsgate Spa called society. By six that evening Mrs. Venn had been told the delightful news and trumpeted at poor Henry how lucky he had been to escape the widow's toils, a view which Henry did not exactly share.

Bel walked into Almeria's drawing-room that evening, Mrs. Broughton by her side, well aware of the furor she had caused, and defying Almeria to say anything.

She was dressed to perfection and beyond in lemon silk, the waist a little lower than had been fashionable at any time in the past fifteen years, seed-pearls sewn into the boat-shaped neck of her dress, Marianne's half-moon jewel in her hair, her fan a dream of a thing, lemon in colour with painted porcelain panels showing birds of paradise—it had been Marianne's, and in her state of anger and defiance of all the world Bel had deliberately carried it in as a kind of trophy.

Her red hair she had brushed into defiant curls; her usually ivory pallor was charmingly enhanced by a wild rose blush, for she would not be set down, she would not, and, ruined or not ruined, she would be Bel Merrick still.

Francis's eyes ran insultingly over her, his glance mocking, as much as to say, We have shown the world our true colours, have we not? But he said nothing; indeed, *everyone* determinedly said nothing, although Bel could feel that everyone was thinking everything.

What a strange world it was, that one indiscreet act could ruin one for life, she thought, but was as pleasant as ever, speaking to Marcus, whom Almeria had placed by her, and to Philip, who was on her left at the head of the table, and with all the cool command of which she felt herself capable.

Marcus, indeed, conscious of having saved himself—he gave no credit to Francis—from Rhys Howell's clutches, said to her in a low voice, "My dear Bel—you will allow me to call you Bel, Mrs. Merrick; Almeria does, and it does so suit you—I would wish to have a private word with you before you leave us this evening—after supper, perhaps, when the tea-board comes round?"

Francis, who sat opposite, bodkin between Mrs. Robey and her daughter, frowned his disapproval at what he saw as a tête-à-tête between Marcus and Bel, which had the effect of making her begin to flirt desperately with his nephew, just to show how little she cared for all the lowering glares he was throwing in her direction.

"Did you ever visit Astley's when you were in London, Lord Tawstock?" she enquired sweetly, fluttering her eyelashes at Marcus, who began to think that, widow or not, travelling in Howell's phaeton or not, the little widow might be worth pursuing.

"Marcus," he replied gallantly, "do call me Marcus, I beg of you," and he said this loudly enough for Francis to hear him and to grind his teeth as madam brought her trollop's ways to the sanctity of the vicarage supper table. Was she thinking of Marcus as a possible protector? Were Howell and himself not enough for her to try her claws on, without attracting his ass of a nephew?

Marcus went on to recite the delights of Astley's at some length to an apparently entranced Bel, who could not resist laying a pretty hand on his arm, and fluting at him with much eye-rolling and grimacing, "Oh, never say so, Lord Tawstock—I mean Marcus," when he told her of the pretty female equestriennes who ended their act by standing on one leg on the back of their prancing steeds. "I should feel quite faint at the sight. But you, I suppose, would enjoy it. Female and hippic beauty in one joyful caracole must always be a delight."

Bel knew that she was behaving badly, and that she was leading Marcus on in the most dreadful fashion, but the sight of that damned canting aristocrat, the unfrocked monk, as Howell had dubbed Francis, was responsible for her wickedness. It was not her fault at all, it was he who was provoking her, and he who, once the meal was over, would, she was sure, be pouring recriminations and unwanted advice over her, while being himself ready to fall on her in the most disgraceful manner, ready to relieve her of her virtue in quick-march time.

Philip spoke to her too, quietly and kindly, which made her feel a little ashamed, and she tailored her response to him, being the sedate Bel Merrick she had always been until first Francis and then Captain Howell had arrived to deprive her of sense by pursuing her, each in his own inimitable way.

Not that her measured replies, and discussion of her helping to decorate the church for the following Sunday, brought her any credit with Francis; rather, indeed, his expression as he surveyed her grew more and more sardonic, so that when she turned to speak to Marcus again she was wilder than ever.

Fortunately for Bel, when the meal ended it was Marcus who escorted her out, almost pushing Francis over when his uncle made a dead set at Bel, taking Bel into a corner of the room, to say confidentially, "I know you will not take this amiss, Bel, I only speak for your own good, but I understand that you went driving with Captain Howell this afternoon. Ladies are not aware of such things, I know," he added sagely, as though he had suddenly acquired the wisdom of Solomon, "but the man has a wicked reputation and you should avoid him by all means in your power, not encourage him. You do not mind my saying this," he went on anxiously, "but a lady alone..."

"No, not at all," said Bel, amused that Marcus, in Rhys Howell's toils until a few days ago, should now constitute himself a protector of the innocent. It was, she thought, almost flattering that Marcus should see her as such an innocent.

"I am always—" she began rapidly, laying her hand on Marcus's arm again, for she saw that Francis had stopped hovering and was advancing on them, a determined expression on his face, ready, she assumed, to hand her yet another sermon to digest, and she thought that she and Marcus might hold him off.

No such thing, for, interrupting her in his most high-handed way, "My dear nephew, you have monopolised Mrs. Merrick all through dinner; now you must let someone else have a turn with her. Good manners require no less."

"Suppose, Lord Francis," retorted Bel sweetly, "I told you that I preferred to continue my discourse with Marcus, rather than move on to another?"

"Then," said Francis glacially, "I should be compelled to conclude that the lack of wisdom which impelled you to share a carriage with such a blackguard as Captain Howell was still working in you this evening, madam."

"Steady on, Uncle," protested Marcus. "No way to treat a lady, and Bel has a right to stay talking to me, if she wishes to do so."

"Do you wish me to read you a lesson on good manners, too?" asked Francis, aware that he was behaving as badly as Marcus and Bel, but unable to prevent himself. "Go and help Almeria hand out the tea cups—that should cool you off and provide you with an occupation which, if not as exciting as whispering nothings to Mrs. Merrick, is at least useful."

This pedantic speech, delivered in Francis's best manner of captain reproving a misbehaving midshipman, had Marcus retreating and muttering, and Bel wanting to giggle, the manner and the matter being so at odds with one another.

Francis, seeing her mouth twitch, said dangerously, "And what is amusing you, madam? The spectacle of yet one more of your victims caught in your toils? What a mermaid you are, to be sure. Have you tired of respectability, that you should allow Rhys Howell to ferry you about? Where was all that noble virtue you used with me the other afternoon? Left behind on the couch where you entertained him, I suppose."

This was delivered in low tones and through his teeth, after such a fashion that, no one being near to them, no one could have any idea what he was saying to her.

The most appalling and delightful rage ran through Bel. How dared he, how dared he say such things to her? And then he said, again through his teeth, "I warned you about Howell, madam, I told you that I knew him to be a villain of the first water, but what notice did you take of me? Recklessly, wantonly, you put yourself in the way of danger...."

"Pray stop," said Bel, also in low tones, reduced to whispering for fear that if she raised her voice it would be to tell him, and the room, exactly what she thought of Lord Francis Carey, unaware that love, desire, a care for her safety and plain green-eyed jealousy were all at work in her tormentor.

Francis opened his mouth again, and what would come out this time? thought Bel despairingly. She must stop this, she must, for her sake, and Almeria's and kind Philip's—she could see his thoughtful eye on them and was suddenly persuaded that he was understanding more than he ought.

Invention struck. She dropped her fan, gave a loud wail, clutched at her bosom—was that the right place to clutch? she wondered—said faintly, "Oh, dear heavens, what is coming over me? Oh, I feel so faint; the heat—" and, speaking thus, her voice dying away, she allowed her knees to sag, and began to fall forward, head hanging, into Francis's arms. He, face disbelieving, caught her as, eyes rolling into her head, she willed herself to turn pale by holding her breath, which had the effect of her turning purple, an even more awful sight, while Francis, enraged, certain that madam was at her tricks and doing this to confound him, was perforce compelled to carry her to a sofa and deposit her reverently on it, with Almeria fetching smelling salts, which did cause Bel to turn pale, and various gentlemen, Marcus the loudest, then to offer contradictory forms of assistance.

Marcus caught his uncle by the arm and hissed at him, "And what were you saying to poor Bel, to overset her so?" for he had been watching them like a hawk, and was sure that Francis had been bullying her; he knew that look of his uncle's very well, having had to endure it so many times himself.

"I, you damned young pup?" returned Francis. "I have said nothing to cause this. I'd take a bet there's nothing wrong with her but a desire to attract attention."

For one moment Francis thought that his tongue had run away with him to the degree that Marcus was about to strike him, but Marcus restrained himself with difficulty, contenting himself with saying, "What the devil do you mean by that?"

To which Francis replied wearily, "Oh, never mind," turning to look at Bel, who was now propped up against some cushions, offering the company a weak and watery smile before closing her eyes and moaning gently.

He had to hand it to her. What a devious bitch she was, to be sure. She had stopped him in his tracks—or anyone else who might try to reproach her—and had thoroughly disarmed everyone. He was not deceived by all this, and tomorrow he would let her know, and no mistake.

Bel opened one eye. She closed it again hastily when she saw Francis's disbelieving stare trained on her. "I really do feel," she announced bravely, "a little better. I cannot think what came over me. It was all so sudden. One moment—" and she sighed as though words were too much for her "—I felt quite well, and then the next moment..." And she gave a delicate shudder as she spoke.

Privately she was again appalled at her own deviousness—and wondered, as before, where all this was coming from. It was Francis Carey's fault, she was sure. If only he would let her alone—or rather would *not* let her alone, but would treat her as he should, respectfully and lovingly—then she could go back to being well-behaved, innocent Bel Merrick again. As it was, she had to protect herself, and if throwing a fainting fit in Almeria's drawing-room was the only way to do it, then so be it.

"Let me assist you upstairs to my room," said Almeria, who had no reason to doubt the truth of Bel's behaviour. "And then Francis can take you home when you are feeling a little better. I shall send Mrs. Broughton on to prepare a warm bed for you, and a restorative cordial. I have a splendid bottle of my own brewing which I shall give her—excellent with a little brandy before retiring—it always ensures a good night's sleep."

Privately, and irreverently, Bel thought that a good draught of brandy might accomplish that for her without the cordial, but said nothing, only sighed gently, and when Almeria called on Francis to carry her upstairs she smiled up at him so limpidly that he almost began to laugh himself. Just let him get madam alone, and she would find out his opinion of mermaids who behaved as she did, he thought, as he laid her lovingly on the bed—he could not help but be loving, only wished that he could stay to...to...and he hurriedly left her to Almeria's ministrations before he forgot himself completely.

CHAPTER FOURTEEN

"YOU ARE BETTER today, then?" Almeria asked Bel anxiously the next morning. Bel was lying on the sofa looking prettily *distraite*—she thought that she had better keep up the farce of being a little unwell. Not only Francis, but Captain Howell, could be kept at bay by it.

Mrs. Broughton had been reading *The Curse of the Comparini* to her when Lady Almeria had arrived, and Bel replied to her question by saying in a low voice, "Oh, I am a little recovered. Rest will assist me...I think," and she lowered her long dark lashes over her eyes in what she hoped was an interesting fashion.

"I bring messages from us all," went on Almeria, a concerned expression on her face. "Marcus was particularly disturbed by your malaise—and Philip and Francis, too, it goes without saying. I am sure you are in good hands," she ended, looking at Mrs. Broughton.

"Oh, yes," said that lady vaguely. "I am breaking the habit of a lifetime by reading dear Bel a novel in the morning to comfort her." And she waved a hand at *The Curse*, which was lying open on her knee.

This distracted Almeria, who picked it up and said eagerly, "Oh, the *Comparini*—too exciting, dear Bel, for an invalid, I would have thought. That scene where the cowardly and dastardly Paolo Neroni blackmails poor Sophia Ermani ... words fail me—such a brute. I thank God we live in dear quiet Lulsgate Spa where such dreadful events do not occur."

Bel thought that, though she and Almeria might laugh together at the goings-on in Gothic novels, Almeria also enjoyed them on a different level ... and what would she think if she knew of the pother Bel was in? It was not so different from Sophia's. Oh, if only there was someone in whom she could confide!

She thought that if Philip Harley had not been her friend's husband and Francis's brother-in-law she might have gone to him for advice, but, as it was ... no such thing.

Later that afternoon, putting on a big bonnet, and venturing out when no one was about, she went to her little class, not so much to teach, but to ask the advice of Mr. Birch.

Unworldly he might seem, but Bel thought there was an iron core to him, seldom shown, revealed a little when he had recently queried Francis's intentions towards her, in the most discreet fashion, of course.

After she had dismissed her class, taken indoors, for the weather was growing chilly, Mr. Birch brought her a cup of tea and a slice of the cake which she had brought with her.

"What is it, my dear?" he asked her mildly. "I cannot help but see that you are troubled in spirit. May I assist you in any way?"

Well, that showed percipience, Bel thought wryly, since no one else about her seemed to have noticed *that*.

"I have a problem," she said simply. "But it is not one which I can properly confide to anyone." She paused, and said, "Is it ever proper, or truly Chris-

tian, to deceive people, even for the best of motives?''
For this was one of the questions which occupied her
thoughts more and more; it was a series of deceits, un-
dertaken mostly with the best of motives, which had
landed her in her current predicament.

Worse, she was beginning to feel more and more
uncomfortable about the false face she presented to
Almeria and her Lulsgate friends, the face of a widow,
not the young untried girl she really was.

"As a Christian and a minister," said Mr. Birch
gently, "my answer must be, of course, no, as you are
well aware. But, as a man of the world, living in the
real world, the answer cannot be so clear-cut. Suffering human beings may feel it necessary to engage in
them. I have to say that if they do so they must be prepared to take the consequences which must inevitably
follow."

"Yes," said Bel, in a hollow tone, heart sinking.
"And suppose, only suppose, that one's heart is fixed
on someone who may have the wrong view of one—"
for this was, she felt, as far as she could go "—what
then, Mr. Birch, what then? Should one abandon one's
feelings, or try to overcome the error?''

Mr. Birch, as Bel suspected, was no fool. "If," he
said, "your object of affection were someone like the
gentleman who has called for you lately, I would think
it unwise to try to trick him. Perfect candour would
answer better. From his looks and conversation he is
upright to a fault, if a minister may properly say such
a thing."

Bel's answering, "Yes, I suppose so," was hollow
again. "Then one should never do a wrong, however
slight, hoping that good might come from it?" she
asked feverishly, feeling that her conversation was be-

coming more and more obscure, but, paradoxically, feeling also that Mr. Birch somehow knew exactly of what she was speaking.

"Truth is always the best," he answered, "although sometimes it may be inconvenient to tell it. Only you, my dear, and no one else, save only God, can help yourself. I may advise you to be perfectly candid, but if, in your opinion, being so would be destructive to yourself, then in the real world one might have to think again. On the other hand, you may find that truth and only truth can save you. Put your trust in God, and He will tell you what to do."

Bel took his old hand and pressed it. "Oh, you are kind," she said fervently, "and wise. For many in your condition would simply have given me a stern answer without understanding how difficult my situation might be. You will forgive me if I do not tell you exactly what it is, but..." She hesitated.

Mr. Birch looked at her agonised face. "My dear," he said, "we have been friends for nearly two years, you and I, and I know you to be that rare thing, a good woman. But you are a woman on your own. I understand that you have no near relations, no family on whom to fall back, who might advise you, and, that being so, your conduct has been admirable. But you are very young, and the young may be foolish, impulsive. It is for you to try to remedy that by letting your head as well as your heart advise you, and God is there for you to ask for succour."

Bel withdrew her hand and drank her tea. Having spoken to him, her heart felt lighter, even if he had only told her what she already knew.

"Thank you," she said, her voice low.

"My dear Mrs. Merrick, you know that here you may always find refuge, should you need it. The children and I owe you at least that. You bring sunshine into our lives every week of the year."

Well, that was that, she thought, walking home, and even as she breathed a sigh of relief she heard carriage wheels and knew that Francis had been waiting for her to leave Mr. Birch's cottage, and that the hour of reckoning for last night's naughtiness was on her.

Francis stopped the curricle, leaned down and said roughly, "Come, you cannot refuse my offer of a lift. Almeria said that you were too overset to do anything today, but I was sure that you would not neglect your children. What a strange mixture you are, to be sure." His face was rueful, and she knew that he was as tormented as herself, but for quite different reasons.

"No more so than another," she said quietly, only to be met by his disbelieving face.

"And what does the old man make of you, madam? I should dearly love to know. And the trick you played on me and the company last night—what would he have made of that?"

Bel thought of the conversation which she had had with Mr. Birch and decided to tell Francis the truth— or at least a little of it. "I could think of no other way of quietening you," she said. "Another moment and you would have ruined the pair of us."

His eyebrows rose haughtily. "Ruined me, madam? I can see how I could have ruined you, but how should I have ruined myself?"

"To let the company know of what you think is the truth of me would be also that you had known of that truth for some time, and had said nothing, had allowed the woman you think of as a Cyprian not only to continue as Almeria's friend, but as the friend of her little children, polluting a pure home," Bel said, wondering why this had not occurred to her before. "What would Almeria think of your conduct then?"

Francis, mouth tightening, stared at the passing scenery, then, "Not only a witch, madam, but were females allowed to be diplomats you would make a masterly one. Your mind is as sharp as it is devious. You admit, then, that you were shamming last night?"

"For a good reason," said Bel wearily, "although I do not think that Mr. Birch would agree with what I did, were I to tell him of it."

Francis was silent again, then finally he said in a stifled voice, "Since I met you again in Lulsgate I think that I have run mad. I think only of you, want to talk only with you, be with you, want only you in my bed, wish that you were...honest, that we could have met in some other way. *That* is my ruin, madam, and you have worked it."

How strange, thought Bel; last night I blamed Francis for destroying my usual good conduct, and today he is blaming me for doing the same thing to him, and his thoughts are my thoughts: he wishes, as I do, that we had met under a different star.

"And now I must say again what I have said before," he went on. "That you should have nothing to do with Captain Howell. Most unwisely you choose to receive him, drive out with him, and I suppose that I shall be hearing next that he is taking you to the grandest Assembly of the year—the September Ball."

Bel was silent, for that lunchtime a note had been delivered to her from Rhys Howell, stating that he expected her to attend the September Ball with him as a proof of her good faith.

Francis read her silence aright. "No!" he exclaimed violently. "Do not say that I have hit the nail on the head! You *are* going with him. Why, Bel, why? You, with your excellent judgement, must know that the man is a blackguard—will ruin you..." He fell silent, suddenly conscious of the absurdity of what he was saying.

"Now how can that be," wondered Bel, "when according to you I am ruined already? What a mass of contradictions you are, Francis."

"No contradictions at all," he almost groaned. "I cannot bear to think of you in his arms, or, indeed, in any man's. There. I have said it. You have wrung it from me. I shall not be answerable for the consequences if you go with him. I know what he is, I see the way in which he looks at you. He wishes to run you, to be your pander, to sell you to the highest bidder, that is plain to me, as plain as day, and do not ask me how I know, for I cannot tell you. Do you wish to be run by him, Bel? Do you wish to out-Marina Marina? Are you not content to stay virtuous in Lulsgate Spa? Does that...life...still attract you, call you back?"

She could not tell him that his intuitive guess about Rhys Howell's intentions towards her was correct. It trembled on her lips; she almost told him of Captain Howell's blackmailing of her—but could she trust Francis, either?

Had their relationship been different, been what she knew it ought to have been, then and only then could she have asked him for help. As it was... She hesitated and was lost; the moment passed. She saw his grim face. No, she must solve this problem herself. She could not beg for help from a man who thought her a trollop; pride alone prevented that.

They had reached her home. He helped her down, said hoarsely, "Remember, Bel, if you go to the ball with Howell I shall act. What I shall do, God help me, I don't know. But I saved Marcus from him, and I do not intend to do otherwise with you." He saluted her with his whip, and was gone, Cassius at the back clinging on for dear life, favouring her with a wink as he flew by, which had her laughing despite her very real misery.

Oh, damn all men, good and bad, thought Bel as she entered her home. How much better if this world were peopled only by women, and the odd notions of men did not obtain, and babies did appear under the gooseberry bush—and all of them female!

JUST TO MAKE LIFE more exasperating than ever, Mrs. Broughton met her with a long face. The postman had been and brought her a letter from her sister. She was ill, and Mrs. Broughton was needed to help her, for her sister's husband was an invalid, the housekeeper had deserted them, all was at sixes and sevens, and only Mrs. Broughton's presence would help.

"Dear Bel, you will allow me leave to go, I trust. I would not ask if the case were not dire. I shall return as quickly as may be. And you do have dear Lottie."

Bel refrained from pointing out that dear Lottie was growing old, was nearly at pensionable age, if not beyond it, but she had no mind to do other than accede to Mrs. Broughton's wishes, even though she used that lady as a bulwark against the man she loved and the man she hated.

"Of course you must go," she said, "and of course I shall manage. Stay as long as is necessary, my dear.

Lottie will help you to pack. You wish to go on tomorrow's stage?"

"Indeed, as soon as I may. You will be careful when I am gone, dear Bel. You are usually the soul of discretion, though I cannot say that I fully approve of this new friendship of yours with Captain Howell. I do not feel that he is quite the thing. Lord Francis, however..." And she trailed up the stairs, murmuring benedictions on Bel, Lord Francis and Lady Almeria—already seeing me as Lady Francis, I suppose, thought Bel ruefully. Oh, dear, what a tangled web we weave, when first we practise to deceive. I never thought much of that verse in the past... but now...

BEL WAS THINKING of this again while waiting for Captain Howell to call for her to take her to the Grand Assembly. She had not seen Francis in private again; she did not know that he was almost afraid to be alone with her, and when they met in public they were icy cold to one another—anything less and there was the danger that they might be in each other's arms, and for their own reasons neither wanted that until the difference between them was resolved.

"Oh, dear," mourned Almeria to her, "I am so disappointed that you and Francis have not taken to one another; at first I thought..." And then, mindful of Philip's strictures, she said apologetically, "I do not mean to meddle, but you seemed so suited to one another."

She wished that she could ask what had gone wrong, but sitting with Francis at breakfast that morning she had thought that one of the things which he and Bel had in common was an indomitable will, allied to a pride which was so strong that it could almost be felt.

Perhaps *that* was what was wrong, thought Almeria; they are too much alike, so strong, so independent. For she had begun to see beneath the surface gloss of Bel's gentleness to the steel core it covered.

The doorknocker went in the middle of Bel's musings over this conversation and Lottie came in.

"That nasty piece is here to take you to the dance," she said bluntly. "I cannot imagine why you encourage such a low creature."

And what to say that? I have no alternative but to do as he wishes, so do not pester me with reproaches? Instead Bel said gently, "He asked me before anyone else did, and it was difficult for me to refuse him without offence."

"You have never found much difficulty in holding off those you do not care for before," returned Lottie with incontrovertible and inconvenient truth.

"No matter," said Bel, drawing on her long lace gloves, and seeing that the small circlet of silk flowers in her hair was in place—she was as fresh and lovely as she ever was, even though all this was put on for her to be escorted by a man she despised. For Francis was there, and she wished to be absolutely *à point*, even though he was not to know that she had dressed for him, and thought it was all for Rhys Howell.

Bel had long since lost the wish to provoke Francis Carey—except, of course, when he deliberately set out to provoke her.

"Oh, you are magnificent tonight, my dear," sighed the captain gallantly over her hand, admiring the delicate blue silk of her dress, the creamy gauze which covered it, the new way in which she had made Lottie dress her hair—that unhappy servant trailing along behind them on the short walk to the Assembly Rooms, to sit with the other servants in an ante-room until the dance was over, seeing that there was no Mrs. Broughton to protect her mistress.

They were early. The party from the vicarage had not yet arrived. Some of Rhys Howell's disreputable court was leaning against the wall, yawning, such small beer of excitement as Lulsgate could provide already boring them. Several more hangers-on had arrived during the week, although one hard-faced gentleman whom Bel had seen disputing with the captain in Lulsgate's main street was not there; nor, she discovered, did he later favour the dance with his presence.

Slowly, the room filled up. The Venns arrived, and Henry, on seeing Rhys Howell leave Bel to join one of his boon companions for a moment, and then go to the supper-table for a cool drink for them both, took the opportunity to come over to her to say, "Is this wise, my dear? Your escort, I mean. My mother..."

Bel was tired of being hectored by everybody from Francis Carey downwards, all of whom seemed to know her own business better than she did herself.

"Your mother never approves of anything I do, as you well know, my dear Mr. Venn. Now if she were to approve, you might trouble me about the matter. Otherwise, I will take her censure as read."

Henry turned a dull red. "She and I only mean you well," he said stiffly, "whereas I doubt whether the same can be said for Captain Howell. You choose your companions badly."

The worst of it was, thought Bel, that so far as Rhys Howell went he was in the right. But all this was handed down from on high, and she also knew quite well that if Henry knew the truth about her—and

Marianne—he would throw her over without a thought.

"I will take note of what you say," she replied, attempting to be a little conciliatory, "but it is for me to make my own decisions, as you, Mr. Venn, make yours. I do not choose to lecture you on what you are to do."

"But then I am not a young woman who needs advice lest she be led astray, women being so prone to that if not guarded with loving care," was his swift response.

Fortunately, before Bel could say something unforgivable, Rhys Howell returned, a glass of lemonade for her, and a cold stare for Henry.

"Happy to see you are guarding Mrs. Merrick for me," he said. "Now that I am back I thank you, and you may return to your mama."

Henry turned red again, bowed stiffly and walked away to speak to the said mama, who turned her baleful and disapproving gaze on Bel.

I shall be ruined before Captain Howell gains his ends, she thought, and then had not time to think more, for the vicarage party arrived, Almeria and Philip leading, Francis and Marcus behind, Francis throwing every other man in the hall into the shade, and consequently had every female eye, married and unmarried, young and old, on him.

He was quite unmoved. Took it as his due, doubtless, thought Bel exasperatedly, and was far more exasperated when Captain Howell, who, seeing Francis's eye, even more baleful than Mrs. Venn's, upon them, said loudly, "Come, my dear Bel. Stand up with me, I beg. It is the waltz next, and none but your humble servant shall dance it with you."

Bel tried to hang back, began to mutter some feeble negative, only he turned *his* baleful stare on her, saying, "Remember what I have promised you, my dear, if you fail to co-operate with me."

There was nothing she could do. Resigned, if inwardly mutinous, Bel stood up with him, and as the small group of musicians began to play she and the captain were the first on the floor, every eye upon them, as he had intended.

Bel was quite aware that if she allowed the captain to monopolise her it was as good as announcing that she and he were an engaged pair—or that she, Bel, was on the loose side of good behaviour. Lulsgate Spa was as narrow-minded as most small provincial towns, and breaches of etiquette were severely frowned upon.

She could almost feel Francis's eyes boring into her back, and was relieved when Mr. Courtney, the Master of Ceremonies, waved his hand and the music stopped. Fortunately, she and the captain were not near the small group from the vicarage, and she was walked back to her seat by him, feeling that she was treading on eggshells or grenades, at the very least.

The captain began small talk, in the middle of which she saw Marcus Carey crossing the floor towards her, a purposeful look on his face.

He reached her, bowed, and said, "You will allow me to reserve a dance with you, my dear Bel. I am sure that your card is not yet full."

Bel's card, given to her as she entered the hall, was hanging from her wrist; she detached it and began to examine it, only for the captain to take it, saying, "Mrs. Merrick's card is reserved for me tonight, Tawstock."

"No," Bel protested without thinking, "not so. I shall be happy to stand up with you in the quadrille, Marcus."

"Marcus, is it?" said the captain nastily, snatching the card from Bel's hand and beginning to write his name beside every space. "Well, you may stand up with this popinjay for the next dance, but the rest will be mine."

"You are a very oaf, Howell, and how I endured you for so long I shall never know," said Marcus indignantly. "I shall speak to the MC. I understand that such monopolies are not allowed at Lulsgate Spa's Assembly Rooms. Things are done in proper form here. You have no right to take Bel's card from her."

Bel was by now in her feet herself, furious with the captain, who she suddenly realised intended to compromise her hopelessly, so that she would be compelled to receive his protection, decent society being sure to cast her out once it saw her apparent relationship with him. "Dear Marcus, I will stand up with you, and as for the card, rest assured that I shall dance with whom I please," she said.

"Not so," said the captain again with a grin, "and dancing with raw boys without manners or money is not what I intend for you at all."

To Bel's horror, she saw Marcus begin to square up to the captain in protest at the manner which he was using to her, but before he could do anything a new actor arrived on the scene.

It was Francis Carey. His baleful stare took in the three of them.

"You are in danger of becoming the talk of the ballroom," he said coldly. "Are you at your tricks again, Howell? I understand that Lord Tawstock came over to ask Mrs. Merrick to dance with him. The rules of the Assembly say that it is her choice with whom she dances. What is your wish, Mrs. Merrick?'' And his hard eyes were on her, pitiless, challenging her, she was sure, to state her position.

''I have already said that I will dance with Lord Tawstock,'' Bel replied, as cold as he. ''You will hand me back my programme, Captain Howell. No one but myself shall fill it in.''

It was a declaration of war, and Bel knew it. She also knew that, faced with Francis Carey, Rhys Howell might not go so far as he had done with Marcus, and she read him aright.

For all his bravado the captain had no wish to fight with a man whose reputation was as great as Francis's. Francis had, he knew, killed the man who had wantonly shot down one of his young officers in a duel not of the young man's making, and his bravery as a naval officer had been recognised on more than one occasion.

The captain had come to the Assembly Rooms with the half-formed idea of ruining Bel Merrick on the spot by his behaviour to and with her—but not at the risk of being killed himself. He would wait to finish her off when the mealy-mouthed aristocrat seeking to protect her was not about.

But Francis's expression was so grim that Bel feared for a moment that worse might befall, except that the MC, Mr. Courtney, whose duty it was to see that such scenes did not occur, now joined them.

''Gentlemen,'' he said, severely, ''may I remind you that before you were allowed to share in the pleasures organised here you signed a set of rules which demanded certain standards of behaviour and agreed to adhere to them? It is my duty to see that you do so. You will observe them, will you not?''

Mr. Courtney was, in may ways, a silly, pompous man; nevertheless in a town like Lulsgate Spa the wishes of the MC was law. Those not agreeing to be bound by them were banned from the official festivities of the place, were banished from the very society which they had come to enjoy.

All the gentlemen, including Rhys Howell, bowed together to signify their submission to the MC's wishes. Marcus took Bel's hand to lead her on to the floor as the music began.

Like all reformed rakes and gamesters, Marcus wished to reform others. "Dear Bel," he said, "you must know what a blackguard Rhys Howell is, as I now do, and I cannot understand why you should give him such encouragement."

His voice was so sorrowful that Bel did not know how to answer him, and was reduced to saying, rather cryptically, "I fear that he asked me for more than I wish to give, and it is hard to refuse him."

Marcus mistook her meaning a little. "Oh, you have no man to protect you," he said. "Why do you not ask my Uncle Frank to look out for you? I am sure that he would be only too pleased to do so," and when Bel shook her head he said ingenuously, "Oh, he is such a good fellow, I am sure that he would not mind. Look how he cared for me, and I am sure that I did not deserve it, whereas you..." And he paused, his artless face aglow with newfound goodwill.

Bel could see Francis watching her as she danced. He was almost the only man in the room not on the floor, and she could almost feel what he was thinking of her, and she was sure that it was not favourable. But at least he and Marcus, by their intervention, had saved her, for she was certain that the captain was frightened of Francis, and Marcus had given Francis the opportunity to intervene without it appearing that he was doing so for himself.

Marcus said nothing more after that, concentrating on the dance, until, the dance over, he said to her, "Join us, Bel, dear; you surely do not wish to remain with a man who treats you in such a fashion."

Bel hesitated; then, looking across at the captain, who was now talking angrily to one of his cronies, she knew that, whatever else, he would not ruin her tonight. He was too frightened of Francis and what he might do to him. He had backed down over Marcus the night that Francis had taken him away, and tonight he had let her go without making any real threats.

If she joined the Harleys' party she was sure that he would make no attempt to haul her back this evening, would do so on another day.

Well, that other day was not with her yet, and—who knew?—by then she might have thought of something to thwart him in his designs on her. What that might be she could not foresee, but meantime Marcus was offering her salvation.

"Thank you," she said. "You know, I really do not care for him at all, Marcus, but he asked me to come here tonight before anyone else did, and in politeness it was difficult to refuse." Which was, she thought, as good an excuse as any, and was the one which she had offered to Lottie.

Marcus nodded, satisfied. He knew how strict were the rules of etiquette which governed women's conduct, and that lone women like Bel were at particular risk. They were, by now, with Philip and Almeria, who both rose, Almeria saying, "Oh, I am so happy to see that you no longer wish to remain with that man. Come and tell me what you think of *The Curse of the Comparini*. Did Mrs. Broughton find time to finish it before she left? It is a pity she had to go. Captain Howell could not have been so particular with you had she been present."

Bel nodded agreement to all this, before Almeria carefully seated her beside Francis, who was as glacial as ever. When Philip and Almeria had taken the floor, and Marcus had engaged Miss Robey, he said to her coldly, "You put yourself in a false position, Mrs. Merrick, accompanying such a creature as Howell is. Young Marcus did well to lead the column of relief for you."

"Oh," said Bel. "The pair of you manoeuvred that, then?"

Francis nodded. "I admit I was the instigator, once I saw that you had come with him as you had said that you would. But Marcus needed little prodding. He is thoroughly converted to good behaviour at the moment, is disillusioned with all such as Howell—and how long that will last is another matter. But you—what has got into you—unless it is a hankering for your old ways?"

"My old ways!" said Bel vigorously. "I have no old ways—as one day you will realise."

"And you will promise to avoid Howell from now on and save...Almeria...and myself from worry in the future."

Bel went white. "I cannot promise you that," she said faintly, knowing that the captain would begin his campaign to persuade her to throw in her lot with him once Francis was not about.

"I cannot understand you," he said passionately. "Until he arrived you were discretion itself, in your public life at least. Now you worry all those who care for you by your odd conduct."

"And do you care for me?" queried Bel, eyes agleam, for oh, how wonderful it would be if he did—if he could abandon the false belief he had of her—which to be fair to him was one which she, and none other, had created. Oh, how she regretted the hasty words at Stanhope Street with which she had deceived him—and the trick which she had played upon him.

Francis wanted to cry, I more than "care for you," I adore you, but I cannot tell you so. I want to protect you, as well as love you, and now I know that my love for you is more than lust I am beside myself.

Controlling himself almost visibly, he said instead, "I do not care to see anyone exploited by such a cur as Howell," and she had to be content with that, and with his invitation to her to dance the next waltz with him, to which she agreed with alacrity.

Oh, bliss for Bel to be in his arms, to be so near to him, and yet purgatory that she could be no nearer—and Francis? He, too, felt as Bel did. The intoxication of the music, the passionate feelings both were experiencing were, unknown to them, written on their faces; all the signs of their profound and mutual love gave them away to the watchers.

By God, the monk's in love with her—and she with him, thought Rhys Howell savagely, having taken a little more port than he ought in an effort to forget that he had once again given way to Francis Carey, while Philip and Almeria—and a hundred others—came to the same conclusion.

How lovely she is, thought Francis distractedly, and how brave, even in her wilfulness. The red hair, the green eyes, the damask cheek, the ... I grow maudlin. While for Bel the athletic body, the strong face, straight mouth and hard grey eyes of the man whom she had come to love were more pleasing to her than the softer features of the other men who surrounded her. And each thought with longing of the other: male and female both *beaux-idéals* of beauty and strength.

The dance over, Francis led her back, thinking hard, at the last, of anything but the woman he so inconveniently loved, lest his arousal betray him to all the world. A period away from her and a cold drink might restore him, he thought wildly, and so he said to Almeria, who had been watching them, "A drink, perhaps, Almy, and you, too, Bel?" The two women assenting, he and Philip strolled off to the supper-room together.

Neither Bel, Almeria nor Marcus, who stayed behind with them, to talk lightly of Queen Caroline, the weather, and various inconsiderable topics, ever knew exactly what passed in the supper-room, which stood at some distance from the ballroom itself.

The supper-room was laid out with tables containing food more substantial than, if not so fashionable as, the light fare found at similar places in London. As in London, long sideboards containing drink stood at the side of the room, and Francis and Philip made for these.

Rhys Howell, his pack of toadies about him, had abandoned the dance-floor and was drinking fairly steadily, even though he was, as yet, still relatively sober. His eyes were ugly as he surveyed the brothers-in-law choosing their partners' drinks after drinking themselves—Philip sticking to lemonade, Francis taking a glass of port.

"Enjoying the pretty widow, are you, Carey?" he said jeeringly; he could not restrain himself at the sight of the man he disliked, but was content to address Francis's back—though not for long.

Francis swung round. "I told you before not to call me Carey, Howell," he said coldly, "and I will also thank you not to speak of any lady before the scum whom you call friends." He felt Philip's hand on his arm and threw it off. The anger mixed with jealousy which he always experienced when he thought of Bel having anything to do with this piece of filth was strong in him. He was sure that Howell wished to be Bel's pimp, and the desire to kill him with his bare hands was almost overwhelming.

Howell went purple. Even he could hardly swallow such an insult.

"Damn you . . . Carey. I'll call you out for that."

"As I told you before," returned Francis, "I'll not fight you, ever. A horsewhip, now that would be a different matter. Shall I send for one?" If this was Drury Lane heroics, he thought savagely, then he was enjoying them. He felt Philip's restraining hand on his arm again, and threw it off once more.

"By God," swore Howell, "if you think to continue insulting me with impunity, you are vastly mistaken," and, made bold by the drink he had taken, he threw himself on his tormentor, to be met with Francis's iron fingers on his throat.

"Francis, think of what you are doing!" Philip was trying to pull his brother-in-law off his victim, who was slowly turning purple; men were shouting, and, fortunately for Howell, the MC himself came bustling in, mewing fearfully, "Gentlemen, gentlemen, remember where you are. There are ladies near by. Shame on you, sir," he addressed Francis, and, strangely, the MC's fluttering tones restored him to sanity.

Francis let go of Howell, who fell to his knees, clutching his throat and croaking, "By heaven, Carey, another minute and you'd have killed me."

"Pity I didn't, for the sake of all the men you've cheated and the women you've seduced," retorted Francis, cold again.

Mr. Courtney said, tremulously, looking at the pair of them, "I shall have to ask you to leave, both of you, and you must seek my permission before you are admitted again."

Francis replied in a more normal voice, "I regret, sir, that what I did was done here. I cannot regret the doing. All the same, I beg your pardon, and I shall leave at once."

He swung towards his brother-in-law. "You were right to try to stop me, Philip, and you will give my apologies to Almy and Bel, but whenever I see that man—" and he indicated Howell, who was being led away by his cohorts "—reason seems to leave me."

Philip nodded. In all the years he had known Francis, he had found him stern but always perfectly in control of himself, and the savage who had nearly strangled Howell was unknown to him. His belief that there was more than met the eye between Francis, Bel Merrick and Rhys Howell was further strengthened.

As if he knew what Philip was thinking, Francis said ruefully as Philip walked him to the back door, "Pray forgive me but it is most unlike me to behave as I did. The devil seems to be in me these days."

Philip thought, but did not say, that since Bel Merrick had come into Francis's life his whole world seemed to have turned upside down, but it was Francis's problem, not his, and Francis would have to solve it.

Meantime he must return to Almeria, Marcus and Bel, and try to gloss over what had happened in the supper-room, and over the fact that Bel Merrick was the main cause of it—for of that one thing Philip was quite sure.

CHAPTER FIFTEEN

BEL, HOWEVER, was soon made aware that whatever had happened in the supper-room between Francis and Rhys Howell must in some way have concerned herself.

She had suspected it ever since Philip Harley, in his quiet fashion, had told them that the MC had asked Francis and Captain Howell to leave. She remembered what Francis had said—that if she persisted in attending the September Ball with Rhys Howell he would take action. The stares and curious glances which she received all evening, the triumphant expression on Mrs. Venn's face, and Henry's mild, forbearing one, almost as though he were saying, I told you so, at a distance, carried their own message.

She was determinedly gay, but the gaiety had something febrile in it. She was almost sure, now, that Philip Harley, alone of all the people she knew in Lulsgate, thought that there was something a little strange, subtly out of place, in her relationship with Francis, and it was that which troubled him, as much as her apparent friendship with Rhys Howell.

Suppertime arrived, but she could not eat or drink, and suddenly everything seemed intolerable, even Almeria's kindness and protection, for, while the Harleys approved of her, Lulsgate would always accept her.

She rose, saying to Almeria, "You will forgive me if I leave you early. I have a headache coming on, and an early night will suit me." She had stayed long enough she knew, to remove suspicion that the fracas in the supper-room had driven her away early, and Almeria, looking at Bel's suddenly white face, had not the heart to persuade her to stay longer.

"Of course," she said, then, "Bel, dear, do not worry over what passed tonight. Francis has been... impulsive, I know, but I am sure that whatever he did was done to protect you. Most unlike him to act as he did, but I believe that that, and only that, lay behind his conduct."

Bel saw Philip Harley, almost unconsciously, nod agreement. She fought an impulse to cry, knowing that what Almeria said was true—despite his suspicions of her, the mixture of desire and hostility which were the staple of Francis's dealings with her, he genuinely wanted to save her from Rhys Howell. She almost wished that she had confided in him.

"Thank you, Almeria," she said through stiff lips. "Now you will excuse me, I trust. I will go and fetch Lottie. It is time that she went home; she is growing too old for late-night sessions such as these."

"And that is what I like about Bel Merrick," remarked Philip as they watched her go, bowing to those who bade her goodnight. "She has a true consideration for all those about her. I suppose," he added slowly, "that that might account for her taking up with such an unlikely person as Rhys Howell...." But he did not believe what he said.

BEL FOUND LOTTIE looking weary as she had expected, but also surprised at Bel's relatively early departure from an event which was the height of Lulsgate's small season.

"I thought that you were going home with him, or with the Harleys, Miss Bel," was all she said when it became apparent that she was Bel's sole escort.

"No." Bel was brief. "I am tired and do not wish to stay longer. You may accompany me home. After all, the journey is not far, and Lulsgate streets are safe at night."

Once home, bone-weariness took over. She felt as though she had run the sort of race she had done as a youthful hoyden before ladylike considerations took over to make her the model of a parson's good and proper daughter.

When Lottie would have followed her into her bedroom to ready her for the night, she shook her head. "No, we are both tired, you more than myself. You may go to bed at once. I will look after myself."

She thought that Lottie was growing old and would have to be pensioned off, found a little home, but she was the last link with her old life and she did not wish to lose her. She watched the old woman struggle upstairs to her bedroom on the second floor. The temporary loss of Mrs. Broughton had never seemed more annoying, for it had thrown more responsibilities on to her old servant.

Sighing, she pushed open her bedroom door, the candle she held throwing strange shadows about the room, her own, monstrously distorted, moving with her. She placed the candle on the dressing-table, undid her pearl necklace—only to see a movement in the shadows reflected in her mirror.

Startled, Bel swung around, a scream on her lips as she saw that a male figure was seated in the armchair by her bed, a scream she stifled when she saw that it was Francis, his face white and drawn, his whole mien one of barely suppressed pain.

"You!" she exclaimed. "How came you here? And, more to the point, what are you doing here?"

He answered her first question, not her second, standing up as he did so, all his usual formality of manner quite gone.

"I came through the connection between your garden and Almy's. I noticed the other day that one of the glass doors in your drawing-room had a faulty lock. It was the work of a moment to force it and to enter. I have done no permanent damage. In any case, for your own safety the lock needed replacing."

There was nothing apologetic about him. Nothing to suggest that the last thing he ought to have done was to break and enter a house, force his way into a lady's bedroom.

Shocked though she was, Bel could not help saying sharply, before she asked him to leave at once, before she called for the constable to remove him, "You took a great risk. Suppose Lottie had come in with me? She usually does. What would you have done then?"

"Then I should have hidden in the curtains, or in the closet yonder, until she left." He gave a humourless smile. "You see, where you are concerned, Mrs. Bel Merrick, I am full of wicked invention, and I have no conscience or honour left at all. You have deprived me of it."

"Oh, I see," said Bel, fascination replacing fear. "It is all my fault. I might have expected that. I have provoked you to this dishonourable conduct, unworthy of a man of your reputation, character and station in life."

Why was she bandying words with him? she wondered. She must order him to leave, although how she could compel him to go if he chose not to she could not think. To scream, to call for Lottie, or Ben, the boy who did the odd-jobs for her—a handyman rather than a footman—would destroy the last shreds of her reputation in Lulsgate Spa, to say nothing of the humiliations which such an act would heap on Francis himself. A supposedly honourable man who had arrived, uninvited, in a lady's bedroom, presumably to force her... or so the world would think. She did not really believe that that was why he had come.

"Yes, you have provoked me," was his reply to that, "by encouraging that damned swine Howell. God forgive me, I nearly killed him tonight, after seeing you with him. You must know only too well what a blackguard he is, that he can only mean you harm—"

"And what harm do *you* mean me?" flashed Bel. "It is you who are in my bedroom, uninvited, at nigh on midnight, not Rhys Howell—who, of course, I know to be a villain, and one who means me harm. And now I ask again that you leave me, at once."

"Not before you have heard me out," he replied hoarsely, his face full of an almost physical pain. "It has been murder, pure murder, for me to watch you tonight—aye, and all the recent days when I have seen you with *him*. Do not you know how you affect me, madam? Oh, Bel, I burn for you, feel how I burn," and he grasped her hand, held it against his forehead for a moment, and it was true, he was on fire.

Bel wrenched her own hand back, for through it the fire had passed from him to her, and she was suddenly shaking, consumed by the same flames. Her breath had shortened at his touch, and the sight of him, here in her most secret place, the room where she had dreamed of him so often, was rousing her to the same pitch of excitement which Francis was suffering—or enjoying. Perhaps the two sensations were the same, pleasure so exquisite that it was almost pain.

Francis saw her state, saw everything about her as though she had become transparent, open to him, felt her desire for him in the same measure that he felt his for her.

"Oh, you feel as I do!" he cried exultantly. "Oh, Bel, you must not torment me longer. The more you hold me off, the more you inflame me, particularly when I know that you are deceiving me when you deny me. I vowed two years ago that I would enjoy you without paying you anything, that as a punishment for cheating me you would lie with me willingly, would beg me to do so, as I am now begging you. I told myself that I hated you for being a cheating whore, but I was wrong. I cannot pretend any more. I wish to be in your arms so strongly that I will gladly pay any price you name to be there."

He loved her with all the passion of a passionate nature long denied, but he could not say so. He could not confess that he loved a Cyprian, and the sister of a Cyprian so notorious that two years after her death her name was still remembered—that was beyond him. Besides, he feared that she might laugh at him if he made any such confession; she had mocked him so often for much less than that.

Bel swallowed at his words, especially at the word "price." He *still* thought her a whore after all these weeks together. How could he, oh, how could he? Her unconsidered acts of two years ago had ruined the future for both of them. Suppose she had said then, I am

Marina St. George's innocent sister, and can prove it—
then they would not be standing here, dying of love for
one another and unable to do anything about it without each violating his or her most inward self.

For if Francis felt that he was betraying himself by
loving a whore—for Bel now had no doubts that he
loved her—she too would betray herself, destroy her
own virtue by consenting to lie with him in other than
honourable marriage, because now she knew that she
loved him beyond life, beyond reputation.

Love's cross-currents flung them now together, now
apart—except that tonight, alone at last, hidden from
the prying world, Bel knew that nothing could prevent
her from giving him what he wanted so desperately to
take—and she had desperately to offer.

He would not, she knew, keep her, take her as his
mistress. She knew that his dead wife stood between
him and a lesser permanent union. He would have her
for one night, she thought—to assuage what? Was he
strong enough to love her and leave her—was she
strong enough to accept him as a lover, without marriage, risking social disgrace, and perhaps preg-
nancy—which was possible from even one night's
loving?

And if she gave way to herself, as well as to him,
what price would she demand of him—and of herself?

Francis had grasped her hand again, and again she
pulled it away. She said coldly, denying the passion
within her, "Why do you ask me, Francis?" and her
voice was almost cruel. "We are here alone. You may
take what you wish, with or without my consent. Many
would not hesitate to take a whore without her consent. Why do *you* hesitate, Francis, thinking so little of
me as you do?"

"Oh, God, not that, no, never that," he said violently, putting his hands over his eyes. "Not rape, Bel, never rape. Only with your consent, ever. You must accept me willingly, or not at all. If not for love, then for money, and you may name your price."

She could not take him in the name of love—for she thought that he might not believe her if she told him that she loved him, and that would be to dishonour love. Knowing that, she also knew that in the end she would take him for the lesser reason. For, against all logic, all common sense, she was as determined to have him as he her, and if that meant the surrender of her chastity, then so be it—but he must pay in another coin first.

"Then beg me, Francis," she said fiercely. "Would you care for me to give you brandy, as you gave it to me at Almeria's table that first night? Beg me, Francis, beg me on your knees for me to take you to my bed, if you wish to lie with me, for whore though I *might* be, though any may offer me payment, I and only I choose who may visit my bed—and I am not yet sure that I wish to choose you."

Francis fell on his knees before her, put his head in her lap, before looking up at her to see her face almost saintly in the halo created by the candlelight behind her.

"Oh, Bel, be merciful. Would you have me walk through the fire as well as burn?"

As I would walk through fire for you, and as I burn for you, was her unspoken reply. Yes, I would have you do that, so that we might be equal.

Instead, she answered him gently. "No, not for mercy, Francis, but for payment. Whores have no pity, look only for payment. Your payment is—that you should beg again.''

Bel thought for a moment that she had gone too far. He lifted his head, stared at her, rose; pride had returned. He saw her white face, disembodied in the mirror, saw with astonishment that she was suffering as he did, for she was beside herself, lost in her own torment—and feeling his.

He was not to know, even though some strong message, unspoken, passed between them, informing him of the depths of her feelings, but untried, chaste though she was, she would have taken him in love and was now, as she thought, prepared to take him in despite, seeing that there was no other way in which she could accept him.

Francis had no means of knowing this. Love's crosscurrents were now so strong that both were drowning in them.

"I ask you, Mrs. Bel Merrick, for I have no other name for you, to take me, Francis Carey, as I am, as your lover, for whatever reason, for love, for pity or for money, so long as we may enjoy together what I now see that we both so palpably want. Beyond reason, beyond honour, what I feel for you—and I have no name to give it—is so strong that you alone can give me something which I never thought to feel again.''

He fell silent, and Bel knew that, mistaking what she was, it was as near to a declaration of undying love as he could make to her. She thought of his dead wife and child, of her dead sister, and all doubts, all hesitations and resentments, were burned away.

"Yes," she said simply, "Yes, Francis, you need say no more. No payment of any kind is needed. Now it is my turn to beg you to come to me, to assuage *my* longing, *my* desire, for I, too, am beyond reason and honour and need no payment for what I so dearly wish.''

Francis's eyes, wide already from his body's arousal, widened still further, for he had thought that she was about to inflict the final humiliation on him—either refusal, or an acceptance so insulting that their loving would be bitter.

"*You* beg *me?*''

"Yes, Francis," she said quietly, her voice so full of love for him that he ached at the sound, her face as soft as an angel's in a painting. "That was what you wanted, was it not? For me to beg you? Shall I beg you again? Love for love, Francis, not hate for hate. No payment needed on either side. We are to meet as willing equals.''

Bel saw that she had cut the Gordian knot, broken down all the barriers which had arisen between them. She had, at one stroke, freed them from the hateful past, for now his eyes were glowing, triumphant, but loving, too.

"Equals, Bel? You mean that?''

"Equals, Francis. As though we meet for the first time, no taint of our mutual past upon us, free to enjoy one another without bitterness, revenge or the desire to hurt.''

"Then I kneel to you willingly," he said, and proud Francis Carey went down before her, and this time when he took her hand she let him keep it. He kissed it, and said, looking up at her, "Oh, you are generous, my heart, and now let me see all of you; not only that which you show the world, but the treasures which you normally hide—except from your lovers, of whom I am humbly one.''

Bel shivered under his ardent gaze, internally quaked at the thought of stripping herself before him. But after all that she had said she could not refuse him, even though her modesty shrank before the act.

She stood up, he still kneeling, pulling her dress over her head, removed her underclothing, her stockings, until she stood naked before him. His gaze on her had never wavered. His eyes were wider than ever, and as her last garment fell away, and she instinctively dropped her hands to cover herself—there—he was there before her, had clasped her round the knees and was kissing her where the red-gold fleece hid her most secret parts.

"Oh," he said fervently, looking up at her perfect, unspoiled body, a very chaste Diana as she was, although he was not yet to know that, "you are even more lovely than I had dared to hope. Bel, you are *belle* indeed," and he rose, saying, "And now you may prepare me for the sacred rite we are about to undertake, for there shall be nothing between us, nothing, all subterfuge stripped away."

Again Bel could not deny him, and it was she who undid his cravat, peeled off his coat, undid the buttons of his shirt. Then, when he bore her to the bed, between them they reduced him to the same state as herself, so that now she saw all of him, and as they came together nothing, no, nothing lay between them, symbolic of the fashion in which they had mentally stripped themselves before beginning the physical act of loving and finally offering to one another two perfect bodies.

The fierceness of her passion surprised Bel, who had thought herself a calm and reasoned soul. But she could not have enough of him, as he wished to have all of her; mouth, hands, legs, eyes and voice, all played their part, and as he loved and caressed her breasts and her mouth, so she too rejoiced to stroke his hard body, kissing and caressing his torso, the muscles which stood on his arms and shoulders, ran her hands up his inward thighs—as he had done to her—so that as she cried out for surcease, so did he, and finally his passion, so long restrained, could be held in check no more and he entered her.

To find, too late, that she was the virgin she had always said she was. But there was nothing he could do; the very shock of the forced entry brought Francis relief, a relief so strong and fierce that Bel, too, shared in it, immediate though it was, for the strength of their passion and their preliminary loving, and the frustrations of the previous weeks, would brook no delay for either of them.

Time and space disappeared. The sense of separateness disappeared, too, as they achieved the truest union of all, not given to many to experience. Francis was too far gone in sensation to register his shock at finding his lightskirt, his ladybird, his bit of muslin, his courtesan a virgin, although when, shuddering and gasping, the first transports were over, Bel, who regretted nothing, found him still shaking, but this time in grief, not in love.

"Oh, God forgive me, Bel, for you never can, for what I thought, said and did to you. I have wronged you for months in thought, and now in deed. I have seduced an innocent girl. I am Rhys Howell's worst."

Bel clasped him to her. "Oh, Frank," she said, the pet name coming naturally to her lips, "my darling Frank, there is nothing to forgive. I misled you first, and tonight I freely invited you to love me, as we both wished, and there is nothing you say which can change that."

He lifted his ravaged face from the pillow in which he had buried it. "Oh, you are an angel, my darling, to speak so, but for weeks I have miscalled you, taunted you, and now... I have ruined you. Now you must marry me."

"Marry you!" Bel sat up. "Oh, I cannot do that. You cannot marry me. It would not be fitting. I bring you a dishonoured name. I have told so many lies, not only to you, but to all the world. You must marry someone truly innocent. Captain Howell..." she began, then hesitated, finally said resolutely, "Captain Howell has been trying to blackmail me, about Marianne and my supposed past; that is why I was compelled to endure his advances. You cannot wish to marry someone who may have other such creatures arrive in the future to soil your good name."

"My good name?" said Francis bitterly. "And what is that, pray? I have, in effect, seduced you, bullied you until you gave way to me. If you marry me, then I will protect you from any who might try to harm you—or me. Oh, my love, you should have come to me for protection from him—but how could you, speaking to you and treating you as I did?"

He does not say that he loves me, thought Bel—but then he turned towards her, kissed her, and said hoarsely, "Oh, I worship you, Bel, worship you, so gallant as you are. Why did you pretend to be the same as your sister, *why?*"

"Because," said Bel, inwardly joyful at the declaration which he had just made, "I was so angry when you treated me as a courtesan that I pretended to be one—and then cheated you, something which I have regretted ever since, for after that you could never believe me innocent. But I had no idea that I should ever meet you again, or that you had affected me so strongly, so quickly—as you did. You see, I am shameless where you are concerned.''

"Then," said Francis, kissing her on the cheek, "with you feeling as you do, I fail to see why you refuse to marry me."

"You could . . . keep me," said Bel gently.

"No, indeed. It is bad enough that I have ruined you, without proclaiming it to all the world; besides, it is not a thing I am prepared to do. I despise the immorality I see all around me, and now you may laugh at me for saying that, in view of my behaviour to you. I fail to see why you cannot accept my honourable proposal when you have accepted my dishonourable one—against all your beliefs, I am sure."

"Because I love you," Bel said, "and because I accepted your dishonourable one, then the other is forbidden to me, and besides, although I come from a good family and my father was a parson, think of what my sister was, and what you are. You cannot marry such as myself." And she leaned forward and kissed him on the cheek.

They were both now sitting up, and he took her face in his hands and said, "It is not your sister whom I hope to marry, but you. Let me try to persuade you otherwise," and he kissed her on the lips, gently at first, and then with renewed and rising passion, so that, all his good intentions forgotten, he turned her beneath him again, and they resumed where they had so recently left off. Only this time he treated her with such loving and patient care that in her transports she almost wept beneath him.

And when, sated, they lay in one another's arms, and he would again have asked her to marry him, Bel put her fingers on his mouth and said, "Go to sleep, Francis, let us have tonight."

He nodded his head, but replied, "But I must leave soon, I must not ruin you completely," and they fell asleep, sitting up, propped against the pillows, arms round one another, as though to be parted physically was death itself.

BEL SLEPT AS SHE had not done for weeks, and Francis too, so deeply that dawn came and went, and the door opened, for Lottie had knocked, and Bel had not answered, nor did she wake until her old servant, worried, entered the room—

To see Francis still there, sleeping, his head now on Bel's breast, and Bel's gaze, steady, unashamed, meeting hers, left hand to her lips commanding silence, for she knew, instinctively, that Francis was at peace as he, too, had not been for years.

The old woman, who had seen even more of the world than Bel suspected, nodded her head and left, but the closing door broke Francis's slumbers. He sat up, looked at Bel, saw the daylight through the curtains, and said, "My God, Bel, whatever is the time? I said that I would not ruin you, but I am like to do so," and he sprang out of the bed, alternately pulling on his clothing and demanding that she marry him.

Bel rose from the bed, pulled on her dressing-gown and began to help him, buttoning his shirt, tying his cravat, assisting him into a tight, fashionable coat, shaking her head, finally saying, "Then give me leave to think on the matter, Francis."

He began to kiss her passionately. "Yes, my darling, for that answer is better than last night's refusal, but not enough!" And then, "But I must be away, before I am seen."

Together they stole downstairs—it was now eight-thirty on a fine morning—and Bel let him out through the glass doors in the drawing-room, for him to escape, not by the way to Almeria's garden, but through a small gate to a side-alley, so that he might steal back unseen—after claiming yet another kiss.

Then Bel went back indoors, to meet Lottie's reproving stare. "I might have known," said the old woman resignedly. "You are not your sister, but you are loving enough. Could he not wait for you, then, or were you only too ready to make him your lover without so much as a wedding-ring or a betrothal?"

"He has asked me to marry him," began Bel, "but—"

"But?" said Lottie. "What but is there? The man is besotted. Has been since he met you as was plain for all to see—who had eyes, that is, and were not full of their own consequence. To be Lady Francis—what 'but' can there be? Your wits are addled, Bel Passmore, for I will not call you by a name that is not yours. Does he know that yet?"

"No," said Bel, "and I do not think that he cares. I have promised to think on the matter."

"Think for one minute and then say yes before he changes his mind," said her servant acidly as Bel walked by her, clutching to her the memory of the night, and with the intention of considering carefully what she ought to do. Impulsiveness had brought her to this day; would careful thought do better for her?

FRANCIS MADE HIS WAY to the vicarage as warily as he could. No one was about, and he knew that neither Almeria nor Philip would rise early after last night's junketing. With luck he could slip in—he possessed a door-key—and be up the stairs before anyone stirred.

Good fortune was not with him. Little Frank had been ill in the night, and though he took all the care in the world Francis had no more luck than to start up the stairs just as Philip and Almeria arrived on the landing, early risers after being awake most of the night caring for the little boy.

They both stared at the sight of him, still in last night's clothes for the hall, dishevelled, not at all his usual orderly self, walking in after a night spent— where? To try to explain would make matters worse. Neither his half-sister nor his brother-in-law said anything. Francis smiled ruefully and continued on his way. It was only too patent that he had spent the night away from the vicarage. He shrugged his shoulders. Well, that could not be helped; after all, he was more than of age.

Only to meet Marcus's accusing stare as he, too, arrived to see his uncle coming in after a night's debauch. Marcus's smile was knowing, almost derisory, and the only consolation was that not one of the three of them could have any idea in whose bed he had actually spent the night.

"Celebrating?" said Marcus, thinking he had caught his high-minded uncle on his way home after a bout with one of Lulsgate Spa's rather seedy Cyprians. Never say the old fellow has turned human at last! was his inward thought.

Francis cursed his ill luck, said, "Good morning," as cheerfully as though he were not rumpled, unshaven, and full of a goodwill brought on by a thoroughly satisfactory night's loving—of which he could say nothing to anyone. Neither Marcus's broad grin nor Almeria and Philip's faint expression of shock had the power to move him. He was suddenly sure that his heart's desire would be granted, that Bel would agree to marry him, and his lonely years would be over.

BEL DID NOT HAVE LONG to debate over Francis's proposal, or over her own surrender of her virginity. She had expected to feel some faint regret, but could only feel pleasure. Francis's loving had been so kind and careful, as well as passionate—exactly what she might have expected it to be.

But could she really accept him? Eating breakfast, dressing for the day, a sense of well-being lapping round her, she was coming to feel that perhaps she could—but that she must not hurry her decision.

Just before luncheon, however, Lottie came in, her face one big O, bursting with news. "Oh, Miss Bel, you would never guess what has happened!"

"No," said Bel, smiling, "I refuse to guess, for I am sure that you are determined to tell me."

"It's that Captain Howell. He was found shot dead in his room at the White Peacock not an hour ago. They had to break his door down when he failed to rise this morning, and his man could not make him hear. Such a thing to happen! And him taking you to the ball, last night! I can't say that I'm sorry to hear the news, I disliked the man greatly, but I hope no one thinks Lord Francis had anything to do with it, after his quarrel with Captain Howell last night."

"Goodness!" said Bel. "That's the most unlikely thing I ever heard."

Lottie looked at her, and said, "Well, at least, Miss Bel, *we* know that Lord Francis couldn't have murdered Captain Howell...." And she almost winked at her mistress.

Bel was not surprised that Captain Howell had been murdered. Given the way in which he had behaved towards her, and what Francis had hinted about his career in London and Paris, it was perhaps to be expected that someone should see fit to dispose of him.

One more thing which I do not need to worry about, thought Bel. I don't like to be relieved that a man, even a man like Rhys Howell, was murdered, but his death has saved me from further difficulties—and perhaps may change my intentions about marrying Francis.

She suddenly had a desperate, aching desire to see him, to be with him, and her resolve not to marry him was shaken. Oh, to love someone was so all-consuming, how could she bear to wait to see him again? Thank God, she thought, that I am to dine at the vicarage tonight, when we may meet at last in friendship, even if we are not able to acknowledge our love openly.

Her smile was so purely happy that Lottie, looking at her, thought wisely, No need to worry about Miss Bel. He's an honourable man, for all that he got her into bed before he asked her to marry him, but he'll do the right thing by her, I'm sure, and whatever she says I'm sure that she'll accept him.

She sighed sentimentally. She knew that she should have been shocked, but the sight of Bel with Francis in her arms had warmed her, not shocked her, for Lottie's view of life, like that of many servants, was earthier than that of the gentry whom they served. I know Miss Bel, she thought; she'll make a good wife, and a good mother, not like Miss Marianne—she always wanted things easy...not surprising that she went wrong in London.

Which was Marianne's epitaph and Bel's eulogy.

CHAPTER SIXTEEN

CAPTAIN HOWELL provided Lulsgate Spa with as much scandalised and excited gossip in death as in life. From the moment he was discovered on the floor, a pistol thrown down by him, which had been held close to his body when it fired, presumably to muffle its noise of the shot, speculation roared about who had done the deed. Opinion was divided between whether the murderer ought to be hanged or rewarded, the innkeeper's belief inclining to the latter since it turned out that Captain Howell had left nothing behind him with which to pay his huge bill.

Inevitably the discord between Lord Francis Carey and the dead man, ending in the fracas the night before the murder, was also discussed in gleeful tones. Among those worried by the news was Almeria, remembering that Francis had spent the night away from the vicarage. Of course he could not have murdered Captain Howell, could he? But where had he been, what had he been doing?

Speculation even invaded the vicarage itself at the dinner which Bel attended. There had been talk of sending for the Bow Street Runners, but Mr. Thomas Fancourt, a local landlord, who was one of Lulsgate Spa's magistrates, said that he had been informed by Sir Charles Walton, the chief of them, that that would probably not be necessary. He knew no details, but Sir

Charles had been on his high ropes, had said that the identity of the murderer would cause great excitement, and he would not move against him until he was sure of his case.

Mrs. Venn informed the table, "The sooner such a creature is apprehended the better; we are none of us safe in our beds."

Ever inwardly inflamed by Mrs. Venn, Bel wanted to retort, On the contrary, we are all safer now that he is dead, and he has probably been killed by someone whom he has bammed, this last delightful piece of slang having come from her latest novel from the subscription library, partly set in London's underworld, *The Bells of St. Giles*.

Almeria had sat her by Francis, and his speech and manner to her at dinner were so loving that Bel almost feared that they would cause comment; but no such thing—everyone was too busy dissecting the dead captain. For once she saw little of Francis after the dinner, the men congregating together to discuss the day's news; and the women, too, in their own excited huddle, wondered at it, and said how little surprised they were, the dead man having become universally disliked, although a few had favoured him at first.

Over the tea-board, Francis took the opportunity to pass her cup to her and sit beside her, saying in a low voice, "You have thought of what I said? You have reached a decision?" and the hard grey eyes were suddenly so soft and full of hope that Bel hardly knew him. She could see Philip and Alméria watching them, presumably also hopeful, and she felt compelled to say, "Not yet, Francis, not yet. I have had not time to think."

"No time?" he said tenderly. "You have had since morning. An eternity. If all time passes as slowly as this while I wait for you to make up your mind, I shall have a white beard down to my knees by the week's end."

Bel choked back a laugh and said severely, "You are as naughty in your admiration as you were when you despised me."

"No," he said, suddenly deadly sincere in his manner. "I never despised you, however hard I tried—that was the trouble. Oh, I cannot see why you hesitate; we are two halves come together, and my life will be incomplete without you. Ever since my dear Cassie died I have lived without love—and now I see what a half-life it was, and how hard it has made me. Marry me, Bel, and save me."

Almost she said yes on the spot, but Mrs. Venn came up, spiteful eyes on them. She did not want Henry to have Bel, nor did she want Francis Carey to succeed with her either.

"So," she said to Bel, "you have lost your admirer, Mrs. Merrick. Not that I can say I cared for your taste, but then Lulsgate Spa probably contains few who can please you, you being so discriminating in all things." The last was said in such a manner that it indicated Mrs. Venn believed that Bel was nothing of the kind.

Bel was fearful of what Francis's reaction might be, but he merely bowed—he had risen on Mrs. Venn's approach—and said lightly, "I believe that Mrs. Merrick has always a good reason for even her lightest decisions, and one must remember that, whatever else, Captain Rhys Howell once held the King's Commission."

That Mrs. Venn was annoyed at Francis's refusal to be ruffled went without saying; she tossed her head and moved on, Francis remarking mildly when she was out of earshot, "I am so near to happiness today that even such arrows as Mrs. Venn cares to loose at us cannot touch me. Have we reached harbour, Bel? Say that we have, I beg of you," and even though she shook her head at him her eyes were giving him another message—and it was the one he wanted. Paradise seemed near.

Those around them thought so, too. Almeria kissed Philip when Francis had retired for the night, saying joyfully, "I do believe, my dear, that my good little Bel is going to make Francis a happy man. You could not but notice his manner to her, and hers to him. And you must not say that I interfered to arrange it, for I followed your instructions, and left them to solve their problems together."

"Better so," said Philip gently, "and I agree that Bel will do Francis the world of good. He was in danger of becoming a lost soul, and I feared for him a little."

"So, we go to bed happy," said Almeria gaily, kissing him again, "and the thought that Francis will have someone, as I have you, and will no longer be lonely, is a comforting one."

BEL THOUGHT of Francis's proposal the next day when she sat reading a letter from Mrs. Broughton, who said that although her return was delayed it would not be many days before she was with dear Bel again. Bel put the letter down and thought that if she accepted Francis he would almost certainly help her to find a place for Mrs. Broughton somewhere in his vast establishment. Almeria had told her of his wealth, and the great house in the north which his mother had left him.

Which means, she told herself joyfully, that I have made up my mind to accept him, for he is right, we are two halves and must come together. I am foolish to let what Marina was come between us. After all, we came from a good family, and in normal circumstances there would be no bar to our marriage. We love each other, our minds meet as well, and that is all that matters in the end. Oh, I can hardly wait to tell him.

A comic thought struck her: Cassius will be so pleased that we have stopped wrangling, so there is another good thing! She must remember that he would appreciate it, and now they would share their jokes, not hurl them at one another—as she hoped they would share everything else.

While she had been reading there had been noise in the street, and now she heard the sound of running footsteps, and the door flew open.

It was Lottie, her face white. "Oh, Miss Bel. Such terrible news. Sir Charles is at the vicarage, with the constables. Betty from the kitchen has told me that the pistol found by Captain Howell's body was Lord Francis's. He says it was stolen from him in Paris, but they knew that he was out all night, will not say where he was, and they are threatening to arrest him for murder, for all the world knows how much at outs he was with the captain, and that he had attacked and threatened him only the evening before. Betty says that were he not who he is they would have had him in the lock-up by now!"

Bel rose to her feet, mouth trembling. "Francis, murder Captain Howell! Are they all run mad? Besides, he can have done no such thing. He was with me all night, as you know. Oh...!" And the implications of *that* struck her immediately, and she knew, though no one else did, why Francis would offer no explanation of where he had spent the night.

It was her honour, her reputation which he was protecting, at the expense of his freedom—possibly of his life.

White to the lips, her whole body shaking, she said hoarsely, "You must be mistaken, Lottie. Sir Charles cannot believe that Lord Francis would do such a thing."

"And so he apparently said, Miss Bel, but the evidence is so strong.... Why? What are you about to do?" For Bel had picked up her shawl, thrown it around her shoulders and was making for the glass doors and the back path to the vicarage.

"Do?" said Bel energetically. "Why, go there at once, and tell them the truth—that he was with me."

"No," said Lottie, barring her way. "Oh, no, Miss Bel. Think; your reputation will be gone in an instant. You will be no better than poor Miss Marianne. You will have to leave Lulsgate."

"I cannot allow them to try Francis, possibly hang him, for something which I can prove he did not do," said Bel, her heart sinking into her pretty little kid slippers at the thought of what telling the truth might do to her.

But Mr. Birch had told her that there might come a time when she ought to tell the truth, and now she had no choice—that time had come.

Ironically, what Francis had thought of her would shortly come true. She would be a pariah, a light woman, not fit for society. She would almost certainly have to leave Lulsgate, forfeit her friendships here, and her good name...but what was that against what might be done to Francis if she kept silent?

She could not allow him to do this, she could not, and, pushing by Lottie, she ran towards the vicarage, praying that she was not too late.

FRANCIS, AT BAY IN THE vicarage drawing-room, Philip and Almeria with him, was at his haughtiest.

He had laughed contemptuously at what he called the so-called evidence, said that the pistol with his arms and initials on it was one of a pair stolen from him in Paris, and he could prove it, that he was certain that Howell had been killed by someone he had cheated, almost certainly from outside Lulsgate. And no, he could not deny that he had not been in his bed at the vicarage the night that the captain was murdered, but would not, on any account, say where he *had* been.

"You leave me to no alternative but to arrest you, my lord," said the harassed Sir Charles. "You threatened him more than once, before many witnesses, the last time on the night before the murder when you had to be pulled off him before you killed him. Your pistol is found by his body, and you refuse to say where you were—hardly the action of an innocent man." He refrained from adding that were he anyone but *Lord* Francis he would not be debating the matter at such length before taking a man with such a wealth of evidence against him to the lock-up.

"Francis," said Philip gently, "is there nothing you can tell Sir Charles of your whereabouts on the fatal night? Nothing at all?" He was suddenly sure where Francis had been that night, but, in the face of Francis's own silence, he too could say nothing, could offer no hint.

"Only," said Francis, and his voice was stone, "that I was troubled in my mind, and spent the night walking and thinking."

"All night?" said Sir Charles, with Philip's expression echoing his words. "You must see that that beggars belief."

They had reached this impasse when there was the sound of an altercation outside, the door was unceremoniously thrown open, and Bel almost threw herself into the room.

Francis took one agonised look at her and knew why she had arrived, what she was about to do. The haughtily indifferent languor which had infuriated Sir Charles and his brother-in-law flew away in an instant.

"No, Bel," he said, walking towards her and seizing her hands. "No, you have no business here. You know nothing of the matter," and then he saw her implacable face, felt her trembling at what she was about to say, and said loudly, "No, I forbid it, you understand? I positively forbid it. You are not to speak."

He swung on the startled spectators, his face anguished. "Tell her to leave. She has no place here," and he tried to push her to the door. Neither Philip nor Almeria had ever seen him so moved before. Stern, implacable Francis Carey had disappeared.

Bel freed herself from his clutching hands. "No, Francis, I cannot allow this. You must not lie yourself to the gallows by refusing to speak."

She turned to Sir Charles, who knew her a little and was staring at her wild manner and informal dress with astonishment. Not in such a fashion was Mrs. Bel Merrick wont to be seen abroad in Lulsgate Spa.

"Do I collect, sir, that the gravamen of the case against Lord Francis is that he cannot prove, or will not say, where he was on Thursday night when Captain Howell was murdered?"

Sir Charles nodded. "Yes, madam, but I fail to see—"

"You will see this, sir," said Bel steadily. She was aware, for all the world suddenly seemed hard and clear, that Francis had sunk into a chair, his head in his hands, compelled to realise that nothing he could say or do would stop his gallant love from ruining herself for him. "Lord Francis could not possibly have killed Captain Howell, for he spent the entire night with me. I arrived home with him a little time after eleven o'clock, and we were together until gone eight the next morning. He is refusing to speak in order to save me, but I cannot allow him to do so at the expense of his freedom and his life. I must tell the truth."

The world, from being so sharp, became dull and blurred. She heard Almeria's indrawn breath, saw Philip's kind and understanding face, and Sir Charles's almost disdainful one as she finished speaking.

Francis lifted his head, said hoarsely, "Not so, I say. It is good for her to do this, but she is lying to save me."

Sir Charles, seeing how matters must stand between them, began to say, "Just so—"

Bel interrupted him, shaking her head and looking steadily at Francis.

"It is useless, Francis," she said gently, "for you must know that my maid Lottie came to my...room while you were still sleeping in the early morning, and I was awake and she...saw you there. And so she will testify. I appreciate the sacrifice you have been making in order to save my reputation, but it is your life which might be at stake, and I cannot allow you to save me at such an expense.''

She saw Philip's approving nod, heard Almeria give a half-sob, but nothing mattered to Bel except that Francis must be saved. The passion which had ruled since Lottie had told her of Sir Charles arriving to arrest Francis, and his refusal to say where he had been, was beginning to fade. There was a ringing in her ears, and she was fearful that she would disgrace herself by fainting. And this time the faint would be a true one....

Philip, indeed, looking at Sir Charles, moved forward and took her hand; he could see that she was *in extremis*.

''Look at me, my dear Bel,'' he said gently, an expression of infinite pity on his face which had her fighting against tears. ''You are telling the truth, are you not? You are not simply trying to save Francis by sacrificing yourself?''

Bel looked at him, beyond him to where Francis had turned his back to them all, and was, she knew by his whole stance, fighting for his composure.

''Yes,'' she said, and her voice was suddenly strong. ''I have told you so many lies, dear Philip, as you will shortly discover, but I am not lying to you over this, I swear it.''

Philip looked over the top of her head at Sir Charles and said, ''I am sure that Mrs. Merrick is speaking the truth. Everything which she had said bears the stamp of veracity, and, that being so, it would be most unwise to arrest my brother-in-law before her servant has been questioned. Best to make enquiries about the theft of the pistol as well. You really have no case against him now.''

He released Bel's hand, but not before, with a look of infinite compassion on his face, he had kissed it. Almeria was looking from Bel to Francis, and the glance which she gave her half-brother was a fierce one, all the usual affection which she felt for him quite banished.

Sir Charles bowed to them all, gestured to the two constables to leave with him, but not before saying stiffly to Francis, "You will forgive me the accusation I made, but your refusal to answer me, or to divulge your whereabouts, made it inevitable that I did so. Mrs. Merrick's evidence, given that her servant supports it, leaves you innocent of all accusations relating to Captain Howell's death. I shall make enquiries about the theft of your pistols. I am inclined to the belief that if they were, as you say, stolen in Paris, then someone from that city may have come here to murder him. I understand, and not only from yourself, that his reputation was a bad one."

And so it later proved. Captain Howell's death was a nine-day wonder, ended only when it appeared that he had been engaged in criminal activities in both Paris and London, and his associates, whom he had cheated, had found means to dispose of him—Francis's pistol, bearing his initials and arms being a useful red herring.

The door closed behind them. Bel, around whom Almeria had placed a protective arm, had begun to shiver. Francis swung towards her, his face ravaged.

"Oh, my darling Bel!" he exclaimed. "You should not have done what you did—the accusation against me could never have stood, I am sure—but oh, how I honour you for it." And he fell on to his knees before her, clutching her hand as he did so, ignoring Philip and Almeria who stared at him in wonder.

Proud and stern Francis Carey, almost fighting tears, was saying to the woman he loved and who had destroyed herself for him, "You cannot refuse to marry me now, Bel; it is the least that I can offer you...if I thought that I loved you before, think what I feel for you now."

Bel snatched her hand away, and turned impetuously from him to face Philip and Almeria. "No! You cannot marry a ruined woman, and one of such a bad reputation. I must tell you all the truth, I must."

She was thinking of what Mr. Birch had said as she poured this out. "I have told you so many lies. I am not even Mrs. Merrick—there is no Mr. Merrick. I am Bel Passmore, a respectable clergyman's daughter, but I am also the younger sister of Marina St. George, the noted courtesan, as Francis knows, and until two days ago I was virtuous, but am no longer. Francis cannot marry such a woman, a woman whom Rhys Howell felt free to blackmail. No, do not argue with me, Francis; you know that what I say is true, and that is why I refused to marry you two days ago, and do so now." And before any of them could stop her she ran from the room.

Francis rose, started to follow her, but was stopped by Philip, his face stern. "No," he said. "Leave her alone, Francis. You seduced her, did you not? And that you wished to marry her afterwards does not mitigate what you did." And Almeria's eyes were as accusing as her husband's.

Francis turned toward them again, his face a mask of torment, tears in his eyes, quite changed from what he had been.

"I love her to distraction," he said hoarsely. "I first met her two years ago, shortly after her sister died. I never thought to meet her again, and then here she was in Lulsgate. I thought at first that she was unworthy, but it is I who am that, not my dear Bel. You are both right to despise me. And now you must let me go to her, for I shall not rest until she consents to become my wife. I have mourned my dear Cassie too long; it is time to let her go—in any case she would hate what I have done to Bel as much as you do. I cannot spare her scandal, but with my name she may face the world down."

"Oh, you do love her, Francis," said Almeria wonderingly. "Why did you seduce her, then? All you needed to do was offer her honourable marriage."

Francis could make no reply to that without giving away the tangle of his relationship with Bel. He saw Philip raise warning brows at his wife, and then, like Bel, he ran through the door, out into the garden to take the path to Bel's glass doors. To find her, to ask her to forgive him—and become his wife.

Almeria turned to Philip, bewildered. "I do not understand him at all," she complained. "If he loved her, and wished to marry her, why did he do what he did? He had no need—" And then, as Philip looked at her steadily, she said, "Oh, you always thought that there was something odd about them, did you not? And you would not wish me to pry, I understand . . . or rather I don't."

"There are some things about others," Philip said, "which it is best for us not to ask about, or even to know. I said once before that Francis and Bel must solve their own problems, and despite all that has passed this morning I think that they are about to do so. And now we must think of other things—and try to stop Lulsgate from tearing them both to pieces, for this morning's doings will be all about Lulsgate in the hour.''

BUT FRANCIS discovered that Bel was not at home. He only found Lottie there, who had just confirmed Bel's story to Sir Charles, for if Miss Bel had sacrificed her good name to save Francis then she could do no less than tell the truth.

''Where is she?'' they both said together, Francis recovering himself first. ''She has not come here?''

''No,'' said Lottie, staring, ''I thought that she was still with you.''

''Oh, God,'' said Francis frantically, ''where has she gone, if she has not come back here?''

''And why should I tell you anything,'' said the old woman fiercely, ''seeing that you have ruined her with your wickedness? Such a good girl, my dear Miss Bel, not at all like that silly Miss Marianne. Shame on you if you thought Miss Bel was no better.''

''You cannot despise me more than I despise myself,'' said Francis humbly. ''Have you no idea where she may have gone?''

Lottie shook her head, and Francis ran back to the vicarage, his head on fire, to enquire frantically. ''Oh, Almy, my dear, do not look at me like that. I have no idea where she has gone, and I must find her, I must.''

''Before every tabby-cat in Lulsgate rips her to bits when today's news leaks out, as it will,'' said Almeria. ''I hardly know you, Francis. Such a good girl as my dear Bel was. How could you treat her so?'' And then she was silent, remembering what Philip had counselled.

"But none of this helps me to find her," said Francis grimly, and he looked so distressed that Philip, who had come in while they were talking, pushed him gently into a chair, pouring him a glass of wine from the bottle which he had brought in with him, then handed the glass to his brother-in-law, who refused it.

"No," said Philip gently, "drink it. You look as though you are about to drop dead any minute. Think, Francis, think. You know her as well as anyone. Where in Lulsgate Spa could she have found refuge?"

Francis drank the wine, shuddering. Something in Philip's words struck him, and he stared at him. Even Almeria was beginning to show a little pity for him in his distracted state.

"Not in Lulsgate Spa," he said slowly, "but in Morewood."

"Morewood!" they both said together, then Almeria asked, "Why Morewood?"

"Because," said Francis, "and I see that you do not know this, she helped the Methodist minister, Mr. Birch, to run a small dame school for poor children at Morewood twice a week. She extended her love and compassion to them—as she did to me."

"On Wednesdays and Fridays!" said Almeria. "Which explains why she was always unavailable on those days."

"Exactly," said Francis, colour returning to his cheeks. "Morewood, I am sure of it. To the old man there. I know that he thinks a great deal of her, and she respects him. I will go there at once. Not in the curricle. To take that would be to emphasise the difference which once existed between us." And before Philip and Almeria could stop him he ran out of the room again.

Almeria turned to Philip, shocked. "I would never have believed it," she said slowly. "He adores her, that is plain. And if so, why did he ruin her? For that is what he did. I shall never understand him, ever. So upright he was, and now this."

"He is human," replied her husband, "and he has been so severe with himself for so long—and now he must try to find his salvation—for this is what Bel is, I suspect. And, as I said before, he must do it himself."

FRANCIS FOLLOWED Bel, who, as he suspected, had gone to Mr. Birch at Morewood for succour. Like her, he ran through the streets unheeding, surprised spectators turning to follow his progress, as they had followed Bel's.

Bel, indeed, had had only one idea in her head, and that was to get away from everyone, and find absolution with Mr. Birch. Why this was so she did not know. Only, at the moment when she had told the truth about the night which Francis had spent with her, she had had a kind of revelation—that it was important to tell the truth about everything; there must be no more lies, however good the reasons she might once have had for telling them.

She must go to see Mr. Birch, to tell him what she had done, and only then could she allow herself to think about Francis and his needs—for she knew that she could not abandon him, only that before she could speak to him again she must clear her conscience, and she could only do that when she had spoken to the old man. Philip Harley would not have done at all, for it was not Philip to whom she had earlier hinted of her dilemma, but Mr. Birch.

Mr. Birch was in his garden when Bel arrived, panting, her eyes wild, nothing of the refined young lady left. She threw open the garden gate and ran to him, half sobbing, "Oh, Mr. Birch, dear Mr. Birch, pray let me speak to you."

He put an arm around her, led her gently into the house, sat her down in his big Windsor chair, and brought her a glass of water to still her shaking and sobbing.

"Now what is it, dear? How can I help you?"

"I have told the truth," she wailed, "and I feel worse than ever. Not only am I ruined, but I have told the whole world of it, and more besides." And she broke into the sobs which she had held back for so long. "And it is all my fault. Oh, dear Mr. Birch, I did a wrong thing two years ago; I told a great lie—or rather implied it—to the gentleman who has come here for me several times, and though I love him dearly I cannot marry him."

"He rejects you, then," said Mr. Birch gently. "I told you I thought that he was not a man to play with."

"Oh, no," said Bel, showing him a tear-stained face. "He wishes to marry me, but I feel so unworthy."

Mr. Birch looked puzzled. "But you said that you were ruined. You mean that there is another suitor, of whom you have not told me?"

"Oh, it is all so difficult," wailed Bel again. "I allowed him to ruin me because I loved him so, and he thought that I was not virtuous, but then he found out that I *was* virtuous after all, and now he wishes to marry me. But it would not be fair to him. Oh, I have done my duty, and even that does not answer."

This muddled explanation served to enlighten Mr. Birch a little. He handed poor Bel a man's large handkerchief and said, "And if you truly care for him, my dear, and he wishes to marry you, and you are—or were—virtuous then I do not see your problem. But always remember that virtue and telling the truth are their own rewards—although sometimes God sees fit to give us more."

He had hardly finished speaking when there was a hammering on his front door. Bel heard the housekeeper answer it, and then Francis's agitated voice echoed through the house.

Bel rose to her feet, turned towards the door, and said to Mr. Birch, "It's Francis." Her lip trembled. "Should I see him?"

"It is your life and your decision, under God, of course," said the old man gently.

"Yes," said Bel, and as Francis came through the door he saw them together, Bel's hand in Mr. Birch's, a look of peace on her face such as he had never seen before.

And what did Bel see? She saw that Francis had in some strange way found his peace, too. The mixture of desire and pain which had driven him ever since he had first met her had disappeared.

He bowed to Mr. Birch, and said, "You will allow me to speak to Mrs. Merrick, I trust."

"Miss Anne Isabella Passmore," said Bel. "I must not deceive either of you, or the world, any more. I am the daughter of the Reverend Mr. Caius Passmore, sometime rector of Brangton in Lincolnshire, who was cousin to Sir Titus Passmore of Dallow in Cheshire. It is little enough to claim, but I must tell you at last who I really am."

"Miss Passmore, then," said Francis gravely. "I have something which I wish to say to her privately, sir. We have had too much discussion in public today."

"If Miss Passmore wishes it," said Mr. Birch, "then it shall be so. It is your wish, Miss Passmore?"

"Yes," said Bel, suddenly and unwontedly shy. "If Lord Francis wishes it."

"Then I will leave you," said the old man, and, as he reached the door, he added, "May the Lord be with you both."

Francis bowed again. His punctiliousness and care for the old man pleased Bel more than she could say. All his pride and hauteur seemed to have leaked out of him. She thought that they might return, but that he would never again be entirely as he was.

And now he bowed to Bel. "I am pleased to make your acquaintance, Miss Passmore," he said, as though they had never met before. "I have something to say to you, to which I hope you will give your most earnest consideration. You will allow?"

Bel bowed her head, signed for him to continue. She felt barely able to speak.

"Yes," she achieved, "pray do," as though, she thought, they had not so recently been together, as close as a man and woman might be.

"Miss Passmore, I have known you long enough now to be aware that above all things I would wish you to be my wife. You are the woman I have always wanted to meet; kind, brave and generous. You have borne my recent intolerable behaviour after a fashion so admirable that it gains my utmost respect. More, I know that I love you as I have never loved any other woman.

"What I felt for my dear Cassie was quite different, if not less true. Today you honoured me by offering up your reputation in order to save me obloquy, pain and possible death. If you can bring yourself to accept my suit you will make me the happiest man in Britain, as I hope to make you the happiest woman. I cannot say fairer than that." And he took her hand and kissed it, bowing his head, then lifting it to show her his eyes, brimming with love. "Please, my dear Miss Passmore, marry me, as soon as possible."

Bel could not speak. Her throat had filled. What he had said to her was said so humbly, so differently from all his previous offers to her, either honourable or dishonourable.

She lifted his hand to her lips, kissed it, and said, "If you can bring yourself to offer for me, Francis, knowing my true circumstances, then, loving you as I do, I cannot refuse such a noble offer. Yes, I will accept you."

Francis broke on that. The perfect courteous calm which he had shown to her ever since he had entered the room was suddenly gone; he took her in his arms and began to kiss her, kiss away the tears which ran down her face—tears of joy, not of sorrow.

"And you will not regret this," said Bel, pulling back a little, "knowing of me, and mine, what you do?"

"I would regret not asking you," he said. "And if you can bring yourself to forgive me, then some time, perhaps, I can forgive myself."

Bel put her hand on his lips. "The fault lay in both of us," she said, "and we have a lifetime to repair it. And now, sir, we must be decorous. It is Mr. Birch's home we grace, and it is time that we informed him that we intend to behave honourably in future."

"Indeed," he said, putting an arm around her and kissing the top of her head. "We must behave ourselves now, until we marry. I shall go to London for a special licence, and Philip shall marry us if you think you can face the world here. If not, we can be married at my home in the north."

"I think," said Bel steadily, "that it would be only fair to Philip and Almeria, whom we have both deceived, to be married here as quietly as possible."

As she spoke, there was a knock at the door and then Mr. Birch came in, carrying tea-things for three on a small tray.

He looked at them shrewdly, and said, "I thought that you might like to celebrate with me. You *are* about to celebrate, are you not?"

Francis and Bel stared at him, astonished. He gave a dry chuckle. "Come," he said, "I have lived in the world these many years, and I know the faces which men and women assume. You are a man and a woman of sense; I could not but think that you would behave sensibly in the end, and so it proves."

He handed the cups around, and said, "I toast the pair of you, and I firmly believe that you will soon be Lord and Lady Francis, and happy together."

Francis Carey had never expected to become betrothed to the woman whom he so passionately loved in a Methodist minister's shabby parlour, nor that the minister's prophecy would come as true as it did when he forecast a happy life for him with the Cyprian's sister.

NOTES FOR THE READER

MARIANNE PASSMORE'S death from a "fulminating stomach" was, in modern terms, from a burst appendix. Appendicitis in the early nineteenth century usually resulted in death.

In the early nineteenth century, the famous courtesan, Harriette Wilson blackmailed her famous lovers just as Marianne did in the novel. She was also in league with dubious adventurers of good family, come down in the world, very similar to Rhys Howell.

Lulsgate Spa is an imaginary town; it does not exist in Leicestershire or any other country. Its environment, social life and characteristics are based on many of the spas which were popular in the eighteenth and nineteenth century. The MCs in such towns were very powerful people who controlled social life in them, keeping it respectable.

Morewood also is imaginary, although again there were many small and depressed villages like it in the Midland counties, both during and after the Napoleonic wars. Beacon Hill, however, does exist, and may still be visited.

Fifty red-blooded, white-hot, true-blue hunks
from every State in the Union!

Look for MEN MADE IN AMERICA! Written by some of
our most popular authors, these stories feature fifty of
the strongest, sexiest men, each from a different state in
the union!

Two titles available every month at your favorite retail
outlet.

In August, look for:

PROS AND CONS by Bethany Campbell
(Massachusetts)
TO TAME A WOLF by Anne McAllister (Michigan)

In September, look for:

WINTER LADY by Janet Joyce (Minnesota)
AFTER THE STORM by Rebecca Flanders (Mississippi)

You won't be able to resist MEN MADE IN AMERICA!

If you missed your state or would like to order any other states that have already been
published, send your name, address, zip or postal code along with a check or money
order (please do not send cash) in U.S. for $3.59 plus 75¢ postage and handling for
each book, and in Canada for $3.99 plus $1.00 postage and handling for each book,
payable to Harlequin Reader Service, to:

In the U.S.	In Canada
3010 Walden Avenue	P.O. Box 609
P.O. Box 1369	Fort Erie, Ontario
Buffalo, NY 14269-1369	L2A 5X3

Please specify book title(s) with your order.
Canadian residents add applicable federal and provincial taxes.   MEN894

This September, discover the fun of falling in love with...

love and laughter

Harlequin is pleased to bring you this exciting new collection of three original short stories by bestselling authors!

ELISE TITLE
BARBARA BRETTON
LASS SMALL

LOVE AND LAUGHTER—sexy, romantic, fun stories guaranteed to tickle your funny bone and fuel your fantasies!

Available in September wherever
Harlequin books are sold.

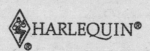 HARLEQUIN®

MILLION DOLLAR SWEEPSTAKES (III)

No purchase necessary. To enter, follow the directions published. Method of entry may vary. For eligibility, entries must be received no later than March 31, 1996. No liability is assumed for printing errors, lost, late or misdirected entries. Odds of winning are determined by the number of eligible entries distributed and received. Prizewinners will be determined no later than June 30, 1996.

Sweepstakes open to residents of the U.S. (except Puerto Rico), Canada, Europe and Taiwan who are 18 years of age or older. All applicable laws and regulations apply. Sweepstakes offer void wherever prohibited by law. Values of all prizes are in U.S. currency. This sweepstakes is presented by Torstar Corp., its subsidiaries and affiliates, in conjunction with book, merchandise and/or product offerings. For a copy of the Official Rules send a self-addressed, stamped envelope (WA residents need not affix return postage) to: MILLION DOLLAR SWEEPSTAKES (III) Rules, P.O. Box 4573, Blair, NE 68009, USA.

EXTRA BONUS PRIZE DRAWING

No purchase necessary. The Extra Bonus Prize will be awarded in a random drawing to be conducted no later than 5/30/96 from among all entries received. To qualify, entries must be received by 3/31/96 and comply with published directions. Drawing open to residents of the U.S. (except Puerto Rico), Canada, Europe and Taiwan who are 18 years of age or older. All applicable laws and regulations apply; offer void wherever prohibited by law. Odds of winning are dependent upon number of eligibile entries received. Prize is valued in U.S. currency. The offer is presented by Torstar Corp., its subsidiaries and affiliates in conjunction with book, merchandise and/or product offering. For a copy of the Official Rules governing this sweepstakes, send a self-addressed, stamped envelope (WA residents need not affix return postage) to: Extra Bonus Prize Drawing Rules, P.O. Box 4590, Blair, NE 68009, USA.

SWP-H894

Harlequin® Historical

LOOK TO THE PAST FOR
FUTURE FUN AND EXCITEMENT!

The past the Harlequin Historical way, that is. 1994 is going to be a
banner year for us, so here's a preview of what to expect:

* The continuation of our bigger book program, with titles such as
Across Time by Nina Beaumont, *Defy the Eagle* by Lynn Bartlett and
Unicorn Bride by Claire Delacroix.

* A 1994 March Madness promotion featuring four titles by
promising new authors Gayle Wilson, Cheryl St. John, Madris Dupree
and Emily French.

* Brand-new in-line series: DESTINY'S WOMEN by Merline Lovelace
and HIGHLANDER by Ruth Langan; and new chapters in old favorites,
such as the SPARHAWK saga by Miranda Jarrett and the WARRIOR
series by Margaret Moore.

* *Promised Brides*, an exciting brand-new anthology with stories by
Mary Jo Putney, Kristin James and Julie Tetel.

* Our perennial favorite, the Christmas anthology, this year featuring
Patricia Gardner Evans, Kathleen Eagle, Elaine Barbieri and
Margaret Moore.

**Watch for these programs and titles wherever
Harlequin Historicals are sold.**

HARLEQUIN HISTORICALS...
A TOUCH OF MAGIC!